QUEEN OF SORROWS

Book One in The Living Legends Series

A. E. James

For Megs.

CONTENTS

Title Page

Copyright

Dedication

Prologue   2

WALES   4

Chapter 1   5

Chapter 2   10

Chapter 3   14

Chapter 4   22

Chapter 5   30

Chapter 6   42

Chapter 7   47

Chapter 8   56

Chapter 9   64

Chapter 10   68

Chapter 11   78

Chapter 12   84

Chapter 13   92

Chapter 14   98

Chapter 15   106

Chapter 16   112

Chapter 17   117

Chapter 18   123

Chapter 19   128

Chapter 20   136

Chapter 21   139

Chapter 22   144

Chapter 23   149

Chapter 24   153

Chapter 25   163

Chapter 26   173

Chapter 27   180

Chapter 28   185

Chapter 29   191

Chapter 30   196

Chapter 31   201

THE IN BETWEEN   206

The In Between   207

ALBION   210

Chapter 32   211

Chapter 33   221

Chapter 34   228

Chapter 35   236

Chapter 36   246

Chapter 37   253

Chapter 38   256

Chapter 39   262

Chapter 40   270

Chapter 41   279

Chapter 42   283

Chapter 43   287

Chapter 44   290

Chapter 45   298

Chapter 46   305

Chapter 47   308

Chapter 48   311

Chapter 49   314

Chapter 50   323

Chapter 51   324

Chapter 52   331

Chapter 53   338

Chapter 54   341

Chapter 55   346

Chapter 56   352

Chapter 57   358

Chapter 58   364

Epilogue   371

Acknowledgement   374

About The Author   376

The Living Legends Series   378

One for sorrow
Two for joy
Three for a girl
Four for a boy
Five for silver
Six for gold
Seven for a secret, never to be told
Eight for heaven
Nine for hell
Ten beware it's the devil himself.

TRADITIONAL NURSERY RHYME

Will he make many supplications unto thee? Will he speak soft words unto thee?

JOB 41:3

KING JAMES BIBLE

PROLOGUE

Taliesin speaks ...

When Gertrude Springate was just four years old, a god came to visit her.

Of course, looking back, she convinced herself that he only *seemed* like a god, but we know different, don't we, my loves?

Left alone for the first time by her grandmother and feeling an equal mixture of terror and relief, Gertrude curled herself up into a ball and pulled the bed covers over her head.

And then *he* appeared, singing her name.

With his shining golden hair and eyes that changed colour, he was the most beautiful being she had ever seen.

The first night, he made her laugh by producing fire from his hands. He drew chocolates out of thin air and fed them to her. He told her she was beautiful. He told her she was a princess. He told her she must not fear her grandmother, but she should try to avoid upsetting her, at least until he could come and rescue her.

On the second night, the golden-haired man wrapped stories around her. Tales of dashing princes, cruel kings, wicked queens, and beguiling maidens. Stories of young girls, cruelly treated, who eventually became the princesses they were destined to be.

'Like you,' he whispered. She clapped her hands in delight

when he opened the bedroom window and woke the birds up to come and sing for her.

On the third night, he swept her up into his arms and holding her, as she had seen fathers do with their children, he danced around the small bedroom, making fireworks bounce off the walls. He whispered in her ear,

'I love you. You are my true love.'

Her grandmother had burst in. The old woman screeched like a banshee and attacked him, raking her nails down his beautiful face. Ice covered the walls and the ceiling. The golden-haired man screamed in rage and pain, his visible breath a cloud of despair.

He disappeared.

Her grandmother turned on her. Later on, in the hospital, Gertrude's grandmother told the doctor that the dog next door had attacked her granddaughter. The doctors and nurses liked Gertrude's grandmother, because of the work she did with her church group. They urged her to contact the police.

Neither of them ever spoke about the golden-haired man again.

Nevertheless, every night, when she closed her eyes, Gertrude would dream of the beautiful, golden-haired man, whose eyes were like the sunrise, and who had conjured magic with his hands.

But he was not the only man who haunted Gertrude's dreams.

WALES

CHAPTER 1

Gertrude really should have known better.

She should have known, after seeing Magness the magpie on his own that morning, that today was going to be hell.

One for sorrow.

Not that any day was particularly good, but she should have been more prepared.

As she pressed her face into the concrete, she felt the first kick catch her in the ribs. The crowd laughed and jeered. As they emptied her bag, Gertrude braced herself. She tried to move her head, but hot sweaty hands pinned her down, as they rubbed her fish paste sandwiches into her hair.

Another kick, a retching noise and now spit, as well as fish paste, landed in her hair. She would have to make a trip down to the pool before going home. She hated feeling dirty and it was hard enough keeping her frizzy mane of hair clean. Inevitably the name-calling started and she almost chanted along with them.

'Freak! Ginger minger! Fat slag!'

Fat chance, Gertrude thought. *A slag is a girl who sleeps around. No boy will look at me, at least not in the eyes.* But Gertrude would not look at boys either or anyone else if she could help it. She always kept her head down and avoided eye contact. She knew every pair of shoes in the school and the truth was, she liked looking at the floor. The floor was for discarded things, like the pink bobble that kept her hair out of the way or the one-pound coin which had allowed her to buy some nice smelling soap. That had been a good day. That day she was sure that she had seen Magness *and* Agnes.

Two for joy.

But not today. More rummaging in her bag and they found her book.

'*The Lion, the Witch and the Wardrobe?*' said the familiar, sneering voice.

Tara Wilcox. The bottle blonde bombshell of year eleven and Gertrude's tormentor since year three. Gertrude's nemesis in stilettos was the ringleader of the three most stupid, vindictive girls the school had ever seen. Gertrude called them, '*The Petty Four.*'

Another kick had Gertrude crying out.

'What are you, six?' said Samantha Howard, her breath hot in Gertrude's ear. One of Tara's minions, Samantha was arguably prettier than Tara and just as vindictive. She grabbed Gertrude's hair and yanked it back, pulling her face up off the ground. Tara gave Gertrude a stinging slap and Samantha slammed Gertrude's head back onto the concrete. Team work.

Please do not rip my book. It took me so long to steal it. The sweaty hands were roaming over her body now, slapping and punching. One large hand, burrowing under her body, found her left breast, and squeezed it, hard. Another hand crept up her leg. She had seen boys look at her with a look she never could quite identify and now some understanding dawned on her.

High above her in the sky, a crow cawed. For the first time that day, Gertrude smiled.

One.

'Only retards read kid's books,' barked Tara. 'Jacky! Turn her over!'

Jacky Streatfield, Tara's personal guard dog, and not pretty at all, grabbed Gertrude's arms and rolled her onto her back. Jacky's hand formed into a fist.

Two.

Jacky's fist pulled back. Gertrude closed her eyes and let her smile spread.

Three. Gotcha.

'Oh my god, that bird just shat on my head!' screamed Tara.

'Get it away from me! Get it off! Call it off, freak!' yelled Jacky. Billy Yates, Samantha's skinhead boyfriend, roared in disgust.

'Ugh! Tara that is, like, actually disgusting,' said Michelle Lewis, the fourth and dumbest of Tara's terrorists. Tara retched and the crowd dispersed, shouting and swearing, but none of them could compete with the obscene words streaming from the crow's mouth.

Standing up, Gertrude checked herself over. Laddered tights, ripped shirt, no blood on her clothes, which was good. Blood was hard to get out. Looking up at the sky, she watched the crow flying away over the school playing field. Gathering up her stuff, she cursed herself for being a fool.

When she had seen Luke, the boy with the limp, underneath the pile of bodies, she had waded in without a moment's thought. She had actually hit Billy Yates. He clobbered her back, of course, and then the pile of bodies had jumped up and attacked her. Luke had shrieked with laughter as they wrestled her to the ground. She had been as gullible as Snow White and she should have known better, after Magness' solo visit that morning. At least her book was still intact and she still had time to go up to the field.

Luke stood there, leaning against the wall, his hands in his pockets. She lifted her chin and stared down at him.

'Why?' she said. The boy looked down at his feet.

'Because it's not me anymore,' and turning round he walked off, dragging his useless leg behind him.

❊ ❊ ❊

'Breathe,' said the tree.

'I am,' said Gertrude. The leaves rustled. Gertrude pressed her back into the trunk, took a deep breath and released it. The leaves sighed and swished above her matching her rhythm. In. Out. In. Out. Opening her eyes, she caught a movement to her left. The crow took two steps towards her and stopped. He held a fat, wriggling worm in his beak. The crow took another two steps and stopped again, looking round. *If he could whistle,* Gertrude laughed to herself, *he would.* Another two steps and he drew up beside her. He dropped the worm, which grunted as it hit the ground. The crow bowed his head.

'Queen Girly.' Gertrude bowed her head back.

'King Jim.'

'I saw they stole your lunch again.'

'Yes.'

'So, I have brought you mine.'

'You shouldn't have.'

'Go on, take it.'

'Oh no, I couldn't.'

'Go on. Get it down you.' Fighting nausea, Gertrude gave him a polite smile.

'No, you have it. I could not possibly deprive you. It's so plump.'

'Really?'

'Really. I'm not hungry.'

'You used to love eating worms.'

'I was four, Jim.'

'Oh well, if you're sure?'

'I'm sure.' The crow looked down at the fat wriggling worm.

'Please don't kill me, Mr Crow, sir,' the worm said. 'I have a wife and family.'

'Lying bar steward,' Jim said. 'Everyone knows the only thing a worm loves is his self.' He stabbed it with his beak and gulped it down.

'You were right, it was plump.'

'I know.'

'Anyway, you could always do with losing a few pounds.'

'Thanks, matey.'

'You're welcome, Queen Girly.' Gertrude allowed herself to relax against the tree. She had fifteen minutes left before break finished. The scent of new grass and flowers yet to unfurl, filled her with excitement. Spring was her favourite season. In the shelter of the tree, the cold March wind did not trouble her. Nor did anyone else. Not even the smokers came this far up the field.

'There's a surprise waiting for you at home.' She opened her eyes and looked at her friend.

'My grandmother's not there?' Jim cocked his head to the side.

'Nah, the old bitch is still there. No, it's something else actually, or rather *someone* else. You'll see when you come home. Just don't dawdle like you normally do.' Gertrude ran her hands through her matted hair.

'I will have to stop off at the pool, Jim. I smell awful.' Jim hopped away.

'Cor! Like an old fishwife with scampi knickers.' Gertrude laughed.

'Always the gentleman.'

'I'll see you later.'

'Jim?'

'Yes, Your Majesty?'

'Thank you for saving me.' Jim puffed his chest out.

'I live to shit on bullying cocktweazles, so don't mention it. Remember to hurry home,' and as he ascended into the sky, Gertrude yearned to do the same. She followed his flight with envious eyes until she could no longer see his black body in the sky.

'I don't think I have ever hurried home,' she murmured to the tree. Its leaves rustled in answer. Taking a deep breath, she stood up and prepared to go back to class.

CHAPTER 2

The walk home from school took forty-five minutes. Gertrude tried to make it last an hour. She loved this time of day. It belonged to her. The nightmare of school had finished and the nightmare of home had yet to start. She always walked. Only once she had gone on the school bus. Never again.

Removing her clothes and hiding them behind a bush, she waded into the pool and, steadying herself, dived under. The cold water pushed all the breath out of her and she surfaced, gasping. Laughing, she floated on her back, allowing the water to take her weight. The clouds scudded by, promising rain. She moved her head back and forth to wet every strand of her thick red hair.

Kenfig pool had been Gertrude's bath since she was five years old. Her grandmother had kicked her out of the house one afternoon and Jim had led the sobbing child to the pool. She needed no encouragement that hot day and had dived straight in. Later, she learned to remove her clothes first. Jim laughed and dive bombed her all afternoon. They hid in the reeds, whenever anyone passed by, and for a while, the legend of Kenfig pool had grown, with local people rushing home with tales of disembodied laughter. A drowned city was supposed to lie beneath the water, and the locals said you could hear the submerged church bell tolling, just before a storm. Gertrude had never heard the bell, but sometimes she felt there were people down there. Something had caressed her foot once. Jim said it was a reed, but she was sure she had also felt unseen hands helping to wash her hair. She sensed no malice and put it down to her overactive imagination. Anyway, the sensation had been pleasant.

A dark shadow appeared above her.

'Come on, fat girl! Stop dawdling!'

'Shut up, Jim! Let me wash my hair, scampi knickers and all that.'

'Okay, just hurry up.' He flew off and alighted on a branch. She washed her hair with the shampoo she hid in a bag behind the bush. With no more conditioner left, her hair was going to be a frizzy mess, but at least it would be a clean mess. Climbing out of the pool, she dried herself with her school jumper dressed herself. Jim jumped down and hopped around on the ground.

'Okay, Jim, let's go. Bye, pool.' She ran, following Jim who had taken off.

'Goodbye,' the reeds whispered.

Clambering over the dunes, she crossed the road and instinctively looked up at the sky. Dark, glowering clouds hovered above the church tower.

Grandmother was home.

As she reached the small copse of trees by the entrance to her road, a movement caught her eye. She turned towards it and dropped her schoolbag.

A man and an enormous black horse stood on the grass by the church. He stared at her with such intensity, her face grew hot. The horse tossed its head and the breeze lifted its dark mane. The man's long black hair also lifted, until she could no longer distinguish where the horse ended and the man began. Her ears buzzed and her heart hammered so fast she thought it would give out. She blindly reached for the wall enclosing the copse, as her legs gave way.

And still he stared.

In that instant, she knew him. She had dreamed about

him often enough. Whilst it was the golden-haired man who chased her through her dreams, this man was never far behind. How could she only have remembered him now?

Something moved across her with lightning speed, and then something else moved the opposite way. She tore her eyes away from the man and looked up. Blurred shapes danced all around her and with a rush of joy, she realized who they were.

The swifts spun around her, their little bodies weaving in and out. Her heart stopped racing and the buzzing faded. She looked over towards the man but he and the horse had vanished. She pulled herself shakily to her feet.

'Jim? Did you see –?'

'Told you there was a surprise waiting for you. You know what this means don't you?' She drew her attention back to the whizzing little bodies that were now dive bombing her from all directions.

'Spring,' she said and smiled, putting the dark-haired man and horse out of her mind. The leader of the swifts sang as he weaved in and out of the trees.

'Spring is sprung. Spring is sprung. We are back. We are back!' Gertrude laughed.

'I am so glad to see you. Did you have a good holiday? Did you relax? Did you have lovely warm weather?'

'It was wonderful. The bloody German swifts kept nicking all the best branches, but after a few aerial fights, we got it sorted. Taught us a few good moves as well.' He turned in mid-air and rushed towards the earth, pulling up just at the last moment.

'Wow,' Gertrude said.

'Show off,' said Jim. Gertrude chuckled.

'Welcome back. I have missed you, and now spring is just around the corner.' Jim jumped up onto the stone wall.

'That means it's your birthday soon, Queen Girly. How old?'

'Sixteen. I wonder what I will get this year? A broken nose perhaps? Or a rib? Perhaps something special, since I am sweet sixteen. What was it last year?' Jim shifted on the wall.

'Broken wrist, I 'fink.'

'Oh yes. How could I forget?' She looked down the road that led to her grandmother's house. Jim turned to the lead swift and tried to catch his attention.

'Could you teach me some moves, fella? I want to dive bomb that black demon cat from hell that lives at number seven.' The swift laughed and then yelped as Jim took to the air to chase it.

'Breathe,' whispered the tree nearest to her. Gertrude pushed down her irritation and patted the tree. Saying goodbye to the swifts, she walked down her road. She passed the field where the horses were usually grazing, but she could not see Duke nor Esmeralda. They must be in the far field. The unopened daffodils, nestled against the fence, danced in the breeze. When she came to the huge tree on the grass verge, she stopped. Throwing her arms around the tree, she kissed its trunk.

'Soon, my darling,' she whispered. The tree's budding leaves swayed joyfully. In just a few weeks she would start to blossom.

'Here she comes, spring is sprung,' Gertrude whispered and squaring her shoulders, she walked into her grandmother's house.

CHAPTER 3

Silence greeted her, but not a peaceful silence. The sort of silence that holds its breath, waiting. Gertrude paused by the kitchen door and tried to sense her grandmother. Despite the dark clouds above the church, the old woman was not in the house. She would not be far though. Gertrude maybe had about ten minutes.

She rushed to the, *'Cupboard-that-was-not-for-her.'* In the cupboard were biscuits with chocolate on them. She grabbed the tin and wrenched it open, hunger making her bold. She put one biscuit in her blouse pocket for later and stuffed a biscuit into her mouth. She ate it so quickly, she hardly chewed. A second biscuit followed and a third. She closed her eyes and let out a moan of satisfaction. The hand came from nowhere, crashing down onto her head so hard she almost choked.

Idiot! A second slap knocked her to the floor. She stayed down, knowing better than to get up.

'You will clean up this mess,' her grandmother said in a voice soft as snow, 'and then you will go to the shops and replace the biscuits you have stolen.' Gertrude tried to swallow her biscuit down but ended up coughing and spluttering the crumbs all down her blouse.

'I have no money, Grandmother, to replace them,' she replied in a hushed voice. Gertrude and her grandmother always whispered to each other. Her grandmother never raised her voice, even when she beat her. Gertrude sat up slowly, making no sudden movements. Anything could set her grandmother off. Her grandmother's face showed no signs of anger. Only the blazing arctic blue eyes revealed the rage beneath.

'Stick or hot hob ring?' Gertrude did not hesitate.

'Stick,' she whispered. Her grandmother nodded.

'Be thankful I am in a forgiving mood and allowing you to choose. Go and choose wisely and then come back in. Twenty canings should do the trick.'

'Thank you, Grandmother.' Scrambling to her feet Gertrude walked to the back door.

'Gertrude?'

'Yes, Grandmother?'

'Do not dawdle,' and she left the kitchen. Gertrude turned the key and pulled down on the handle.

Okay, choose wisely. If I come back with a thin stick, I will only be sent out again and anyway, the thin ones sting more. If I come in with a stick too big, Grandmother will still be able to lift it. For all her scrawniness, Gertrude's grandmother had incredible strength. Gertrude, in one of her few rebellious moments, had once dragged in an enormous branch, hoping to avoid a whipping. Her grandmother had managed to lift it and sent Gertrude through the paned glass doors leading through to the lounge. She had to pick up the glass afterwards. Lesson definitely learned. She ran to the end of the garden, to the silver birch. The branches moved.

'Breathe,' said the tree.

'Not now, Birch, I really can't. I am sorry, but can I have one of your branches?' Birch shuddered.

'Why?' the tree asked. Gertrude shook her head.

'You do not want to know.' Birch shuddered again.

'No, you can't. I won't be used in violence against you.' Gertrude flung her arms around the pale trunk and kissed the papery bark.

'Now listen, it is either your branch or the hob again and I hate being burned. Wouldn't you? This is easier. You are helping me really.'

'Are you really talking to that tree?' a posh pompous voice said.

Gertrude's heart jumped and she wheeled around. On the other side of the chicken wire fence, in the neighbour's garden, sat a golden retriever. His mouth opened in a smile and he cocked his head to one side.

'Yes. She's a friend.' The dog cocked his head to the other side.

'Are you really talking to me?'

'I don't see anyone else here.'

'You can hear me?' Gertrude moved away from the tree and crouched down on her side of the fence.

'Not only can I hear you, but I have something for you.' She pulled the hidden biscuit from her blouse pocket. 'What she doesn't know won't kill her … unfortunately,' she murmured. 'I was saving it for later, but I would love to share it with you.' The golden dog hesitated only a moment before trotting over to the fence. Gertrude broke the biscuit in two and pushed it through the chicken wire. The dog wolfed it down and Gertrude, chuckling, wolfed her half down almost as fast. Green eyes looked into brown and they both grinned. The dog gave a slight bow.

'My name is Sam.'

'Mine is Gertrude. Hello, Sam.'

'Hello, Gertrude.'

'We've never had neighbours before. That old house has been empty since I moved here. When did you move in?' The dog lay down on the grass.

'Yesterday. It is a lovely house. You should come round.' Gertrude frowned.

'I've been in that house. I used to go exploring in it. It's full of damp and cobwebs.'

'Not now. Mrs Eccles has made it beautiful.'

'Mrs Eccles?'

'My friend. She has worked her magic. I have never lived in such a cosy, beautiful house and I have lived in a lot.'

'You have not always lived with Mrs Eccles?' The big brown eyes looked mournful and his face grew long. He let out a sigh and dropped his head onto his paws.

'Mrs Eccles is my sixth owner.'

'Oh.' Gertrude looked at the big dog and recognized another victim. 'Is she nice?' He lifted his head, his eyes shining again.

'Oh yes, the best, just lovely. I love her.'

'How long have you been with her?'

'Three weeks and I totally love her.' Gertrude grinned.

'I'm sure she loves you too.' He sat up, his tail wagging.

'Oh yes, absolutely. She calls me her big golden boy and she really listens.' Gertrude raised her eyebrows. 'I mean she seems too.' He pushed his nose through the fence and Gertrude put her hand out so he could sniff it.

'How come you can hear me?' he asked. Gertrude crossed her legs, settling herself on the grass.

'I have always been able to hear animals. I can hear the trees whispering and the birds laughing and swearing. I can even hear that evil cat at number seven. I can hear him cursing everything in sight.' Sam shuddered.

'I saw that cat on my walk today. He is not right in the head.'

'It's always wise to avoid Satan. Magness and Jim will not go into his garden. Agnes says that if you go in there, you will never come out.'

'Who are Magness and Jim?'

'My friends. Jim is my oldest friend.'

'What does he look like?'

'He's completely black with the wisest eyes I have ever seen and swears like a sailor.' Sam frowned and Gertrude laughed. 'He's a crow.' Sam's eyes widened.

'Oh, so that is why I was sent outside.' Sam turned to look at his house. 'He is in there now, talking to Mrs Eccles.' Gertrude followed his glance.

'Jim's in there? *Talking* with Mrs Eccles?' Sam swung his head back to her.

'Well, no, I mean not talking … I mean she is … I mean he is just in there. I guess if he is your friend, he is checking up on who has moved next door to you.'

'Gertrude Emmeline Springate, you will step away from that mangy beast this instance. If you do not have the branch, which I politely asked you to get, you will have ten more canings, though I would dearly love to make it forty. However, I have no desire to kill you … yet.'

Gertrude scrambled to her feet, her heart pounding, and her mouth dry. Twice in one day, her grandmother had sneaked up on her. Usually, she was tuned into her grandmother's whereabouts. Sam leapt back from the fence so quickly he fell over his paws. He pulled back his lips and bared his teeth. Gertrude heard a low growl coming from his chest. Her grandmother's head turned and she fixed her cold blue eyes on Sam. The dog whimpered and he dropped down into a submissive position.

'Up you get, Sam, no need for that,' a lilting Irish voice said. Her grandmother's head snapped up and her eyes widened, as she took in the little old lady standing on the other side of the fence. Sam ran over and sat by the woman's feet. She smoothed his golden head and murmured,

'It's all right, I'm here now.' She lifted her head and fixed Gertrude's grandmother with a long cool stare. 'Mrs Winter, I presume.' Her grandmother became still.

'Mrs Eccles, I take it?' The two women exchanged a long look. Gertrude watched her grandmother narrow her eyes and give Mrs Eccles a look that turned most people's blood cold. Gertrude turned her head and watched with amazement, as Mrs Eccles' piercing blue eyes glared back. Sam and her looked from one old woman to the other, as the glares and the stares went on. Incredibly, her grandmother looked away first, her left eye twitching. Gertrude let out a long breath and looked with respect at the little old lady who stroked her new friend's head.

She was tiny. Dressed completely in white, she wore her platinum white hair in a neat bun. *If angels ever get old, they would look like her,* Gertrude thought.

'Mrs Winter? It seems we are to be neighbours. I would like to point out that although Sam is a beast, he is not mangy. Not anymore.' She rubbed the retriever's ears and Sam let out a low growl of pleasure.

'Be that as it may, Mrs Eccles, he was near my granddaughter. I do not want Gertrude catching fleas. My granddaughter has a fear of dogs. One attacked her when she was four.' Her grandmother had said it often enough it was almost believable.

Knowing she would be made to pay for what she was about to do, she found her voice and turned to Mrs Eccles.

'On the contrary, I was getting to know your lovely dog. He is indeed clean and there are no fleas on him as I would have heard – I mean he looks clean.' Trembling, she stepped forward and extended her hand. 'My name is Gertrude and it is lovely to meet you, Mrs Eccles.' Mrs Eccles closed her eyes for a moment and let out a sigh. Stepping forward she clasped Gertrude's hand with both of hers. Gertrude had never felt such warm hands.

'Gertrude, I cannot tell you how delighted I am to make your acquaintance. What an absolute honour to finally meet you,' and as she smiled, she did not look old at all. Up close the old lady's eyes were nearer to violet than blue. Mrs Eccles let go of her hand and then gave her a quick wink before turning back to her grandmother.

'Mrs Winter, I have heard such lovely things about you already. Someone told me you help in the church and the hospital. In fact, a little bird told me, you are often away doing good deeds. I am sure you have passed on your good values to your lovely granddaughter and therefore, may I be presumptuous in asking you a favour?' Gertrude never thought her grandmother could turn paler than she already was, but she did. Her thin lips clamped together and she seemed to be fighting an inner battle. At last, a sickly smile spread across her face.

'But of course, Mrs Eccles, ask away.' Mrs Eccles drew herself up.

'My legs are not what they were and I wondered if your granddaughter would be willing to walk my lovely boy, Sam?'

'Yes,' said Gertrude.

'Maybe you should have thought of that when you took on the animal. My granddaughter is my only help around the house and I really cannot spare her. She is very dear to me.' Mrs Eccles swept her bright glance up and down Gertrude and took in the frizzy hair and torn clothes.

'I am sure she is a constant delight to you and I normally would not ask, except everyone told me that if you are ever struggling, you would be the lady to turn to. Your reputation is known throughout the neighbourhood it seems.' Mrs Eccles flashed a mischievous grin and, in that moment, Gertrude knew she had made another friend.

'Well … but of course … I suppose I could spare her, and the good lord knows the girl could use more exercise. Fine. Tomorrow morning suit you?' Mrs Eccles clasped her hands together and bowed her head.

'But of course.'

'Five thirty? Or is that too early? She has a lot to do before school.' Mrs Eccles smiled.

'Tomorrow is Saturday, Mrs Winter.'

'As I said, five thirty in the morning?' Mrs Eccles smiled and turned to Gertrude.

'Is that all right with you, my dear?' and again Gertrude caught a wink.

'Yes, wonderful. The birds wake me up anyway.' Mrs Eccles gave her a warm look and clapped her hands.

'Excellent! Then it is settled. Come on, Sam, teatime. Lovely to meet you, Gertrude.' She gave her grandmother another cool stare. 'Mrs Winter, until next time.' Clasping her cardigan around her shoulders, Mrs Eccles turned and walked into her house. Sam stood up.

'See you tomorrow, Scamp. Watch out, your grandmother

looks like a storm cloud,' and he trotted after his mistress.

The daylight was fading and Gertrude could not see her grandmother's expression. The old woman did not move, staring at the door Mrs Eccles had entered. Eventually, Gertrude gave a small cough. Her grandmother flinched.

'Straight to bed. No supper.'

'Of course, Grandmother.' Gertrude walked into the house and ran upstairs to her small bedroom. Diving onto the bed, she burst out laughing. She had escaped a whipping and made two friends. What a woman Mrs Eccles was and Sam was a lovely dog. She could not wait to walk him. It would be like having a pet of her own. Wait until she told Jim. Today had turned out not so bad after all. Maybe Agnes had been hiding and Gertrude had not seen her.

With a pang, she realized she had left her schoolbag downstairs with her book in it, but not to worry, as she knew the first chapter off by heart. She recited it to herself until sleep became a breath away.

Listening to the birds calling good night to everyone, she fell into her dreams, where she knew the golden-haired man would be waiting.

Except this time, she would also look out for the dark horseman.

CHAPTER 4

J im once told Gertrude that birdsong changes in February. After all, there is a lot of waking up to do. Trees, drowsy from winter's sleep and flower bulbs, deeply slumbering in the cold earth, need to be roused. Birds have always taken their job of guardians of the dawn and dusk seriously and they sing songs of awakening in the second month of the year, heralding in the new season.

'But,' said Jim, 'In March we go bleedin' crazy.'

Jim had explained to her that the energy of the earth starts to build again. The trees all get ready to blossom and the first flowers start unfurling their hearts for all to see.

'As the days approach the first turning point of the year, Queen Girly, us birds get impatient and any lazy blighter stupid enough to sleep through this waking up time is told to, "*Get up and get out!*"' Therefore, by five thirty, the birds would have easily woken Gertrude up. However, such was her excitement at walking Sam, that she woke up before the first bird had even sung. She lay in her bed for a moment, as she always did, trying to capture last night's dream.

She sat bolt upright.

The dark man with the horse had been in it and this time the dream stayed with her. His eyes were grey, like summer storm clouds. She had been imprisoned in a room with bars on the window. He had climbed up the wall and torn through the bars to reach her. His blood had covered her face as he kissed her, over and over again. He murmured her name but it was not '*Gertrude*.' She frowned as she tried to remember it. The golden-haired man had not been there. She felt guilty as if she had betrayed him.

Shaking her head, she jumped up from her bed and opened her wardrobe door. She took out the one outfit that hung there. Old brown trousers, a mustard yellow shirt – that clashed hideously with her red hair – and an itchy brown jumper with a big hole in the armpit. The jumper ripped some more as she shoved her head through it.

Kneeling, she put her hand under the bed and feeling with her fingers, found the pink bobble she had rescued from the school floor. Gathering up her hair with her hands, she tried to pull it into a ponytail. Her hair was so thick, she had to wrestle to get it through the pink elastic and the bobble snapped. Letting out a sigh, she felt a pang of loss. She got up and went to a jar on the windowsill that contained red elastic bands the postman had dropped. They ruined her hair, but they would have to do. She grabbed one and once more tried to get her hair out of the way. Finally succeeding she whispered,

'The mane has been tamed.' She had no idea what she looked like, for there were no mirrors in her room.

'Why on earth would you want to look at yourself?' her grandmother once said. Having seen herself in the mirrors at school, Gertrude was inclined to agree with her. Padding over to her door, she turned the doorknob and opened it. Creeping across the landing, she stopped outside her grandmother's room. No sound escaped suggesting the old woman was in there, but she took a breath and tuned in. Moving closer to the door, she nodded to herself. The malevolent energy was there, creeping over her like fingers of ice. Feeling it, she could not believe how she had not sensed her grandmother yesterday. All her life Gertrude had been able to sense when she was near. Shaking her head, she crept down the stairs, put on her shoes, grabbed her coat, and escaped outside into the street.

The sun had not risen yet, but the birds were singing their

'*Get up and get out!*' song. Jim and his Crownies were in a tree, cawing outside the window of the house opposite.

'Get up you lazy old son of a motherless goat!' Jim crowed. 'Get up and stop stewing in your sweat, you big fat shiznit!'

'Oi, Jim,' croaked a big crow, 'Brilliant! A Shiznit! That's a good one. Come on boys, join in!' and the other crows cawed and croaked. The upstairs window opened and a head with a dark mess of hair leant out.

'Shut up!' the head screamed. 'Shut up! Every bloody morning it's the same. Shut up or I'll shoot you!' The head disappeared. Jim and his friends let out caws of raucous laughter.

'Oi, Fred,' yelled Jim, 'go and get Magness and Agnes. If he loves our voices, he's going to love theirs.'

'Right you are, boss,' and the big crow took flight. Gertrude called up to him.

'Hiya, Fred. Bye, Fred.' Gertrude ran over to the tree where Jim was holding court, and looked up at her friend.

'Jim, you should leave that man alone. He works really hard. He's up at six most days and doesn't get home until seven. He wants a lie in.' Jim flew down to her and alighted on the man's wall.

'Now, just you listen here, Gertrude Emmeline Springate,' he said doing his impression of her grandmother. She laughed. 'Listen, Queen Girly, that sod in there aimed a kick at Sid's head last week all because Sid was digging up worms in his front garden. I ask you, who the hell tries to kick a crow?'

'Oh, in that case then …' Gertrude cupped her hands to her mouth and gave a couple of caws. The head appeared again and Gertrude crouched down behind the wall.

'For the love of god shut up!' the head yelled.

'Don't kick crows then!' Gertrude yelled back.

'Who said that? Who's there?' Gertrude lowered her voice.

'It is I, your conscience. Do not kick crows or you will be cursed by their king.' She nodded to Jim, who puffed himself up.

'I'm coming down there and if I find you, I'm going to punch you.' Gertrude and Jim looked at each other.

'Scarper!' cried Jim. He and his Crownies flew up into the trees next door. Gertrude ran back to her grandmother's house and hid behind the wall.

'Where are you? Who said that?' the man yelled from his drive.

'Will you keep that racket down?' yelled another voice. 'Some of us work hard all week!'

'It's not me, it's those bloody birds!'

'Well, I can only hear you, so shut up!' A window slammed shut. She waited and then a door slammed. She peeked over the wall and giggled quietly in relief. The coast was clear.

'Och, it will turn out bad for us all, you know.' Magness the magpie sat on the wall, shaking his head. Gertrude quickly looked around.

'Where's Agnes?'

'Left me. Left me all alone. I am bereft. I am in grief. I am –'

'A silly blighter who would not wait for me.' Agnes landed on the wall and Gertrude greeted her with a relieved smile. 'Hello, Gertrude. You're up early lassie.' She gave her husband a nudge. 'Idiot! As if I would ever leave you.'

'Och, I know,' Magness said in a bright tone. 'I don't know what came over me. So, who are we waking up then?' Gertrude shook her head.

'I really think you should let that man sleep. We have caused quite a stir already and I don't want to wake my grandmother up.' The three of them turned their heads to the upstairs window of Gertrude's house. The curtains remained closed.

'No, lassie, we do not want that at all,' said Agnes.

Gertrude walked over to the wall enclosing Mrs Eccles' front garden. The front lawn was a deep verdant green, beautifully mowed. Herb bushes dotted along the borders, and already crocuses and daffodils were singing quietly. Gertrude drank in their fragrance.

'In answer to your comment, Agnes, I'm up early as I am

walking Mrs Eccles' dog.'

'Did I hear you say Mrs Eccles?' said Fred, flying down to sit on Mrs Eccles' wall.

'Mrs Eccles?' said Sid joining him. As if the name was a summoning spell, Gertrude soon found herself surrounded by all the Crownies, and Christopher the robin. All the birds murmured her neighbour's name and sat watching the little old lady's front door.

'Do you know her then, Fred?' Gertrude asked.

'Oh yes. All of us knows her. She lived in the next village. She always put out food for us and she really listened to us.'

'Listened?' Jim hopped down onto the ground and then up again onto the wall.

'Er … well what Fred means is that she seems to. I met her yesterday and she seems nice enough, for an old 'un.'

'She nursed me when I was shot,' said Fred with a tremor in his voice. Jim shook his head.

'Oh gawd, here we go.'

'It was a Sunday. In March. No! May – or was it April?'

'It was a spring morning,' Jim said, glaring at his friend.

'It was a spring morning. The light was luminescent and played mildly over the new seedlings that Old Sod Jones had just planted.' Gertrude shuddered. Old Sod Jones owned Satan the cat. They were a good match. 'The new seeds called to me in their deliciousness and who was I to resist? I dive in and gets a mouthful when Old Sod Jones comes out wiv' his rifle and tries to blast me back to heaven.'

'Or hell,' muttered Jim.

'I wandered about, my wing broken, my heart as well and soft hands gathered me up and took me to a warm room with cake and sunlight.' Jim raised his wing and touched his head.

'Delirious,' he said.

'No,' said Fred, still caught up in his story 'Delicious. The cake was delicious. Anyway, I went down a black tunnel and I saw the light. The light beckoned me on. And then, do you knows who I see? Me mam. And she says, "*Go back, Frederick.*

You are too important to leave the world. Go back and spread your light so all will follow." So, I did return and Mrs Eccles restored me back to the full healthiness you see before you now.'

'You know what, Fred?' said Jim hopping over to him. 'Next time you sees a light, keep going towards it and close the bloody door after you!' All the birds burst into laughter. Gertrude tutted at Jim.

'I think it is a great story, Fred, and I'm glad you are here. Where would Jim be without you? So, Mrs Eccles is a good 'un?'

'Oh yes,' said Christopher. 'She even rehomed some sparrows.' Jim made a noise.

'Argh, sparrows. I hates them. Common tykes taking all our trees.'

'Jim,' said Christopher. 'You know where all those new houses are being built down the road? That was where the sparrows used to live, so give them a break. Be welcoming. Take them under your wing.'

'You robins have such bleeding hearts.' Jim turned his back on the robin and looked at Gertrude. 'So, you walking the big furball, are you?'

'His name is Sam, Jim.'

'Samjim? What a weird name.'

'Sam. His name is Sam.'

'We birds not good enough for you then? Four legs rather than two? You've got two and don't you forget who taught you how to run with them and who took you to the pool and –'

'Jim, are you jealous? You have friends other than me. It will be nice for me to have another friend and it will free you up to spend more time with your Crownies. You won't have to worry about me so much.'

'Worry? Who says I worry? I don't care if you want to hobnob with the furries, all I'm saying is –'

'Jim, I won't forget you. I don't forget. Any of it.' Gertrude went over to the crow who was looking at the ground. She leant down and whispered,

'My oldest friend,' and kissed him. He sprang away.

'Get out of it! Less of the old and stop with the kissing. I don't know where those lips have been.'

'Yes, you do. They have been with me all night. No one has kissed them. Not in real life,' and remembering her dream she flushed red. Jim and her exchanged a look.

'All right, darling,' he said softly. 'Where are you going for a walk?'

'Down the beach, I think. Dogs like beaches, don't they? Do you want to come?' Jim recoiled in shock.

'Gertrude, my fat flower, it's Saturday.' Gertrude nodded.

'So what?'

'So what? So what, she says. Saturday. S-a-t-u-r-d-a-y.' Gertrude shrugged. Jim peered at her.

'Old Sod Jones washes his car.'

'Oh god, how could I forget?' said Gertrude with a smile. 'Old Sod Jones loves his car.'

'Takes pride in it!'

'Washes it.'

'Buffs it.'

'And then you lot ruin it.'

'Five points for the bonnet, two for the boot, six for the windscreen and if you manage to get a shat in as he shoots you, it's ten points and you've won.'

'Car clean roulette is dangerous, Jim. I wish you wouldn't.' Jim puffed himself up.

'It's my duty; he shot at our Fred! Come on, boys, away we go. See you, Queen Girly!' The flock of crows took off, their black bodies moving across the sky like a dark cloud.

'Crows,' sighed Christopher. 'They never forgive.'

'Or forget,' said Gertrude watching them settle outside the old man's house. 'Do you want to come to the beach, Christopher?'

'No, I best keep an eye on everyone here, just in case anyone needs the last rites. I suppose you're going, Magness?' The magpie shook his head.

'No. Me and my lassie are off looking for shiny things. I want to get you something nice today, Agnes. Spring is sprung. The swifts are back!'

'Och, I know!' said Agnes. 'Little blighters chased me down the street yesterday. They only stopped when I threatened to get you, Seamus and Demetrius.' Magness nodded.

'The boys are enough to scare anyone off. See you later, Gertrude.' The magpies flew off.

'Right, Gertrude,' said Christopher, 'I better see that they keep themselves safe. Mind you, how I can hope to control a load of crows I do not know. Enjoy your walk, sweetheart.' He flew up the road to join the crows, leaving Gertrude standing alone outside Mrs Eccles' house, as the sun rose.

CHAPTER 5

All Mrs Eccles' curtains were closed.

Should she knock on the door? Maybe Mrs Eccles had forgotten her. Twisting her hands and looking at the front door, a movement caught her eye. Relieved to see Sam's golden head peep through the curtains of the front room, her face broke into a grin and she waved. He grinned back and disappeared. A moment passed and the front door opened. The golden retriever trotted out and the door closed behind him. Disappointed not to see the old lady, she crouched down and welcomed the dog by scratching him behind the ears, as she had seen Mrs Eccles do.

'She's an early riser then,' Gertrude said.

'Who?'

'Mrs Eccles, but why did she not say hello?'

'She's not up yet.'

'How did the door open?'

'I ran upstairs and nudged her and she said it would open for me.' Gertrude frowned.

'Is she a witch?' she blurted out. Sam stepped back.

'People in glass houses …'

'What do you mean?'

'You are the last one to call anyone a witch. Plus look whom you live with.'

'Are you calling me and my grandmother witches?'

'Actually, just you. Your grandmother is a … I am not sure

yet.'

'I'm going to take that as a compliment then. Me and Mrs Eccles could form our own coven.'

'Mrs Eccles and I,' Sam corrected 'But yes, do it!'

'I will talk to her when I return you.'

'When I return *you*, you mean. It is *me* taking you for a walk actually.'

'Where is your lead?'

'Oh please, come on. It smells as if it is going to be a beautiful day and I feel like chasing rabbits.'

'I thought we would head down to Sker beach,' said Gertrude standing up and walking up the road.

'Are there rabbits?'

'Tons.'

'Lead the way, Scamp,' and laughing, they broke into a run. They came to a halt outside number seven.

By now a huge gathering of birds were in the trees outside Old Sod Jones' house. Jim was leading them in a rude song about old men and their bowel movements. Gertrude burst out laughing and Jim flew down to meet her, landing on the stone wall that enclosed the old man's front garden.

'Like it, Queen Girly? It's a new song I've been working on.'

'As always, King Jim, your poetry inspires.' Sam tossed his head.

'Well, it is not Shakespeare, but the rhythm is good. Jim, we have not been formally introduced. I am Sam. Thank you for lending me Gertrude for the day.' The crow hopped down from the wall and went up to the dog. He peered up at him.

'Listen, furball, she's only on loan. Bring her back wiv' no scratches or bruises and you and me will be just fine.' Sam drew himself up, his hackles rising.

'I am sure Gertrude will be pleased to have some civilised company for a change and some proper conversation that does not involve swearing.' Jim flew back up onto the wall so that now Sam had to look up at him.

'Oh, here we go. You're a dog, so you 'fink you have the last word on civilised conversation. Bloody snooty furries, always looking down on us winged fellas, when all we're doing is teaching the young 'un what she needs to know. All I'm saying is, I'm leaving her in your care and you bloody better look after her or I'll peck you a new arsehole.'

'Jim!' Gertrude snapped. 'Manners! We're only going for a walk and I want you two to be friends. I'm not a library book to be lent out and returned. Neither of you owns me. If anything, I own you. I am the human after all.' Both Sam and Jim gave Gertrude such a horrified look she instantly felt ashamed.

'Sorry,' she said, 'I don't know what came over me then. Obviously, it's standing near Old Sod Jones' garden. I came over all funny then.' She shook her head trying to clear it and took a step back. 'He honestly thinks he rules the world.'

'Don't they all?' said Jim.

'Don't they just?' said Sam at the same time.

'Dump one on the bonnet for me, Jim,' said Gertrude. The crow bobbed his head.

'And for me,' said Sam. Jim gave a mocking bow. Gertrude blew him a kiss.

'Come on, Sam, let's go. Have fun, Jim, but be careful.' She looked up at the birds sitting on the branches. 'All of you.' Sam and her continued walking up the road.

'You must forgive Jim. He's my oldest friend and we have been through a lot together.'

'Why does he call you Queen Girly?'

'It's a game we play. He is King of the Crows and I am Queen of the Girlies. We hold court, wage wars, and pass laws. He taught me how to curtsey. There is more to Jim than meets the eye.'

'Well, I admire his protectiveness of you, even if I do not care for his language. What are the birds doing exactly?'

'They're playing car clean roulette. Old Sod Jones—'

'Who?'

'He owns Satan, that big black furry cat. They're as evil as each other, just horrid. He cleans his car every Saturday and the birds ruin it. He shot Fred you know. Come on, I will introduce you to some other friends.' They reached the top of the road. Gertrude looked up at the church tower and saw the dark cloud hovering above it. Her grandmother was still in the house. She stood up on the fence enclosing the field, where some horses were grazing and yelled a greeting.

'Hola!' A beautiful chestnut stallion raised his head and with a friendly whinny, made his way over to the fence. A white mare followed shyly behind.

'Chiquilla mia, you look beautiful today,' the stallion said nuzzling Gertrude's outstretched hand. 'Azúcar?'

'Sorry, Duke, I forgot. There's someone I would like you to meet. This is Sam. He's moved next door to me and his owner, Mrs Eccles, is lovely. I have to walk Sam every day and—'

'Actually, sir, it is me that is walking her.' Sam put his front paws up on the fence, standing up on his back legs. 'Very pleased to meet you, sir. And you Señora. Usted es tan bella como la primera nevada.' Gertrude gave Sam an impressed look.

'Blimey, Sam, what did you say?'

'He said my Esmeralda is as beautiful as the first snow. Un placer conocerlo, Señor Sam.' The stallion bowed his head. 'Now, Gertrude, it must be the weekend, no? Because you only smile coming up the road when you don't have school. Am I right?'

'Yes, it's Saturday. Best day of the week.'

'Being retired I do not know what day it is. Every day is just blissfully content.' He turned to the white mare beside him and nuzzled her. She gave a soft whinny.

'I'm glad, Duke. You deserve it. I promise next time I come up I will have some sugar.' Esmeralda shook her head.

'You are supposed to be giving up, my love.'

'No, bring loads next time,' Duke said. 'I need to keep my strength up.' Gertrude reached forward and stroked the stallion's nose.

'I will bring some, Duke. You know what he's like, Esme, he

will only sulk.' Esmeralda shook her head.

'It is true, the sulks are bad things. But I just found you, my love, and I want you to live long.'

'Ah, mi reina, I have all the sweetness I need.' The stallion and mare started nuzzling and kissing each other. Gertrude jumped down off the fence.

'Time to go. Bye, you two. Enjoy your day,' but the horses did not even look up, so Gertrude and Sam continued on their journey. They came to the copse at the top of the road and the swifts attacked them from all sides, two even chasing Sam across the road onto the dunes.

'What if there had been a car?' Gertrude yelled, but they laughed and chased her across the road as well. Panting, she caught up with Sam.

'What the hell were the swifts doing?' she asked him.

'Reenacting the Battle of Britain. It is my fault. I told them all about it.'

'What fun!' Sam shook his head.

'Not really. The Germans won yesterday.'

'Jim says they have no sense of propriety.'

'What, the Germans?'

'No, silly. The swifts.'

'*Jim* says that? Good god, they must be bad. It is the coming of spring. Makes everyone wild.' Sam suddenly sat down and sniffed the air.

'Rabbits! Coming?'

'You run; I'm just going to walk. I will catch you up. We're going down to the sea, remember? Do you know the way?'

'I have my nose.' His head jerked around as a rabbit ran across the path. He sped off like a golden flash of lightning.

'I wish I could run like that,' Gertrude muttered. She followed the dog and gave herself up to the glorious morning. Away from her street, the sky was blue. She listened to the birds singing – mostly dirty limericks – and her thoughts wandered to the horses.

To be in love like that! If she ever found half of what

Duke and Esmeralda had, she would count herself lucky. She thought back to the dark horseman in her dream who had kissed her. Her stomach flipped at the thought of him. Sam kept running back to check on her and then bounding off again.

Finally, being caught up in his enthusiasm, she ran a little bit. It was not as bad as she thought. She ran up the final dune and looked down onto Sker beach.

As always, it was nearly deserted. Two dogs and their owner were walking away from them in the distance to the right. A lone horseman on a black horse galloped along the shore, towards her, but he suddenly turned and galloped away. Gertrude watched him recede into the distance, her stomach fluttering.

It isn't him ... whoever him *is. Get a grip girl.* Apart from the dark horseman, and the dog walker, they had the whole beach to themselves.

Sam bounded down the bank of pebbles that lead to the beach, with Gertrude following. She slipped and slid down on her bottom, giggling. The sandy beach stretched out before her and she chased Sam all the way down to the water's edge. The tide was out so they had a long way to run. The retriever bounded into the waves.

'Isn't that cold?' she asked.

'Not for me. Throw me that stick.' Gertrude looked at her feet and saw a bit of driftwood. Picking it up, she drew back her arm. Sam came bounding out of the waves and went down on his front paws, his back end up, his tail wagging furiously.

'Be warned, I throw like a girl, Sam.'

'You are a girl. Do not worry. I retrieve like a retriever. Throw it!' Putting all her strength into it, Gertrude threw and was pleased to see it land quite a way into the sea. Sam bounded off the moment it left her fingers and he danced across the water. He felt the seafloor with his paws. The stick floated away and he bounded through a wave to retrieve it. Triumphant, he trotted back to her with his sodden tail held high. She applauded him and reached for the stick, but he would not give it to her. He gave a playful growl as she tried to wrestle it from his mouth.

'Sam, how am I supposed to throw it again if you won't give it back?'

'I know,' he growled through gritted teeth. 'It is just that I won it and I do not see why you should have it.' Gertrude tugged again, but Sam just tugged back.

'So why did you come back to me? You want me to throw it again, don't you? Isn't that how it's meant to work?'

'I know. It is just I cannot let go of something once I have it. Distract me with something.' Gertrude looked along the beach. Spotting some big pebbles, she ran towards them. Sam dropped the stick and chased her. Shrieking, she managed to get to the pebbles before him and threw one. It plopped into the sea. Sam bounded in and once more felt the seafloor with his paws. Finding his prize, his head disappeared under the waves for a few seconds. Gertrude ran for the stick and nearly had it, but Sam ran out of the sea. Dropping his pebble, he snatched the stick from her hand.

'God, Sam, give me a chance!' she squealed. For the next half hour, they chased each other from stick to pebble, Gertrude screaming with delight and Sam giving a throaty chuckle every time he beat her.

Gertrude could never remember a time when she had felt so happy and free. There was just the beach, Sam, the sea, and the sky. Nothing else existed and she found an energy she never knew she had.

Finally, she flopped down onto the sand and just lay there, laughing. Sam stood over her with a big pebble in his mouth and the sea dripping off him onto her face. He started to laugh with her, his laugh deep and warm, and he opened his mouth. Gertrude moved just in time, as the pebble fell on the sand where her head had been.

'Whoops! Sorry, Scamp.' They both laughed all over again. Gertrude lay back on the sand and Sam lay down next to her.

Their laughter ebbed away. After a quiet pause, Sam tentatively put his head on her chest. She stroked his head and they both let out a sigh of utter contentment.

'You live totally in the present,' Sam said, after a moment. 'I have never met another human like you.'

'What do you mean?'

'You take everything in. I watched you walking down to the beach. Not a bird flew past that you did not acknowledge—'

'That would be bad manners.'

'Or a tree or bush you that you did not touch—'

'They're all so friendly.'

'You really look and hear. Most humans I have seen walking, have things in their ears or they are bent over looking at little square metal things.'

'Mobile phones you mean? I don't own one, Sam. I mean who would I call?'

'Whom, you mean. It is *whom* would I call.'

'Anyway, if I want to talk to anyone, I just stick my head out of the window and talk to the birds.'

'That is what I mean. Humans seem so distracted all the time as if they do not want to be here. They are never ... here.'

'Well, I'm here.'

'That you are. You know I chewed a saying once, *"All animals, except man, know that the ultimate of life is to enjoy it."'* Gertrude sat up on her elbows.

'Chewed?' Sam lifted his head proudly.

'I have chewed my way through quite a number of books. I consider myself extremely well-fed.' Gertrude shifted onto her side. Sam took his head off her chest and lay down beside her. They looked into each other's eyes. Leaning on one elbow, she asked,

'Is that why you are so wise?'

'You are what you eat. My first home was with a bookseller. Harmless enough, but a drunk. He had me as a puppy and was a bit absent minded. He would take me to work with him. However, one Saturday evening, he shut up shop in his haste to get to the pub and forgot about me. By the time he came back on Monday, I had devoured the reference section, the self-help section, the poetry section and was halfway through the complete works of Shakespeare. In fact, I was halfway through Hamlet. I hope it ends happily.'

'It doesn't.'

'Oh, what a shame. Well, needless to say, the silly old drunk was not happy and I was placed in a dog home. But I have a lot to thank him for.'

'Where did you go next?' Sam turned and looked out towards the sea. Gertrude gave him a moment and then gently stroked his head.

'You don't have to tell me if it's painful.' He swung his head round to look at her.

'After the bookseller, a man bought me. I was young and a hell of a boy. He took to chaining me outside and would feed me when he remembered, which was about once a week. Then some friends of his came round. They thought it would be funny to burn me with cigarettes.' Gertrude stilled. 'That night I worked that chain loose. I did not sleep. The next time he came near me, I went for his throat. I escaped but was picked up again and taken to the kennels. Then a nice young couple bought me.' Gertrude let out a breath and tried to calm her trembling.

'Good.'

'And gave me to their one-legged uncle.' Sam fixed Gertrude with a stare. 'Well, you can imagine how that worked out. So back to the kennels I went. Then they decided I would be a good father, so I was sent to a farm. I thought my luck was in, but the ladies there seemed sad and tired. The farmer's wife took one look at my tail and said it had a kink in it, so back I went. I mean look at my tail.' He stood up and moved around so his tail wagged over Gertrude's face.

'I think it's magnificent,' she spluttered through the fur.

'Okay, it is a bit more *feathery* – I think that was the word she used – than most other retrievers' tails, but it does what it is meant to do.' Sam flopped back down.

'So back you went?'

'Back I went. They started nicknaming me boomerang, as every time they sent me away, I came back.' Gertrude smiled. 'Then a young couple picked me. Steve and Jane had a little girl called Amy, who was lovely and sweet. One day we all went to a park and Amy had run off. I was keeping an eye on her and I saw a man loitering in the bushes. He had a dark cloud above him like your grandmother does, and he did not smell right. He watched Amy in a way that made my hackles rise. He came out of the bushes and reached out to touch her.' Sam turned his head again to look out to sea. Gertrude did not move.

'I went for his throat.'

'Of course you did.'

'I had no choice.'

'No, of course not.'

'He was the park keeper. I had drawn so much blood that they reported me. The police came and I was taken into custody to be killed.'

'But you saved Amy.'

'It did not matter. I had a record already and the kennels said they could not home me again.'

'Did you escape?'

'No. They put me in a police cell and left me. I shivered and cried all night. I had let my mother down.'

'How the hell had you let your mother down?'

'Because she taught me to love. *"Love humans,"* she told me, *"They need it more than any other creature on this planet."'*

'We don't deserve that love, Sam.'

'It is what dogs do, Gertrude. It is what we are made for. We are made in the image of love. If we do not show you, how will you learn? But I had nearly killed ... twice.'

'A psychopathic sod, who watched his friends burn you and a paedophile? I only wish you had killed them, then there would be two less scum for us to worry about.'

'I lay in that cell feeling more wretched than I have ever felt in my life. That is when she came in.'

'Who? … or whom?'

'You were right the first time. Mrs Eccles came in. Do not ask me how she got in, but she was there. She opened my cell and said I had suffered enough. I was to come and live with her. She said she had been looking for me for ages and that it was time.'

'Time for what?' Sam shook his head.

'No idea.'

'She reminds me of the fairy godmother in Cinderella.'

'More true than you know.' Gertrude lay back on the sand and looked up at the sky. One fluffy cloud floated across the brilliant blue sky. She drew in a deep breath and let it out as if she was blowing the cloud on its way.

She loved this time of year. March was full of promises; the promise of leaves on trees, the promise of lighter nights to come and the promise of maybe, just maybe, a warm summer. She could sense the hesitant growth of everything.

'Gertrude?'

'Yes, Sam?'

'Do you like the sea?'

'Uh-huh.'

'Good, because she is about to say hello!' Sam leapt up and bounded away, but Gertrude was too slow and the tide rushed over her feet and legs. Screaming with laughter, she jumped up.

'Blimey, how long have we been here for?'

'Long enough.'

'We better make a move. I have chores to do and I want to check on Jim.' She gazed at Sam. 'I have loved this morning.' Sam gazed back and winked.

'Me too. Come on, Scamp, otherwise, Jim may come looking for us and I do not want a lecture on how wet you are.' Gertrude turned and looked out to the sea, telling herself she was watching it make its way up the beach. However, her eyes scanned the beach for the dark horseman. Sam and her were the only ones there and ignoring the stab of disappointment, she turned away.

'Bye-bye sea.' She made her way back up the bank of pebbles.

They had just crossed the road to the top of her street when they heard the gunshot.

CHAPTER 6

Gertrude ran down the road with Sam chasing after her. Chaos greeted them outside number seven. Old Sod Jones lay on his back in his drive, his car gleaming behind him, except for a huge white splat over his windscreen. He held his shotgun in front of him, as a shield, as bird after bird dive-bombed him. The language from him and the birds were as black as the crows, who led the attack. Gertrude spotted Magness and Agnes, the two wood pigeons, Roy and Joy, and a group of sparrows. The swifts were circling high above. Gertrude could hear the swift leader relaying instructions.

'Swift seven, report position. Swift five, report.' Another shot went off and Gertrude rushed forward. She threw herself onto the prone man and tried to wrestle the gun off him. As if waiting for her signal, the birds dive-bombed en masse, including the swifts. Old Sod Jones yelled in rage, as he moved his gun back and forth, tossing Gertrude from side to side as she clung on. Sam raced up beside her and grabbed the man's shirt between his teeth. Out of the corner of her eye, Gertrude saw a black shape moving forward. Satan hissed and sprang. Gertrude jumped back, but she was not the target. The cat scrammed his claws down his owner's cheek and then left as quickly as he had come. The old man screamed in pain.

'Call them off, or I will kill them all.' Gertrude leapt off him and cried out,

'Friends, to me.' Every single bird turned in mid-flight and settled about her, some on the trees, some on the wall and Jim on her shoulder. Trembling, she watched the old man stumble to his feet. He slowly levelled the gun. Gertrude found herself staring down the barrel.

'Your dog is dead.' Gertrude lifted her chin and glared down at the old man.

'He has done no wrong to you.'

'He has drawn blood.'

'That was done by your own cat.' The old man snorted.

'Fluffykins? My cat would never harm me.' At the cat's name, the birds all burst into laughter. The man, hearing the cacophony, pointed the gun up to the sky and took a shot. The whites of his eyes showed and spittle gleamed on his chin.

'Tell them to shut up.' Gertrude tried to steady her breath.

'Quieten down, my loves.' The birds hushed. The man turned his wild gaze to Gertrude.

'You really are a freak, aren't you? Your grandmother will be hearing about this. And that—' he pointed his gun at Sam, '—that beast is as good as dead. I shall inform the police. A dangerous dog should not—' Gertrude stepped forward and was pleased when the old man stumbled back.

'It wasn't Sam who drew blood! It was your bloody sod of a cat, Satan. You want to talk about dangerous? Your cat is a menace! Curses me every time I pass—'

'Freak! Get off my land! Or you will join your dog.' Again, he lowered the gun and pointed it at Gertrude's face. Sam growled and the birds all moved their wings, readying to attack. Gertrude looked at the deranged man and pulled back her lip into a sneer.

'Men and guns. You are pathetic. Let's go. Stand down, Sam. Jim, call off the attack. Stand down, swift leader, I don't want anyone getting hurt.' The birds all took off in a cloud of wings. She turned away and walked towards her grandmother's house.

A wave of weariness crashed over her and her legs buckled.

Sinking to the ground, she felt sick and put her head in her hands.

'Breathe,' said the big blossom tree beside her. Sam nuzzled her head.

'She is right, Scamp, breathe deep. It is the adrenalin hitting you. You just looked down the barrel of a gun so it is bound to affect you. I know it shook me up the first time.'

'What?'

'Do not worry about that now, just take in deep breaths. It will pass.' She heard the flap of crow's wings.

'Queen Girly, you okay? Blimey! Old Sod Jones got out on the wrong side of the bed this morning, stupid moron. All because Sid did a shat on his windscreen. I mean it was a huge one, granted, but even so—'

'You bloody stupid, irresponsible, feathered son of a sparrow!' barked Sam turning so fast on the crow that Jim squawked in alarm. 'You could have got her killed. After lecturing me about looking after her, you then put her life at risk, just so you can have a bit of fun on a Saturday morning.'

'Now just a minute, you big snotfish of a furball. We've been doing car clean roulette long before you graced us with your presence, Your Royal Furriness, so don't you go all high and mighty on me. Gertrude was never in any danger.'

'No danger? What else would you call having a gun pointed at your face? You are as mad as that old bloke is. I am surprised the girl isn't dead.'

'I've done all right up to now and we don't need you, do we, Queen Girly? You're okay, Gertrude, aren't you? She loves the excitement. She's not some baby to collywobble. She's a lot braver than you think. Bah! What's a gunshot now and again anyway?'

'The word is mollycoddle!'

'Stick your fine words up your arse!' Gertrude lifted her head.

'I'm all right. Honestly. Please stop shouting, my head is hurting.'

'Tell him!' they both said at the same time.

'Get up,' said an ice-cold voice. Knowing the voice, as she knew her own, Gertrude leapt up. Swaying, she faced her grandmother. The old woman's eyes swept up and down her.

'You are filthy.' Gertrude swallowed and felt Sam take a step back. Jim flew off.

'I went down the beach. I thought Sam would like—'

'You are filthy.'

'I know. I will brush my clothes down before I come in and wash them today.'

'You are not entering the house with those clothes on.' Sam moved forward and sat, pressing his trembling body close to Gertrude's thigh.

'Lean into me and we will tremble together,' he whispered. Drawing strength from the brave heart beside her, she put her hand down to stroke his head. Her grandmother flicked a glance at the retriever and then looked back at Gertrude.

'Take them off.'

'I will.'

'No. Now.'

'I'm in the middle of the street.' Her grandmother raised a white eyebrow. With shaking hands, Gertrude grabbed the bottom of her jumper and pulled it over her head.

'My loves! You're back. Did you have a nice time?' Gertrude stopped and looked at Mrs Eccles. The tiny old lady walked towards them; her arms outstretched. Gertrude had to stop herself running into them, but Sam had no such reserve. He bounded joyfully up to her.

'Do something,' she heard him whisper. Mrs Eccles winked at him and made her way over to Gertrude, who stood with her jumper in her hands.

'Oh look, Gertrude dear, you're covered in sand. You must have had such fun, but you are messy. Let me take you in for a hot bath and a clean-up.' Gertrude dared a look at her grandmother. Her face had blanched and she stared at Mrs Eccles with absolute hatred.

'That will not be necessary, Mrs Eccles. Gertrude has to learn —'

'Look! The vicar! Hello, Reverend, lovely weather for this time of year. I will leave you two to discuss church business. Come along you two dirty scamps,' and taking Gertrude's hand in hers, she led her away. Gertrude could feel her grandmother's eyes boring into her back and went to look round.

'Just keep walking, lovely girl,' Mrs Eccles said squeezing her hand. 'Fancy being saved by a vicar, now that is a first,' and she laughed. Her laugh sounded like little bells. They reached Mrs Eccles' front door and Gertrude stared at the knocker. The face of a man covered in leaves held the knocker in his mouth. Mrs Eccles followed her glance.

'That's Jack. He's a friend. Say hello if you want and when you are ready, come into my home. Come on, Sam.' Dog and owner pushed the door open and closed it behind them. Gertrude stood staring at the leafy man and sprung back in shock. The face had closed its eyes and sighed.

'Aeyociminginirnit?' Gertrude looked around. Again, she heard a sigh. She took hold of the knocker and jumped when it came off in her hand. The man puckered his lips.

'I said, are you coming in or not?' Aware that she was gaping she closed her mouth and nodded.

'Knock then and enter. And be most welcome.' She replaced the knocker between the lips of the leafy man and knocked. The door opened. Looking back, she saw her grandmother, the vicar, and Old Sod Jones, staring at her from across the road. Turning her back on them, she took a breath and entered the house of Mrs Eccles.

CHAPTER 7

The hallway sparkled with light.

Rainbows bounced off the walls and the house smelled of spring. A vase of dancing daffodils sat on the hallway table. Gertrude blinked twice. They *were* dancing. Looking towards the hall window, she saw several crystals hanging down. They captured the spring sunshine and threw rainbows across the walls.

Sunshine. This house, it seemed, escaped the dark clouds of her grandmother. A sense of calm descended on her. She bent to smell the daffodils.

'We smell sublime, don't we? Oh, divine we are. We smell of spring and happiness. We're everybody's favourite.' Gertrude smiled.

'Well, my lovelies, you are in Wales,' and she bent to smell them again.

'They are beautiful, but rather full of themselves I'm afraid,' the soft lilting voice said. Gertrude lifted her head. Mrs Eccles stood in an archway that Gertrude presumed led to the rest of the house. Her hand was on Sam's head and he grinned up at her. Up close, in the bright light, Gertrude could see that Mrs Eccles had smooth, wrinkle free skin. Her face was radiant, as though lit from within.

'Are you Irish?' Gertrude blurted out. The old lady's eyes flashed amethyst and she smiled.

'Sometimes.' Gertrude nodded, as though this made perfect

sense. Mrs Eccles gazed at her with such ferocious tenderness, that she felt uncomfortable and made a show of looking around.

'I love what you have done with the house and—'

'There is no need to whisper here, my darling.'

'Sorry I did not realise I was. Sorry—'

'And stop apologising to me.'

'Sorry. I was saying … this house always looked so sad and decaying before. Sam said you had worked your magic.' The old lady continued staring and Gertrude looked at the ground not knowing what to do.

'You, my darling girl, do not have to say or do anything, except go upstairs, get out of your sandy clothes and run yourself a bath.' The sound of fast footsteps from upstairs made Gertrude jump.

'Don't worry, that's just the bath running.' Sam started to edge away from her. 'Sam, my boy, don't think you're getting away with it. You are full of sand and smell like a dead fish. Gertrude is our guest, so she will have the bath. You are outside with me and the hose.' Sam still tried edging away, shaking his head. Gertrude laughed.

'Sam, I could not get you out of the water this morning. A hose is nothing compared to the Bristol Channel.'

'Well said, my dear. Now, Gertrude, go upstairs and run yourself a lovely warm bath. There are lots of potions up there so …' Mrs Eccles cocked her head to one side and looked Gertrude up and down. 'Is it time?' she murmured to herself. 'Yes, I think so. The purple bottle for you, my darling. Put three drops into the water, no more mind, just three, and then wash your hair with the shampoo and conditioner that is up there. It is especially for you. Soak for at least twenty minutes. Then go into the guest bedroom and there will be some clean clothes for you to change into. After that, come downstairs and we will have a nice cup of tea and some of my chocolate cake I made this morning.' Sam nudged her. 'That my friend made this morning.' Gertrude did not move. 'Well go on, girl!' and smiling Mrs Eccles turned, pushing Sam thorough to the back of the house.

Holding the wooden bannister, Gertrude made her way up the stairs. She stopped to look at the pictures lining the wall. The pictures were of trees and were the most vivid, lifelike paintings she had ever seen. When she came to a painting of a huge gnarled oak tree, she stopped and jumped back. The leaves of the tree moved! She rubbed her eyes and looked again. *No, just a painting.* She carried on up the stairs and heard a rustling sound. Turning, she saw each painted tree move, as if a breeze blew through them. Shaking her head and putting it down to not having had any breakfast, she reached the top of the stairs and went to find the bathroom.

It was easy to find.

It glowed. It had so many crystals hanging from the ceiling it was like stepping into a rainbow. A beautiful smell greeted Gertrude. In the middle of the spacious room, stood an enormous bath with clawed feet. Around its edge were candles, their dancing flames adding to the glow. Their scent floated across the room. On the walls were more pictures, this time of sea creatures. On the windowsill, a row of coloured glass bottles sparkled in the sun. Elegant and tall, they threw different coloured lights onto the walls. Gertrude picked up the purple bottle and read the label.

PURPLE! for Passion, Potency and Power.

Pour 1-7 drops, (depending on how much power you think you can handle and how walked upon you currently are,) under meandering water and breathe deep.

Soak for twenty minutes, (or thirty if you dare.)

Creators Note: I am not responsible for your behaviour afterwards. If you think you rule the world and start throwing your weight around, I do not want to know. Remember less is more, (unless it is chocolate.)

Bemused, Gertrude turned the gold dolphin taps on and put in the heavy gold plug. The water cascaded down into the deep bath and taking the top off the bottle, she carefully poured in three drops of the purple liquid. The water turned a deep purple and a smell of violets wafted up. Breathing deep, she felt lightheaded and a rush of warmth came over her. Her stomach fluttered and skipped as if she had a flower there and one by one the petals were unfurling. She put her hand on her stomach and felt the fluttering beneath her skin. The flower felt fully open and she felt as if she could indeed deal with anything that came her way. It was a most bizarre feeling.

Removing her damp clothes, she saw two red bottles by the side of the bath. Picking one up, she read the gold writing.

Are you a redhead? Are you a ginger? Are you a titian marvel? Are you on fire? Let this special shampoo, (which contains real beams of a glorious sunset that occurred sometime late August,) light your fire.

You stand out anyway, ginger, so really stand out, tall and proud.

For best results, follow with super, special, splendid, sunset conditioner.

Creators note: I am not responsible for the heads you will turn. If you are chased down the street and whistled at, I do not want to know. Leave me alone.

The bath filled up and the violet water sparkled, inviting her in. Clouds of purple steam filled the bathroom with a heady scent. She turned the tap off, stepped into the bath and submerged herself. The flower in her stomach started dancing and she felt queasy. Then it settled down and she let the knots of tension soak away. *I really can accomplish anything. I must remember how this feels.*

'I could stand up for myself if I tried,' she said aloud to a picture of a dolphin. She held her breath and went under the water. She shook her hair from side to side. Coming up for air, she reached down and found the shampoo bottle. The shampoo was deep red, with sparkles of gold that seemed to dance.

'Everything dances and sings in this house,' she mused as she massaged it into her thick hair. Her head tingled and felt warm. Diving under again she rinsed out the shampoo. Emerging, she reached for the conditioner and massaged it in. She felt the knots jump out of her hair and for the first time in her life, she ran her fingers through it. Piling the heavy hair on top of her head, she sank back into the bath and let the conditioner do its work.

Her stomach still tingled and felt warm. Sighing, she luxuriated in the scented purple water. Tara and the '*Petty Four*' stole into her mind and Gertrude laughed out loud. She imagined them in a bubble and watched them float away.

'Stupid girls! What have I been afraid of all these years?' Her grandmother's face floated in front of her and Gertrude tried putting her into a bubble too. She would not go. Frowning she tried harder, but her grandmother's face would not budge. Shrugging, Gertrude decided to ignore her and dived under the water. Swishing her hair, she rinsed all the conditioner off. She felt so strong and sure of herself that she laughed underwater.

As her mouth opened the purple water gushed down her throat.

A rush of energy shot down her and back up and she flew out of the bath onto the mat beside it. She coughed and began to dance and sing, spinning around the bathroom. She grabbed a fluffy red towel off the heated rail and wrapped it around her body. Her wet hair spun out all around her and she jumped over the bath.

Hearing a polite cough, she stopped with a start to see Mrs Eccles standing in the doorway with a frown on her face. Sam, looking damp, had his head cocked to one side and his white eyebrows raised.

'I can do anything you know,' Gertrude said and coughed.

'Oh, my word,' said Mrs Eccles coming over to her, 'You swallowed some didn't you? All right, my lovely girl, sit down, I'll get you some water. And put a towel around your hair, would you? You're dripping everywhere.' Gertrude skipped over to the towels. The fluffy red towels were a welcome change from the scratchy brown ones her grandmother allowed her to use. Mrs Eccles held out a glass of water.

'Drink this down, it's good Welsh water. Get it down you.'

'But I feel just wonderful. I could fly if I wanted to.'

'Exactly! Drink. Now. Before you do take off.' Gertrude gulped down the cool water and felt the energy die down a little. She coughed again and a little cloud of purple mist came from her mouth. It formed into a hand and gave her the thumbs up. Then it waved goodbye and disappeared. Mrs Eccles cast a beady eye over the bathroom and walked over to pull out the plug. Placing her hands on the bath Mrs Eccles gave Gertrude a searching look.

'I should have told you not to swallow the water, but at least you didn't get all arrogant and want to rule the world. That, my girl, speaks volumes. Dry yourself off and help yourself to moisturiser. You will find some in the cabinet. Then go into the spare room, my darling, where you will find some lotion for your hair. Run it through, right to the ends. Put on the dress laid out for you and then come downstairs.' She turned and walked away. 'Come on, Sam, leave Gertrude in peace.' Sam waited until he heard the old lady's footsteps recede downstairs and then winked at Gertrude.

'You look all different, Scamp. All glowy and rosy.'

'Sam?' a voice came from downstairs.

'Coming!' He turned and scampered down the stairs. Gertrude opened the cabinet and picked up a midnight blue pot. She read the label:

Silky moisturiser made from silkworms who weave starlight. Fragranced with midnight jasmine, picked during a blue moon. It is ridiculously expensive but since when did you have any luxury in your life, Gertrude?

Gertrude nearly dropped the pot.

'This really is the most curious bathroom.' She opened the pot and felt lightheaded at the scent that floated up. Little blue flowers glided upwards and popped in front of her, releasing more of the beautiful scent. She dipped her fingers into the thick white cream and smoothed it over her arms. The cream quickly absorbed, leaving her skin with a subtle sparkle. She slathered it on and rewrapping herself in the towel, put the pot back in the cupboard. In the cabinet, a little yellow packet had appeared. It said;

Oh dear, you have been thinking too much again, haven't you? Taking on everything and now you have a headache.

Take two Starflower tablets and for Goddess' sake sit down!

Gertrude closed the door. 'Poor Mrs Eccles.' She walked out of the bathroom and through to the guest bedroom.

It was like walking into a meadow. The carpet was deep green and her feet sunk into it. The wallpaper had little flowers all over it as did the curtains and bedding. A large double bed dominated the room. It gave off a sweet floral fragrance. As she padded across the carpet, the flowers on the wallpaper all turned their heads, as if following the sun. On the white dressing table stood two bottles; one labelled straight and one labelled curly. Gertrude picked up the curly one and smiling read the label.

Oh, good choice! Pre Raphaelite curls it is! Put a daffodil size portion in your palm, rub together, and work through your hair, (head upside down,) and feel your hair remember how to behave! Then fling your head back in total abandonment and just glory in those locks.

Gertrude turned her head upside down and smoothed the white lotion through her hair. She felt her hair move, as though rearranging itself. She hung upside down until the sensation stopped. She flung her head back, she hoped in total abandonment, and put her hand up to feel her hair. It was already dry and she felt silky curls instead of frizz. She walked over to the bed and picked up the satin grass green dress that lay there. She shook her head. There was no way she would fit into it. She took her towel off and put it in the linen basket. Taking the dress, she edged it over her head and smoothed it down. It rippled like water and she was overjoyed to find that it fit.

Walking over to the full-length mirror that stood by the window, she dared a glance at herself. She had not seen herself for years, but even so, she did not recognise herself.

'I have a waist,' she murmured. The dress clung in all the good places. Her breasts looked full and round and her waist curved in and out. And her hair! It sparkled and shone. It looked like a sunset. Highlights and lowlights glistened and the curls corkscrewed and twirled down her back. Her green eyes glittered with a fire she had never noticed before and Gertrude felt dizzy and excited.

'She *is* a fairy godmother,' and then realising she was keeping the fairy godmother waiting, she twirled once more in front of the mirror and floated down the stairs.

CHAPTER 8

In the hallway, the daffodils oohed and aahed.

'Still not as pretty as us!'

'Shut up, you vain things,' but Gertrude laughed as she said it. Wandering through to the kitchen, she followed the sound of Mrs Eccles' voice. She found the old lady and Sam sitting in a conservatory at the back of the house.

Gertrude did not know where the glass room ended and the outside garden began. Flowers and bushes crowded the room in abundance. Butterflies danced in the air. Dragonflies and damselflies chased each other, in and out of pink and purple flowers and the whole room was warm and fragrant as if it had captured summer. Statues peeped from beneath bushes. They looked like they were playing hide and seek. She tore her eyes away from a statue of a faun and looked at Mrs Eccles.

The old lady stood up and leant on a wicker chair for support. She had gone pale and was breathing hard. Tears flowed down her cheeks and she trembled.

'Oh, Mrs Eccles, what's wrong?' Gertrude ran forward but Mrs Eccles waved her away.

'No,' she said, 'Let me look at you.' Gertrude stayed still and allowed herself to be scrutinised. 'In all my days, I never thought – it took so long – I lost you and I thought … she has not won, Gertrude, oh no, she has not won.' Gertrude listened to her without moving. Only when Mrs Eccles sat back down, did Gertrude look over to Sam with her eyebrows raised. He shook his head and went to sit by his owner.

'Please be seated, my dear,' Mrs Eccles said as if nothing had happened. The old lady poured out tea from a silver pot.

'Milk?'

'Yes please.' Gertrude took the bone china cup from the now steady hand of her host.

'Cake?' Covering half the table was the biggest chocolate cake Gertrude had ever seen.

'Oh yes, please. You made this?' Mrs Eccles nodded. Sam grunted.

'Oh, very well,' she sighed, cutting a huge slice. 'I have a friend who can bake and cook like no one else in all the worlds, but the proof is in the pudding. Eat and tell me what you think. I know she will want to know. She baked it for you.'

'Does she know me?' Mrs Eccles sipped her tea and peered over the rim of her cup.

'She used to.' Questions bubbled up on Gertrude's lips, but Mrs Eccles put her cup down.

'There is only one use for a mouth when there is chocolate cake in front of you. Eat.' She handed the plate over to Gertrude. Gertrude sunk her teeth into the cake and closed her eyes as the dark rich fluffiness floated around her mouth. The chocolate frosting and buttercream melted over her tongue. Gertrude grinned with sheer contentment.

'Can I have some? Please?' asked Sam. Mrs Eccles shook her head.

'How many times have I told you, Sam, chocolate is bad for dogs. It's poisonous.'

'But Gertrude gave me a chocolate biscuit the other day and your friend said she would make one especially for me. Isn't this it?'

'Oh, she did too. I did not ask her. Better not risk it, I mean if anything happened to you, I would never forgive myself and – Gertrude? What on earth is the matter?' Gertrude was staring wildly at Mrs Eccles. She coughed and choked as the cake went down the wrong way. Mrs Eccles jumped up and ran behind her. Giving her a good hard slap on the back, she dislodged the piece of cake and Gertrude caught it in her hand.

'You can hear him?' she croaked.

'Pardon?'

'Mrs Eccles,' Sam said, 'We have slipped up. Oh, how we have slipped up.' Mrs Eccles came from behind Gertrude and walked slowly back to her chair. She sat down. A strange light shone in her violet eyes.

'Yes. Yes, I can hear him. And the daffodils boasting in the hall, and Jim and his Crownies swearing, and the swifts shouting battle formations to each other. I can hear the trees whispering and laughing, as the wind caresses them. I can hear the blossom tree down the road preparing to unfurl in her glory and the Spanish stallion, whispering endearments to his white mare. I can hear the stars sing, the moon pine, the sun roar and I can hear the sea calling to the river like a lover. I can hear all this and more, much more than you can imagine. Just. Like. You.' Gertrude stared at her and the old lady met her gaze with her proud violet eyes.

'You're a freak. Just like me.'

'Freak? Who said anything about being a freak?' Mrs Eccles smashed her arm down on the armrest. 'The freaks are the ones who can't hear these things. They walk around, their heads full of the mundane and the banal, totally oblivious to the murmurings and secrets around them. They are the freaks, child, not you and I.'

'But all my life people have beaten me and—'

'And you are lucky I found you before Morgan did, otherwise they would all be a pile of smouldering ash by now, or worse. You are lucky I have more self-control.'

'Who is Morgan?'

'Have another cup of tea.'

'I don't want another cup of tea.' Mrs Eccles ignored her as she poured out another cup. She added three sugars.

'I don't take sugar.'

'You have had a shock. Hot sweet tea is the remedy. Now

drink it down.'

'I don't want it.'

'You know I had almost forgotten how stubborn you are and how you never seem to want what is good for you. Drink it. Now.' The violet eyes blazed and Gertrude took the outstretched cup and obediently drank. She felt better and placed the cup down.

'What are we? I mean how come no one else hears these things? How is it that only you and I can?'

'There are plenty of people who can do as we do. I grant you there are not many in this part of the world and certainly no one you know, but there are many people who talk to trees, flowers and animals as easily as you and I are talking right now.'

'All my life I have heard these things. My grandmother beat me, my teachers mocked me, calling me special—'

'You are special, more special than you could imagine.'

'Special is a polite way of saying freak. I stuffed my ears with cotton wool to drown out the voices, but Jim sang and swore at me. He pulled the wool out of them.' Mrs Eccles gave a soft chuckle. 'All my life, thinking I was a freak, that I was mad, insane. And now you – you say it's normal?'

'Well, all right it's not normal. Not round here anyway. I know what you must have gone through.'

'No, you don't.'

'You're right, I don't. I can only imagine what torture you have been through.'

'Where do I come from?' Mrs Eccles stared down at her hands. 'Who and what am I, Mrs Eccles?' The old lady shook her head.

'You really have no inkling? You can't remember who you are?'

'No.'

'Then you will know who you are when the time is right.'

'You can't leave me hanging like this.'

'I can't tell you *who* you are. That is always for us to figure out alone. But I can tell you where you are from.' She raised her head, gave Gertrude a piercing look, and then looked up.

Two yellow butterflies danced between them. Mrs Eccles' eyes followed them, darting back and forth and Gertrude began to think the old lady's eyes were making them dance. Mrs Eccles put her hand out, palm up. The dancers settled there, huddling close and becoming still. She smiled down at them.

'Go on and dance. There's not much time left.' The butterflies flew upwards and resumed their dance, moving out into the garden. Not taking her eyes off them and ignoring Gertrude's fierce stare, Mrs Eccles said,

'There is another Britain, one that exists within this one. It is a deeper reflection of this one, where we have not forgotten the old ways. We live with the land, not on it. We joke with the birds and we listen to the flowers and the plants who tell us their healing stories. Animals are brothers and sisters and the women there ...' Mrs Eccles' eyes found Gertrude's. 'The women are strong and proud and create magic and storms. And the men protect them, gloriously, creating a magic of their own and doing great deeds that the worlds sing about.

'There are no legends there, for all the legends are real. King Arthur no longer sleeps, Morgan Le Fay still conjures magic and mischief; Lancelot still rides like the wind; Merlin talks to the stars and I ... I still give swords from the lake to the heroes of our land.' Gertrude edged forward on her chair.

'What's it called?'

'Albion.' Gertrude felt a stirring in her mind, like a curtain being blown back by a passing breeze. Mrs Eccles stared intensely at her and Gertrude closed her eyes.

'Albion,' she whispered. The stirring became a fluttering. Wings of memory beat at the corner of her mind, but no matter how hard she screwed her face up and concentrated, her memory refused to take flight.

'It's gone,' she sighed, opening her eyes.

'Almost,' said Mrs Eccles softly. Gertrude frowned.

'Fifteen of your world's years ago we were called into Elphame—'

'Elphame?'

'Within Albion, there is another land and within that one, another, endlessly going on, each one deeper and richer than the one before it, until it reaches the source. These are mysteries you would learn if you were at school.'

'I am at school.'

'You are not at *my* school. We went into Elphame where the Elven dwell, to celebrate Midsummer Eve. We – I– should have known better. The gate from this Britain to Albion was wide open that evening. I should have left a sentinel but such was our arrogance and laziness. We all left to feast with the Elven. And what a feast it was. Dancing and loving, drinking, and singing. Songs to break your heart in two and songs to put it back together again. The Elven loved us again and shone their light upon us.' Mrs Eccles looked down at her hands. They were trembling.

'Oberon felt it first. I will never forget the look on his face. He dropped his cup of wine and shook violently. *"Something has come,"* he said and I knew then, that we were undone.' Gertrude leaned closer.

'What was it?'

'Not a what, but a who. It was a girl. A girl who had slipped through the gate between this Britain and Albion. And she brought death and winter with her.'

'What girl?'

'We don't know. We still don't know. We don't know where she came from or how she got in or who she is, but she is more powerful than all of us. She sealed the gate between Albion and Elphame trapping us. The Elven accused us of betrayal and demanded we left. But we could not and they wanted to kill us for the pain they felt we had caused.' Mrs Eccles' face softened. 'Only Oberon protected us, and Finn and Nuada, the Elven pixie princes.'

'But you escaped?'

'Time passes differently in Elphame. It passes differently in Albion as well, compared to this world. For three moons she trapped us but when we found a way back to Albion, fifteen winters had passed. Those who did find their way back went mad with grief at what Albion had become.'

'What did the girl do?'

'She froze the sea and the lakes. She destroyed the sacred groves and hunted down the wolves, the wolves who were our first teachers. She brought a plague with her and people died in their thousands. And then she healed them, so they believed her to be their saviour and took her as their queen. But the land never recovered. Albion is dying. She is the queen of a wasteland.' Gertrude's heart constricted in the silence as if an icy fist had closed over it. No butterflies danced; no bush stirred.

Mrs Eccles rose from her chair and went through to the kitchen and opened a drawer. She came back with a newspaper and put it on the table. Gertrude picked it up and read the headline.

'*MASS BREAKOUTS IN SECURE WINGS LEAVE POLICE BAFFLED*'

'You won't remember it, Gertrude. It happened the year you were born. The secure prison wings that housed the most desperate and depraved criminals, were broken into one night. In the morning, every prisoner had vanished. One minute they were there and then they were not. There were no clues, no evidence, physical or forensic. They simply disappeared.'

'Where did they go?' but Gertrude already knew the answer.

'She brought them through. She made the most hated and depraved men in Britain her army. And those brave souls who had survived the plague and rebelled against her, fell before them, like lambs.'

'But King Arthur?'

'Missing.'

'Morgan?'

'Goddess only knows.'

'Merlin?' A pause.

'Became mad.' Mrs Eccles poured herself another cup of tea and drank it, not taking her eyes off Gertrude. Gertrude was counting on her fingers.

'Fifteen years ago, you say?'

'Yes, my dear, in your world.'

'And I'm from there?'

'Originally … yes.' Gertrude nodded.

'I'm fifteen.'

'I know.' Gertrude looked around the conservatory. She caught sight of the faun statue and saw how sorrowful he looked.

'How can I help? What can I do?' Mrs Eccles put down her cup and leant forward taking Gertrude's hands in her own. The violet eyes searched her face.

'Stay alive.'

CHAPTER 9

Gertrude gazed into the violet depths of Mrs Eccles' eyes. She felt dizzy and opened her mouth to ask another question but Mrs Eccles jumped up.

'I'm going to wash up. You sit here and make sure Sam does not eat any cake.'

She collected the crockery and went through to the kitchen. Gertrude leant back in her chair and looked at the flowers and plants, but they did not bring her any peace. Her mind spun and danced like the butterflies earlier. Sam put his head on her lap and she stroked him. Mrs Eccles came back and handed Gertrude her dry clothes. Gertrude sat up straight and looked the old lady in the eyes.

'I'm not going back to my grandmother's.'

'I know you don't want to, but I have enough to contend with, without the wrath of your grandmother. Do you know what yesterday was?'

'Friday.'

'What date?'

'March the twenty-first.'

'Good lord, I have a lot to teach you. Who did you meet?'

'Whom,' muttered Sam. Gertrude frowned.

'The swifts.'

'It was the first day of spring. Yesterday was the spring equinox when the dark and light are in perfect balance. From today, the light grows stronger.' She smiled at Gertrude. 'When do you turn sixteen?'

'April the thirtieth.'

'Is there any point me asking you if you know the significance of that date?'

'Look, I'm sorry I don't know this stuff—' Mrs Eccles waved her hand impatiently.

'April the thirtieth is May Eve. Beltane. It's another time when the gate between Britain and Albion opens. Stay alive until then. If I can just get you to sixteen. Mind you, I have so much to teach you. Fifteen years of wasted time. I have to teach you everything and I have less than six weeks to do it. From now on, you will come to see me every day. Homework can wait. Your real education starts now.' Gertrude grinned.

'I can miss school if you like.'

'No, we need to keep up appearances that everything is normal.' Gertrude's face clouded. 'What is it, dear?'

'My grandmother.' Mrs Eccles' hands gripped the back of the chair until her knuckles went white.

'Leave her to me. Now go and change. You will have to go back and although that dress is stunning on you, I do not want to arouse too much suspicion. If you look as if you're having too much fun, no doubt your grandmother will stop you coming.'

'She can try,' Gertrude muttered.

'Gertrude, never underestimate your grandmother. Now away with you. Get upstairs and change.'

'She will notice my hair. I better make it messy again.'

'Impossible, I'm afraid. No matter what shampoo you use, or what conditioner or even if you never wash it again, your hair will stay like that for the next seven years, shining like copper.'

'You can say ginger, you know. I've never had a problem with being ginger. It just seems to upset other people.'

'Copper, titian, red, ginger – whatever you are, you glow like a sunrise. And after seven years all you will have to do is reapply that lotion and away you go – curls to make your heart sing! Now go.'

Dread settled in Gertrude's stomach like a stone as she trudged her way through to the stairs. The daffodils giggled as she climbed them.

'Lovely hair, but what a misery guts. Not like us.'

Not like anyone. But that wasn't true anymore. Mrs Eccles was like her. She ran up the stairs, taking them two at a time.

At last, there was an explanation. At last, there was a way out and a light in the darkness. Stepping into the meadow room, she took off the green dress and put her old clothes on. They smelt fresh and were so soft, she almost did not mind. Her hair looked wonderful and she plaited it, as she did not want to draw her grandmother's attention to it. Looking around for a bobble she turned and jumped when she saw Sam sitting there with one in his mouth.

'You scared me! I didn't hear you come in. Thank you.'

'Mrs Eccles sent me up. She guessed you needed it.'

'Mrs Eccles knows a lot.' She carried on plaiting her hair and stole a glance in the mirror. She looked different. It wasn't just her hair, there was a glint in her eyes that had never been there before. She turned and crouched down rubbing Sam's ears.

'I have had the most wonderful day. I don't want it to end.'

'It is not ending, Scamp; it is just beginning. Come on, you better get home.' The stone in Gertrude's stomach shifted a little.

Mrs Eccles waited for her at the bottom of the stairs.

'Right, my girl, keep your hair up and your head down. We have a lot of work to do. Call for Sam again tomorrow and then come to me for lunch.' She pulled Gertrude into a fierce embrace and then shoved her towards the door.

'Go! Go before I kidnap you!' and smiling she pushed her out of the front door. Gertrude saw Mrs Eccles raise her hand to a forehead.

'You have a headache coming, don't you?'

'Yes, dear, it's this air. Now run along.'

'Mrs Eccles? What happens when I turn sixteen?' Mrs Eccles took her hand away from her forehead and looked hard at

Gertrude.

'If I believed in hell, that is when it breaks loose.' She shut the door, leaving Gertrude standing on the step with more questions than answers.

CHAPTER 10

'**G**ertrude. Gertrude! Wake up. Come on, I have to show you something.'

Gertrude moaned and turning over, buried her face in the pillow. She chased the tail of the dream before it left her. Her eyes flew open.

In her dream, the dark horseman had stood behind the golden-haired man. He had reached out for her, but the golden-haired man had clicked his fingers and the dark horseman had vanished.

'Who are you?' she whispered.

'Gertrude! Gertrude! For the love of all that is holy, *get up!*'

'Sam!' She scrambled out of bed and rushed to the window. Opening it, she peered out into the darkness. She could just make out the golden retriever sitting on the pavement below. 'God, Sam, what time is it?'

'Early. As Rumi says, "*The breeze at dawn has secrets to tell you. Don't go back to sleep.*"'

'Who's Rumi? Is he coming?'

'I doubt it. Now hurry up and get out here. I want to show you something.'

Closing the window, Gertrude threw on her clothes and thanked Mrs Eccles for the hundredth time, as she bound her hair up into a ponytail. True to her word, Gertrude's hair had stayed silky and bouncy. Even after sleep, it still felt soft. Gertrude tiptoed out of her room and stopped.

Her grandmother was not in the house.

After returning home yesterday, she had done her chores under her grandmother's watchful eye. When she went upstairs to her room in the afternoon, as she did every Saturday, she heard her grandmother pottering around downstairs.

At some point in the night, she had disappeared.

Long ago Gertrude had grown to sense when her grandmother was on one of her mysterious visits away, but she did not usually leave as abruptly as this and had said nothing to Gertrude. Gertrude grinned and skipped down the stairs.

Mrs Eccles was going to teach her. What she was going to teach her, Gertrude did not know, but she was already excited about lunch and listening to the old lady talk and now she didn't have to worry about her grandmother for a few days.

Grabbing her coat, she opened the front door, put the key in the pot outside and pulled the door too.

'Sam, what could you possibly want to show me at this time in the morning?' The golden retriever's tail swished on the pavement.

'Good God, girl, only the miracle that happens every morning. Come on.'

Bounding forward the dog took off and Gertrude started to jog to keep up with him. Sam turned left and ran up Heol Broom Lane. They jogged in silence until he stopped at a metal gate that led to the farm.

'Right, open it for us, Scamp.' Gertrude drew back the bolt and swung it wide enough to let them both through. Shutting it behind her, she asked,

'Where on earth are we going?'

'You will see soon enough. Now come on, it is almost time.' Trudging over the field Gertrude hugged herself. The early morning chill made her shiver and she could hear the grass crunch with frost beneath her feet. Sam broke into a run.

'Come on. Keep up.' Gertrude jogged as fast as she could and got a shock as she ran into a cow.

'God, I am so sorry.'

'Watch where you're going,' said the cow 'Some of us are still trying to sleep.' Gertrude apologised again and could now make out the large shapes in the field. She always got up early to do chores, but to be outside at this hour was enchanting. There was a peacefulness. The world belonged to her and Sam. Rounding the corner of a stone wall, she found herself in a courtyard in front of a large farmhouse. Sam skidded to a halt.

'Made it,' he panted. Gertrude looked around. In the front garden stood a hencoop. Nothing stirred.

'Sam,' she whispered, 'What exactly is it we're here for?'

'Not it – who – and here he comes.' Out of the hencoop swaggered the biggest cockerel Gertrude had ever seen. On seeing them, the massive bird stopped. He cocked his head to one side as if questioning their presence.

'Louis, you do not mind an audience do you?'

'Why, Monsieur Sam, I am honoured that you would join me on what will be a fine morning. Who is the charming young lady you have brought?'

'Louis, may I introduce Miss Gertrude Emmeline Springate. Gertrude this is Louis … the sun king.' Gertrude smiled and dropped into a deep curtsey.

'Your Majesty,' she murmured. The cockerel bowed his head

'Mademoiselle. Now, if you would please step back and let me do my thing.' The magnificent cockerel strode forward and planted himself facing across the field. Sam backed away,

'Gertrude, stand by me, keep quiet, and watch.' Gertrude moved next to Sam and followed the cockerel's gaze over the field. The sky showed a finger of light. Dawn was about to break. Louis shook himself and seemed to root himself to the earth. He threw back his head and gave a crow so loud that Gertrude felt the sound vibrate through her. Over the horizon, the first glimpse of the sun appeared. Louis crowed again and the sun moved up a little. It then seemed to sink below the horizon. Louis stamped his feet.

'Oh no, you don't. Get up. Come on, mon ami, you can do

it. Follow my call.' Louis shook himself and gave a crow so deafening, Gertrude knew that whoever was in the farmhouse and within half a mile, would be awake now.

And then the sun rose.

Light spilled over the field and the first ray hit Louis. The whole orange orb heaved itself over the horizon and hung like a huge lantern. Louis gave a deep bow and Gertrude swore she saw the sun wobble in return. Taking a deep breath, Louis turned to his enraptured audience and bowed.

'Wow,' breathed Gertrude.

'Oh, Louis,' said Sam, 'You outdo yourself every time. That was a joy to watch and an honour.' Louis nodded his head and then swaggered over to Gertrude.

'Mademoiselle, would you like a fresh egg for your breakfast? My wives would be honoured to give you one of their treasures.'

'How very kind. Yes, I would love one.' The front door of the farmhouse slammed. Whipping round, Gertrude saw the farmer striding over to them. He tipped his hat to Gertrude and Sam and said, without stopping,

'Good one, Louis. Nearly slept in.' He carried on striding over the field towards the cows.

'Can he hear you?' asked Gertrude.

'The whole village can hear me, little one.'

'No, I mean can he talk to you like I can?'

'Not as well as you, but there are moments.'

'It comes from working with the land,' Sam said. 'Good farmers are the closest humans to the earth. They are always going to be able to hear nature.' He turned to Louis. 'I thought you were going to have a problem there, getting the sun up.'

'Pssht! You should see him in winter. He is lazy. Have you ever got up, Mademoiselle Gertrude, and thought that even the sun cannot be bothered to get up today? Honestly, we have to charm him and cajole him and some mornings the moon even has to intervene. She shows herself full on to entice him and promises to stay there so he can see her for the next few hours.

Oh, he is a lazy one. But since two days ago, he is much happier and soon he will be bouncing up. Then we cannot get him to bed! Now let us get that egg for you.' The cockerel sauntered back into the hen coop. Gertrude could hear him cooing.

'Get up, my darlings. Get up. Another day has begun. Chantal, have you a treasure to give our friends outside for their breakfast? Oh, my darling girl, what a big egg. Magnifique!' An egg rolled down the ramp of the hen coop. Gertrude went over and picked it up gently. It was warm.

'Thank you, Chantal,' she called. Louis emerged, followed by a big fat red hen who dipped her head shyly. Gertrude gave a little curtsey.

'Nice to meet you, Chantal and thank you so much.'

'You are welcome, Mademoiselle. I grew it all myself.'

'Now, my friends,' said the cockerel, 'I must leave you. I have a lot of hens to do. I have to get all the naughty girls out of bed and then put them all back into bed, if you know what I mean.' Chantal let out a giggle and scampered back into the coop. Gertrude could hear the other hens giggling and clucking.

'No problem, Louis,' Sam said. 'We have things to do as well. Enjoy your day.' Gertrude curtseyed again.

'Yes, enjoy, Your Majesty, and it was an honour.'

'Au Revoir, Mademoiselle. Au revoir, Monsieur Sam,' and he bowed. Turning round he swaggered back up the ramp to the coop. 'Who wants the Louis love first?' The whole hencoop erupted into giggling and clucking.

'Come on, Scamp. I like Louis, but I really do not want to listen to him start his day.' Both of them turned and walked back the way they came.

Mist rose from the ground as the sun warmed the frosted field. Gertrude looked up at the sun as he continued to rise in the sky. There was so much she did not know.

'Did you get any hassle from your grandmother after?' Sam said, breaking into her reverie.

'No. She's gone. She must have left last night.'

'Does she often go away and leave you alone?'

'Not often enough.' They reached the gate and Gertrude pulled back the bolt letting them both through.

'What do you do when she leaves?'

'Breathe, run wild, muck around with Jim and stay up all night reading, until my eyes hurt.'

'You are not scared?' Gertrude snorted

'I'm more scared when she's there.'

'How old were you when she first left you?' Gertrude grew quiet.

'Scamp?'

'Four.'

'Four? You were a baby. That is awful. Were you scared?'

'Yes ... for the first hour. Then Jim turned up. He sang nursery rhymes to me. His version of Bo Peep is quite disgusting, but at the time, it went over my head. It was only when I sang it at nursery, I realised it was rude. Stop frowning, Sam. He has always been great company.'

'But what about night-time? You were all alone.' Gertrude fell silent. The two of them neared her grandmother's house. Sam looked over at her.

'Gertrude?'

'I wasn't alone the entire time. I had company that first night.'

'Whom?' For a moment Gertrude wanted to blurt the whole story out about the golden-haired man. But he was her secret. Her treasured memory to hang onto. One day, perhaps. But not today.

'Come on, Sam, let us run the rest of the way. I'm starving and I have a fresh egg to eat. I met the hen who laid it ... and now she's getting laid.' Gertrude laughed and began to jog. Sam barked and followed her. He soon overtook her, beating her to her house. Panting and laughing, Gertrude located the key from the pot and opened the front door.

Soon she was tucking into boiled egg and soldiers whilst Sam devoured some ham they had found in her grandmother's fridge. They ate in silence, apart from them both making appreciative noises. Finishing, Gertrude leant back on the chair and wiped her mouth with a tissue.

'That was the most fantastic breakfast I have ever had. That egg was delicious. The yolk was so yellow.'

'Natural you see, not tampered with. You lot love tampering with nature when she has it all perfectly worked out. Like this morning with Louis. That cockerel and thousands like him get the sun up every day. And at night, the birds put him to bed. Have you ever heard the birds at dusk? They sing a particular song, different from the rest of the day. They sing the day to sleep. Nature is constantly whispering her secrets to us.'

'Sam, I know. I hear her all the time remember?'

'You said you tried to block it out though.' Gertrude brought her chair down with a crash.

'Sam, I thought I was mad. Until yesterday I never knew there was anyone else like me.'

'How did you feel when you tried to shut nature out?'

'I felt lost and isolated. Anyway, Jim bombarded me with jokes so it didn't last long and I love nature, Sam. I love her and every moment she creates. I drink her in.'

'You are so like a dog.'

'That's what the girls at school say.'

'How nice.' Gertrude decided not to enlighten him.

'Let us go out into your garden.' Gertrude jumped up and unlocked the back door. Sam stepped out and then reversed back into Gertrude.

'Good god! It's an abomination.' Sam jumped off the step and wandered amongst the neatly trimmed bushes and flower beds. 'Your grandmother is nuts. There is gardening and then there is trying to destroy nature. There is no energy in this garden. It makes no sense. Oh god, what flower is this?' He sniffed an ugly orange flower and recoiled. 'Ugh, awful. Sorry flower but what are you?' The flower gasped but did not reply. 'The poor thing cannot speak. What is it, Gertrude?'

'It's one of her experiments. She says she's trying to improve nature.'

'Nuts. The woman must be stopped. Why has that tree got a red cross painted on it?' Gertrude followed his gaze to the silver birch.

'Oh my god, no.' She ran down to it. 'Tell me she isn't?' she said addressing Birch. The tree sighed and her bare branches rustled.

'She has been wanting to get rid of me for ages. I am twisted and old, she says.'

'She could only say that if she was looking in the mirror,' said Sam, joining them. Gertrude flung her arms around the tree and squeezed her tightly.

'Sam! What can we do? Maybe Mrs Eccles could do something?'

'I will ask her. Poor tree. Madam, if I may say so, I would not say that you are twisted. I would say sculpted by the wind, but no less the beautiful for that. All of us are sculpted by life's storms in some form or another.'

'Spoken like a true philosopher,' croaked a rough voice. Sam jumped and Gertrude laughed. Looking up, she grinned at the crow sitting among the branches. 'What you lecturing about now, you big furball?' Sam tried to recover his dignity and sat down. His tail swished along the ground and Gertrude had a vision of him as a professor, with a cane behind his back.

'Just sharing some wisdom, crow, if you do not mind. I was saying that—'

'Yeah, yeah, yeah. Storms come and go and the best of us bend wiv' 'em rather than fight 'em, just like the tress. Oh? Surprised? Surprised I should know some philosophising meself? I'm a crow ain't I? Ain't no bird cleverer, ain't that right, Queen Girly?' Gertrude grinned.

'No one comes close, King Jim.' Jim nodded and puffed up his feathers.

'Anyway, what you all looking so serious about?' Birch stirred her branches.

'Jim, dear, Gertrude's grandmother has marked me. She wants to cut me down.' Jim jumped down and landed amongst them. Looking up at the tree, he shook his head.

'She bloody can't! Buggering old witch. Birch, old girl, you're my lookout tree. I'll peck her eyes out.' Sam snorted and Jim turned on him. 'Oh, you don't think I can do it, do you? I could you know.' Sam glared at Jim.

'Then why, in all the gods' names, have you not done so before?' Jim stammered and shut his beak. He looked down at the ground and slowly raised his head to look at Gertrude.

'I did try once, Gertrude,' he said in a different voice. Gertrude crouched down next to him.

'When was this?'

'After your tenth birthday, when she broke your thumb. I got the boys together and we arranged some payback. I – I don't want to talk about what happened, but we lost Stan.'

'I thought he went on holiday.'

'For five years?' Gertrude went red.

'Oh god, Jim why didn't you tell me? No, Sam, don't say anything. That was very brave, Jim and thank you, but never, ever, go up against her again. None of you. Not Magness, Agnes or you, Sam.' Sam stood up and put his nose down to Jim.

'Leave her to Mrs Eccles. She will sort her out. She sorts everything out.' Jim snorted and shook his head. Gertrude stood up and stretched her legs. She ran her hands down the birch's trunk.

'Birch, I will not let her hurt you.' Birch sighed and whispered,

'Breathe.' Gertrude patted her.

'Fancy going down the beach, Sam? Shame to waste the day. What time is Mrs Eccles expecting me?'

'Lunchtime.'

'What time is that?' Sam cocked his head.

'When it is time for lunch. Come on then.' He turned to go and stopped. Looking round he gave Jim a long look.

'Would you like to come with us crow – I mean Jim?' Jim's head snapped up.

'Er … I'm very busy, what wiv' organising Sid and Fred and

...'

'All right, Jim, no problems. Come on, Gertrude we can go and chase rabbits.'

'Oh, rabbits! Well then, you need a sentinel. You know? Someone to show you where the rabbits are. I can do that. I will just go and get the boys. Keep strong, Birch.' And he flew off. Gertrude rubbed Sam's head.

'Bye, Birch. If I can help, I will,' she said. The tree sighed and with a heavy feeling, Gertrude and Sam made their way out of the garden. As they passed the ugly orange flower she heard Sam mutter under his breath,

'Buggering old witch.'

CHAPTER 11

'To me!'

'To you!'

'Sam, fella, he's near you now, you almost got him. Oh no, he's coming back to me.'

'To you, Jim?' Sam barked

'No, to me,' yelled Fred.

'No, back to me,' cried Jim. Gertrude was laughing so much she thought she was going to burst something. Sam ran in circles trying to catch the rabbits, who ran in circles the opposite way. The bunnies howled with laughter before they disappeared down their holes that seemed to be everywhere on the dunes.

'I cannot believe the fluffy blighters have so many homes,' complained Jim. 'There must be hundreds of them.'

'Hundreds of rabbits,' panted Sam. 'They multiply like—'

'Like rabbits?' said Jim. Sam nodded.

'Blighters,' Jim said. 'Ah well, we're near the sea now, so we may as well give up.'

'I did like your sentinel idea, Jim.'

'Ah, Sam fella, it needs trees and a herd of something to work proper. Little bushes and crazy rodents ain't the best of circumstances for it. But if you ever want to hunt cows, I is your bird.'

'Oh god, just stop, I can't take anymore,' said Gertrude flopping down on the pebbles that led to the beach. 'Why on earth would Sam want to hunt cows?' Jim settled down on her right.

'Plenty of reasons.'

'Yeah,' said Fred, settling on her left.

'Name one.'

'Milk,' said Jim.

'Wool,' said Fred. Jim snorted.

'That's sheep, you daft oaf.'

'Same 'fing ain't it?' No one knew how to reply to that, so they all sat getting their breath back.

Sker Beach was almost completely deserted, although Gertrude could make out a solitary horseman, on a dark horse, further down. She idly watched as the horse turned and started riding up at a gallop towards them. Tearing her eyes away and ignoring the sudden thudding of her heart she looked up into the high, brilliant sky.

'He is riding fast,' Sam said. The horse was now thundering along the shore, spray leaping up from its hooves as it drew nearer.

And that was when it hit her.

A buzzing in her ears alerted her first. She could not breathe. She reached out for Sam, but her hand found emptiness. Her heartbeat changed, becoming erratic. Her mouth dried up and she tried to speak but as she opened her mouth, she thought she was going to throw up. All the while the dark horse and its rider came closer and closer until they were level with her. With a sudden movement, the man brought his horse to a complete standstill.

The dark horseman.

As his long black hair flew out behind him, he stared straight at her.

Her heart caught fire.

A rush of heat enveloped her body. Her heart shuddered so hard she shook. She reached out her hand to him but whether it was to greet him or to ward him off, she did not know. Her movement caused him to grow still as he stared at her across the wide beach. After a long moment, he leant down and spoke to his horse. The huge horse tossed its long black mane and turned. They galloped back along the beach, away from her.

It was at that point Gertrude decided it would probably be better if she passed out. Closing her eyes, she fell back onto the pebbles.

In her dream, the man stared at her so intensely, she did not know whether it was with love or with hate. His grey eyes burned into her. She wanted to move closer to him but there seemed to be an invisible barrier between them.

'You must come to me,' she heard herself saying. 'You know that. It is, as it always has been.' The dark man closed his eyes briefly. When he opened them, she read such pain in their stormy depths that she stepped back in shock.

She fell.

He screamed her name, but it was not *Gertrude.* She fell deep into an abyss. As she fell through solid darkness, she screamed out a name and knew it belonged to the grey-eyed man above. She sobbed as she knew she had condemned him to fall as well. Hitting the bottom of the abyss, she felt herself shatter.

And then – blissfully – nothing.

'She is coming round.'

'Lick her again, Sam.' A warm wet sensation on her face – like tears. No, like a dog's tongue.

'Oh gawd, step out of the bloody way. Queen Girly!' A stab of pain went through her forehead. 'Queen Girly, get up.'

'You cannot just peck her like that, you uncivilised brute.'

'Your gently, gently approach, Your Royal Furriness, wasn't working.' Gertrude groaned and moved her hand to where Jim's beak had stabbed her. Her forehead felt warm and sticky.

'Get out of the way, crow. You made her bleed.' Sam's tongue began licking the wound.

'Yeugh, get off her!' Fred said. 'We don't know where that tongue has been.'

'We know exactly where that tongue has been, Fred, my boy.' Jim said. 'We all know where dogs like to lick.' The licking stopped.

'Everybody knows that dog's saliva is full of antiseptic,' huffed Sam, 'and I would appreciate it if you would not discuss my grooming habits in front of a lady.'

'Why do dogs lick their balls?' asked Jim.

'Because we can – oh hello, Scamp. How are you feeling?' Gertrude sat up and allowed her eyes to focus on the three friends who surrounded her. She looked over to the beach where the rider had been, but she could not see him. Sam nudged her arm with his wet, black nose.

'What happened, Scamp? I mean you had breakfast, so it cannot be a lack of food, and it is not that hot, so it cannot be dehydration. Maybe you should have drunk more orange juice?'

'There wasn't any orange juice, Sam.'

'Maybe that was the problem.' Gertrude shook her head and then wished she hadn't, as the world went fuzzy.

'I'll be all right. Just the hilarity of seeing you lot trying to hunt rabbits.' She forced herself to smile, but she felt shaken. That was the second time she had seen the dark horseman in the flesh and the reaction had been the same; one of total helplessness. She closed her eyes, chasing the dream down the corridors of her mind, but it was fading and she could not grasp onto it. 'Go on, go and play. I'll be fine.'

'Play?' squawked Jim. 'Crows do not play, Queen Girly. Dogs play. Cats play. Us crows have to work all day long, toiling and tilling over the earth, looking for food to keep our loved ones alive. And we have to keep order and peace and—'

'Peace?' Sam laughed. 'Never have I met such breachers of the peace as yourselves. And what do you call car wash roulette if that is not playing?' Jim puffed up his feathers.

'That is our sacred duty. We have to keep twonks like Old Sod Jones in his place, as who knows what havoc he could create.'

'You create enough havoc for the whole street and another thing—' Gertrude groaned.

'Could you keep this argument for another time? My head is

throbbing.'

'Yes, of course, Gertrude,' said Sam, throwing a furious look at Jim. 'Let us get you home. Do you think you can stand?' Gertrude got to her feet and after swaying a couple of times, she felt herself root into the earth.

'Okay, I'm grounded.' Sam lifted his eyebrows.

'Odd expression.'

'No, it isn't. You know sometimes you feel you are floating and other times you can feel yourself rooted in the earth?' Sam shook his head and Jim let out a caw.

'Gawd no. I would hate to be grounded. I hate the ground, full of muck and worms and rubbish. Nah, give me the air to float upon, the wind in my wings, the sun on my back, the moon to guide my way—' Sam snorted.

'What are you, an owl? Crows don't fly at night.' Jim rounded on the dog.

'And just what the hell do you know, dog? Of course we fly at night. We is black, we is the colour of the night. No one can see us.'

'Yeah, Jim, you tell him,' said Fred. 'Mind you, we ain't good at it. Last time we flys at night, Jim here goes straight into a telegraph pole.'

'Shut your mouth, Fred. They must have bloody moved it.'

'Nah, Jim, you was just showing off and you went right into it and oi—' Fred took off in fright as Jim flew at him. The two crows chased each other in the sky above the sand.

'Come on, Scamp, let us walk home slowly. Mrs Eccles will be waiting.'

'Is it lunchtime then?' asked Gertrude. She looked up at the sun in the blue sky, as if she could tell the time by it.

'I am hungry, so yes it must be lunchtime. You do not have to look at the sun, Gertrude. You just have to ask your stomach what time of day it is. Best clock in the world.'

They turned away from the beach, with Jim and Fred's curses ringing in their ears. Gertrude looked back along the sand, but there was still no sign of the horse nor its dark rider.

It was as if they had never existed.

CHAPTER 12

Gertrude leant back in her chair to allow the food she had consumed to settle properly.

She fixed Mrs Eccles with what she hoped was a determined look.

An amazing lunch had greeted her and Sam when they returned. There had been a cheeseboard with a yellow creamy one, a strong orange one and a white crumbly one with apricots through it. There was a warm crusty loaf with creamy butter and an array of different salads. Sam and Gertrude had fallen on the food and Mrs Eccles had laughed.

'You could swear you two had never eaten before.' Gertrude gulped down the hunk of bread she had torn off.

'It's the sea air, Mrs Eccles. This is lovely. Thank you.' The old lady had smiled and bowed her head,

'Oh, it was nothing, dear.' Sam snorted. 'All right, it really was nothing. My friend prepared it. She lives to feed people.'

'Her vocation is well chosen. I would live just to eat like this every day.'

Afterwards, Gertrude had helped clear up and then sat down with a strong cup of tea. She heard Sam muttering about, *'a funny turn,'* to Mrs Eccles in the kitchen. She put her cup down and waited patiently for the old lady to sit back down. When she did, Gertrude began her inquisition.

'I have questions.' Mrs Eccles smiled at her.

'Of course you do.'

'Are you the Lady of the Lake?'

'One of them.' Gertrude's eyebrows shot up.

'How many are there?'

'About nine in all.'

'Are you the leader?' Mrs Eccles smile grew wider.

'Some would say so … others would not. I agree with the latter.'

'Are they all like you?'

'No. We are all different. But together we make a whole.'

'Are you human?' A slight pause.

'Almost.' Gertrude took a deep breath and leant forward.

'Am I human?' Another pause.

'Almost.' Gertrude let out the breath she was holding.

A big fat bumble bee entered the conservatory and Mrs Eccles clapped her hands with delight.

'Hello friend, you are early, aren't you?' The bee settled on a leaf. Mrs Eccles got up and danced over to him. 'Try that big pink flower over there, sir. You will find all you need and she's ready.' The bee buzzed thank you and flew over to a deep pink flower.

'Mrs Eccles, please. I need to know who I am. Who were my parents?' Mrs Eccles did not take her eyes off the bee. The pink flower bent over with the bee's weight. Gertrude flung herself back on the chair and closed her eyes. The old woman had crashed into *her* life, not the other way around. It had been Mrs Eccles who said she was going to teach her, and now it seemed she did not want to share anything. *This is like drawing blood from a stone,* Gertrude thought angrily.

'Or Merlin from the stars,' Mrs Eccles murmured.

'Pardon?' Mrs Eccles sat back down and poured another cup of tea.

'I know I am being vague. I know you have a million things to ask me. I can answer some of them, others I cannot.' She took a sip of tea.

'Who are my parents?' Mrs Eccles shook her head.

'I was hoping you could tell me, as I know who they *were*, but not who they *are*.'

'I remember nothing of my parents. It has always been me and grandmother.'

'My grandmother and I,' said Sam.

'Did you ever ask your grandmother?' Gertrude dropped her eyes and looked at her hands. A tremor passed through her as a memory crashed in.

'Only once, and that was enough.' Looking up she caught a look of rage flicker across Mrs Eccles' face and then it was gone. 'Who *were* my parents then?'

'You don't remember?'

'No.'

'Then I can't tell you.' Gertrude let out a shout of frustration and jumped out of her seat. She paced around the conservatory and came to rest before the pink flower with the bee still busy in its centre.

'You told the bee what he needed to know.'

'Yes, I did, and I will tell you what you need to know. But I cannot tell you what I do not know myself. Everything I do know, I will impart to you.'

'Except who I am.'

'Except that. There is a reason for you not knowing. Far be it from me to tamper with that, even if I do not understand it.'

'But if you are the Lady of the Lake, isn't that what you do? Tamper with things?' Mrs Eccles burst out laughing.

'By the stars, you haven't been reading Malory, have you? Or Tennyson? Stupid old buffoons. And damn Taliesin for telling tales. I prefer the word, *intervene* to tamper but, yes, I think some people would agree. I have tampered enough, in my many lifetimes, for all eternity. I am tampering now. I wonder if I should have left you in ignorance? What business do I have to drag you into a war in a land that you know nothing about? Who am I to pull you into danger, for make no mistake, Gertrude, you are in danger, now more than ever? Who am I indeed?' Sam came up and laid his head on her lap.

'You are the kindest human I ever met. I love you.' Mrs Eccles laughed and stroked his ears.

'You're a dog, so you're biased. You love everyone.'

'I don't love Jim.'

'Of course you do. Well, if not now, one day.'

'If that ever happens, I will grow whiskers and catch a mouse. I have more chance of turning into a cat than I do loving that ignorant, uncivilised oaf.'

'You called?' Jim flew through the open door. Mrs Eccles jumped up in delight and welcomed Jim as an old friend, pulling up a chair for him. She made such a fuss, that Sam got the hump and slunk back to stand with Gertrude. Gertrude tried to take everything in. Her thoughts spiralled to the golden-haired man of her dreams since she was four.

'You mentioned the Elven yesterday? Do their eyes change colour?' Mrs Eccles gave her a sharp look.

'No. When the Elven look at you it is as if the stars themselves have noticed you. Why?' Gertrude shook her head.

'Do they have storm grey eyes?' Mrs Eccles and Jim exchanged a look.

'Where did you see him?' Mrs Eccles said, not looking at her.

'Who?'

'The man with the storm grey eyes.'

'In a dream.'

'And on the beach,' said Jim 'and on the first day of spring. He can't keep away and—' Mrs Eccles cut Jim off with a sharp look.

'Who is he?' asked Gertrude, but Mrs Eccles clapped her hands.

'Right, enough questions, upstairs for a bath.'

'Another one?'

'One can never have too many baths, Gertrude. Back in Albion, I almost live in the lake. Indeed, some people, including that oaf Malory, think I do.' A noise from upstairs made everyone jump and look up. Mrs Eccles tutted.

'I do wish the bath would not run itself. Now, stand up and let me have a look at you.' Gertrude dutifully stood and raised her chin a little.

'Good ... power is there ... now if I can just get your self-esteem up, I have something to work with. The gold one ... yes, use the gold bath oil. No more than five drops mind, I do not want an arrogant love goddess on my hands and goddess only knows I've met enough of them.' Gertrude did not move. 'Well go on with you, girl. Use the shampoo again and dump those clothes outside the bathroom. Afterwards, go into the spare bedroom, where you will find an outfit laid out for you.' Gertrude skipped down the hallway and heard the daffodils sing out.

'Ooooh, look at her. Someone's in a better mood.'

Although again she had more questions than answers, the thought of another bath filled her with joy. Bathing in Kenfig pool was exhilarating, but the sheer luxury of running a bath and soaking in perfumed water delighted her. She ran up the stairs two at a time, nodding to the trees in the paintings and skidding into the bathroom. A knocking noise made her jump and she wheeled round in time to see the bath move a little.

'Okay, okay, I'm coming.' She rushed over, put the plug in and turning on the taps, let the water cascade down. Going over to the windowsill, she picked up the gold bottle and read the label.

Fed up of disliking yourself? Feel you are overlooked all the time? Do you feel ugly? Unattractive? Like a troll that no one wants to come near?

You are probably not, but even if you are a troll, never fear! Self-esteem in a bottle is here!
Pour 3-5 drops into cascading water and immerse yourself in the fragrant golden waters, perfumed with; otto rose, midnight jasmine, ylang ylang, sandalwood and ...

BELIEVE!

For you really are the goddess's gift.

Creators Note: We, the creators, take no responsibility for sudden proposals of marriage, love crazed stalkers and obsessed individuals killing themselves because they are pining for you. If you cause chaos, it is your own fault. Go away. We are not at home.

Excited, Gertrude rushed over to the bath and poured out five drops exactly. Each time a drop hit the water, a firework burst into the air, showering the bathroom in gold stars. Feeling rebellious, Gertrude poured in five more drops. After all, she needed all the help she could get and this might be her only chance to get a marriage proposal. The water sparkled gold and the whole room shimmered and shone.

Gertrude ripped off her clothes and left them outside the door. Turning off the taps, she took a breath of the fragranced air as she slid down into the warm water.

Warmth spread all over her body and she traced her fingers over her arm, marvelling at her smooth skin. Looking closely at her skin, she fell in love with its paleness.

'Like marble,' she murmured. Gertrude had always hated her pasty skin, but in the glowing light, her ivory skin looked beautiful. Extending her right leg out of the water, she ran her hands down its length. Her legs were stunning, curved, and graceful. Smiling, she went under the water to wet her hair. Surfacing, Gertrude reached down and found her shampoo. Massaging it in, she gave herself up to the warm sensations that enveloped her.

'I could be a princess; I am that beautiful.' With a shock, she clamped her hand over her mouth. The words had come from nowhere and she had said them out loud. She blushed with shame and hoped no one could hear her. *Such arrogance!* She could imagine what her grandmother would say to her. Rinsing her hair, she applied the conditioner.

'But I am so beautiful. Even the goddess of love could call me her sister and not be ashamed. The birds get up in the morning to sing

for me—oh good god shut up,' and she clamped her hand over her mouth again.

'*No, I will not shut up. I have been quiet for far too long. Feel how smooth my skin is, see the way it glimmers. Feel how heavy my red hair is, a glorious mane that would make Aphrodite herself covetous and as for my breasts*—' Gertrude dived under the water, horrified at the things she was saying. She could not stop herself. It was as if there was another Gertrude, one that was full of herself. She rinsed out the conditioner as fast as she could. She swallowed some of the water and surfaced, coughing and spluttering.

This time she did not fly out of the bath. She rose, majestic and graceful. She went over to the bathroom window and threw it open. Two doves flew in and grabbing a towel, they wrapped it around her body. They fetched another one and wrapped it around her head. They settled on the windowsill, cooing gently. She crouched down to the doves and kissed them both.

'Thank you,' she murmured. The doves bowed their heads and flew off.

Floating over to the bathroom cabinet, she opened the door and found a gold pot of moisturiser.

Now you are feeling like a goddess, give your skin a treat with this luxurious moisturiser. Made from desert roses and primroses, which grow on westerly hills, you will feel like you are clothed in silk, even when you are naked,

(and naked is how everyone is going to want you – phwoar!)

Please ignore that last bit. That is very rude. Not everyone gets up to the shenanigans you get up to every night you dirty—
Who you calling dirty you stuck up—
Get off! It is my job to write the labels, yours to stick them on and—OW!

The label stopped. Gertrude laughed and rubbed the silky moisturiser on her skin. It left a golden shimmer and the scent made her smile.

Gliding through to the bedroom, she found a gown of heavy green velvet lying on the bed. She slipped it on and looked at herself in the mirror.

Gertrude reeled back in shock.

'It can't possibly be me.'

'*But it is you. It is me. Look at me.*' Her hair shone even more than yesterday. Her curls were drying already and they gleamed with shades of gold and red. Her hair hung in perfect curls down to her waist, which looked neater than yesterday. The dress showed the top of her swelling breasts and her skin glowed.

Gertrude leaned closer to the mirror and touched her heart-shaped face, taking in the high cheekbones and ivory complexion. Her eyebrows arched perfectly. Her cheeks blushed like roses and her dusting of freckles gleamed like gold dust. Her lips, which she always felt were too big for her face, pouted prettily. She thought that maybe, someone, someday, would like to kiss them. She looked into her eyes, which gazed back, large, and luminous, sparkling like emeralds.

'*Hello, darling. Welcome back,*' said her reflection. '*Where on earth have you been?*'

CHAPTER 13

Gertrude jumped back.

Her reflection trilled out a laugh, whilst pirouetting and curtseying. She winked at Gertrude and her emerald green eyes glittered. The long eyelashes fluttered against her dewy cheek. Gertrude's legs shook and she held on to the mirror for support.

'All right, my darling, I've got you.' Mrs Eccles' warm hands took her gently by the shoulders and moved her over to the bed. The room spun and Gertrude raised her head to look over at the mirror. The other Gertrude danced and twirled, singing to herself.

'Who the hell does she think she is?' muttered Gertrude.

'That, my darling girl, is you. She is a part of you that you have never met. Your grandmother hid her well. She probably thought she had killed her off but I think I got here just in the nick of time.' Sam ran into the bedroom and jumped onto the bed.

'Sam! Gently.' A smell of lavender enveloped Gertrude. Sam laughed.

'Whoops, poor little flowers.' Glancing down at the bedding, the little purple flowers looked real. Feeling sleepy and relaxed she leant over and buried her head in Sam's fur.

'Mrs Eccles? Can Sam sleep at my place tonight? My grandmother is away and it would be such fun and—'

'Gertrude, I could not possibly part with Sam. He takes a lot of looking after.' Gertrude nodded and tried to smile. She made to get up, but Mrs Eccles put her arms around her and pulled her in for a hug. Gertrude stiffened. The last time anyone had held her, she had been four years old. Mrs Eccles let her go. She brushed Gertrude's hair back from her face.

'You could however sleep here ... that is if you want to?' Gertrude looked around the room. It was fresh and light and the bed felt so soft.

'Do you really mean it?'

'Gertrude, I never say anything I do not mean. Now go and get your school stuff and anything else you might need for the night. In fact ... bring back what you need for a week. I have a feeling your grandmother will not be back until next week – or maybe even later.' Gertrude frowned.

'It feels like she's gone away for a long visit but how do you know?' Mrs Eccles looked Gertrude in the eyes.

'I saw her yesterday. She mentioned she was going to be away for a while.' It was a lie but Gertrude felt too excited to pursue it. 'Now go on, away with you. We will have a nice cup of cocoa and then off to bed for all of us.' The old lady yawned, which started Gertrude off yawning and then Sam joined in. Even Gertrude's reflection let out a yawn. They all burst into laughter.

It did not take long for Gertrude to gather up her stuff from her grandmother's house. She stuffed *'Fairy Tales From Around the World,' 'King Arthur and the Knights of the Round Table'* and *'The Lion the Witch and the Wardrobe,'* into a bag, but she doubted she would read as she felt so drowsy. She found her school uniform and realised with all the excitement of walking Sam she had forgotten to wash it. She looked around her grandmother's house and tried to sense the old woman, but she was definitely not there and the house had an empty, forlorn feel to it as if it missed its mistress.

Running back, she flew into Mrs Eccles' house and the feelings of warmth and comfort were even more apparent after standing alone next door.

'I am really sorry; may I use your washing machine? I forgot to wash these clothes on Friday. It does not matter if they do not dry, I usually wear them damp.'

'You will do no such thing. Give them to me and I will sort it, no arguments. Let me look after you, just a little. I know you are perfectly capable of looking after yourself but it would please me to do so.' Gertrude handed over her clothes with a smile.

'Right go through to the living room, by the fire and I will get the cocoa on.'

Gertrude followed Sam who led the way, his tail held high.

She stopped in shock at the doorway. The living room was huge. There was no way it could fit inside the house. She went back out through the door and walked in again, to make sure she was not hallucinating. Paintings of trees and animals covered one wall, whilst books from floor to ceiling covered another. Latticed arched windows with padded window seats let the remaining light in. There was a table near one of the windows. Opened books, papers and pens covered its surface. Mrs Eccles was obviously studying something.

'I am in heaven,' Gertrude murmured. She stepped in and her feet sunk into a deep pile cream carpet. The cheerful fire flickering in the grate, gave the room a cosy, warm feel, despite its great size. Sam settled down in front of it. He gazed at her, grinning. Above the mantelpiece hung a tapestry depicting a lion and a unicorn. The room smelt of sweet applewood. Gertrude wandered over to the books and ran her fingers over the beautifully coloured spines. *The Power of the Nine, The Healing Powers of Plants, The Book of Leviathan,* and *The Poems of Taliesin,* were just a few of the books that caught her eye. A movement made her look over to a painting of a lion. The proud haughty face looked down his nose at her. She tilted her chin up and gave him a defiant stare of her own. Then realising what she was doing, she turned away. A low growl had her quickly turning back but then Mrs Eccles came in with a tray.

'Never mind about Ariel,' Mrs Eccles said, whilst carefully

placing the tray onto the table. 'He's a proud one but he has a heart of gold. Now sit down by the fire and drink up.' Gertrude took the steaming mug from Mrs Eccles' outstretched hand and sat down in one of the chairs by the fire. Mrs Eccles sat on the other side of the fire so that Sam stretched out between them.

'No cocoa for you, Sam, but I brought you some warm milk. And here you are my dear.' The cocoa smelled delicious, but that was nothing compared to how it tasted. It was rich, smooth, and chocolaty and Gertrude let out a sigh. She stretched her legs out and wiggled her toes that poked out from beneath the long gown. The fire warmed them up and heat spread all over her until she felt quite flushed.

There were so many questions crowding her mind, but in that moment of contentment, she did not care about anything. She had never known the simple joy of sipping a warm drink by an open fire and she relished in the sensual delight of it. Sam let out a sigh and, having gulped his milk down in a matter of seconds, stretched out in front of the fire.

'How was Jim this afternoon?' Gertrude asked.

'Full of fun and jokes. What a wonderfully bright friend you have there.'

'He is, isn't he? Sam doesn't think so.'

'Dogs get so jealous you know. Their lives revolve around us and they expect ours to do the same.' Sam snorted.

'I am listening you know and that is so arrogant. Typical human.'

'You know I speak the truth, Sam. What is the most important thing in your life?'

'You and Scamp.' Mrs Eccles smiled and got off the chair to kneel by the golden retriever. His feathered tail banged on the floor, sounding like a drum.

'And we love you too. Dogs are amazing. Here is Sam, six homes, a life full of abuse and yet still he loves. If he was human, he would be a saint, for is that not what the saints teach us? To forgive? And yet we struggle with it, we who are supposed to be more aware and intelligent.'

'God is dog spelt backwards,' Sam said sleepily.

'Well *Tac* is cat spelt backwards, so I don't think that means anything, Sam.' But he had drifted off and started to snore. Gertrude felt her head drop and she shook herself awake. Mrs Eccles touched her arm.

'Now come on, upstairs with you. Go into the wardrobe and there will be a nightgown for you to wear. In the bathroom, you will find a toothbrush. Go on now.' She took Gertrude's empty cup away from her. Feeling heavy, Gertrude slid out of the chair and trudged upstairs. Going into the bathroom she cleaned her teeth with a green toothbrush and made her way to the bedroom. Opening the wardrobe, she found a long white cotton nightdress, hanging on a padded hanger. It felt crisp and clean and smelled of lavender. She stole a glance at the mirror and saw the other Gertrude still dancing and singing.

'I hope you're not going to sing all night,' she snapped. She hung up the green velvet gown and slid into bed. Bursts of fragrance enveloped her as she settled herself down on the soft pillow. The duvet floated down over her. *This is what it must feel like to sleep on a cloud,* Gertrude thought dreamily.

There was a soft knock at the door and Mrs Eccles came in. She looked down at Gertrude, her violet eyes sparkling. Sam jumped on the bed releasing more of the wonderful fragrance. He licked her face. Mrs Eccles bent down and placed a kiss on her forehead.

'Sweet dreams, dear heart. May your sleep and dreams be blessed. Come on, Sam,' and they left the room.

Turning over onto her side, Gertrude let out a sigh and closed her eyes. The floral scent floated around her and she was on the brink of dropping off when the other Gertrude started singing a new song.

'Oh god, girl, get over yourself.' The singing stopped and a voice near Gertrude's ear said,

'You are going to shut me out again, aren't you?' Gertrude leapt out of bed and stared at the other Gertrude, who was sitting on

the bed. She looked at the mirror. It only reflected the room.

'Oh my god, what are you? What do you think you're doing?' Looking hurt, the other Gertrude sat up and hugged her knees to her chest. Gertrude could not help but notice how pretty she was.

'I am desperately trying to get back with you. I have not been allowed near you for years. The last time I was close to you was when we were four and he *came to us and sang and made fire with his hands and danced—'* Gertrude leapt back on the bed and clamped her hand over the other girl's mouth.

'Shut your mouth. Don't. Don't talk about him.' The other girl wrenched Gertrude's hand away. Angry tears filled her eyes.

'Are we never to talk of him? Are we never allowed to admit to ourselves that we were beautiful? That we were once enchanting as well as enchanted? That we were loved? You are living half a life! I am the best friend you could ever have because if you love me, love will find you. Don't you get it? Love me and love will follow. Please let me in.' She began to cry. Gertrude knelt staring at her. Then she took a deep breath and put her arms around the other girl.

'You don't have to go. You can stay. You make me laugh actually. Come on, lie down and let's go to sleep. This bed is making me sleepy.' The two Gertrudes burrowed down under the covers.

'You won't regret this. I am really good to have around.' Turning on her side Gertrude murmured,

'I know,' and fell asleep hugging herself.

CHAPTER 14

Aweekend can change your life.

Gertrude remembered reading that phrase in a romantic novel and, at the time, thought the author stupid. She had returned the book to the library the following day, but it turned out the author was correct and she made a mental note to borrow the book again and give it another chance.

Gertrude entered the school on Monday morning and tried to assume her normal position of head down and eyes averted. The other Gertrude had other ideas.

'*Head up, keep on walking. You are just as good as anyone else,*' she prattled in her head. Gertrude could not help but obey.

The reactions were laughable.

The boys' mouths dropped open as she sashayed by.

'*Keep your hips swinging ... you're doing fine.*' The girls' mouths snapped shut, their lips disappearing into mean, thin lines.

She floated down the corridor and, on a whim, let her hair down. The thick mass of red curls tumbled down and swung below her waist and she heard gasps and whispers. A group of boys' heads turned to watch her pass by. They reminded her of the flowers on Mrs Eccles' wallpaper. Gertrude blushed and kept walking down the corridor, her face getting hotter. She found the level of attention uncomfortable. Used to being whispered about and sneered at, this positive attention was no less embarrassing and she faltered for a moment outside her form room.

It is only the uniform.

She did not know how she had done it, but Mrs Eccles had found her a brand new uniform and for the first time in fifteen years, Gertrude wore clothes that fitted her. Her blouse did not gape and the skirt hugged her hips, and even if her shirt had gaped open, Gertrude wore brand new underwear. Her bra was brilliant white and lacy, with knickers to match. She found it amazing that lovely underwear could make her feel so confident. A new pair of ballet pumps had also been at the end of the bed when she had woken up. Maybe they contributed to the fact that Gertrude almost danced down the corridor.

She walked into her form room and, keeping her eyes straight ahead, walked to her desk at the back of the room. Two boys sprang up from their desks and fought to pull her chair out. She flicked her eyes up and tried to read any mockery in their faces but all she saw was undisguised awe. She blushed, murmured thank you, and sat down. Fighting the other Gertrude all the way, she put her head down and stared at the graffiti on the desk. Someone had scrawled the word '*Skank*' and looking up she caught Tara Wilson smirking. The blonde girl turned to face the teacher for registration. Gertrude got her eraser out of her school bag and tried to rub the offending word off, but all she created was a mess of rubber shavings. Mrs Pope called out the register and when her name was called, Gertrude dutifully said,

'Here.' Charlie Evans turned around in his chair and let out a long wolf whistle.

'You so are,' he grinned. Gertrude flushed and turned her head to look out of the window.

'*He paid you a compliment! Turn back around and smile,*' the other Gertrude hissed. Gertrude swallowed and turning round gave him just a ghost of a smile. His mischievous grin disappeared to be replaced by an almost reverent look. She lowered her eyes demurely and turned back around.

'*You've made his day now.*' Gertrude put her hand over her mouth.

'Pipe down,' she said through gritted teeth and looked to make sure no one had heard her talking to herself.

'*You pipe down. Anyway, we have games next and they will all go mad for your legs, once they see them.*' Gertrude's stomach clenched. She had forgotten her games kit and, magical as Mrs Eccles was, she would not be able to conjure up a games kit in time for Gertrude's next lesson. Mrs Macready, the games mistress, was cut from the same cloth as her grandmother and would honour no excuses. Gertrude would have to wear an old games kit from lost and found, all from children who were skinnier than she was. Last time there had not been any shorts that had fitted her. Mrs Macready had made her play netball in her knickers. The huge grey pants had been the source of many jokes and their comic value had kept the *Petty Four* in snide comments for months.

No. She could not go through that hell again. But what to do? The class became noisier and she looked out of the window in despair. The sky was a brilliant blue and the day held the promise of spring warmth. A lovely day for cross-country. Gertrude groaned and watched as a little fluffy cloud made its way across the sky.

'I wandered lonely as a cloud,' she murmured. Were clouds lonely? How did Wordsworth know? Was that cloud as lonely as she was in that classroom? What if that cloud had a friend? What if another cloud, which was also lonely, joined it? As she thought this, another cloud slid across the sky, moving up to the other cloud. The clouds were fluffy and white but would they be friends with a dirty cloud or were clouds as bullying as her schoolmates? What if a dirty grey cloud came and— Gertrude blinked. A big dirty grey cloud slid across the sky and joined the other two clouds and, what do you know? They accepted him and even allowed some of his greyness to mingle with their whiteness. But what about a big rain cloud? Or one full of hail? Or what if a cloud full of snow came up and asked to be friends? Would they push him away to his own lonely part of the sky?

Gertrude tore her eyes away from the window and looked around the room. Billy Yates was throwing paper at Jacky Streatfield. Tara was whispering in the corner with Samantha Howard and everyone else was talking about a party they had gone to on Saturday. Gertrude turned back and looked with astonishment at the clouds that were now forming outside the window. She recognized a rain cloud and one hail cloud, the colour of slate. Some seagulls flew in front of it and they looked like stars against the darkness. More clouds appeared, filling up the sky. The blue sky disappeared and the classroom darkened.

'Goodness, it looks like snow,' said Mrs Pope, raising her head from her paperwork.

What a good idea. Looking down at the rubber shavings, Gertrude took a breath and blew them off the table. A howl of wind whistled outside and cries from her classmates and the scraping of chairs made Gertrude look out of the window.

It was snowing.

Huge fat flakes floated down from the sky and began to settle on the playground. The wind rose and the trees bent in the sudden furious snowstorm.

'Snow? Snow in March? Oh, my word,' twittered Mrs Pope. 'Global warming class, I am telling you now, we have mucked around for so long with nature—'

'There's nothing warm about that, Miss,' yelled David Hughes.

'You will still have to do games. Nothing puts Mrs Macready off, as you know.' The girls groaned and Gertrude, thinking about Mrs Macready, gripped her pencil so hard it snapped in two. Minutes passed as the children watched the snow whirling outside the window. The classroom door banged open and Mr Lake, the headmaster, stood there looking wet and weary.

'Games are cancelled, Mrs Pope. You are all to go to the assembly hall and wait there. Mrs Macready has fallen over in the snow and broken her leg, snapped it right in two. The ambulance is on its way.' He left, banging the door behind him. Gertrude looked down at her broken pencil and then back out of the window.

'Leave in an orderly fashion please and try not to look too happy. Poor Mrs Macready will be in awful pain.'

'Serves her right for putting us through awful pain then, the ugly cow,' said Tara as she left. For once Gertrude agreed with her. Scraping her chair back, she gathered up her stuff. Any traces of guilt she felt disappeared when she remembered the way Mrs Macready had smirked at her big grey pants.

She dumped the broken pencil in the bin as she sashayed out.

❊ ❊ ❊

Running through Mrs Eccles' house, that afternoon, Gertrude called out for Sam. He barked hello from the conservatory and she ran through, skidding across the floor to meet him as he ran into her arms.

'How was school?' he panted. Gertrude looked up at Mrs Eccles who stood still amongst the flowers.

'Oh, you know, the usual.' She stood up, still ruffling his ears and looked warily at the old lady, but Mrs Eccles had not registered her presence as she was listening to two dragonflies hovering in the air. After a while, the old lady nodded and said,

'That is outrageous. Leave it with me and I will see what I can do.' The dragonflies both put their tales in the air as if bowing and flew off through the open doors into the garden.

'Beach?' said Sam, his golden face smiling up at her. Gertrude looked at Mrs Eccles and decided a quick exit would be best.

'Yes, the beach definitely. I will just go and change and—'

'Hello, Gertrude. How are you? How was school?' Mrs Eccles turned round and stopped Gertrude with a piercing look. Her violet eyes blazed for a second and then softened as she read the trepidation on Gertrude's face. Gertrude swallowed.

'You know, the usual.' Mrs Eccles moved to the beautiful bush with the deep pink flowers. She caressed the blooms with her hand and then buried her face in them. Taking a small spray bottle from the table, she doused them with water and the flowers sighed happily.

'Lovely weather, isn't it?' Mrs Eccles said. 'Not a cloud in the sky.'

'*Careful now,*' giggled the other Gertrude. Gertrude cleared her throat.

'Yes, it is indeed lovely and that is why I'm taking Sam down the beach now. You never know when it could change.' Mrs Eccles turned and stared at her. Gertrude looked down at the floor.

'Tell me everything, child.' Gertrude looked up and saw a flicker of fear in the old lady's eyes but then it passed and a look of pride replaced it. She shrugged.

'I don't know if there is much to tell.'

'A freak snowstorm? In Porthcawl? In March? I think you have plenty to tell me.' Mrs Eccles sat down on one of the wicker chairs and folded her hands in her lap.

'I really do not know how it happened or even if it was me—'

'It was you all right.'

Gertrude sat and proceeded to tell Mrs Eccles what she had thought about and how the clouds had gathered.

'And then I blew the rubber shavings off my desk and all hell broke loose.'

'You were daydreaming?'

'Yes, that's all, so you see—'

'That's all? Oh, my girl, daydreaming is the most powerful and dangerous magic to be had. Why do you think this world tells you off so much for doing it? Thoughts have power, Gertrude, serious power. If people knew how much power their thoughts had, they would not be thinking the things they do. And daydreams are thoughts gone wild.'

'But everyone daydreams.'

'No, not everyone. The mystics and the poets and the geniuses daydream. Need I say more?'

'But people must go around all the time thinking things like, *I wish she would die*, or other things and it doesn't happen.' Mrs Eccles narrowed her eyes.

'Doesn't it? Is there anything else you would like to tell me?' Gertrude shook her head, trying not to think of the broken pencil.

'Are you sure?' Gertrude nodded and looked over at Sam to escape Mrs Eccles' searching look.

'Every time you have a thought, Gertrude, it grows from your head and can become real.' There was a long pause as Mrs Eccles looked down at her hands.

'Once, long ago, when this land and Albion were still as one, an Elven girl went a wandering.' Mrs Eccles' voice dropped to a whisper and Gertrude leant forward to catch what she was saying.

'Tired, hungry, and thirsty, she came upon a small fishing village and begged for a drink of water from their well.' Mrs Eccles looked up. 'Terrified by her wildness and beauty, they refused and threw stones at her. Then three young men rushed at her and carried her off into one of the houses.' Mrs Eccles' hands trembled and she clenched them as if to stop them, her knuckles turning white.

'When they had finished with her, they threw her, like a piece of rubbish, into the surrounding forest and left her, torn and bleeding, to the wild ones. But the men from the village could not have known that the wolves and the bears love the Elven as their own. They took her gently on their backs and took her home.

'A year later, to the day, I lay down with an Elven prince in a green meadow by a stream.' Gertrude's eyebrows shot up and Mrs Eccles gave her a ghost of a smile.

'Afterwards, the Prince got up and fetched two chalices of water from the stream. I gulped mine down but he sat and gazed into his. I must have yawned because he said to me, *"Sleep, Vivienne and do not mind me, I am just going to daydream for a while."* He swished the water round and round in his chalice and I fell asleep beside him, as he daydreamed and sang.

'I later found out, that across the land, the worst storm in time remembered, came crashing down on that village. Ships were lost at sea and houses fell on the people who lived in them. Lightening set the village on fire and there was not a man, woman or child that escaped the fury. The very sea, I am told, rose up and crashed down upon them all, with waves as tall as oak trees. The bears and the wolves came out of the forest and devoured the bodies. The only thing left standing was the well.' Gertrude shivered. The temperature had dropped in the conservatory as if the sun had gone behind a cloud. Mrs Eccles held Gertrude with her stare, her violet eyes lit up like jewels.

'Everything you do comes back on you. Everything you give out will find its way back to you.' Gertrude thought of the Elven girl and how she had suffered. Then she thought of the broken pencil and people who gloried in the humiliation of others. She lifted her chin as she returned the penetrating stare.

'That, Mrs Eccles, is what I am hoping for.' Standing up, she motioned for Sam to follow her as she walked out of the conservatory, leaving Mrs Eccles sitting with her hands still clenched.

CHAPTER 15

The walk to the beach had been quiet and uneventful, with no sign of the dark horseman.

Sam had left her to her thoughts, which she was grateful for. The sky remained cloudless, even above the church tower.

She wondered if perhaps she had dreamed the whole thing, but it had been dreaming that had caused the snowstorm to happen. If daydreams were the key to making things happen, why could she just not daydream that her grandmother never came back? Or that the *Petty Four* became ugly? She remained silent on the way home, only breaking her brooding mood when she came to Duke and Esmeralda's field. Standing on the fence, she found the two horses snuggling together under the trees. They were unaware of their guests until Sam barked hello. With a soft whinny, Duke came up to the fence, followed by his white lady.

'Ah, Señor Sam, I did not see you. I was otherwise engaged.' He turned and nuzzled the white mare. Gertrude felt a stab of envy and pushed it away. She felt her thoughts drift to the dark horseman and shook her head as if to empty her thoughts of him. Since talking with Mrs Eccles, she had monitored every thought and was surprised at how many negative ones floated through her mind. She made a fuss of the two horses until Sam pulled at her jumper.

'Come on, Scamp, my stomach says it's teatime.' They said

their goodbyes and walked down the road. Sam stopped in his tracks.

'You know Duke?'

'Yes,' Gertrude said.

'Good god! He's not—'

'Yes, he is *the* Spanish Duke, four times grand national winner, the top racehorse in the country until ... *the unfortunate incident.*' Sam shook his head.

'When he kicked the queen? Into the next enclosure?' Gertrude nodded. 'You know I thought he had been put down. I mean *the queen,* Gertrude.'

'Esmeralda has told me that the queen begged for his life. The queen loves horses you know and she could see he was upset.'

'But why did he do it?' They had stopped at the blossom tree. Gertrude looked up at the pink buds. In a couple of weeks, she would be out in full bloom and Gertrude could smell her hesitant fragrance. She traced her hand up and down the trunk and the tree sighed.

'On his last race, he watched one of his friends die. His friend lost his footing at one of the bigger jumps and Duke heard his neck snap. His friend died instantly and the jockey just stood there, whipping his dead friend. Duke's grief and rage spurred him on to win. Then, in the winner's enclosure, he spotted the horrid jockey. Esmeralda told me that this jockey was notorious for his brutality. Duke broke free and kicked the jockey into the next enclosure. He only kicked the queen because she got in the way. She had gone forward to calm him down.

'It was terrible after that. They beat him and were going to put him down but as I said, the queen herself—'

'Lord bless her.'

'Lord bless her indeed, said no. But when he raced again, he could not jump. Can you imagine that? One of the greatest racehorses this country has ever seen, unable to jump? He was so traumatised, even now he will not talk about it. I heard all this from Esmeralda. He won't ever have another human on his back. He was quite mad when he arrived here, but Esmeralda has loved him back to sanity.'

'How awful. Poor Duke.'

'I know, but he is happy now, him and his Esme.' Gertrude sighed. 'Do you think anyone could love me like that?' Sam fell silent. 'I hope one day I am loved. I mean really loved. I want to be the most loved woman in all the world.'

'Be careful what you wish for.'

'How could that be an awful thing? To be loved so much?' Sam pranced off.

'Mrs Eccles is right; you do have a lot to learn.'

'What the hell do you mean? I have never known love and all I want—'

'I know what you want, Gertrude, but just be happy with one man loving you. Do not wish the whole world to love you as well.'

'As if they would? It was only a thought.' Sam rounded on her.

'And what did Mrs Eccles say about thoughts? Has today not taught you anything? To be the most loved woman in the world – do you really think that would bring you happiness? People fighting over you and destroying themselves to have you, is that what you want?'

'God, Sam, I was only thinking out loud.'

'Exactly! Just wish for a happy contented life. That is all most of us can hope for.' Angry tears prickled in her eyes.

'Mrs Eccles wants me to be strong and beautiful and powerful and yet the moment I show any real power or desire, I get told off like a child.'

'You are a child.' Sam trotted off. He halted and his head bowed down. He turned and slunk back to her. Sitting down, he held out his paw and after a moment, Gertrude took it in her hand.

'Look, I am sorry, Scamp. You must feel so confused and I know that your mind must be reeling. You have had years of being repressed and now you are free, you must feel explosive with all the possibilities. It must be dizzying.'

'Dizzying is the word,' she said, her anger forgotten as she heard Sam describe exactly as she felt.

'Just listen to Mrs Eccles. She will guide you and show you the way. You are not a bad person, Gertrude, but it is so easy to get caught up in your own power. To think you can do anything you want or have anything or anyone you want. Do not go down that path, for it is the path of destruction and despair.' Gertrude felt that Sam was no longer aiming his lecture at her and she put her hand down to soothe him. He flinched and then relaxed into her.

'Come on, let's get you fed, Sam,' and they raced each other to Mrs Eccles' front door.

✻ ✻ ✻

There had been no magical bath that night, just a quick hot shower.

Gertrude felt she was being punished, although Mrs Eccles had kissed her goodnight when she went to bed. The next day at school, she had been quiet and oblivious to the hungry eyes that followed her every move.

Following her afternoon walk with Sam and a dinner of soup and bread, she went through to the living room and sat by the fire. Mrs Eccles had her head down in a book and so Gertrude also curled up and read a book called *Horse Tails* by *Rhiannon.* Sam stretched out in front of the fire, his snores rumbling and Jim, who had popped in for dinner, sat behind Mrs Eccles on her chair. He drifted off and fell onto the floor. Gertrude picked him up and put him on her lap, stroking him. She had been engrossed in her book for some time when she looked up to find Mrs Eccles staring at her.

'What did you think of dinner?' the old lady asked. Gertrude politely closed her book.

'The vegetable soup was golden and warm and the homemade bread delicious. I just love your cooking. I love eating vegetables, but my grandmother won't let me.' Mrs Eccles put her book down.

'What does your grandmother feed you?'

'Kids food, chicken nuggets and fish fingers, but piles of them, whole platefuls. It's as if she wants me to be unhealthy.'

'Humph, no doubt. Well, it is not your fault you're not as fit as you could be, and that kind of food only dulls the senses. The atmosphere in this world is so heavy, I myself have put on weight—'

'Fatty,' chirped Jim.

'—If only to protect myself, and I thank my body for it. In Albion, the air is lighter. You are already getting to know your body better and to appreciate it, but in Albion, you will really notice a difference. However, before you go there, I need to get you fighting fit and I have six weeks to do it in.'

'You would need six years with Queen Girly.'

'Now it's going to be tough,' Mrs Eccles continued, blatantly ignoring Jim, 'And it's going to hurt, but you have power now and self-esteem. Today is Tuesday, so the timing is right. Tuesday belongs to Mars, one of the gods of war, so it seems appropriate that we start your training tonight. It is time for a bath.'

Gertrude jumped up knocking Jim squawking and swearing to the floor.

'I am forgiven then?' Mrs Eccles smiled.

'Nothing to forgive. I showed you this door, but it is you who knocked upon it and walked through it. Now come on, upstairs.' They heard running footsteps above them, but this time no one flinched. Gertrude, Sam, and Jim followed Mrs Eccles up the stairs and entered the bathroom. The bath stood in the middle of the room bouncing up and down on its clawed feet. Mrs Eccles gave the bath a tap.

'Calm yourself otherwise *you* will have to have a bath.' The bath stopped bouncing and Gertrude wondered what that would be like. Mrs Eccles danced over to the windowsill and picked up a red bottle. She bit her lip as she read the label and then shrugged. Dancing back over to the bath, she turned the taps on and waited until the bath was half full. Muttering under her breath something that sounded like,

'Cat is going to kill me,' she poured the whole bottle into the running water.

A spicy scent filled the room. The smell made Gertrude's body tingle. The bathwater turned red and began to boil until it looked like lava. Even when Mrs Eccles turned off the tap, the water boiled and bubbled. Hugging herself, Gertrude looked over at Mrs Eccles.

'You put the whole bottle in.'

'And I stand by my decision. Get in and soak as long as you like. Normally this takes months of training, but we do not have that luxury. When you come out, change into the clothes I will lay out for you on your bed. Oh, and you will need this.' She went over to the sink and opened the cabinet below. She returned with a bucket, placing it by the side of the bath.

'Come on boys, let's leave Gertrude in peace. It might be the last chance she gets.'

'Good luck, Scamp.'

'Yeah, it was nice knowing you,' Jim said. Giving Gertrude a curt nod, Mrs Eccles left her alone in the spicy scented bathroom.

CHAPTER 16

Gertrude stared at the mass of red liquid for a long time and it was only when the bath bobbed impatiently, that she removed her clothes and stepped in.

The water pulled her under.

Gasping for breath, she swallowed the water. Her insides exploded in pain. She fought to get out, but the water fought back. It pinned her down in the bath and wrestled with her.

I am going to die.

Her lungs burned. Her eyes streamed and her throat closed. Even though she was in water, it felt as if she were being consumed in flames. She stopped fighting. The water loosened its grip on her and she splashed to the surface. Clinging onto the side of the bath, she took in great gulps of air.

The water pulled her under again. The pain became sharper and she screamed. Hot red water flowed into her mouth, making her cough and splutter. Red hot needles burst through her stomach. Again, the water released its hold on her and she leant over the bath. She retched up the contents of her stomach into the bucket. Thick black liquid spurted out of her mouth and nostrils. The stench was foul and decaying, smelling like rotten meat. She vomited again, splattering the floor and half the wall. Groaning, she felt the water tighten around her legs and she gripped onto the bath, but the water was stronger and she went under again.

This time she became still straight away. She felt the water move over her body, exploring her. Invisible hands held her face, whilst other hands pinned her to the bottom of the bath. She tried not to panic, but her air was running out and she began to thrash. The water lifted her and slammed her down onto the porcelain beneath. Something broke inside her. Feeling herself released, she just made it over the side of the bath to vomit. The liquid was lighter in colour, a brown rather than a black, and the stench had lessened. Bracing herself, the water pulled her under again and subjected her to the invisible hands.

Time and again, she resurfaced to throw up. The bucket began to fill and she wondered how she could have anything left in her stomach. Each time she went under, the hands became softer until they fluttered over her in soft caresses. She came up and finally vomited a clear liquid that smelled sweet. The water calmed and she tentatively sunk back into it. Hot tears poured down her face. One tear dropped into the water and the red colour disappeared, leaving Gertrude sitting in fresh, clear water.

The door opened and Mrs Eccles entered. Without looking at Gertrude, she went straight to the bucket and looked at the contents. She flinched.

'All done?' she asked.

'Eventually. It took some time.'

'There was a lot to come out.' Gertrude leant back and closed her eyes.

'What was that stuff?'

'All the poison you had been fed over the years.' Gertrude opened her eyes and saw Mrs Eccles look with disgust into the bucket.

'Worse case I have ever seen. Right, I will deal with this. Get out, change, and meet me downstairs. Well done by the way. People stronger than you have died during one of Cú Chulainn baths.' Leaving Gertrude with that thought, she walked out of the bathroom.

It took Gertrude half an hour to change. Her body felt raw,

the light blinded her, and any noise made her cover her ears in pain. Mrs Eccles came up and helped Gertrude into the black trousers and white shirt. The clothes itched and scratched on her skin. The shirt billowed and looking at herself in the mirror, she thought she looked like a pirate. Her reflection mimed fighting with a sword.

'Drink this,' Mrs Eccles said, handing her a glass of something. Gertrude gulped down a clear liquid. The sensations receded a little and the light did not blind her so much.

'What is it?'

'Good old Welsh water, cure for all ills.'

'Why is everything so loud and bright?'

'You're like a newborn. Your senses have heightened. No warrior can fight with dulled senses.' Gertrude sat down on the edge of her bed and then stood up again as the released scent overwhelmed her.

'What was in that bath?'

'Cú Chulainn's blood, amongst other things. You would not believe what I had to do to get him to give me some.'

'Was it painful?' Mrs Eccles looked down at the carpet and a faint flush crept across her cheeks.

'Parts of it were, but there is a thin line between pain and pleasure and I have been subjected to worse. In fact, I will be once Cat finds out I've emptied the whole bottle.'

'Who is Cat?'

'My sister and my friend. Now speaking of cats and friends come downstairs. Time to begin.' Gertrude fell back on the bed with a groan and let the floral scent wash over her. The scent did not have its usual effect. She did not feel tired at all. She felt energized and her leg restlessly moved up and down. She bounded off the bed and ran downstairs.

Bursting into the living room, she reeled back as the flames of the fire blinded her. Blinking, she made her way to her chair and sat down. She picked up her book to read, whilst she waited for Mrs Eccles, but the words swam in front of her eyes. She jumped up again. Sam and Jim entered the room and watched her pacing up and down.

'Gawd, Gertrude, slow down, Queen Girly. You'll wear a hole in the carpet.'

'I can't, Jim. I feel as if I have jumping beans in my belly. I am going to have to go out and run.'

'That is exactly what you are going to do,' said Mrs Eccles as she entered the room. Gertrude stopped pacing.

'Did you get rid of—'

'All gone, and the bathroom clean.'

'You should not have had to handle that. I should have dealt with it.'

'You had dealt with it long enough. Now this running lark … have you ever run for fitness or done any form of exercise at all?' Jim let out a cackle.

'That will be a no,' said Gertrude. 'I did try once. When I went to the comp, I tried to get fit by running home every day from school. Then my grandmother found out and increased my chores so much, that I was exhausted by the end of the day. But I did enjoy it. Jim used to chase me and I remember reading that if you wanted to keep running, you had to imagine you were being chased by a ferocious dog.' She smiled at Sam who pulled his lip back in a joking snarl.

'I think we can come up with something like that.' Mrs Eccles' eyes gleamed in the firelight. They glanced behind Gertrude.

An explosive roar ripped through the room.

Gertrude leapt into the air, whirling round. She dropped into a defensive crouch, her arms out in front of her.

'Brilliant reactions,' commented Mrs Eccles. Gertrude focused on the picture of the lion. He roared again. Straightening up, Gertrude watched as he backed away, becoming smaller in the picture. He broke into a run coming straight for her and came crashing through the picture frame, shattering it. Glass and wood fell onto the floor. Gertrude sprang back as the snarling lion paced around the room.

Jim passed out. Sam backed up against Mrs Eccles. His hackles rose and his lips pulled back in a real snarl. The lion went up to the fallen crow and with surprising gentleness, pushed Jim with his huge paw. Jim came round, cawing. He flapped his wings and flew up onto the chair.

'Get off me, you big hairy barstool.' A deep rumble came from the lion and Gertrude realised he was laughing. Mrs Eccles came forward.

'Jim! Your manners are terrible! Sam, Gertrude, I would like you to meet Ariel. Ariel, you are most welcome. These are my friends, Gertrude and Sam. Sam is not to be harmed in any way. As for Gertrude? I will leave her in your capable paws.' The lion gave another deep-throated laugh and Gertrude had a longing to bury her head in the thick mane. *This is how Lucy must have felt when she first met Aslan.*

He turned and faced her, his tail swishing back and forth.

'I will give you five minutes,' he growled.

'Five minutes? For what?' asked Gertrude.

'Five minutes head start. Although now it is four and half minutes.' Gertrude stared at him without moving.

'Four minutes,' the lion said, never taking his eyes off her. He licked his lips.

'I should warn you; I am very hungry.' Gertrude looked at Mrs Eccles who was beaming at her.

'You said you wanted to run, so run.' Gertrude looked back at the lion.

'Three and a half ...'

Gertrude turned and ran.

CHAPTER 17

Two weeks later saw Gertrude streaking up Heol Broom Lane.

Any moment now she would reach the gate. She could not hear Ariel, but she knew he was there. She took a sharp turn right and in the dark, saw the moonlight glint off the farm gate. Gathering up her energy she ran and jumped, sailing right over it. Letting out a whoop of joy, she turned left and ran across the field. Ariel would catch her, he always did, but by god, she would make him work for it. As always, Sam ran beside her, weaving in and out of her legs, so she had to jump over him. This was her favourite part of the nightly chase. Yesterday she had cleared this field and entered the second one before the lion had caught her. Tonight, she was determined to make it halfway through the second field.

'Every day set yourself a goal to go just a little bit further,' Ariel had told her on that first night. That was after he had battered her up the lane. He had toyed with her exactly like a cat with a mouse. Sam had gone mad, attacking him. Ariel had pulled the retriever away from Gertrude and talked to him. Afterwards, they had walked back to Gertrude, the best of friends. Sam had told Gertrude to fight the lion as it was for her own good.

'You're bloody joking, aren't you?' she had said. For an answer, Ariel had launched himself at her and she had tried to defend herself. At first, she spent most of the time on the ground, but after a while, even in the dark, she began to anticipate his next move and even dodged a couple of blows from the huge paws.

'Soon I will not sheath my claws, little lioness. Then we will see how good you are at dodging.' After that first night, Gertrude's life settled into a routine, but she doubted if anyone else had ever experienced one like it.

Her day would start when the first bird sang. Usually, it was Jim swearing. No matter how early that was, Mrs Eccles would be up and waiting for her in the kitchen. She would hand her a glass of hot water and lemon saying,

'Drink up and go. Run like the wind.' Gertrude and Sam would run out of the house and across the dunes to Sker beach and back. Sometimes she spotted the dark horseman far away in the distance. One day she promised herself she would run all the way across the beach to him.

At first, only Sam had come with her. He would run in front of her and she would jump over him, like leapfrog on the move. Soon, Jim had joined in and appointed himself as her coach. He would fly above her shouting helpful statements such as, '*move your fat arse,*' or '*try harder, you big lump.*'

By the end of the first week, the swifts thought it would be great training for them if they joined in, so they began to dive bomb the three of them, all the way down to the beach. Gertrude loved it and asked them to target her specifically, to see if she could dodge them. She was getting better at it, but the swifts' accuracy was awe-inspiring.

Coming home one morning, they had found Duke pawing at the grass and leaning over the fence, his nostrils flaring. Gertrude had gone up and stroked his nose.

'Who are you racing?' the horse demanded.

'Sam and Jim, the swifts, the wind … everything.'

'I will race you.' Esmeralda and Gertrude had gone very still. Gertrude bowed low.

'Duke – Spanish Duke – it would be an honour.'

The next morning, as Gertrude, Sam and Jim flew past the

field, Britain's greatest racehorse ran at the fence and cleared it effortlessly. Gertrude felt his energy as he streaked past her and glorying in it, she increased her speed. She knew she did not have a hope in hell of catching him, but she reached down and pushed herself. Of course, after that, Esmeralda had asked to join in and then so had Magness and Agnes. Word got around and soon flocks of birds flew with them. Even Satan chased them some mornings and the swifts would dive bomb the cursing, fluffy black cat until he turned back.

Every morning Gertrude would question Duke about running and jumping.

'How do you clear a fence?'

'You see it coming towards you,' the racehorse said, 'You gather your energy into your centre. You say, "*I must clear this fence.*" See yourself doing it, before you do it. See yourself flying over it. Push your heart over first and you will follow.' After that, Gertrude had cleared the farm gate for the first time.

When she arrived home, after the mad morning chase, Mrs Eccles would be there with a bowl of steaming porridge. Gertrude would joke that it was *just right,* and then the morning debate would start.

'Do I really have to go to school?'

'Yes,' Mrs Eccles always replied. 'How else will you measure your progress? Your peers have always regarded you in a certain way. Watch their reactions and you will see how much you are changing.'

'But it's so boring.'

'I know. I have read the curriculum and how you all manage to stay awake is beyond me. There are no spell lessons, no fighting or plant lore. Honestly, no wonder this world is full of dullards, but go you must.' Mrs Eccles would shoo Gertrude off to school with a lunch of bread and salad.

The only welcome distraction Gertrude had at school was Jonathan Winterbourne. The golden boy of year twelve had been, until recently, Tara Wilson's boyfriend. Gertrude had smiled as she watched Tara sob and hold onto his leg as he tried to escape her. Although the *Petty Four* had left her alone, their glares across the playground were disturbing. She knew it was because Jonathan watched her every move. Wherever she was, she would glance up and find the blond boy staring at her. He had even begun smiling at her. She knew a showdown with the *Petty Four* was coming and, despite her training, her stomach still clenched at the thought of it.

However, she really did not have much time to think about it. When she arrived home from school, she would start her exercises. Squats, lunges, sit-ups, press-ups and crunches. She would pull herself up on the door frame whilst Mrs Eccles kept count. The first time she had managed five. Now she was up in the hundreds. Her curves were still there, but now they were even more pronounced. She feasted every night on vast bowls of vegetable stew and hunks of brown bread with lashings of creamy butter.

In the evening, there would be two hours of reading. Mrs Eccles had given her books with titles such as '*The Art of Hand to Hand Combat, by Scathach.*' It had moving pictures of people fighting. Gertrude had been pleased to see as many women fighting as men. '*Fighting With Weapons When You Do Not Have Any, by Scathach,*' had become a personal favourite, as it was about battling with everyday objects such as pens or keys.

One night Mrs Eccles had handed over a book with a proud look, titled, '*Herbs and How They Can Improve Your Performance.*' The author had been a '*Vivienne Myrddin.*' Gertrude had devoured it in one sitting.

Around nine at night, the books would fall to the floor and Gertrude would pace up and down. Ariel would spring into the house, always from a different entrance and Gertrude would have to wrestle him, escape, and run. Every night she would get further until he caught her.

Tonight, it looked as if she would make it to the second field. Spurred on she gave a burst of speed and gave herself up to the pure pleasure of running. The border of the second field was in sight. She ran through an opening in the hedge that separated the fields and turned sharp left. She caught hold of Sam by the scruff of his neck as he streaked after her and waited.

Ariel sprang through the hedge and Gertrude leapt off the ground, grabbing him around the neck. The lion bucked, throwing her off. Landing on her feet, she wheeled round and felt a draught as his unsheathed claws came down towards her face. She leant so far back, she toppled to the ground. Ariel leapt and she rolled out of the way, but he trapped her by her hair, pinning her beneath him.

'How many times, little lioness, must I tell you?' he growled. 'Hair up and head down. Your hair is a weapon for your adversary.' Gertrude went still as if shamed. The lion loosened his grip. She sprang out from under him and flew at him again. Chuckling he swiped at her and she felt his claws rake her arm. Ignoring the pain, she ran and jumped, somersaulting over his back and came round to face him again.

For the next half hour, they engaged in hand-to-paw combat. She leapt over him and under him. She jumped on his back and then buckled under his weight as he jumped on hers. He knocked her down repeatedly, but Sam had told her this did not mean failure.

'A wise man once said, Scamp, *"Our greatest glory is not in never falling, but in rising every time we fall."* So, keep falling down, Scamp. Who knows ... maybe there is something you are meant to find down there.' Having no choice in the matter, Gertrude would get up every time she fell, although she did question whether Confucius would have said that if he had been fighting a lion every night. Only when her legs started to shake and she physically could not get up anymore Ariel would call a halt.

Walking home that night, with Sam and Ariel padding beside her and Jim somewhere in the sky above – he had been determined to improve his night flying – she asked Ariel,

'Has anyone ever beaten you?

'Only two. One I love more than life itself, the other is the greatest knight who ever lived. I would bow to him if he would let me.'

'Who is he?'

'You don't remember?' Gertrude sighed.

'No. I do not remember. Do I know him?'

'Know him? You *are* him,' but the lion would not be pressed anymore and for the first time since her training, Gertrude did not fall asleep straight away. She had been too exhausted lately to dream, but when sleep finally came that night, she dreamt of the two men. One with golden hair whose eyes changed colour and the other, the dark horseman, whose eyes were the colour of storm clouds.

CHAPTER 18

Entering Mrs Eccles' house the next day, Gertrude sensed a new presence.

Her senses were now in a constant heightened state and they were screaming at her that there was someone new in the house. Someone different. She crouched down, but hearing laughter coming from the conservatory, she tiptoed her way through the hall. Pausing in the kitchen, the laughter stopped, as if they were also aware of her. Reaching into her bag, she pulled out a pen and held it up in front of her chest as she crept into the conservatory. Someone grabbed her arm and dragged her into the room. She fell to the ground, pulling her arm out of the assailant's grip. Mrs Eccles yelled,

'Out! Not in here! Take this into the garden.' The unknown visitor lifted and propelled Gertrude out of the door. She fell onto the grass and went into a forward roll.

Springing up she put her hands in front of her face. At least she still had the pen. She flicked her eyes over her attacker. A tall, muscular woman with a mane of tawny hair stood with her hands on her hips. She wore a chain mail vest with tight brown trousers. Gertrude took in the thigh holster, which contained a knife and the baldric crisscrossing her chest, which no doubt held more weapons. A snake bracelet wound its way around the woman's bare upper arm. Her topaz eyes flashed and the wide mouth pulled back into a feral smile of delight. Ariel padded out onto the lawn with Mrs Eccles and flicking a glance between him and the warrior woman, Gertrude did not know who looked the most lion-like.

Gertrude and the mysterious warrior circled each other. Gertrude closed her eyes to centre herself. She sensed the woman move to her right and she twisted her body and leapt, feeling smug. *Get out of that!*

The woman stepped aside almost as an afterthought and Gertrude landed in a heap at her feet. The woman yanked her hair, pulling her face upwards.

'What has Ariel told you about your hair?' she said in a Scottish accent. The woman lifted Gertrude up and threw her down the garden. Twisting in mid-air Gertrude managed to land, without winding herself. The warrior ran at her and Gertrude sprang to her feet, watching as the woman's eyes flicked to her left. Gertrude defended herself from that side but at the last moment, the warrior changed direction and hit her from the right, this time winding her. Cursing her stupidity, Gertrude pulled herself up and launched straight into an attack. Her pen snapped on the warrior's chain mail and an iron grip caught her wrist. Gertrude let go of the broken pen, along with a howl of pain. Her assailant twisted her arm behind her and forced her, face down onto the ground. The woman jumped on her back. She hardly weighed anything at all but Gertrude could not move.

'Say sorry,' the woman said.

'Go to hell,' Gertrude snarled. A wave of dizziness and nausea crashed over her, as the woman pressed down with her fingertips on her neck.

'Pardon?'

'Go – to – hell.' The woman jumped off her. Slowly Gertrude rolled over and looked up at the fierce creature standing over her. The woman's face radiated such pride and love Gertrude frowned.

'Oh, my little sister, it is so good to have you back. My name is Scathach, but all my friends call me Cat, so you, of course, call me that.' She held out her hand, all fierceness gone.

Gertrude ignored the hand. She stood up and lifted her chin, but her legs betrayed her and gave way. Scathach caught her and gently took her into the conservatory. Mrs Eccles fussed around them both, pouring tea and yelling at Scathach for being too rough.

'Viv, stop. Stop! She fought brilliantly. I have trained warriors for a year and a day, who have not fought as well as she just did. How on earth did you get to be so good so fast?'

'I had a bath in Cú Chulainn's—' Gertrude stopped as Mrs Eccles made a slicing gesture with her hand across her throat. 'Er ... and Ariel has been training me.' The lion purred and jumped up on Cat's lap, obscuring her from view. Groaning, Cat said,

'Get off me you big cat. You're not a cub anymore.' She pushed the lion off her and fell to the floor, rolling around with him. Teacups and plates went flying.

'Oh, my goddess, why must you always cause chaos wherever you go, Cat?' Mrs Eccles bustled around, picking up the fallen crockery, whilst Cat and Ariel rolled beneath a bush. Gertrude found herself laughing when Cat reappeared with leaves in her hair. They grinned at each other and any ice Gertrude felt, melted. They both helped clear up and then settled back in the chairs, whilst Mrs Eccles went to prepare dinner.

'You were clever back there,' Cat said, her fingertips trailing over Ariel's mane. 'I deliberately fooled you, but most fighters are not as skilful as I am.' There was no arrogance in her voice. 'I looked over to your left, so you correctly thought I was going there. You anticipated what I was going to do, but not what I actually did. Most people you come up against will give themselves away all the time. Eventually it will be almost boring.' She sighed. Her face brightened. 'Great use of the pen, though. You liked my book?'

'You're *the* Scathach? Oh, yes, *'How to fight with weapons when you do not have any,'* is my favourite.' Cat's grin spread from ear to ear.

'Do you like it better than *'Phases of the Moon and How You Can Transform Yourself Within a Month?'*

'I have not read that one.'

'It's very good,' said Cat leaning forward. 'I will have to ask Viv to give you a copy.'

'Did she write it?' Cat's voice dropped to a whisper.

'Morgan did. It's fab.'

'What are you two whispering about?' said a voice from the kitchen. Cat put a finger to her lips and then shouted,

'Nothing! Just hurry up with that soup you have been slaving over.' She put her head close to Gertrude's. 'Morgan is a sore point at the moment.'

'Who is this, Morgan Le Fay?' Cat sprang back.

'You don't remember?'

'God, not you too.'

'Bloody hell, she really has done a number on you.'

'Who?' but Mrs Eccles interrupted them, bringing through bowls of steaming tomato soup and a loaf of warm bread. Cat fell on the food tearing the bread and gulping the soup. Mrs Eccles frowned.

'Goodness, anyone would think you have not eaten for days, Cat.'

'I haven't.' Cat tore off some bread and shared it with Ariel. Sam, who had been looking adoringly at the warrior since she had arrived, edged closer.

'Okay, my other golden boy.' She tore off another chunk and gave it to him. He wolfed it down as fast as she had. Sitting back, she wiped her mouth on the back of her hand and smacked her lips.

'Vivienne that was wonderful. Remind me to thank Nell.'

'Er – excuse me. I actually cooked that.' Cat raised one eyebrow. Mrs Eccles looked away. 'All right, all right,' she muttered. 'I will thank her.' Gertrude did not even bother asking who Nell was. She would only get the usual evasive reply.

Restless, she sprung out of her chair and stalked into the

garden. A moment later Cat joined her, clapping her so hard on the back that Gertrude nearly fell to her knees.

'It must be hard,' the warrior said, steadying Gertrude with her hands. 'We expect so much from you and yet keep you in the dark. Viv has her reasons. I do not agree with all of them and Morgan doesn't agree with any of them, which is why they fell out. But Viv is seldom wrong and knows so much more than I do.' Cat took Gertrude by the shoulders and looked deep into her eyes. 'I must ask you to put all your trust in me, Gertrude, because for the remaining three weeks until your birthday, I am going to be your best friend, the older sister you never had and your worst nightmare. By the end of it, you will not know whether you are in love with me or if you hate my very soul.

'I expect you to rage against me, curse me to your hell and become so enamoured of me, you sob when I am not there. All I ask of you is that you trust me. Trust me with your life, because I am going to teach you how to save yours.' The sun shone on Cat's hair making a halo around her. 'Will you trust me?' Cat held out her hand and Gertrude put out her own to shake it. Cat pulled her in tight and flung her onto her back. She leapt on her, straddling her chest and pinned her hands above her.

'Lesson one, cub; never, ever trust anyone and never leave your guard down.' She grinned her feral smile, looking so like Ariel that Gertrude groaned out loud.

It was going to be a long night.

CHAPTER 19

If Gertrude thought for one moment that she had reached her physical limit, she was wrong.

The past two weeks now seemed like a warm-up compared to what the leonine warrior had in store for her.

'You run down to Sker beach every morning? Brilliant. Now do it twice. Doing two hundred crunches? Well done. Make it three hundred. You walk to school? How lovely. Now run it.' Every time Gertrude reached a goal, Cat moved the goalposts further away. The repetitive exercises were the worse.

'Bend your knees over your toes,' Cat would say, pacing up and down, her hands clasped behind her back with Ariel padding silently beside her. 'Advance, lead off with your right foot, retreat, move back with your left leg, lunge, kick off with your right foot – kick I said! What in all of Cú Chulainn's bunions was that? And twirl that stick. It should be a flowing movement! You look like you're stirring porridge.' And so it went on, drill after drill, bending and lunging. Gertrude went to sleep with Cat's voice ringing in her head and the sequence of moves juddering through her brain.

The warrior was right though. Gertrude adored her. The love she felt for Mrs Eccles was a warm, deep, grateful love. With Cat, it was infatuation and worship. Cat's very energy made the air around her vibrate as if it had speeded up, and Gertrude's heart joined in. She would have slept by Cat's feet if she had asked her to. But there were days when Gertrude hated her. She felt so angry towards her that she would avert her eyes from the flashing topaz stare but Cat would know and on those days she would attack Gertrude, pushing her onto the ground.

'Let it out, girl!' Gertrude would try, but it was like a lion cub fighting off the alpha male in the pride. Afterwards, exhausted, and sore, Cat would ruffle Gertrude's hair.

'Your passion is commendable. You have fire in your belly and I love you for it, but if you do not learn to channel it, then you are of no use to anyone. Control the blaze, do not let it control you. Direct it to where *you* want it to go. Do not let the flames run amok like a forest fire. Be the fire in the hearth. After all, you are defending your home. Learn to turn the fire down, but never out. And remember, there is a fine line between defeating evil and becoming evil and you must dance along that line all your warrior days.'

In the rare times they had a break, Gertrude would bombard the two women with questions about Albion.

'Why can't I go to Albion now?'

'Because you are not sixteen yet,' Cat said. 'When you turn sixteen the gloves will come off.' Gertrude frowned and looked down at her bare hands. Mrs Eccles smiled.

'What Cat means is at the moment getting you to Albion would be difficult. There have been … certain restraints, shall we say, set upon your person to prevent you from leaving this land.'

'Why will it be different when I'm sixteen?' Mrs Eccles put down her teacup.

'Because at sixteen summers you become a woman. You will no longer be a child and that will make all the difference.'

'But I'm only a kid.' Cat shook her head.

'Not in Albion you're not. It's bloody ridiculous treating sixteen-year-olds like kids. I watched you come out of school the other day—'

'You came to my school? What if someone had seen you?' Cat fixed Gertrude with the same look she had seen Satan use towards Jim.

'I am only seen if I wish it.'

'You still took a risk,' muttered Mrs Eccles. Cat rounded on her.

'By the goddess, I cannot believe you said that. You of all people—' but the tirade was cut short when she took in Mrs Eccles' laughing face.

'By the Morrigan, Vivienne, do not awaken the beast,' purred Ariel, nuzzling Cat's knee with his huge head.

'Can I continue please?' Cat said, her topaz eyes still flashing. 'I went to your school and saw all your schoolmates. I could not believe what I was seeing. They are still acting like kiddies and some of them were at least seventeen summers old. Swearing and spitting and running around like loons. No discipline, no stillness, no self-control. You go to school with idiots.'

'Tell me about it.' Gertrude bent down to stroke Sam who had curled up on her feet. 'What is Albion like?'

'Wondrous, magnificent. Well, it was. Now it's beginning to resemble this land. It is no longer the sanctuary it once was.'

'Why?' Cat's eyes glittered with sudden tears.

'Because the queen took the most horrific people from this land and introduced them to our land. Now there is conquering, raping, battles, and child killings. The sacred groves have all but disappeared, our brothers and sisters of the wild are hunted and cruelly killed and she is building everywhere she can. The queen hates anything natural. She hates nature.'

'Sounds familiar.'

'What do you mean?' asked Mrs Eccles.

'So does my grandmother. Talking about her, where is she?'

'Londoninum,' said Cat.

'Jerusalem,' said Mrs Eccles at the same time, shooting a fierce look at Cat. 'We sent her on a trip to the holy land. She was over the moon about it.' Gertrude knew they were lying but she did not say anything.

'Do you miss your grandmother?' Cat asked. Gertrude barked out a laugh.

'You have obviously never met her.' The truth was Gertrude had hardly given her grandmother a passing thought in the last few weeks. Her old life seemed surreal, like a bad dream. However, the drills with Cat were a nightmare.

One Sunday, they were going through the drills and Jim dropped by to croak encouragement.

'Advance, retreat, lunge, arm up, arm down – no arm down, you big daft arsemonger!' In between Jim yelling, Cat and Ariel fired off questions at Gertrude.

'Does Britain have an army?'

'What do you do for food?'

'Is there a war on?'

'How can people eat meat?' Gertrude answered the best she could and tried to keep her momentum going.

'Yes, there is an army, a huge one. We also have the Navy and the R.A.F., which stands for the Royal Air Force. We have planes … like big birds that drop weapons.'

'I'm a big bird that drops weapons. Ask old Sod Jones,' cackled Jim.

'We have supermarkets where you go and pick what you want from the shelves. Everything is wrapped and prepared for you. You don't have to do any work at all to get your food.' Cat made a face and shook her head.

'How stupid is that? You're eating food prepared by some blighter you do not know? Who may have had a bad day? Goddess only knows what vibes you're eating.' Gertrude did not pursue it. She concentrated on getting her lunge right.

'As for eating meat, don't you, Cat?'

'When have you ever eaten meat with Viv? You try eating something you only just had a conversation with.' Gertrude frowned, twirling her stick, up and down, behind and in front.

Gertrude grew aware that Cat and Ariel had stopped speaking. A proud look came into the warrior's eyes and a slow grin spread across her face. Gertrude realised she had not seen that grin for a long time. Ariel made contented huffing noises. Mrs Eccles came out of the conservatory, beaming at her.

'She's ready, Viv,' Cat said. Mrs Eccles' smile grew even larger. Ariel padded over.

'That she is,' he said, his deep voice rumbling. 'She did not put a foot wrong, despite all the stupid questions we asked her.'

'I shall go and get it,' Mrs Eccles said and disappeared inside. She returned carrying something covered in a white cloth. At a nod from Mrs Eccles, Cat whipped the cloth away to reveal a sword in a scabbard. Gertrude swallowed hard. She felt a spasm of fear and excitement.

'Of course, normally there is a huge ceremony,' Cat said, 'And you oversee the making of your sword with the Elven. It takes several moons to make. The Elven discover what sort of fighter you are and they make sure all the energies are aligned correctly. They cast it during the phase of the moon that suits you best.' Mrs Eccles' violet eyes blazed.

'And then you throw your sword into the lake of Avalon, to see if you are blessed. If you are, I retrieve it and give it to you.'

'Morgan is brilliant. She makes the scabbards and sews the symbols and protection—' but a sharp look from Mrs Eccles cut Cat off midstream.

'Anyway, it is yours,' continued Mrs Eccles. 'I mean it was … I mean it is. Oh, just take it and congratulations for getting this far.' Gertrude reached out her hands and took the sheathed sword. The scabbard was deep green and embroidered with silver symbols and words Gertrude did not recognise. Trembling, she pulled the sword free and for the first time heard her sword sing. A note like a plucked harp string hung in the air between the three women. It had a golden pommel and a hilt studded with emeralds. They glittered in the spring sunshine.

'Name it,' breathed Cat. Gertrude turned it over in her hands and felt a slight vibration, which ran up through her arms and into her heart. Her heart thudded and Gertrude burst into uncontrollable laughter. This sword would guard her.

'I shall call it Joyous – Joyous Guard.' Mrs Eccles and Cat exchanged a look.

'Good choice,' said Cat. 'It is well named.' Cat gestured for Gertrude to try it out. Stepping back, Gertrude waved it from side to side. The sword made a slight sound as it sliced through the air. She twirled it in her hand and brought it over her head and behind, repeating the moves she had learned in the drills. Mrs Eccles and Cat stood quietly, as Gertrude's moves became bolder and she moved around the garden. Sam had to dash out of the way, as the sword came whistling down past his head.

'Sorry, Sam, she is so eager.'

'Yes, well, be that as it may, she can be eager for someone else. Go near Jim.'

'Oooh, you cheeky bar steward. She would have to catch me first. I'd be off before she had even got near—oi watch it!' The crow flapped into the air as Gertrude narrowly missed him. Laughing, she apologised and stood away from her friends.

She had always presumed that swords were heavy, but the weight was reassuring, even comforting. After five minutes, it began to feel such a part of her body that she could not imagine doing her drills without it.

Another sharp note like a plucked string made Gertrude wheel round. Cat had pulled out her own sword. Grinning the warrior advanced and said,

'Right, cub! Let's see if you really have been paying attention to my lessons.' Giving her opponent a bow, Gertrude dropped down into the en garde stance and smiling, beckoned Cat on. Raising Joyous Guard above her head, she brought it down with a satisfying clash against Cat's sword.

'Come on, boys, give them space.' Mrs Eccles said and, Sam, Jim, and Ariel moved to the door of the conservatory. Gertrude knew she would not beat Cat, but as long as she stayed upright and kept her arm moving, she would be satisfied.

'Watch yourself,' Cat said, bringing her sword down to Gertrude's chest. 'You left yourself wide open there. Come on, concentrate. Face me with your head, not with your body. Turn your body away from me.' Gertrude followed her instructions and managed to block a sudden thrust.

'Good girl,' murmured Cat, 'Get closer to the earth. Remember that is where the energy comes from. Lower your centre of gravity.' Gertrude bent her knees further and sure enough, a surge of energy come up through her legs. She welcomed this new energy with a sudden parry aimed at Cat's ribs. Cat blocked it beautifully, but only just. She gave a grunt of approval.

'I love it. Long time since someone surprised me like that.' As if to prove a point Gertrude waded in again, but there was no discipline and Cat lazily disarmed her with a flick of her wrist.

'Damn.' Gertrude stomped over to retrieve her sword.

'You lost your focus that's all. You let your pride take over. Remember, fights are battled with words as well as with the sword. After all, as someone once told me, words and sword contain the same letters. Think about it.' Gertrude thought she saw a flicker of sadness in the warrior's topaz eyes, but it disappeared as fast as it had come.

'I should block out what people say?' she asked.

'Yes. You will be goaded, insulted, provoked, and mocked. All that matters is you and that sword. Do not waste energy exchanging words. Use your breath for breathing, not chatting.'

'Like you're doing now?' and Gertrude leapt at Cat, this time aiming for her legs. Cat jumped up and the sword whipped underneath them. Landing perfectly, Cat threw her head back and laughed. She rushed forward and reined several blows down upon Gertrude. Despite her best intentions, Gertrude found herself disarmed and on the ground with the point of Cat's sword by her throat. Angry tears sprung to her eyes and Cat fell to her knees and clasped her in a fierce embrace.

'By Cú Chulainn's callouses do not be so hard on yourself. You have only been fighting with a sword for ten minutes and you are already further along than anyone I've ever taught … well with a few exceptions. Quite a few actually but that's not the point. We have another week and a half of this and believe me, you are already showing signs of being a great warrior.'

She leaned back and roughly wiped Gertrude's tears with her hand. 'Beltane Eve will soon be upon us. The veil will thin. You, me, and Viv will go over to Albion and if you can fight well here, just wait until you arrive home. The air is so much lighter.' Gertrude looked over at Sam and Jim.

'I am not leaving my friends. Can they come to?' Jim hopped over to Gertrude and looked up at Cat.

'If you say no, I'll peck your eyes out.'

'Idiot, of course *you* are going. You out of all of us.' They exchanged a wink.

'And how could I leave my Sam?' said Mrs Eccles, crouching down next to them and smoothing her hands over Sam's golden head. Feeling left out, Ariel nudged his big head underneath Cat's arm and toppled everyone over. They lay in a heap of feathers, legs, and fur, laughing. A contented silence fell over them as they stared up at the blue sky.

'Just eleven more days,' Gertrude murmured.

'Eleven days until Beltane,' Cat said.

'Eleven days and you will be a woman,' said Mrs Eccles.

'Will she smell better?' asked Jim, which of course started everyone laughing again. Eventually, they calmed down.

If Gertrude had known what was to come, she would have held on to that laughter for a lot longer.

CHAPTER 20

I t is a known fact that when you want time to pass quickly, it knows this and deliberately slows down.

It is the same when you wish time would slow down, it knows this, and speeds up. The best way to deal with this is to live in the present moment, neither looking back nor looking forward. It is something Mrs Eccles drilled into Gertrude every day, but it did not work. Albion and her sixteenth birthday became her holy grail, and she could not wait to get there. The days passed in agonising slowness, and only the blossom tree, unfurling her glory every day, indicated that time was passing.

Not surprisingly Gertrude had no trouble at school anymore. Her schoolmates still kept a distance from her, but it was for different reasons than before. From being at the bottom of the heap, she found to her surprise, that being at the top was just as lonely. No one knew how to talk to her, especially after she had beaten the school record in cross-country. The boys all but dribbled as she walked by and the girls almost hissed. Only Jonathan Winterbourne smiled and she really wished he wouldn't. For every smile he gave her, she would catch Tara glaring at her. Gertrude wished she would just get the confrontation over with, but she would be damned if she was going to initiate it. If Tara and her, *'Three Silly Girls Rough'* wanted to have it out with her, then Tara would have to act first. Cat had drummed it into her that the first move should be made by your opponent.

'You can sum up what kind of fighter they are within seconds. It gives you the advantage.' Every lunchtime Gertrude would sit on the wall in the playground, reading her book and waiting for the attack. It never came and she wished it would, just to break up the boredom she felt during school hours. Who the hell cared about the Industrial Revolution? There was a mad queen running amok in Albion. Who cared about long division, when there was division going on in her homeland? As for Newton's laws of motion, did no one realise that the great man of science was a magician?

'Oh, without a doubt,' Mrs Eccles had said, peeling apples one day in the kitchen. 'Apples are very sacred to us. The fact that one fell on his head shows he was one of us. He studied at Avalon you know.'

'I don't think I'll bring that one up in physics tomorrow though,' Gertrude had said, grabbing an apple and biting into it.

But eventually, time relented and the last day of school arrived. Just as well, Gertrude thought as she dressed for school. Her uniform hung off her. She plaited her long hair, as Cat had pulled it often enough to make a point. Smoothing down her skirt, she looked at herself in the mirror. She waited to see if the other Gertrude would appear. She had not seen much of her in the last few weeks and found herself missing her. Mrs Eccles had explained the other Gertrude's vanishing act one morning.

'It's because she is now a part of you. You've accepted her, so you and her are now one, just as it should be.' However, just as she turned to pick up her school bag, she saw a movement in the mirror. The other Gertrude stood there, hands on hips, smiling. Gertrude thought how lovely her smile was.

'Go and enjoy the last day. Leave them wanting more,' and waving, she faded away, until it was just Gertrude standing there with her hands on her hips.

Gertrude found Mrs Eccles in the kitchen, holding out her packed lunch. The old lady's violet eyes brimmed with tears.

'Last day, my darling and then tomorrow … oh, the birthday celebrations we shall have. We will have a little party. In fact, Cat is making arrangements now and when the sun sets and the veil thins, Cat and I will take you home. Then your life, your true life, will begin.' She came up to Gertrude and threw her arms around her. Gertrude tensed, but not for long.

'Thank you for everything. I … I just do not know …' She stopped as her voice broke. Mrs Eccles gave her a squeeze.

'Hush now, I know everything you wish to say. It is beating in your heart. I am just so glad I found you in time. And I am so sorry.'

'Sorry? For what?' Mrs Eccles stepped back and held Gertrude at arm's length.

'For it all. For what has passed and what is to come.' Gertrude frowned.

'But you said everything will be fine now. I'm sixteen tomorrow and I get to go home. I will find out everything I need to know. I will finally know who I am.' Mrs Eccles' eyes closed briefly, tears spilling down her cheeks.

'That, my love, is what I mean.'

CHAPTER 21

Before she made the journey to school for the last time, Gertrude returned to her grandmother's house and ran up the stairs to get the books hidden under her bed.

As she crept through the house of her childhood, she waited to feel a sense of loss. None came. The house was cold and empty like her life had been. Each room had borne witness to her humiliations and sorrows. Even the door handles had been cruel, catching her clothes and whipping her backwards, as if to prevent her from leaving the room. Only the books in her hands had been her sanctuary in this house, her way of escape. Tomorrow she would escape for good.

She paused in front of her grandmother's bedroom door and feeling brave, tried the handle. Still locked. Where was her grandmother? Gertrude searched her heart and smiling, found she really did not care. Feeling light and free she made her way downstairs and closing the front door behind her, left the house of her childhood without a backward glance.

❊ ❊ ❊

Time was up to his old tricks and each lesson seemed to pass more slowly than the one before. In History, she gazed out of the window and tried to ignore the rattling and prattling voice of her history teacher. Why on earth anyone would care about factory acts, she had no idea. Mind you, she thought the Luddites sounded a grand bunch of fellas, smashing up machinery that would enslave their fellow men. She must be a Luddite. Whoever had said school was the best years of your life was mad.

Looking around her, she saw the boys gazing and even some of the girls smiling at her. Why? Because she was now beautiful? Had she not been all along? She felt contempt for the lot of them. For years she had been the punching bag for her peers and *she* had not changed. She was still Gertrude Springate, ginger, and certainly not skinny. She could now become the most popular girl in school if she chose to. She could turn the tables and make their lives a living hell. She could have her own gang. Chewing the end of her pencil, she smiled.

'Gertrude Springate, if you are not going to pay attention I will send you out,' snapped Mr Fosse. Gertrude lifted her head and gave him a long cool stare beneath her eyelashes. She saw the man's eyes widen angrily and then another look replaced it, one she did not feel comfortable receiving.

'I was paying attention. Just not to you.' The class burst into laughter and Mr Fosse's face flushed bright red. Pushing back her chair, Gertrude stood up and leant down to pick up her school bag.

'I'll see myself out.' She made her way through the chairs, as her classmates whooped and cheered.

She went straight to the library. As usual, there was only Mrs Groves, the librarian, there. She looked up from her desk and gave Gertrude a welcoming smile.

'Hello, Gertrude, I have not seen you for ages.' Gertrude smiled back.

'I've been busy.' Mrs Groves did not question what she was doing out of class. Gertrude was the only pupil who used the library.

'I have some books to return and – and I am sorry I kept them for so long. You see—' Mrs Groves raised her hand.

'You could not bear to be parted with them. I understand. I

knew you were looking after them for me.'

'They have been my friends.' Gertrude blushed, not believing she had said something so silly. Mrs Groves peered over her glasses at her and nodded.

'C. S. Lewis once said, *"We read so we know we are not alone,"*' she murmured. 'Never apologise for loving books, Gertrude. They are the source of wisdom and love. They can hold us in their embrace when no one else does, and they never judge you.' Gertrude nodded, her throat tightening. She reached into her bag and pulled out *'Tales of Greece and Rome,' 'King Arthur and the Knights of the Round Table,' 'Celtic Mythology,'* and the entire *Chronicles of Narnia.* These last she held onto and then sighing put them on the desk. Mrs Groves picked up, *'The Lion, The Witch and The Wardrobe.'*

'Still my favourite.' Gertrude nodded.

'But a talking lion is a bit farfetched don't you think?' Mrs Groves shook her head.

'I do not care. I love Aslan, always have, always will.' *And Ariel would love you,* Gertrude thought. Gertrude remembered all the times Mrs Groves had let her stay in the library, hiding from *The Petty Four.*

'Thank you. For the books and for everything. Goodbye, Mrs Groves.' She turned and made to walk away.

'Keep it, Gertrude!' Mrs Groves said and thrust *'The Lion, The Witch and The Wardrobe,'* into Gertrude's hand. 'Please, I insist. I have five copies at home, all tear marked. I will see you tomorrow.' Gertrude nodded, finding speech difficult.

At lunchtime, she sat on the wall with her nose in the book. It did not matter how many times she read it; C. S. Lewis' words flowed around her like a caress. She was aware of the boys kicking a tennis ball. As she gave herself up to the magic of Lewis' world, she saw a movement out of the corner of her eye. Without lifting her eyes from the page, she put out her left hand and caught the tennis ball in mid-flight. The boys all stopped and stared. Only when she realised who was jogging over to her, did she raise her head from the page.

'Well caught, Red,' Jonathan Winterbourne said. He put his hand out for the ball. She smiled at him and handed the ball back. He grabbed onto her hand and held it, his thumb tracing the back of her knuckles. Gertrude's heart thudded and heat rose to her face. She yanked her hand away. He stood there, passing the ball back and forth between his hands. A yell from one of his mates made him turn round and he threw the ball back. Gertrude jumped off the wall, but he turned to her and said,

'Don't go.' She stood looking up at him. The sun seemed to find him as beautiful as she did. His blond hair shone in the sun and his brown eyes glowed. *But they aren't grey.* She frowned as the thought came from nowhere.

'Fancy going down the beach after school?' he asked. *Now he decides to ask me? Just as I am leaving?*

Looking across the playground, she saw Tara and her crew staring over at them. She fought an impulse to kiss him on the mouth, just to wind them up.

'You've had ages to ask me, Jonathan. Tara no longer your cup of tea?' He made a face.

'She was not who I thought she was.'

'Neither was I.' He sighed and looked at the ground, kicking a stone.

'You are like a blossom tree that has just blossomed.' Gertrude burst into laughter and his shocked face dissolved into a grin. He shook his head.

'Oh god, how lame was that?'

'It's not Byron, but it's a start.' His face clouded.

'Who's Byron? Does he like you too?' Gertrude repressed a giggle.

'Thank you for never joining in.'

'Joining in what?'

'You know what. But I do not thank you for standing there and doing nothing. You are so popular, Jonathan, a word from you and things could have been easier for me. Remember that.' Feeling tired and wanting to be away from him, she reached down and picked up her bag. She felt him move closer and smell her hair. She came up and gave him a sharp look.

'Goodbye, Jonathan. It could have been a pleasure.' She walked away, her heart heavy.

'I'm free tomorrow,' he yelled. She forced herself to keep walking.

Having not seen any sign of Jim, Gertrude decided to finish the remainder of her lunch hour doing what she had done throughout her school years – hiding. She entered the sixth form toilets and pressed her back against the door, closing her eyes. This deserted toilet was always free from lipstick and gossip. She went over to the sink and splashed water on her face as it still burned from the encounter with Jonathan. She raised her head and listened.

The click of kitten heels and the thud of Doc Marten boots announced their arrival. Gertrude wiped her face with a paper towel and looked at her reflection in the mirror. Her emerald eyes flashed and grew hard. The door slammed open so hard, it hit the wall and bounced back on its hinges. *The Petty Four* entered the bathroom and found Gertrude waiting for them.

CHAPTER 22

The four girls took up position and Gertrude laughed to herself.

Why on earth had she waited for Tara to make the first move? She knew all her moves, having seen them first hand over the years. Michelle Lewis took her lookout position by the door, Jacky stood on Gertrude's left and Samantha on her right. Tara stood in front of her, the mistress of ceremonies. Gertrude assumed the victim stance, eyes on the floor, body folding in on itself and, out of courtesy and to give them a chance, she let them go first. She obediently crumpled to the floor as Jacky kicked her legs from beneath her. She did not move as Samantha went through her school bag. Jacky held her down by placing her Doc Marten boot on her neck. Samantha snorted,

'*The Lion, the Witch and the Wardrobe,* again? Who reads this crap?' She tossed the book over to Jacky.

'Please don't rip my book,' said Gertrude in a pleading voice. Jacky pressed down with her foot.

'Oh dear, are you going to cry like you always do when I rip up your books?' Gertrude closed her eyes and pushed her focus down through the floor, into the earth. And there she found an energy spark that recognised her. She pulled the energy up into herself and said in a different voice,

'For the last time I am asking you – please do not rip my book.' Jacky spat and Tara sniggered. Jacky removed her boot and Tara bent down, grabbing the thick rope of Gertrude's hair. She yanked her head back.

'Watch now as Jacky rips up your book before ripping you up. And maybe we will make you eat it again, as you seem to love books so much.' And it was on that memory of having *Pride and Prejudice* stuffed into her mouth when she was eleven, that Gertrude unleashed herself.

Springing up she kicked the book out of Jacky's hand and backflipped across the bathroom. Coming to a standstill, she caught the flying book in her hand.

'I'll take that.' She placed it on the floor. 'Good faithful Jacky, always Tara's loyal guard dog. But just think what you could achieve if you ran your own gang. What if you were top dog instead of guard dog?' Jacky frowned. Tara screamed,

'Get her, Jacks!' Jacky shook her head and ran at Gertrude, baying like the faithful dog she was. She never saw the punch that broke her nose and sent her flying across the bathroom, but the sound of splintering bone echoed around the room. The spiky-haired girl howled in pain, as she slid down the wall. She tried to hold her splattered nose together with her hands.

Gertrude picked up the book and put it back in her school bag, along with her other belongings. No one moved, then Tara screeched,

'Don't just stand there, Sam, get the bitch!' Samantha hesitated only a moment. She ran at Gertrude. Gertrude wheeled round and with a kick, knocked the girl flying into one of the cubicles. Taking the long black hair in her hands, she shoved Samantha's head into the toilet bowl and flushed it. Hauling the dripping girl out, she slapped her twice across the face. She pushed her across the room. Samantha crumpled against the wall and slid down in a heap, next to the howling Jacky.

Gertrude turned and faced Tara. She saw a flicker of fear in the blonde girl's eyes. It passed and Tara's mouth curled into the familiar sneer.

'So, the worm has turned, has she? Well, you will find I am

not as useless as these stupid cows. You are a fat skank and a slag, Gertrude. You're nothing. No one will ever want you. You're disgusting.' Gertrude smiled.

'Jonathan doesn't seem to think so.' Tara paled. Her face transformed into a mask of hatred. Screaming, she ran at Gertrude, her hands shaped like claws.

Gertrude grabbed the deranged girl's wrists in one hand and punched her in the face. Tara's head snapped back and when it came forward again, Gertrude slapped her face, first on one side and then the other. Grabbing the blonde girl's hair, she rammed her face into the mirror. The glass splintered and Gertrude grinned at the blood now smearing the mirror. She glanced over at Michelle. Michelle gave her a shy smile.

'You're ok, Gertrude, no one's coming. Oh my god, Tara, what's happening to your face?' Gertrude forced Tara to look at her bloody reflection. Huge spots sprouted all over the heart-shaped face.

'Look at yourself. Look at yourself, Tara.' Gertrude spat. 'You're pathetic. You make me sick. You're so pretty, so perfect, and for years I wanted to be you. But it's not fun being you, Tara, is it? Because you're not very beautiful after all. Jonathan saw through the mascara and the foundation and that is why he dumped you. Poor Tara. It's all an act, isn't it? Desperate to be loved, desperate to be noticed. Which is why you let Billy Yates feel you up behind the gym.' Gertrude had no idea where the words were coming from. Samantha spluttered something that sounded like an expletive.

'Is that true?' whimpered Samantha.

'Oh yes. She told Billy he was far better off with her because you were a frigid cow and could not kiss to save your life.' Tara's eyes grew wide.

'How do you know that?' she whispered. Gertrude decided to just go with it and let the words come.

'I know everything about you. I know that your mother loves your little sister more than you. I know your father wanted you to be a boy and has not forgiven you for being a girl. I know you go home most nights and sit in your room, away from a drunken mother, who hardly knows you are there. And you wait for daddy to come home, but he's always late because he's too wrapped up in his work and his new secretary.

'So, you sit and you cry in your room and wish that someone would take you away from it all. And here's the thing Tara' – Gertrude pulled her hair by the roots – 'here's the thing – you and I are not so different after all because that's all I've done in my bedroom for the last sixteen years. You and I could have been friends because I understand what it is to be lonely.'

'How are you doing this? How do you know about Mum?'

'Look at yourself, Tara. Look at yourself.' Gertrude thrust Tara's face into the mirror. 'This is you.'

Tara recoiled when she saw the lumps covering her face. Thick black hair bristled on her top lip that covered stained long teeth. Her nose had grown to twice its size and the famed blue eyes had receded into fleshy folds. Tara screamed.

'People will always eventually see this side of you, Tara. No amount of blonde hair dye or pink lipstick can hide this much ugliness of the soul. You're a spoilt, disgusting, dreadful troll, who made every day of my school life hell.'

'I'm so sorry, I'm so sorry,' Tara wailed 'You were so pretty and clever and – and – oh god please stop. Please.' Gertrude felt no pity for her. She could keep Tara this ugly for the rest of her life. She slammed the girl's face into the mirror again. Some spots on Tara's face burst with the impact, leaving pus and blood on the glass. Gertrude looked and caught her reflection. Her mouth curled into a sneer, similar to the one Tara always wore.

The ice around her heart cracked and she let go of Tara's hair. The girl dropped to the floor whimpering. She lay at Gertrude's feet, pawing and whimpering at her shoes.

'I'm sorry. I'm so sorry.'

Bile rose in Gertrude's throat. She closed her eyes and leant against the sink for support. Her head buzzed. Looking down at Tara, she made a motion with her hand and bent to lift the girl up. Tara's face returned to normal and Gertrude showed her in the mirror.

'Oh my god, what did you do to me?'

'Oh my god, what did you do to yourself?' Gertrude replied wearily. She bent down and retrieved her bag.

'I forgive you, Tara Wilson, for it all, but I will never forget. I feel sorry for you. For all of you.'

She walked to the door. Michelle smiled up at her and moved out of the way. Gertrude paused and looked back. Samantha stared open-mouthed at her. Jacky held her bleeding nose, the blood dripping all over her school shirt. Tara muttered to herself, running her fluttering hands over her restored face.

'You poor, ugly bitches,' Gertrude said. She walked out through the door and as it closed behind her, she heard Michelle murmur,

'I always liked Gertrude.' Samantha let out a scream of hate.

'You bloody bitch. Billy was mine!' Gertrude heard a sharp slap and Tara howled in pain. Allowing herself a small smile, Gertrude walked away from them all.

CHAPTER 23

News of the fight spread like a forest fire.

Tara Wilson went to the hospital with a broken arm. She entered the ambulance, sobbing hysterically, 'I'm not ugly, I'm not ugly.'

Jacky Streatfield accompanied her, holding her splattered nose. She had been strangely silent. The school suspended Samantha Howard for breaking Tara's arm, and no one knew where Michelle Lewis had disappeared to. Rumour spread that the breakup of the popular girl group had something to do with Gertrude.

By the time school had finished, the rumours had grown. Some said Gertrude had defeated *The Petty Four* using her book as a weapon. Others said she had been trained in a Krav Maga. Someone even suggested that Gertrude had used a gypsy curse against Tara. When the school bell rang at the end of the day, Gertrude walked through the herd that had gathered outside. They parted for her, like the red sea.

As she walked through them, she caught Luke's eye. The boy with the limp smiled and began to clap. Everyone joined in. Jonathan Winterbourne winked as she passed by.

'Nice one, Red. Tara had it coming to her.' The applause grew and she went out of the school gates to the sound of people chanting her name.

She left without looking back.

Running home, she shook off the school day and focused

on what lay ahead. The relief of never having to walk through those gates again made her run even faster. She wheeled around the corner and came to a skidding halt at the top of her road.

A dark cloud hovered above the church tower.

Her stomach clenched in fear and she looked up at the tower for Jim. *Not there. Oh God, where is he?* The swifts were absent too, and Duke and Esmeralda had vanished from their field. Looking down at the ground, she saw it was wet.

'Oh god.' Her mouth went dry and she broke into a run. As she ran down the road, she stopped as her feet squelched through mush. The blossom tree had been stripped bare, her pink flowers lying sodden on the ground. Gertrude placed her hands on the trunk. The tree shuddered.

'Breathe,' gasped the tree.

'You just worry about yourself.' She hugged the tree and carried on down the road.

She came to Mrs Eccles' house and stood, blinking, to make sure she was seeing right. The house was in darkness. The garden had returned to its overgrown state and the gate hung off its hinges. Gertrude ran up to the door and hammered on the wood. Jack, the doorknocker was gone and the door had paint peeling off it. She ran to the front window and tried to look inside, but the old yellowing curtains she remembered from years ago, were closed.

'Sam? Mrs Eccles? Please answer me. Can you hear me?'

'I doubt it,' said a soft voice. Gertrude turned and came face to face with her grandmother.

The pale blue eyes glittered like glaciers in her white face. She grinned like a skull. If her grandmother had been thin before she went away, now she was emaciated. A claw-like hand shot out and grabbed Gertrude by the throat. She squeezed so tight, Gertrude eyes bulged and her legs gave way. From somewhere, deep in her mind, she could hear Cat's voice in her head.

'It does not matter if someone is stronger than you. Use their

strength against them.'

Gertrude put her arm up and knocked her grandmother's hand away, but her grandmother's other hand came down and grabbed Gertrude's plait. Her grandmother dragged her into the house. The door slammed behind them. Her grandmother kicked Gertrude down the hallway into the kitchen.

'Get up.' Gertrude rose and looked around her. She saw a plate of chicken nuggets on the kitchen table and her eyes widened as her grandmother took her seat. She motioned Gertrude to sit down.

'Let us have dinner. Eat.' Gertrude stood there without moving. Her grandmother raised her eyes.

'Sit down.' Gertrude lowered herself into the chair and stared at the old woman. Up close, she was skeletal, grotesque. Her grandmother picked up a glass of water and sipped it.

'I said eat.' Looking at the pile of orange nuggets, Gertrude swallowed.

'I can't eat this.' A flash of movement and the old woman leapt across the table. She came down on top of her and Gertrude's chair swung back, toppling to the floor. Fists and nails met flesh and Gertrude tried to fend her off, but her grandmother's cruel hands seemed to be everywhere. Gertrude's lip split and blood trickled into her mouth. Everything Cat taught her drained away, along with her spirit. The weaker she felt, the stronger her grandmother became. The hands slapped, punched, and tore into her. Gertrude covered her face with her hands and tried to turn to the side, but she could feel her grandmother growing heavier as she straddled her. Coming to a stop her grandmother leant over her and whispered,

'That witch thought she was being so clever. What a diversion she caused for me. But in the end, she could not beat me. No one can. And now here we are. I will not have my family torn apart.' Gertrude opened her eyes and blinked back the blood.

'You are no family of mine.' Her grandmother yanked her

up to a standing position by her hair. Throwing her out of the kitchen and holding her with one hand, she unlocked the understairs cupboard. She shoved Gertrude in, slammed the door and turned the key in the lock. Gertrude flung herself at the door and beat against it with her fists. Screaming she yelled one word, over and over.

'Why?'

Gertrude leapt back as she heard the key in the door turn. Hope flickering, the door opened revealing her grandmother staring at her.

'Why what?' the old woman rasped.

'Why do you hate me so much?' Her grandmother stilled. She looked like a hideous statue and although Gertrude thought she should run, weariness overcame her again. Her knees buckling, Gertrude sank to the floor and looked up at her grandmother who still had not moved. Taking a shuddering breath, her grandmother replied in an anguished voice Gertrude had never heard before.

'For being born.' The moment of vulnerability passed and she slammed the cupboard door in Gertrude's face. Hearing the key turn in the door again, Gertrude fell forward onto the floor. Beaten, bleeding and exhausted she let the tears come. Curling up into a ball, she gave herself up to the sobbing and finally, the blessed oblivion of sleep. The hours ticked by.

And so it came to pass, that lying in the foetal position, surrounded by dust and spiders, Gertrude Emmeline Springate, finally turned sixteen.

CHAPTER 24

Morning came, as she always does.

No night, however bad, lasts forever. There was no difference in the darkness, whether her eyes were open or closed, but nonetheless, Gertrude knew that the sun had risen.

Beltane.

For all the good it would do her now. She stretched and winced as the blood rushed into her cramped limbs. Her face felt tight with all the dried blood. She sat up and leant against the wall, stretching her legs out and wiggling her toes to get her blood flowing. She checked herself over, expecting to feel her blood on her hands from the cuts and tears in her flesh but instead, she found a silky, sticky substance covering her wounds. She put her hand up to her hair to push it back from her face.

'Oh, be careful,' a tiny voice said. 'We wove a crown into your hair whilst you slept. And we covered your wounds to clot the blood. You may itch a little but your injuries are well on the mend. We hope you don't mind.'

'Who are you?' asked Gertrude, as she crossed her legs.

'The weaver. I weave words, songs, and dreams. Your dreams are not big enough. I know who you are. Your dreams should be huge. It should take me a year and a day to weave your dreams. Instead, I wove your dreams in a night.' Intrigued Gertrude bent forward, her eyes trying to penetrate the darkness.

'You wove my dream?'

'Yes, that is what we do. We weave stories and dreams and leave them in the morning for you to find. Covered in dew, they glitter like jewels. Dreams are more precious than jewels. Our webs are like your dreams, so fragile and so easily broken.'

'You're a spider.' The voice laughed.

'Are you going to run away?' Gertrude shook her head and then realised the spider could not see her.

'I have never been scared of spiders.'

'So many are. Do you know, we only run at people to remind them of a dream they have forgotten? But we get vacuumed up, or stamped on, or thrown outside, along with the dream the person has been carrying around in their heart.'

Gertrude wondered what dream the spider had woven for her. She had only one dream, and her grandmother had stamped on it.

'You said you knew who I was?' There was a long pause and then something tickled on her hand. She fought the impulse to brush it off and grew still. The spider crawled up her body until she nestled against her ear.

'That is not for me to tell you,' the spider whispered, 'but today you take the first step to finding out. Now, what dream do you think I wove for you last night?' Gertrude's mind raced through the images. She saw Sam's face and Mrs Eccles' and then Cat and Ariel. She saw her grandmother and then she saw the dark horseman. Finally, as always, her mind turned to the golden-haired man from her childhood.

'What is your dream right now, Queen of Sorrows?'

'Right now? It's to get out of this cupboard.' The spider laughed.

'I know. Put your hands up and feel the dream I wove for you in your hair. Touch it gently. What image comes to mind?' Gertrude pressed her fingers into the web. She saw herself putting her hand on the door and opening it. When it opened, little spiders came pouring out of the keyhole.

'I am going to open the door and you are going to help me.'

'Brilliant. Come children, let us help her majesty to escape.' Gertrude shuddered as thousands of little legs ran over her. She willed herself to be still as she did not want to appear rude. The tickling sensation stopped and she got up. She put her hand on the door and waited.

'So, you weave dreams and unlock doors?'

'Not all doors, but your dream to get out of here is actually stronger than the evil one's dream to keep you in here.'

'Have you ever woven my grandmother's dreams?'

'I have never, nor will I ever, weave your grandmother's dreams.'

'Why?' The spider sighed. Her breath sounded like a whispered breeze.

'I had a friend. She tried to weave your grandmother's dreams. In the morning, she wove herself a noose and hung herself. Some dreams should never be. And now, Your Majesty, freedom awaits you. Just think the door open. You have already seen it open when you touched your dream. You already know this dream is going to come true, so put your hand on the door and believe it to be so.' Gertrude closed her eyes and conjured up the image of the door opening. The wood moved and the key on the other side of the door clattered to the floor. The door swung open and Gertrude opened her eyes. It took a moment for her eyes to adjust to the sudden light. Hundreds of baby spiders poured through the lock and over the door. Her friend ran down her arm and Gertrude turned her hand over so that the spider could sit in her upturned palm. The big house spider sat there regarding her and Gertrude smiled.

'Thank you, and please thank your children.' The spider remained still and then moved off her hand onto the wall.

'Go. But remember, start dreaming. And dream big. Watch out for your dreams in the mornings. They will be there, waiting for you.' Gertrude walked out of the cupboard, taking care to make sure she did not step on any little bodies. Turning back, she said,

'I won't forget. Thank you.' Once she was sure she was free of the spiders, she broke into a run and rushed out of the house.

She instinctively looked up at the sky. Dark storm clouds were gathering. Her grandmother stood talking to a man standing by a white van. Money exchanged hands and the man shook hands with her. He got into the driver's seat. The van started up and pulled off. As it passed by, Gertrude heard a bark.

'Sam!' She broke into a run, but her grandmother caught her by her hair, pulling her almost off her feet.

'Yes, Sam. Gone now. All the mess is almost cleared up.' Gertrude turned her head to look at her. Her grandmother frowned.

'How did you get out? Well, it does not matter. Get ready for school.' She let go of her and walked into the house. Gertrude watched the van disappear up the road. She sank down on the ground and feeling the web in her hair, she pulled it out, watching it come apart in her hands. All hope had gone. All her dreams were destroyed.

'She thinks you have nowhere else to go,' a dark velvet voice spoke. 'She thinks she has you beaten, but if we put our heads together and work fast, we can save your golden friend and my kittens.'

Gertrude recoiled as she saw Satan, the big, fluffy black cat sitting there.

'Oh god, Satan, not now.' The cat's eyes widened as she took in Gertrude's bruised face.

'Goodness, she really did go for you, didn't she? My name is not Satan. It really is Fluffykins.'

'What?'

'Now is not the time. That van is scheduled to make two more stops to pick up more poor souls. If we act now, we can save our loved ones.'

'How?'

'Run up to Duke's field and call all the birds.' Gertrude looked at her grandmother's house. Fluffykins followed her gaze.

'You are sixteen now, Gertrude. Mrs Eccles told me that your grandmother's power over you has gone. She won't know that for a while and it gives you an advantage, but only for a while. Use it. Call the birds.' When Gertrude did not move, the black cat hissed, 'Now.' Gertrude jumped to her feet.

'Jim! Jim!' she called, running up the road. 'Swifts. Someone answer me.'

'Oh god, everyone's dead,' a miserable voice spoke from above. Looking upwards, Gertrude stopped as Magness swooped down and landed by her feet. 'They're all dead.'

'Don't listen to the mad, sad old barstool,' a familiar voice squawked. Sobbing with relief, Gertrude opened her arms and held on to the black body that flew into them.

'Jim, where have you been? Mrs Eccles and Cat—'

'I know. Well, I don't know, I ain't got a clue what happened. It was all good and then—' Fluffykins streaked past them yelling,

'Keep moving, Ginger. And you, crow, call all your friends.' Jim flew out of Gertrude's arms and attacked the black cat. Gertrude chased him.

'No, Jim, she's helping. They have Sam in a van and we need to rescue him. It was Fluffykins who told me to call you.'

'Fluffy—?'

'Now is not the time, crow,' the cat hissed, swiping at him with her paw. 'Call the birds. Call them and meet us in Duke's field.' The cat rushed up the road.

'I am not taking orders from that piece of—'

'Jim, please, we have to get to Sam. Call them.' Jim hesitated and then flew up and landed on a telephone wire.

'This is a call to arms,' he crowed. 'A call to arms. We have a code red situation. I repeat, code red. This is not a drill.' Bending down he put his beak near the wire and repeated the call. 'That'll reach them,' he said. From nowhere the swifts came streaming down from the sky.

'Follow me,' yelled Gertrude and ran up to Duke's field. The two horses were there and Gertrude vaulted over the fence. Birds came from everywhere. They poured out from trees, gardens, and the surrounding streets. Roy and Joy, the wood pigeons flew in, along with Magness and Agnes. The Crownies turned up, swearing at a family of sparrows. A hawk glided down silently and landed on a branch near to the sparrows. The sparrows, who had been moving away from the crows, about turned, and moved back towards them, away from the silent hawk.

'Better to be insulted than dinner,' murmured one of them. Only Christopher the robin was missing.

Jim flew down and settled on the fence. He faced his troops and took a breath.

'I ain't got a fanny clue what the Hades arse is going on.'

'I do.' The birds all jumped and flapped, as the black cat stepped forward.

'Don't worry, I'm not going to eat you. I have neither the time nor the appetite. Mrs Eccles and the warrior are missing. Sam is in a van along with my four kittens—'

'You're a girl?' blurted out Fred.

'Yeah, and it's called Fluffykins.' Jim laughed. The cat fixed him with an intense stare.

'Now is not the time, soldier.' Jim shut his beak and looked serious. 'The van will make two more stops on the road that runs alongside the dunes. We are going to stop that van. I need you birds to attack it from the air. I will be on foot, along with the horses and Gertrude.' The cat's voice travelled amongst the trees and no one moved a wing as the velvet voice spoke.

'This is a day when heroes will be made. Look to your leader, Jim, and do as he asks. Jim?' She stepped aside and sat down, tail curling neatly around her. Jim looked astonished and then shook himself.

'Who'd had bloody thought it! Friends, brothers, sisters ... and sparrows, you heard the black bast—cat. Let us fly. Swift leader?' The swift swooped down and skimmed across the ground before coming to a stop.

'Your orders sir?'

'Fight formation mate.'

'Yes, sir.' The swift leader took to the wing, shouting orders as he flew up into the cloudy sky. 'All wings report in. All wings report in.' Swift after swift swooped down from the trees.

'Swift ten, standing by.'

'Swift seven, standing by.' Soon the air became full of circling birds.

'Battle of Britain formation!' yelled the swift leader. 'It's what Sam would want. Stay low. Start attack run.'

'Come on,' yelled Fluffykins as she streaked down the field.

'Follow that cat!' Jim shouted. The hawk took off saying,

'I have your backs,' and seeing the majestic bird take flight, some of the birds followed.

'Right, Magness, you mournful old blighter,' said Jim. 'Get the boys together—' an annoyed rat-a-tat-tat interrupted him.

'Of course that includes you, Agnes, you daft mare. No offence, Esmeralda.' The white horse inclined her head.

'Do I get all of them?' asked Magness.

'Yeah, Magness, you do. Agnes, Angus, Seamus, Maximus, Gluteus, Brutus, Ambrosius, Demetrius – and Bob.'

'Och no, Jim. Bob? That makes ten of us.'

'Desperate times call for desperate measures. Do it, mate.'

'It's done.' Magness and Agnes took off.

'Right, the rest of you with me. For Sam, pompous furball that he is.' Jim took off, followed by a flock of birds so large, the sky darkened as they flew off.

'Gertrude, get on my back.' Gertrude turned to Duke.

'Duke you have not had anyone ride you since—'

'I know that. Get on, cariño. There is no time.'

'But I can't ride,' but as she said this, she found herself running and vaulting onto the stallion's broad back. Her school skirt rode up over her thighs, but that was the last of her worries.

'Grip tight with your knees, hold on to my mane and don't let go. Listen to your body. Feel my energy beneath you and meld your energy into mine. We are one. Esmeralda stay close.' Duke began circling around the field, picking up speed.

Gertrude closed her eyes and tried to make her and Duke's bodies into one. The horse changed direction and opening her eyes, Gertrude felt Duke accelerate as he ran towards the fence.

I am going to die, thought Gertrude. The fence was right in front of them. Duke jumped and soared into the air. Time stood still. *This is what flying must feel like.* The ground rushed up to meet them and the racehorse touched down. He pulled sharp to the left, to avoid hurtling into the wall of the churchyard. Esmeralda's hooves clattered behind them. Duke cantered down the road and, not even stopping to look for cars, turned left and followed the road around the corner.

Okay, thought Gertrude, *this is fast, but I can handle this.* But when the road straightened out, Gertrude realised why this horse had won the Grand National four times in a row. Duke exploded with power. He surged forwards and Gertrude closed her eyes and put her head down, lying as flat as possible. *I am going to die.*

'No, *you are not,'* a deep male voice spoke in her mind. *'You and I used to ride like the wind all the time. Remember? Breathe and relax into it. You and he are one. Say it.'* Gertrude raised her head. *'Say it.'*

'You and I are one.'

'That is right,' said Duke

'That's it. You can do this.' said the voice. And she could. She had a slight flutter of memory of racing someone. No, not someone – *him,* the dark horseman, laughing, and riding so fast she felt free. Then the memory vanished. She gripped Duke with her knees, all fear leaving her.

'I see them. They have them,' Duke said. A black cloud of birds quivered above the white van, which had skidded to a stop diagonally across the road. Above the thundering of Duke's hooves, she could hear the cacophony the birds were making. The swifts dive-bombed the van and the magpies sat on top of it, attacking the roof with their beaks. Gertrude could see Fluffykins pacing back and forth across the road.

Duke gave one final burst of speed and overshot the van.

Skidding to a halt, he wheeled around and reared up. He came down, smashing his hooves upon the van's bonnet. Gertrude just had time to see the driver's eyes widen in terror before she fell off. Ignoring the pain in her back, she sprang up and wrenched the driver's door open. She pulled the whimpering man out by his shirt collar. He fell to the ground.

'Dive!' a voice screeched and the swifts rained down upon him. The man screamed and put his hands up to protect his face. The magpies swooped down next. Gertrude leant into the car and pulled the keys from the ignition.

'Don't kill him,' she shouted. She ran round to the back of the van. Hands trembling, she tried key after key until she felt the door unlock. Pulling down the handle, she opened the door. The stench of animal urine and excrement hit her. Dogs barked, cats hissed and her heart ached at how terrified they must be. She jumped in and felt Fluffykins jump in beside her.

Gertrude tore the first cage open. Sam bounded out of it into her arms and knocked her out of the van. Sobbing, they covered each other with kisses.

'I thought I had lost you,' Gertrude cried into the golden fur.

'I thought I had lost *you*,' Sam replied. The two friends gazed at each other.

'Mrs Eccles—' said Gertrude. Fluffykins jumped in between them.

'Gertrude. The rest of the cages, if you please.' Gertrude pushed Sam off her.

'Fluffykins' kittens are in there.'

'Fluffykins?' said Sam sitting up and staring open-mouthed at the cat.

'Now is not the time' said Gertrude and the cat together. They jumped back into the van and opened all the cages. Cats, dogs, rabbits and even a grey parrot, streamed out. Four little black kittens mewed and Gertrude let them out. Purring they crawled over their mother, who lay down on the ground with them.

A scream broke through the air and Gertrude ran round to

the front of the van. The driver lay on the road with Duke's hoof on his stomach and Jim sitting on his chest. Another scream sounded and looking up, Gertrude saw the magpies chasing a sparrow and knocking it to the ground.

'Good god,' Sam said joining Gertrude. 'How many magpies are there?

'Ten,' said Jim 'You're welcome by the way.'

'Ten?' Sam turned on the crow. 'You let ten magpies come together?'

'It was desperate times,' said Jim, sounding petulant.

'We have to stop them.' Gertrude followed Sam's look. The magpies had surrounded a white rabbit and were taking turns to dive-bomb it. The rabbit's sides were bleeding as it whimpered and cowered down into the grass verge. Gertrude yelped as Magness flew straight at her, his eyes glowing red. She raced through the rhyme,

'One for sorrow, two for joy – oh god, Sam! Ten! Ten for the devil.'

CHAPTER 25

Gertrude and Sam watched in horror as the magpies began to attack the escaped animals and birds.

'Swift leader,' Sam yelled. The swift leader flew down and landed in front of him. He bobbed his head.

'Here, sir. Good to have you back, sir.'

'Good to be back, sir. You and your team have got to stop the magpies. You have to pull Bob away.'

'And Demetrius,' said Jim. 'Two have to be taken down to leave eight. Eight is for heaven.'

'Nine is for hell, of course. Can you do it, swift leader?'

'Leave it to us, sir. Jim, sir, may we borrow some Crownies? Two ought to do it. We need some heavy lads.'

'Fred, Sid, you heard him. Do whatever he asks.'

'Rightio, Jim,' said Fred.

'Okay, matey swift, what do you want us to do?' asked Sid. The swift leader took flight, yelling orders as he lifted off the ground.

'All wings report in.' The swifts and the two crows flew off and landed in a neighbouring tree.

'Gertrude, duck!' Gertrude obeyed Sam's command just in time and felt a rush of air from wings beating above her head. Magness cackled.

'Oh gawd, I have unleashed hell,' Jim moaned.

'Jim, brother, you had to do what you had to do. You saved me,' Sam said.

'Yeah, well it won't be a rescue mission if those shit-stained magpies kill us all.'

'Magness, stop this,' Gertrude yelled as the magpies surrounded a black kitten.

'No you bloody don't.' Fluffykins velvet voice cut through the squawking and she leapt into the circle of magpies. As one, the magpies turned their attention to the cat. Fluffykins swiped Demetrius with her paw, catching him on the face.

'Go to hell you, evil arse.'

'I'm taking you with me, *Satan*.' Demetrius laughed and the magpies surrounded her, stabbing at her with their beaks. Fluffykins leapt up on her hind legs clawing and biting until feather and fur flew everywhere.

'Mama,' cried the kitten. Chuckling, Demetrius turned his attention back to the kitten. Sam went down into a crouch.

'I am going in.' He sprang into the circle, knocking magpies out of his way and picked the kitten up in his mouth. He bounded out and laid the kitten at Gertrude's feet. He turned around and waded in again. Furious, half the magpies turned on him, trying to stab him in the eyes. Gertrude picked up the black kitten and held the trembling body to her chest, murmuring words of comfort she did not believe in.

'Start attack run,' a voice yelled from above. The swifts descended from the sky, flying in and out of each magpie. Gertrude could only marvel at their precision. As one, the swifts turned and circled one magpie. They moved together, circling the bewildered Bob, and edging him away from the group. Magness turned his attention away from Fluffykins and Sam shouting,

'Oh no you don't.' He flew straight into the group of swifts, knocking them out of the way.

'Regroup, regroup,' the swift leader said, but one of the swifts did not get up off the ground.

'Swift leader, swift five is down. I'm going back for him'

'We all go back, swift nine.' Fluffykins crawled forward beneath the magpies.

'I've got him.' She opened her mouth, picked up the injured swift gently, and crawled towards Gertrude. Gertrude put down the kitten and prepared to run in, but Sam yelled,

'Stay there.' With a growl, Sam went up on his hind legs and batted the magpies out of the way. He picked Fluffykins up in his mouth. The cat could not protest or she would drop the injured swift, but her green eyes widened. Sam collapsed in a heap by Gertrude's feet, depositing Fluffykins on the ground.

With Sam and Fluffykins out of the way, the battle raged between the swifts and the magpies. The magpies were huge compared to the swifts, but the swift's little bodies flew in and out of them so fast, the magpies could not get hold of them. The swift leader cried out cryptic instructions to his team and once again, Bob became isolated from the group. The swifts circled him so fast it looked as if they had imprisoned behind blurred bars. The swift leader pulled up from the group and shouted his orders.

'Crows, now!' Fred and Sid plunged from the sky. 'Disengage!'

The swifts scattered in all directions, just as Fred and Sid arrived. Each crow grabbed one of Bob's wings and they pulled the magpie off the ground. Grunting with the effort, they were airborne with the demon magpie stretched out between them. Bob cursed, foul words pouring from his mouth. Hearing a shout of anger, Gertrude looked over at Jim. He was hopping from one foot to another.

'Right, that's it. A bit of cussing's okay, but to call attention to Fred's parentage ain't bloody right.' He flew up and grabbed the flailing magpie by his tail feather. The three crows flew away towards Kenfig pool. The birds all cheered and Gertrude clapped her hands.

'Do not be premature, Scamp,' panted Sam. 'there are still nine.'

'Nine for hell,' Gertrude whispered. The remaining magpies' eyes blazed red. They chanted in a strange language. They took off into the air, flying in a circle and the chanting grew louder.

They landed on the van and the hairs on the back of Gertrude's neck stood up. Her flesh began to creep.

'I think I'm going to be sick.' She bent over and emptied the contents of her stomach. As she retched, she remembered how yesterday she had been full of hope. Now hope had gone, along with her web of dreams. Mrs Eccles had gone, Cat and Ariel were lost, Sam had almost been lost, and her grandmother waited for her at home. She looked round and saw the white rabbit on his side, panting heavily, his flanks torn and bleeding. She looked at Fluffykins, the brave black cat who was lying down, her paw on the injured swift. He did not move. A movement caught her eye and she saw a young sparrow, his wing half torn from his shoulder, stumbling over to her.

There was no good left in the world, no hope. Evil always triumphed. The books had lied. Dropping to her knees and closing her eyes, she made a pact with herself that when this was over, she would walk down to Sker beach and walk into the sea.

'Gertrude,' a faint voice said. 'Do not listen to the magpies. All of you.' She opened her eyes and saw Sam pulling himself up.

'Listen to me. The magpies are trying to create hell on earth. They are removing your hope. Without hope, we cannot get up in the morning. Do not listen to them. Listen to me instead, listen to my voice.' Fluffykins stumbled to her paws.

'And mine. I have been called, Satan. I know all about hell, but love is why you are all here. What do you love? Sam tell them.'

'I love ice cream, cheese, cakes, water, Scamp and Mrs Eccles … ' Sam's voice faltered and the chanting grew louder.

'I love Sam,' cried Gertrude. 'I love Magness before he turned nasty. I love Fluffykins for being brave. I love Jim's swearing, books—'

'Fat worms,' yelled a sparrow.

'Fat sparrows,' said the hawk and everyone burst out laughing, even the sparrow.

'My wife, my four kids and the fifth little one on its way,' cried the driver. He lay on the ground, tears streaming down his face. 'And animals. I love animals.' Two of the black kittens made their way over to him and climbed onto his chest. He clasped them tight and bawled into their soft fur. The magpies' chanting faltered.

'Dreams,' yelled a blackbird.

'Chips,' said a seagull.

'Bread.'

'Esmeralda.'

'My beloved Duke.'

'Sleeping.'

'Mating,' said a rabbit and everyone murmured in approval at that one. The swift leader dived down.

'Swift two and swift seven, cover me.' Zooming over to the van, the swift leader knocked Demetrius off the roof. Fluffykins jumped up and knocked the magpie with her paw.

'To you, Sam.' Sam pounced forward and caught the magpie in his mouth. He tossed Demetrius up into the sky.

'Duke, he's all yours.' With the stallion's kick, Demetrius went soaring into the air, over the hedge and landed with a crash and a curse.

The spell broke. Everyone rose and flung wings, arms, and paws around each other. The remaining magpies all shook their heads and started singing hymns and blessing everyone. Fred, Sid, and Jim came back cawing with laughter as they told how they dropped Bob into the pool.

'Gawd, he didn't half put up a fight. The blighter was not pleased. We left him crying in the reeds.' Sam walked over to Gertrude.

'I thought that was it. I have been in tight spots before but being taken to a laboratory? I would never have escaped. Thank you.'

'You were going to a lab? God, Sam. But it isn't me you should be thanking.' She looked over towards Fluffykins. The black cat was checking herself over and cleaning herself. Sam followed her gaze.

'Satan? That big black demon—'

'Her name really is Fluffykins, and if it was not for her calm thinking and quick action, you would be in the lab by now.' Sam shook his head and walked over to the cat. He looked down at the still body of the swift by her paws.

'He's gone,' Fluffykins murmured. 'He was a brave warrior.' Sam gave her a long look.

'Madam, of all the things that have happened today, you have been the most surprising.' She gazed, unblinking back at him.

'Three times I have given birth to beautiful babies,' she said, 'and three times that old sod sold them. I later found out where. My grief tore me apart. I trusted no one, except Mrs Eccles. I hated everyone. Can you understand this? Cats are not like dogs. We do not forgive nor love as easily.' Sam nodded. 'I have saved four of my babies, although they have a lot to learn about loyalty.' All the kittens were nuzzling up to the driver. He seemed content, lying on the ground and making cooing noises. Their purrs vibrated through the air. Sam turned his attention back to Fluffykins.

'Whatever your reasons, Madam, whatever has passed between us is just that—past and passed. You saved me. You brought me Scamp.' He cleared his throat and went down on his front paws, bowing his head. 'Madam, from this day forth, I appoint myself as your protector and servant. No harm will ever befall you or your kin, whilst there is breath in my body and blood in my veins. My life now belongs to you, to direct as you may. I swear by Sirius and by any other god or goddess passing through.' He paused and everyone looked around. The trees sighed as a breeze passed through them. Sam nodded. 'So be it.'

Fluffykins seemed to be struggling. Her whiskers twitched and her eyes narrowed and then opened wide. The retriever remained bowed at her feet. Twitching her nose, she shook her head and then placed her paw on the dog's head.

'I accept your service. You would have done the same for me, no doubt. You may rise now, Sir Loves-cats-a-lot.' Sam spluttered and got up.

'I would not go that far,' he said.

'And this does not make us friends, canine, so do not get too familiar. I don't do friends,' and with a flick of her tail, she wandered over to her kittens and the van driver.

'Cats,' spat Sam, watching her prance away. 'They have incredible amounts of arrogance and conceit.'

'I heard that.'

'And remarkable hearing.'

'Fluffykins?' asked Gertrude following the cat. 'Is that really your name?' The cat sat down.

'It's what the old sod called me, but would you choose it?'

'I just can't get my head around it. I think I prefer Satan.' The cat laughed.

'So do I, but that part of my life is over now,' and she flicked a glance at Sam.

'What would you like to be called?' Sam asked. The cat's eyes widened into huge green pools of light.

'No one has ever asked me that.' Her tail flicked from side to side and she gazed up at the grey sky.

'Lucinda,' she finally said. Then narrowing her green eyes, she murmured, 'It sounds a bit like Lucifer.' The birds laughed nervously and Sam chuckled. Gertrude had been falling in love with the cat by the minute and she wanted to bury her face in the black fur, but she held herself back. She did not think that Fluffy – Lucinda was that sort of cat. Sensing her thoughts, Lucinda turned to Gertrude.

'You are quite right, I am not that sort of cat, Ginger. I am not a pet.'

'You were bloody Old Sod Jones' pet long enough.' Jim crowed. Lucinda put her nose in the air.

'Anyone who knows anything knows that no one owns a cat.'

'Who the hell would want to own a cat? Anyway, you silly

blighters, this is no time for debates and can you lot stop mucking about?' said Jim. 'We got some urgent matters to attend to. Like what we are going to do with that nastard there.' He pointed with his wing to the van driver.

By now, the driver was sitting cross-legged on the road, playing with Lucinda's kittens. One dangled off his wrist, one curled around his neck, and the other chased a stone he kept throwing. The littlest one was fast asleep in his lap. Gertrude walked over and crouched down beside him. He looked up at her and she took in the twinkling blue eyes and curly black hair. He gazed at her and then a smile broke across his face.

'Thank you,' he said. Gertrude frowned.

'Thank you?'

'For saving them … and me.' The man sighed. He brought the kitten that was dangling from his wrist, to his face. Tears rolled down his cheeks and he sniffed, wiping his nose on the kitten. She did not seem to mind, as her purring grew louder.

'I work for the government,' he said. 'I came back from the war, injured. I was good at science and I was good with animals.' He took a shuddering breath. 'They merged my two skills together. I collect animals for scientific experiments. But I did not realise what they were going to do to them. I thought it would be good stuff. But the things I have seen … I can't sleep. I can't eat. My fifth child is on its way, but to say I needed the money was a coward's way out. I see that now.' He looked at all the animals and birds who glared at him. 'I can't do it anymore.'

'I say kill him,' said Jim.

'What's your name?' Gertrude asked.

'Tom. After my granddad. He would turn in his grave if he knew what I was doing. He loved animals. Oh god …' and he burst into another bout of sobbing.

'Kill him,' said Jim. Gertrude glared at Jim.

'Jim! We have all done things we are ashamed of.'

'That is nice of you to say so, but I bet you haven't,' said Tom, thinking Gertrude was talking to him.

'Plenty,' said Gertrude, thinking back to the sixth form toilets. The man sniffed and wiped his face with another kitten. Lucinda's fur stuck up, but she did not attack.

'That's it though. I'm not going back. Someone must want a soldier with a gammy leg? And you know what? They were not going to stop at animals. They were going to use the homeless next. I read it. I saw a file I should not have seen and I have been so scared. If they know I know, they might hurt my family. How many more innocents will die?' A couple of rabbits hopped closer to him and he scooped them up as well. Agnes flew down and with a sheepish look at Gertrude, sat near Tom. Sam edged closer.

'This man is full of love. He just took a wrong path.'

'And my kittens are good judges of character,' said Lucinda. 'There is no way they would go near a –what did you call him Jim? – a nastard?' Jim grunted and hopped nearer. He sniffed and stomped around the man, then came hopping back to Gertrude. Cocking his head to one side, Gertrude bent down to him.

'He's got Elven blood. He's part Elven.' Gertrude sprang back and stared at the man, who was by now lost amongst the feathers and fur.

'Elven? Are you sure?'

'Yep, I can smell it a mile off. It happens every now and then. Oi, Tom!'

'Yes, Jim?' answered Tom, peering underneath a rabbit's stomach.

'Told you,' said Jim, as he sauntered away.

'Tom, can you hear animals talk?' said Gertrude. Tom flushed and looked down at the ground.

'When I was little, I thought I could. My grandfather used to make the birds come out of the trees. They would sit on his arms and sing for him. But that is a long time ago and I probably imagined it.' He peered at her. 'You can, can't you?'

Gertrude opened her mouth to reply, but the sound of police sirens broke off anything she was about to reveal. Jim squawked.

'It's the filth, scarper.' Jim, Fred, and Sid flew off. Sam looked closely at Tom.

'Ask him if he has one of those mobily things.'

'Tom, have you got a—'

'Yes, here.'

'Tell him to phone the local press,' Sam chuckled. 'Tom is going to tell his story.'

CHAPTER 26

Walking back through the fields, Gertrude fought the waves of exhaustion and heartache that were threatening to overwhelm her.

If it was not for the fact that something was tugging at her mind for attention, she might have dropped to the ground and fallen asleep. She had become used to the ghosts in her mind, chasing each other. The two horses, along with Sam and Lucinda, walked in silence beside her. Jim had returned and remained quiet, perched on her shoulder. Even the crow seemed shattered by the morning's events.

In the end, three police cars, a riot van, two reporters from the local paper and one reporter from a national one, had turned up, along with the BBC. They had been filming in Porthcawl when they had caught the scent of a story. They had rushed over to the scene of the ex-soldier cradling as many animals as he could fit into his arms. Tom had started to explain what the government had done and how he had to look after his kids. He was just on the verge of crying again when the journalist from the national paper told him that if he sold his story exclusively to him, he would never have to worry about feeding his kids again.

Lucinda's kittens would not leave him and after a long heart to heart, with Gertrude as the go-between, Lucinda left them safe in his loving hands. Tom promised to love them forever. He had squeezed Gertrude's hand and cried thank you over and over again. Various animal charities had arrived and gathered up the remaining animals, including the injured rabbit. They promised to find good homes for them all. Even a cameraman had gone home with a rabbit.

Magness had come over and mumbled apologies. He said he deserved to die. Lucinda agreed with him, but Sam forgave him, as it had been an emergency. Everyone had gone still, as they watched the swifts and the sparrows take up their dead. The rest of the swifts did a fly past and Tom had cried all over again.

Now walking through the fields, the first drops of rain fell onto Gertrude's hair and the hopelessness she had felt this morning came home to roost. Her knees buckled and she fell to the ground. Looking up to the concerned friends standing around her she said,

'Where am I going?' Duke nuzzled her.

'Home, chicquilla.' Sam and Gertrude looked at each other.

'I'm not going back, Sam.' Sam huffed in agreement and turned to Duke.

'Scamp and I have no home.'

'What happened, Sam?' Gertrude crossed her legs on the ground and leant forward to stroke the dog's silky ears.

'I fell asleep in the conservatory. Cat and Ariel had gone to Albion to make arrangements—'

'Thank god they're both safe.'

'Well, I do not know that. I heard a bang and there was a flash of light. There was screaming … I must have passed out. When I came to, I was in the under stairs cupboard in Mrs Eccles' house.'

'You too?'

'Yes, and then this morning your grandmother hauled me out and handed me over to Tom. I am sorry, Scamp, I do not know any more than that. My heart aches for Mrs Eccles. I feel so useless. I am supposed to protect her, to look after her and I have failed her.'

'Yeah, you're not a brilliant guard dog, are you?' said Jim.

'Shut your mouth, crow,' Lucinda snapped. 'Gertrude's grandmother is not the easiest person to face.' Gertrude gave Lucinda a questioning look.

'I cursed her once as she walked by with the vicar. She turned and hissed at me. Yes, actually hissed. I fled and I am not scared of anyone. There is something not right about her.'

'That is what we used to say about you,' said Sam grinning at her.

'What the hell has my grandmother got to do with Mrs Eccles?' Gertrude said. 'She said she did not want her family torn apart. She knew Mrs Eccles was going to take me away. She comes back and everything is ruined. Jim, where were you when all this was going on?' The crow looked down at the ground.

'I was asleep.'

'The whole time?'

'I had gone round to see Mrs Eccles. She was laughing and packing up some stuff. Cat and Ariel had already buggered off to Albion like Sam said and—' Gertrude's elusive thought flashed into consciousness.

'Jim, how do you know about the Elven?'

'What?'

'Back there, you sniffed Tom and said he had Elven blood. How do you know what an Elven smells like if you have never been to Albion?' She glared at her oldest friend. Jim stared back at her.

'Oh shit,' he said and took off.

'Damn that bloody bird.' She stumbled to her feet. 'Jim! Jim, King of the Crows, I order you to come back here and talk to me,' but the black body continued flying into the distance. 'I'll get him. He won't be able to stay away.'

'He will have made up a story by then,' said Sam. Lucinda licked her lips.

'There are ways to make a crow tell the truth.'

'Sam,' Gertrude said placing her hand over her heart. 'Do you think … is Mrs Eccles dead?' Sam looked down at the ground.

'I cannot feel her so strong in my heart, but she is still there. A spark of her. No, she is not dead. She is too clever. We know her as Mrs Eccles, but remember, she is Vivienne Myrddin. She's Merlin's wife, Scamp. Actually, it is more like Merlin is *her* husband. She is *the* Lady of the Lake. She will have arranged a backup plan.'

'I feel I am constantly wandering in the dark.'

'Aren't we all?' said Lucinda. The rain had begun to fall in earnest. Duke stepped forward.

'Dear ones, at the top of our field is a copse of trees. You can shelter there, all of you. The swifts make fantastic lookouts, but you need to sit and gather your thoughts.' Sam nodded.

'Duke is right. Later we can go and hide out in the dunes, but we need to rest and get some food. Things will not seem so bad on a full stomach.'

'Spoken like a dog,' said Lucinda.

'Any other bright ideas then, madam?'

'No, I agree. Come on then. I shall lead the way,' and off she pranced tail pointing at the sky.

'The arrogance of the creature,' muttered Sam, but he fell into step behind her. Gertrude looked up at the dark sky and turned her face to the rain.

'I'll never see blue sky again. My grandmother will see to that.' Esmeralda came behind her and nudged her.

'Come. Rest and eat and breathe for a little.' Gertrude placed her arm around the mare's neck and walked silently beside her.

At the copse, Gertrude sank to the ground and pressed her back against an accommodating oak.

'Breathe,' said the oak. Putting her hand up, she patted the trunk, took a deep breath, and leaned her head back.

'Scamp needs to eat,' said Sam. She opened her eyes and took in the dog's concerned face.

'We all do.'

'What day is it?' Lucinda asked.

'Beltane,' said Gertrude, her voice catching. The cat sniffed the air and turned to Sam.

'Fancy coming on an adventure, golden paws? Think you can keep up? Old Sod's neighbour is a fantastic cook and judging by the scent—'

'She is cooking a ham. Come on then, follow me. Try not to get caught.' Sam licked Gertrude's hand and ran off through the trees.

'Me? Get caught? Idiot,' Lucinda snapped and trotted after him. Gertrude closed her eyes and tried to fight the weariness.

'We are just here, cariño. Sleep for a little. We will keep watch.'

'Thank you, Duke.' She hugged her knees to her chest, but sleep would not come. Images of Mrs Eccles laughing and Cat fighting came crashing into her mind. She could picture Ariel swiping at her with his huge paws, then picking her up in the air, and catching her, as she had seen fathers do with their children. They had been her family and now they were gone.

'I don't know what to do, Oak. Please help me, I don't know what to do.'

'Turn round and put your arms around me and breathe in deep.' Gertrude obeyed and put her forehead on the trunk, trying to draw strength from the tree.

'Breathe deep. Blow the panic away.' Gertrude breathed. In, out, deep as she could manage.

'That's it deep breath in and—Oh! Gertrude *do not* breathe.' The tree stilled. Not a leaf moved and Gertrude held her breath. Her name rang out in the air and she flinched.

'Gertrude! I know you are there and I know you can hear me. How long do you think you can hide for, child? How long before the police pick you up or find you? Come here. Now.' Gertrude closed her eyes, fighting the impulse to move towards her grandmother's command. She tightened her arms around the oak's trunk, as if not trusting herself.

Hold on to the tree and fight her, Gertrude thought. *I can do this.*

And she found she could.

She opened her eyes and disobeyed her grandmother for the

second time that day. The exhilaration left her feeling dizzy, so she kissed Oak's rough bark and hugged him even tighter. Turning her head, she watched as her grandmother paced up and down in front of the church. The old woman's hands clenched into fists by her side. The vicar came out and put an arm around her and they bent their heads in conversation, talking too low for Gertrude to hear. The vicar shook his head and patting her grandmother on the arm, he led her off towards the church. As she went, she turned and looked straight at Gertrude. Gertrude's heart banged in her chest. Then her grandmother looked straight past her and carried on walking.

'Breathe again,' said Oak.

'Oak, you have no idea.'

'Was that your grandmother I just saw?' Gertrude jumped as Lucinda came through the trees.

'Where's Sam?'

'Can't you hear him?' Twigs snapped and branches cracked as, panting so heavily he sounded like a steam train, the golden retriever burst through the trees carrying a roasted ham in his mouth. He dropped it on the ground.

'Was that your grandmother walking down the street with the vicar?' Lucinda looked at him with unveiled contempt.

'Could you be any noisier? I do not think they heard you in the next village.'

'Oh, I am so sorry, Your Royal Cattiness. Next time you carry the ham. Oh, that is right, you can't because you are not strong enough.'

'Stealth, dog, stealth. You should be as a shadow. I am only seen if I wish to be seen.' Gertrude felt a pang as she remembered Cat saying the same thing. 'The only time they should get a glimpse of you is when you are leaving. We cats are taught that with our mother's milk.'

'We dogs have other things to learn; like saving the universe. Now, Scamp, was that your grandmother?'

'Yes, and she did not sense me at all.'

'Really?'

'Really. All my life, no matter where I have hidden or run off to, she has always tracked me down. Once she was waiting for me by a bus stop when I had only decided to jump on a bus ten minutes before.' Sam sat down on his haunches.

'So, her power over you is fading?'

'Seems like it.'

'Just as Mrs Eccles said it would. Happy birthday by the way. We got you a ham.' Gertrude made a face. She really did not want to eat meat again, but she was starving. Kneeling forward she tore the ham into three chunks making her hands messy. Licking them, she said,

'I don't suppose either of you has napkins or cutlery?' Lucinda looked down her nose.

'You are living in the wild now. Embrace it. And I thought I was stuck up …' and daintily the cat began to eat.

'Mmmm, golden syrup glaze,' said Sam.

'Maple syrup, I think you will find,' Lucinda said. Gertrude could not speak. The sweet saltiness filled her mouth. Too soon, the ham disappeared. Feeling full and sleepy, Gertrude lay down on the ground. The adrenalin had seeped away and her eyes fought to stay open. Sam nudged her with his nose.

'Sleep, Scamp. I'll keep watch.' Lucinda stopped washing herself.

'No, you need to sleep too, dog. I shall keep watch.'

'I am quite capable of keeping guard, thank you.' Duke put his head over the fence.

'All of you sleep. I'll keep watch.' Grunting in appreciation, Sam nestled down with Gertrude, their hands, and paws on top of one another. As Gertrude was on the edge of drifting off, she felt a small body worm it's way in between her and Sam.

'Do not think this means anything,' Lucinda muttered. Sam chuckled.

'Would not dream of it, madam,' and smiling Gertrude let sleep claim her.

CHAPTER 27

Gertrude woke with a start. She felt a paw on her mouth and Lucinda's voice hissed in her ear.

'Keep still. There is someone here.' Her heart thudding, Gertrude nodded and Lucinda removed her paw. The leaves rustled. Someone was moving through the trees. Gertrude sat up. Sam and Lucinda were like sentinels on either side of her. Sam sat with his hackles raised and his ears forward and Lucinda's fur stuck up so much she looked twice the size. The rustling got nearer and Gertrude moved into a crouch, ready to pounce on whatever came through the trees. A figure appeared, but a black missile dropped from the sky, obscuring it from view. Jim leapt onto the figure and dragged it into the open.

'Gotcha, you son of a—' he jumped off as if burned. 'Oh, my gawd. Christopher – what have you done?' Gertrude sprung forward and scooped the small robin into her hands.

Blood covered the robin. Shards of glass stuck out of his small body and he panted. She could feel his little heart pounding underneath her thumb.

'My darling, what happened?' Lucinda and Sam drew close.

'Mrs Eccles … ' Christopher gasped, 'Mrs Eccles … message, I had to …' he stopped.

'Take your time, little one,' said Sam. The robin closed his eyes and then opened them, looking straight at Gertrude.

'Mrs Eccles gave me a message for you. You must go to the

pool … you must seek help from the spirit who lives there.' Christopher took a big breath. 'He must be drawn out with song. He … get you to Albion … Beltane … the veil …' The robin's heartbeat slowed down. Gertrude stroked the blood sodden feathers.

'Take it easy, Christopher. What happened?'

'Your grandmother caught me. She locked me in her house, but I escaped. I was too clever for her.' He puffed his red chest out, which pumped more blood onto Gertrude's hand. 'I flew through the window.'

'You bloody daft bugger,' said Jim in a raw voice.

'No choice, Jim. Some things are bigger than oneself. Don't let her win, Gertrude. There are some dreams that should never be.' He took a laboured breath and shuddered. Gertrude stroked him, hoping to push life back into him, but the shuddering stopped and the little heart stilled. Gertrude placed him gently on the ground.

No one moved. A teardrop fell on the robin's still breast. It glistened there against the red feathers.

'What do we do, Jim?' Lucinda asked. 'How do you honour your dead?'

'What we do with our dead,' Jim said in a shaking voice, 'is for us birds to know alone. First the swift, and then that sparrow, and now Christopher. It's always the innocents first.' Gertrude wiped her tears away.

'Jim, I am so sorry. Nothing is worth this.' Jim turned on her.

'It's worth everything,' he croaked. 'Don't you dare say that. What did he say at the end? You make it worth it, do you hear? You make everything you do from now on worth it. He died to save you. So did swift five this morning and that bloody sparrow. Damn it, damn it to Hades. Christopher and his bloody bleeding heart.' Gertrude gathered Jim up in her arms and rocked him like a baby. Her tears fell on his black feathers, glittering like crystals. Lucinda and Sam moved closer together and Duke and Esmeralda put their heads together.

When Gertrude wiped the tears away, she saw the swifts had gathered, as had Fred and Sid. Gertrude placed Jim down and wiped her nose on her sleeve.

'I want to make a grave for him.'

'Gawd no, put him in the ground? So that the worms eat *him*? Nothing worse for a bird to be grounded like that. He ain't going to be worm food and no cat is digging him up for supper either.' Jim glared at Lucinda. 'You leave him to us. Come on, Fred and Sid. Lift him up and let's give him a proper hero's send-off.' Jim turned to Gertrude and fixed her with a beady stare.

'Stay here. Don't move. Let me perform the passing ceremony and then I will go with you to the pool. I am going to get you to Albion tonight if it's the last thing I do. Don't ask me any questions as I cannot tell you what you want to know, but I can tell you what you *need* to know. Try to stay alive until I get back.' He turned and looked at Lucinda and Sam. 'I am leaving her in your care. If anything happens—'

'Understood, Jim,' said Sam and Lucinda nodded.

'Good. Right, let's go. Fred? Sid? Gentle with him … he was always gentle.'

Sniffing, Jim took to the sky. Fred and Sid grabbed a wing each and for one horrid moment, Gertrude thought the little body would be torn in two, but with infinite care, they flew upwards, with the heroic little robin between them. The swifts took flight next and Gertrude watched them disappear. She remained staring up at the sky, not trusting herself to speak for a while. Thick angry clouds scudded by, bringing more rain.

'I am going to kill her.'

'Who?' asked Lucinda.

'How?' asked Sam.

'I do not know how, but I know this much, my grandmother is helping that queen. She has chosen her side. I have chosen mine.'

'You do not know that,' Lucinda said.

'I don't know anything, but it's pretty obvious. Why keep

me from Mrs Eccles? Why kill Christopher? My grandmother knows about Albion and therefore must know the queen. And if she is not on Mrs Eccles' side—'

'Then she must be on the queen's side, yes, Scamp I see.' Sam shook his head. 'This is a terrible business, terrible, but if Jim —'

'Gertrude, are you really going to trust that crow?' asked Lucinda.

'Jim knows far more than he is telling us. I have always trusted Jim. Now is not the time in my life to start doubting him and if you don't want to trust him, then stay here.' Lucinda puffed herself up.

'And how far do you think you would get without me?' Sam huffed.

'We have managed to get along quite well without you so far, madam.' Lucinda looked him up and down.

'Really? You are both homeless, living off a stolen ham that I sniffed out. Gertrude has had a horrible life, as have you, so I understand. What has been missing in your lives is a cat. Everyone needs a cat.' Sam dropped to the ground and covered his face with his paws.

'Make her stop, Scamp.' Gertrude tried to fight a smile, but it came anyway. Sam parted his paws and gazed up at her.

'So, what do we do?'

'We wait.' Gertrude settled herself against the oak.

'Breathe,' whispered the oak.

'Why do the trees always tell me to breathe?' she snapped.

'Because,' said Sam, 'by breathing deeply you allow the gods, goddesses and the angels in. Did you know that respiration and inspiration have the same word root? And that some cultures think that trees in their previous lives were great philosophers?'

'Thanks for that, Professor Furball. I can sleep easier tonight,' Lucinda said. Sam shot her a disgusted look.

'Breathe,' repeated the oak. Gertrude took a deep breath.

'Okay, we breathe, and we think. We think about

Christopher and the swift and the sparrow. We vow to do whatever it takes to make sure their sacrifices were not wasted.' Lucinda nodded and settled down in the grass and Sam put his head on his paws.

They were brave words, strong and true and her voice rang out, but Gertrude did not know how she was going to keep her vow. She grasped her hands to stop them from trembling. She leaned her head back and closed her eyes.

Please, someone, tell me what to do. But no answer came. No deep reassuring voice spoke. She closed her eyes and let the drops of rain mingle with her tears.

CHAPTER 28

The surface of Kenfig pool ruffled as the wind blew across it.

The rain had finally stopped, but the clouds were darkening with the promise of more rain to come. The water moved as if agitated and Gertrude felt it mirrored her mood. She stood at the edge of her childhood bathing spot, her stomach fluttering, her heart beating fast. She had frolicked enough in this pool over the years, but even Jim, her pool playmate was quiet. She wondered if he was thinking the same thing she was.

There was a spirit in the pool.

Now the big bath of childhood looked forbidding and Gertrude began to wonder if those unseen hands that had touched her, were more than just a lonely girl's imagination.

'He must be drawn out with song,' said Sam, coming to stand by Gertrude. Gertrude looked down and noticed he was trembling. She had been with Sam long enough to realise that this trembling was caused by the effort of holding himself back from jumping in the water.

'I got a song,' Jim croaked. Cat, dog, and girl turned their heads.

'You?' said Lucinda. 'Crows are not really renowned for their singing prowess.' Sam snorted.

'And cats are? Good god, when you lot sing it sounds like death is having a party.'

'At least we can sing. At least we don't howl.'

'Howling is very underappreciated. If I want to sing to the moon—'

'No wonder the moon disappears every month.'

'Stop it, you two,' Gertrude said. Sam and Lucinda glared at each other. 'Jim, do you have a song or not?'

'Yes, Gertrude, thank you, I have.' He scowled at Lucinda. 'I know how to draw water spirits from pools anyway. I seen it done once. You have to flatter them.'

'Well go on then,' said Lucinda. 'Time is running out.'

'Art cannot be rushed, feline, so shut up.' Jim ruffled his wings and hopped from foot to foot. He faced the pool and made a dreadful noise.

'Just clearing me throat.' Jim stared out over the moving water. He shook his head. 'It's no good, I'm too earthed. I need to be up in the trees or a bush.' He looked around and spotted a bush with white flowers by the water's edge. 'That'll do.' He rose in the air and settled amongst the branches. Again, he made the terrible scraping sound and then, lifting his head up high, began to sing.

'Oh, spirit so kind, oh spirit so fair,
Come up from the water and into the air.
Tell us what we need to know,
Then you can go, back down below.'

'Not bad,' said Sam.
'I ain't finished yet.'

'Hello, undine of the pool,
We think you are really cool.
Come and say how do you do?
'Cos we really are in the poo.'

Sam frowned. Everyone looked at the pool but nothing had changed. Jim took a big breath.

'*Clever handsome water sprite,*
We really are in a load of shite,
Mrs Eccles has gone and we are all alone,
We really don't want to sigh and moan,
But we are poor and you are rich,
So bloody wake up you watery son of a —'

'Jim!' spluttered Sam. Gertrude and Sam rushed over to the bush and jumped up to try and catch Jim.

'Jim,' said a wild, deep voice. Panic flared in Gertrude's heart. Her breath caught in her throat and she stood, rooted to the ground, too afraid to look round.

'Jim,' the voice said again. Jim cocked his head and looked over Gertrude's shoulder.

'Hello?' Gertrude turned and faced the pool.

The surface bubbled and boiled. The bubbles grew bigger and a low humming noise filled the air. It grew louder and she put her hands over her ears. Something shot out of the pool, high into the air, leaving a trail of droplets. The thing twisted, turned, and flipped in the sky. Then it began its descent. It dived back into the pool, soaking them all. The thing surfaced and turned to face them.

And so, Gertrude came face to face with the spirit of Kenfig pool.

His long green hair had reeds and watercress threaded through it. His hair moved as if he was still underwater. His skin shimmered blue one moment and then green the next as if shadows played over his skin. His brilliant green eyes held Gertrude still. Gertrude tried to fight the panic down. She could sense the wildness in him, the alien-ness of him. Raising her chin, she forced herself to meet his gaze and to stare back. She knew if she looked away now, he would disappear under the water again. His eyes bore into her and her stomach squirmed. Emotions bubbled to the surface. He probed each emotion Gertrude had, bringing it to her awareness and letting it claim her totally, whilst he examined it. Feeling after feeling washed over her; he was relentless. He still held her fast in his unblinking gaze and she was aware of nothing but the spirit's eyes. Nothing else existed, except him and her. She felt something bump against her lower leg and breaking eye contact, looked down. Sam blocked her way. Her feet felt cold and with a start, she realised she had begun to walk into the pool. Sam gave a low growl.

'Steady, Scamp.' A long deep laugh came from the water spirit and Gertrude looked at him. She became aware that her cheeks were wet.

'Well met, lady.' The spirit bowed, his hair trailing in the water. She curtseyed back.

'Well met … spirit of the pool.' The water spirit turned his green gaze on Sam and Lucinda. He inclined his head.

'Well met to you, Sam, lover of water and to you, Lucinda, not such a lover of water I think?' and he smiled showing a row of sharp white teeth. Lucinda's whiskers twitched.

'No offence, sir, but water is just not my thing.' The spirit shook his head. He slid his gaze back to Sam.

'You, however, have been desiring to jump into my coolness since you arrived here. Please, feel free.' He opened his arms wide and droplets flew off him. Sam went to spring and then with a momentous effort sat down, pressing himself close to Gertrude's leg.

'If it is all the same to you, sir, I would like to hear what you have to say.' Jim flapped down to join them.

'Yeah, Your Royal Wetness, you need to tell Gertrude how to get to Albion.'

'Ah, Jim, the singer.' The water spirit stared at the crow for a long moment, until Jim started hopping around.

'It was all I could do on short notice, Your Majesty.'

'If you were not who you are and if you did not know who you did—'

'And if Fred had whiskers, he would be a cat.' The spirit frowned and then threw his head back and laughed. Gertrude watched his throat move up and down and a feeling of warmth spread through her. Her breath quickened and she parted her lips. He brought his head down and looked straight at her. Her face grew hot and she looked away.

'My song worked though,' muttered Jim.

'Yes, Jim, King of the Crows, it worked. I am here and you are here.' There was an awkward silence and Gertrude glanced back at him. He still looked at her. She looked down at Sam whose muscles were rippling and twitching as if he would jump in at any moment. Lucinda backed away, shaking off some droplets that had landed on her and Jim looked up at the sky. She met the spirit's gaze again and an amused smile spread across his face.

'I understand Mrs Eccles left some information with you, Your Majesty?' Her voice shook and the spirit continued to smile. 'About how to get to Albion? Tonight is—'

'I know what tonight is. Can you feel it?' he said in a soft voice. This time an emotion surfaced that Gertrude had never felt before. Her breath caught in her throat and her face burned. She felt light-headed. Her legs began to tremble and her stomach flipped. He laughed softly. 'I will tell you all you need to know, Queen of Sorrows, but first, bathe with me. Bathe in my waters. Let my waters soothe you.'

'You are most kind, Your Majesty, but evening will soon be upon us and I need to know how to get through the veil.' He moved through the water towards her. The water receded off his body until he stood naked in front of her. She glanced down and then away again. He leaned in and murmured in her ear,

'What were you expecting, a tail?' Taking her hands into his, he bent his head and kissed them. He had webbed hands and a shot of cold went through her, followed by a wave of warmth. The warm feeling spread everywhere. He smelt musky and sweet.

'Come and bathe in me, you are not usually this shy.' Gertrude swallowed and whispered,

'Normally I would love to but—' He squeezed her hands.

'But I insist.' He leaned back from her, fixing her again with his emerald gaze. A splash made her jump and she watched, in disbelief, as Sam swam out towards the centre of the pool. The spirit gave a low laugh.

'Ah, he could not resist the pull, and now you will have to come in, as I love Sam and might not let him back.' Bowing over her hands, he flicked his tongue around her knuckles. He backed away, beckoning her.

'Come in, the water is lovely,' and with a dive, he disappeared into the depths.

Looking out over the pool, Gertrude could just see Sam's head above the surface. Pulling her school jumper over her head, she said to Lucinda,

'Remind me to get a newspaper on the way home.'

'Why?'

'So I can roll it up and hit Sam on the nose with it.' Gertrude removed the last of her clothes. Trembling, and against her better judgment, she entered the pool.

CHAPTER 29

Gertrude gasped as she waded through the cold water. Mrs Eccles' hot baths had made her soft.

The thought of Mrs Eccles fortified her and she dived in. As the water closed around her, laughter echoed from the depths. She surfaced and hands from behind her suddenly gathered up her hair.

'Too cold, my lady?' The hands turned her around. 'Let me make it better.' The spirit of the pool took her face in his webbed hands and kissed her on the mouth. He took his time, kissing her closed lips, only stopping to whisper,

'I am the first it seems.' Gertrude parted her lips and his tongue flicked gently inside her mouth. She let her tongue meet his and then pulled back, frightened by her forwardness and by the way her stomach reacted. He let her go.

'Warm enough?' Gertrude put her hands in the water. It felt as warm as one of Mrs Eccles' baths.

'How—?' He placed his finger on her lips and stroked her hair.

'Ssh, no questions. Not yet. Let me wash away all your troubles. Turn around. That's it. Now fall back into my arms and let me bathe you.' Mesmerised by the deep wild voice, Gertrude obeyed and felt soft hands catching her. The spirit took her head in his hands and pulled her further towards the middle of the pool, all the while singing a low and sensual song that made her feel sleepy. He ran his hands through her wet hair. Raindrops started to fall, splashing on the surface of the pool.

'Water above me, water below me,' she murmured.

'Water all around you. Feel it caressing your skin. Feel it relaxing your body. Surrender to the calm.' He kissed the top of her head and she closed her eyes, smiling as the pool rocked her. She felt like a child. She felt looked after. Soon she could not distinguish between the spirit's rhythmic hands and the rhythm of the pool. She relaxed and all her worries and fears dissolved in the soft rain.

'I used to do this to you when you were little. Do you remember me caressing you?'

'It was you?' A hand touched her leg and she flinched.

'Ssh, darling, calm yourself. Those are just my children. They love you. They want to help you.' Unseen hands massaged her legs and Gertrude sighed.

'I could stay here forever.'

'That is what we are hoping for.' The hands on her legs gripped tight and pulled her down. The spirit pushed her head below the surface. As she gasped, she took in water. Coughing and spluttering, she thrashed and tried to surface. Looking up through the water, she could see his shadow above her. Someone grabbed her legs again. Looking down through the green water she saw several water sprites grinning up at her, all showing their small pointed teeth.

I am going to drown. Kicking and punching, she managed to break free and propel herself upwards. Breaking the surface, she heard Sam barking in absolute panic. She blinked the cold water out of her eyes just in time to see a black object dive down from the sky. Jim's language was extreme, even for him and the spirit put up his hands to protect his eyes. Yelling directions at Sam, Jim managed to land on the golden retriever's head.

'You treacherous, watery, slimy son of an old trout's daughter. You bloody nastard. How dare you! How dare you try to claim her. After all Vivienne did for you? After all the times

Vivienne saved this pool and made it sacred and protected? And you betray the Lady of the Lake by trying to drown the only person who may be able to rescue her? What in the name of scampi were you thinking?'

'I love her,' the spirit said, looking over at Gertrude. 'I have always loved her.' Gertrude shook her head as she trod water, the shock of nearly drowning robbing her of any words.

'You can't have her. Now tell us what we need to know or so help me god I will destroy you.' The spirit laughed.

'You may be King of the Crows but you can't destroy me.' Jim puffed himself up on Sam's head.

'Do I have to remind you who I work with?' The spirit's smile faltered and he looked around him.

'She loves me,' he said, his voice soft.

'She may do, she loves many. But do you really want to risk her wrath?' Gertrude's legs were tiring and she did not know whom Jim was talking about.

'I need to get to shore,' she rasped. 'You,' and she looked at the spirit, 'Follow me.' She turned and swam. He caught up with her and she flinched as he put his arms around her waist and helped propel her along. Her knees scraped the floor of the pool and she pulled her top half out of the water and lay there, panting. The spirit still held her by the waist. He squeezed her and she sat up and turned around, her legs still in the pool. He kneeled between them and smiled up at her making her stomach flip again. She reminded herself that he had tried to drown her. Lucinda padded up and hiding behind Gertrude, poked her head around Gertrude's body. Sam splashed out of the pool and shaking, covered them all in water, making Lucinda hiss at him and run off to the trees. Sam flopped down next to Gertrude and Jim landed beside her. The spirit ran his hands down her legs making her breath catch again. He massaged her calves and she kicked him off.

'How do we get to Albion?' she demanded. He heaved a deep sigh and placed his hands back on her calves.

'You must open the gateway. You are staying at the copse at

the top of the road. You feel safe there, even though it is near your grandmother. Do you know why?' Gertrude shook her head.

'Because it is a gateway. There are several round here, areas of trees that feel different. You must open the gate.'

'And how do I do that?'

'You must sing. You must sing the Song of the Earth. You must feel the earth's heartbeat and beat it out with your hands. You must bring your energy into alignment with the gateway's energy, and then it shall open for you.'

'What do I sing?' The spirit shook his head. Cold water droplets from his hair landed on her skin and she realised, with a shock, that she was still naked. She put her hands up to cover her breasts. The spirit gave a sad smile.

'I am of water. This song is of the earth. I do not know. You must find the song in your heart. Only do not let Jim do it.' He flashed her a smile. Despite everything, Gertrude smiled back and put her hand out.

'Thank you.' He put his head to one side regarding her.

'Thank you, Queen of Sorrows,' and bending over he kissed her hand. 'Until next time.' Looking around at the small group, he bowed and with a flourish, dived back into the depths.

'There won't be a next time, you crazy cod fillet,' shouted Jim. All at once, the warmth left Gertrude. Goosebumps burst out on her skin and her teeth chattered. She stood up and put her clothes on. It took time as her hands shook. As she was pulling her jumper over her head Sam slunk up to her.

'Sorry, I jumped in, Scamp. I could not help myself.' Lucinda tutted.

'That is why we cats do not like water. You cannot trust it. You never know what it is going to do next. So, what is the plan?' Gertrude looked up at the cloudy sky. Raindrops fell on her face. She was sick of being wet.

'We go back to the copse. We wait until sunset and we sing the Song of the Earth. Why couldn't the gateway be a big door with a key? Why is everything so complicated?'

'We have to sing … again?' asked Sam. Jim hopped forward. Gertrude gathered up her wet hair and wrung it.

'Yes, Sam, we have to sing and before you ask, Jim, the answer is no.'

CHAPTER 30

Gertrude walked through a forest with trees so tall and ancient, she felt humbled by them.

'*Make them sing,*' the deep reassuring voice spoke.

'*How?*' asked Gertrude.

'*Touch them.*' As she passed each tree, she touched it and it sang a note. Soon the whole forest sang. A thousand trees blending their voices in a song so heart-wrenchingly beautiful, that when Gertrude flung her eyes open, they were wet. She looked down at Jim, who pecked at her leg.

'Why did you wake me?'

'You were making weird noises.'

'I was dreaming.'

'Well, weirder noises than you normally make when you are dreaming. What were you dreaming about?'

'I was walking in a forest and each time I passed a tree and touched it, it sang. All the trees were singing, each with their own note until the song was ...'

'What?'

'Words can't describe it.' She leant back against the oak. Sam and Lucinda had gone off to sort out dinner and she was alone in the copse with Jim. He was hopping around, looking for worms.

'I ain't sorry I woke you. You were making a right racket and that bloody grandmother of yours might spring out at any time.' Gertrude hardly heard him. She had only napped for a moment but she was finding it hard to come back to reality. She had always found that stolen naps in the day produce vivid dreams, but this dream felt real. She looked up at the sky. There was no sign of sunset and she was glad. She still had no idea how to sing a '*Song of the Earth.*' She had a flashing image of the spirit of the pool and her face grew hot.

'Jim, what did the water spirit mean when he called me "Queen of Sorrows"'?

'No idea.'

'Whom do you work with? What was that all about?'

'No idea.'

'Rubbish, you just won't tell me.'

'Gertrude, fat flower of mine, it's not that I won't tell you, it's that I *can't* tell you.'

'What do you mean?'

'Go on ask me. Ask me who I work with.'

'Whom do you work with?' The crow opened his mouth and a terrible rasping sound came out.

'See? Not only did she put a geis on me, but she put a spell on me too.'

'What the hell is a geis? Oh god, you're not working for the queen, are you?' Jim swore so violently that the expletives ran into one another.

'Okay, okay, calm down. Sorry, King Jim.' Jim shook out his feathers.

'It's okay, Queen Girly. You're obviously tired and not thinking straight.'

'What *can* you tell me?'

'Watch out for the In Between.' Gertrude frowned and leant forward.

'The what?'

'The In Between. To get to Albion you have to navigate the In Between. It's a strange place, nice but strange. And that is the problem. You can get stuck in there and then we've lost you. Travelling between worlds is a serious business, Queen Girly. Let's hope you're ready.'

'Do I have a choice?'

'No, you don't, but nevertheless, be careful. The most important thing is getting to Albion, rescuing Mrs Eccles, seeing Cat and Ariel again, finding out who you are and defeating the queen. Hold on to one of those thoughts. Hell, hold on to all of them and you will get through the In Between just fine.'

The rustle of branches announced dinner and Lucinda pranced into the clearing, followed by a lumbering Sam, who dragged in a carrier bag. Inside were several kinds of cheese and a baguette

'Blimey!' Gertrude exclaimed, 'You two are brilliant.' Sam dropped to the ground and let out a grunt.

'Our dark friend here certainly knows where to look; I will give her that.' Lucinda's whiskers twitched.

'Years of being starved, golden paws. Come on, dig in. We do not know when we will get a chance to eat again.'

'I'm not hungry,' said Gertrude. The thought of leaving this world and travelling to another made her feel sick. Sam came up to her and licked her nose.

'Eat, Scamp. I mean it, eat. Cat would tell you one missed meal means a loss of a days' worth of energy. We do not know what lies ahead of us, so we must be strong to face whatever it is.'

'That's why I can't eat. I feel so nervous and my stomach is like a washing machine.' Jim pecked at her leg, making her yelp in pain.

'Eat. Listen to your elders. Eat.'

'Sam is not my elder. How old are you, Sam? Three?' Sam sat down and stared at her.

'In dog years I am considered a wise one.' Lucinda let out a snort and then looked away when Sam shot her a look. She looked back and said,

'Golden paws is right – for once. Eat, Ginger, or I will scram you.'

'Oh god, okay, just stop nagging.' Once she took the first

mouthful, her body gave way to hunger and she devoured it.

'Mmmmm, you can taste the onion in this cheese.' Sam said. Lucinda shook her head.

'Chives, I think you will find.' Gertrude told Sam and Lucinda about her dream.

'"*And this our life exempt from public haunt, finds tongues in trees,*" Sam said. At everyone's blank look he sighed.

'Shakespeare, '*As You Like It.*' Never mind. Well, that is it then, you have to get the trees to sing. Why else would that dream come to you? If there is one thing I learned from Mrs Eccles, it is that there is no such thing as coincidence. The universe is always speaking to us.' Jim lifted his head from a piece of cheese he was attacking and cocked his head to one side.

'What's it saying then? To me? 'Cos I ain't bloody heard it?'

'Nor me,' said Lucinda, winking at Gertrude. Sam snorted.

'I am wasted on the lot of you. Get the trees to sing, they are of the earth. It makes total sense.'

'Oh yeah, total sense,' Jim squawked 'Hello trees, do you do requests? I'd like some Elvis, if you would be so kind, or what about The Byrds? Or maybe some Rick Arse-tly!' He laughed at his own joke so much he fell over. Sam sniffed and turned his nose up in the air.

'As I said – wasted.' Gertrude stroked his head.

'Don't mind Jim, Sam. At least you tell me stuff. Jim is under a geis, whatever that means.' Sam's head swung around and he narrowed his eyes at the crow.

'Really? Who did that to you?'

'I can't tell you,' Jim shouted 'That's part of the geis you bloody—'

'Jim, shut up,' said Lucinda. 'What is a geis anyway?' Sam cleared his throat.

'A geis, madam, is an ancient Celtic oath. A person places a geis upon you and if you break it, it can mean death. Jim, whom do you know that would place a geis on you because there are not many people who have that sort of power?'

'I can't tell you!'

'He can't say, Sam,' Gertrude said. 'Look don't upset him. Let's settle down and wait for sunset.' Gertrude looked up at the sky. 'Do we start when the sun is gone?'

'That is traditionally when Beltane begins,' Sam said. 'Twilight is the in between, on a night of the in between.'

'Talking about the In Between, that is something Jim can tell you about.' She settled herself against the oak and listened with half an ear to Jim's explanation. Closing her eyes, she matched her breath to the oak's and let her mind wander, amongst trees that sang.

CHAPTER 31

News travels fast in the world of birds.

By twilight, a crowd had gathered. Fred, Sid, and Jim were sitting above Gertrude, on the branches of the oak tree. They were quiet for once, not a swear word nor a dirty joke between them. Lucinda gazed wide-eyed at Magness and Agnes, who huddled together on the ground, inches away from her. Lucinda licked her lips and then took a few steps back to give the plump birds some space. Every now and then, a swift zoomed in and out of the trees. One word from Gertrude and they would assemble in battle formation, ready to swoop and destroy. But what she was about to face was not an enemy that could be fought. She did not know what she was about to face. Roy and Joy, the wood pigeons were deep in conversation with Duke and Esmeralda. Gertrude wondered if the two couples ever went out for dinner together. She shook her head. She was losing it.

Ever since the sun had set, she had felt a difference in the land beneath her. She felt like a drawn bowstring. An invisible archer held her there, trembling and waiting to release her. Except she was meant to be the arrow, not the bowstring and who was aiming her anyway? *Oh god, I really am losing it.* She wondered if this was how it felt to be drunk, as every thought led to another thought and her mind was winding down strange pathways. Since the dream of the singing trees, she had not felt present, as if half of her travelled to the other world already.

She felt the air change and looking up, she saw the clouds clearing. They revealed a red sky that gradually became purple. Her eyes found Sam and his brown-eyed stare anchored her to the ground.

'It is time,' he said. She nodded and a hush fell over the crowd. Looking around, she took in every one of their furred and feathered faces.

'I have not got a clue what I am doing. I do not know what is going to happen. I do not know what this gate looks like or if I will even be able to get through it. What I do know, is that throughout my life, I have been blessed, because I have had friends like you. You have walked, scampered and flown beside me and I want to say thank you, in case … well … just thank you.' No one made a sound, although a few heads nodded and Esmeralda snuffled. Gertrude wiped her eyes.

'Anyone who wishes to leave may do so, as this may be dangerous.' Only Magness made a move but Agnes gave him a sharp peck. He looked down at the ground.

'Carry on, hen,' he said mournfully. 'No one is leaving you to a certain death on your own.'

'Oh, spoken like a true magpie,' piped up Fred. 'That'll make her feel better.' No one else moved or said anything. Gertrude gazed up at the purple sky. Sam made a noise bringing her back to earth.

'Back to earth …' she murmured. Sam lay down on the ground and his tail wagged, making a swishing noise against the earth. Gertrude sank to her knees and put her forehead to the soft, damp ground.

'Breathe,' said a silver birch.

'Breathe,' said the oak. Silence fell on the copse as Gertrude breathed in the smell of the damp soil. The trees rustled as a breeze passed through them and she felt everyone take a breath and relax. Lucinda started to purr. The Crownies began to caw and the rat-a-tat-tat of the magpies joined them. Duke and Esmeralda whickered and Duke stamped his foot on the ground. Roy and Joy cooed to each other and for a moment, the cacophony of noise threatened to make Gertrude lose her train of thought. Then the noises shifted and, along with Sam's tail, each individual sound merged into a natural rhythm.

Gertrude pushed her awareness deep into the earth. Down below, with the roots of the trees, the moles, and the worms, she heard a faint drumbeat. She chased it. She sent herself down through the layers and called out to it with her heart. The drumbeat stopped running and waited for her. She caught it and it leapt into her body. She brought it back up with her and added it to the rhythm of her friends. She let the beat flow through her veins and become a part of her. Her heart shuddered. It skipped a beat and then took up the same rhythm as the earth's heartbeat.

Planting a kiss on the ground, she stood up. Swaying, as though drunk, she put her hand on the oak to steady herself. As she touched the bark, the tree sang one note. It was deep and rich and spoke of a knowledge so ancient, she felt her head spin. She moved to a silver birch and touched it. A silvery, light voice sang out. Most of the trees in the copse were birches and as she touched them, each added a silvery layer to the existing song. She came before a horse chestnut and placed both hands on him.

'Sing,' she said and he sang a low note that made her think of the changing seasons.

Walking back through the singing trees she came back to her friends who still kept rhythm with the earth's heartbeat. Each tree's note had beautifully blended and the symphony made her feel joyous and free. She knew she would not be able to hold onto her mind for much longer. Thought and reason were about to leave. They had no place here and the wildness flooded her senses.

Something touched her foot and jumping back, she looked down to see a vine creeping around her ankle and up her leg. A vine claimed her other leg and she knew she was lost. She let her body sag and the vines take her weight. She leant back onto the oak.

'Sing,' he commanded.

And so, Gertrude sang the Song of the Earth.

She allowed her voice to climb up with the vines. Then she entwined her voice with the oak's and following him up, reached for the sky. She held the note there, allowing it to swing in the breeze. Then she trilled downwards, coming back to the earth. She sang deeper, pushing her voice down, like roots seeking secret waterways. She held her voice at ground level and sang belly down with the worms and the beings that crawled. Jim raised his voice and catching his eye, she obeyed the yearning she heard there. She spiralled her voice back upwards, through the branches, sending it high into the darkening sky. She let her voice take flight upon the air and looking up, she saw the first evening star.

Her voice changed. It became ethereal and she put a twinkle into it. The star faded a little and then, to her delight and utter joy, the star sang back. Its mystical and glittering voice danced with Gertrude's earthly one. It seemed an eternity that she and the star sang together, but there came a time when she longed for the earth again and saying farewell, she lowered her voice and brought it and herself gently back to earth.

The trees had moved. They had aligned themselves and bent over to make a tunnel. A light emerged from the middle of the pathway and Gertrude knew that this was the gateway. Still singing, she put her hands out and felt Sam beside her and then Lucinda by her legs. As the vines retreated, Jim landed on her shoulder. The light grew stronger and the four of them moved towards it. She stopped singing and so did everyone else.

'I am so scared,' she whispered. Sam nudged her hand. 'Thank you, everyone,' she said, hoping they could hear her, as the light had begun to emit a low hum. Her skin tingled and the space between her eyes grew hot. She felt disorientated and sick and had wild thoughts of turning and running, but the light held her fast. In the middle of the light, a dark spot grew.

Fascinated, she watched as the darkness spread and consumed the light. The hum thrummed in her veins and, unable to fight it, she gave herself up to the encroaching darkness. The last of the light vanished and the hum stopped.

Gertrude found herself in total silence and blackness.

She was alone.

THE IN BETWEEN

THE IN BETWEEN

'Where am I?' a voice asks

'You are here,' a voice replies.

'Who am I?'

'You are me.'

'Oh,' says the first voice.

'Oh, indeed,' replies the second voice.

'You know your voice is very familiar.'

'This is not the first time we have met.' A pause.

'Where am I?'

'I told you, here.'

'I am me then?'

'Yes, and so am I.' Both voices ponder this for a while.

Years go by.

'You know,' says the first voice, 'I am meant to be going somewhere.'

'You are somewhere,' says the second voice, 'So I would say your journey is done.'

'Oh. That's good.'

Three days pass. First voice gasps.

'No! I am not where I am supposed to be. There is somewhere important ... specific

... somewhere I have not been to before. I need to get there. Someone I am looking for ...'

'You found me. Job done.'

One second. Two seconds. Three seconds ...

'Not you. Someone else. Someone I loved.'

'I love you, so you must love me.'

'Oh, I love you very much but I loved that person because … because …'

'Because? Because? That does not sound like love. You love someone, end of. There is no because.'

'Maybe you are right.' Silence. 'No, I am sorry, she did something for me. She helped me. She was my friend, my family.'

'She?'

'Mrs …'

'Mrs?'

'Yes, Mrs.' A hurt silence follows this remark.

'I am your friend,' the second voice whispers. 'I would do anything for you.'

'Yes, I know, but she needs me.'

'*I* need you.'

'Not like she does.'

'Don't you like being here?'

'I love being here. I feel … peaceful,' the first voice sighs.

'Stay then. Don't go back.'

'Back where?'

'Back into the physical. You do not know me properly yet. When you do you will not want to leave me.'

The first voice thinks about this for ten days.

'Sam needs me,' the first voice says.

'I thought Mrs needs you?'

'Sam does too.'

'Do you love Sam?'

'Yes.'

'Because …?'

'No because. I just love him.'

'I'm losing you,' the second voice says.

'I will come back.'

'Not for lifetimes. I am losing you – again. Are you sure you want to go back?'

'Yes.'

'To the physical? To the pain? To the noise and the fear?'

'Yes. I have no choice.'

'There is always a choice.'

'Not for me.'

'Especially for you.' The first voice says nothing. The second voice sighs. The breath sweeps over the first voice and the first voice realises it had a body once. Pictures come in the darkness.

'Sam and Lucinda and ... Mrs ... Eccles.'

'Leave me then. I will be sad.'

'I am sorry.'

'I love you.'

'I love you.'

'Go. Back to the noise, the pain and the fear.'

'Goodbye, you.'

'Goodbye, me.'

ALBION

CHAPTER 32

Gertrude's head itched.

If only she had hands to scratch it. *Oh, but I do.* Her hands lay on something prickly and she moved them. Hay.

Gertrude took a deep breath and took in sweet smelling hay and horses nearby. She tried to sit up, but a wave of dizziness and nausea broke over her and with a long groan, she lay back down.

'Take it easy, Scamp.' Her eyes flew open.

'Sam?'

'Right here. All is well.'

'Yes. We all made it through,' said Lucinda, 'although you took your time.'

'Come on, Queen Girly, get up. Can't you feel it? Can't you feel how good it feels?' Jim's voice was harsh and it hurt her head.

'I feel awful.'

'Right, take it easy, Scamp.'

'I have been somewhere … was I dreaming?' She lifted her head and pushed herself up. Jim danced around on the hay-strewn floor, whilst Lucinda cleaned herself. Sam watched her closely. Gertrude put a hand up to her head to try to stop the spinning sensation.

'What happened to us?' Jim stopped moving.

'Well, a big light came and we all came through the gate and now I'm home and it feels so good. I had forgotten how good it feels. Can you feel it? The air? Clean and light?' Gertrude groaned and put her head in her hands.

'I feel sick.'

'It will pass,' said a deep, reassuring, male voice. Gertrude looked up sharply and then regretted it. She fought through the dizziness and looked towards the voice.

A man leant against the stable wall, his arms crossed in front of him. His white shirt pulled tight over his arms, showing his biceps and the undone laces showed a chest that was smooth and olive-skinned. His hair made her breath catch in her throat. It fell in black waves to his shoulders. He ran a hand through it, to push it back.

The dark horseman. The man from the beach.

Swaying, she went to fall back onto the hay. He rushed over to her and crouching down, caught her by her shoulders. At his touch, all the blood in her body rushed forward as if in greeting. He gasped, as if in shock. His face was young, but his grey eyes were old. They moved all over her face and then settled back on her eyes. His eyes grew thunderous and then blazed as if lightning had lit up their depths.

Gertrude could not breathe. She could not move. His eyes burned into her and lit up her soul. She had not realised the darkness she had been in until this moment.

'I know you,' she whispered.

'You saw me on the first day of spring.'

'No. I *know* you. I have always known you.' For a moment, something flickered in the grey depths, something that yearned for her, but pleaded as well. Then his stare grew colder, turning the grey eyes to stone. His jaw clenched and his fingers dug into her shoulders. A veneer of ice came down over his face, shutting her out. He took his hands off her as if she was diseased and leant back from her. Gertrude broke eye contact and looked down at her hands, which were now shaking. Sam edged forward.

'Sir, I am sorry, we were not aware of you and I would like to take this opportunity—'

'Sam!' The man turned and knelt in the hay, reaching for the golden retriever. 'Sam, so good to meet you at last. Aunt Viv told me all about you.' Gertrude risked a glance at the man's face. He smiled with such warmth it transformed him, making him look boyish. Gertrude took in his powerful arms and the beautiful profile. Sam surged forward and bounded into his arms. 'My name is Tal and you are most welcome, Sam, indeed it is an honour.' Gertrude said the man's name in her mind, but it did not feel right. Why would he lie? She remained silent, watching him through her lowered lashes. Sam had no such reservations. He licked the man's face and wrestled with him in the hay.

'And whom do we have here?' Gertrude's heart thumped, but Tal turned his attention to Lucinda. The cat stopped washing herself and gazed at the dark-haired man, her eyes widening in undisguised adoration. Tal spread his arms wide.

'Oh, my deepest, darkest, darling,' and Gertrude watched, in disbelief, as Lucinda jumped into his arms and began purring. Tal fell back in the hay and cradled Lucinda to his chest, whilst burying his face in her fur, something Gertrude had always longed to do. Lucinda nuzzled his face with her head and purred even louder. Gertrude turned to Sam and Jim and was pleased to see them looking as bewildered as she did. Jim shook his head in disgust.

'Oi, Tal, put the cat down. Believe me, you don't want to know where it's been.' Tal sat up and holding Lucinda with one hand, stretched out his other hand to Jim.

'Jim, King of the Crows! In all my days! 'Tis good to see you, old friend.' Gertrude looked at Jim, willing him to snub the man, but Jim seemed to be under his spell as much as the others were. With a croak, he flew into the man's embrace and laughed as Tal tickled his chest feathers.

'Tal, you great ugly bugger,' Jim spluttered.

'Jim, the bloody crow,' Tal laughed.

Jealousy ran riot through Gertrude, but whether it was because her friends adored him or whether it was because they were getting all his attention, she did not know. Nor did she care to. As the growling, cawing, and purring died down, Tal glanced her way. The warm smile faded and his face shut down again. A muscle flickered in his jaw and his grey eyes grew cold. Another wave of dizziness overwhelmed her again and she fell back into the hay, glad to be away from his penetrating eyes.

'What is wrong with her?' asked Sam.

'She is adjusting to the energy here,' Tal said.

'How come we are all right then?' said Lucinda.

'You, my darkest darling, are in your true element. You usually live with this energy. Her kind will always take longer.'

'What do you mean my kind?' murmured Gertrude, but no one heard her.

'Don't mind Queen Girly. She'll be fine soon enough. She's a fighter, Tal. She'll soon be running around causing trouble wiv' me.' If she could have killed Jim, she would have. As the stable grew quiet, she became aware that her school skirt had ridden up and her bare legs were on show. Sitting up, she pulled her skirt down, but not before she caught Tal quickly looking away. She allowed herself a faint smile. As if sensing what she was thinking, he sprung to his feet.

'You need to change. You stick out like a priest at an orgy. And you all need to eat. You look half starved.' He moved to the doorway and held out a bag to Gertrude. Gertrude tried to reach the bag, but it was just out of reach and she did not want to move as throwing up in front of this man was not an option. With an impatient gesture, he came forward and dropped it by her feet. 'Mind you, your hair will draw attention enough.'

Moving behind her, he knelt down and pushed her further up into a sitting position. Taking her hair in his hands, he began to plait it. He was rough and she let out a cry, as he yanked her hair. Another dizzy spell came upon her and she tried to put her head into her hands, but he jerked her head back.

'Please,' she whispered. His hands became still and she was conscious of his breath on the nape of her neck. She waited until the dizzy spell passed. 'Okay.' He resumed his plaiting, but this time his hands were gentle. She hoped he would not hear the thud of her erratic heart. She concentrated on the pleasant sensation of someone playing with her hair. She closed her eyes and leant back onto him. He pushed her forward, off him.

'Stay still. There is so much of it.' Jim hopped onto her leg and gave her a fierce look.

'You should have plaited it before you came here, Girly.'

'I thought I had.'

'Cat would kill you if she knew you had entered Albion with your hair down.'

Tal's fingers paused at the mention of the warrior's name and then carried on. As he neared the bottom of the plait, he held it with one hand and fumbled in his pocket with the other. She felt him wrap something around the bottom of her hair.

'There.' For a moment, she thought she felt him brush the back of her neck with his fingers, but he jumped up and strode out of the stable, without looking at her or saying farewell.

'What a lovely man,' purred Lucinda.

'Top bloke,' agreed Jim.

'We have no idea who he is,' snapped Gertrude. 'Jim, you should not have mentioned Cat in front of him. He could be on the queen's side for all we know.' Jim turned his head and fixed Gertrude with a disgusted look.

'That man is Vivienne's nephew. Merlin and *the* Lady of the Lake raised that boy and *I* know him. That should be enough for you.' As an answer, Gertrude groaned and fell back.

'Sorry,' she muttered. Jim jumped onto her stomach.

'Pardon? Didn't quite catch that?'

'Sorry, I said.'

'Sorry I did not trust me old mucker mate, Jim, who has never let me down in his wonderful illustrious life? Is that what you mean?' He hopped up and down on her, making her laugh.

'Yes, sorry I did not trust my old mate, now for god's sake get off me before I throw up. Ugh, if only this nausea would stop.'

Sam came up to her head and peered down at her.

'Perhaps some fresh air, Scamp? Come on, get dressed and we will go exploring.'

'Do you think that is wise?' Lucinda said. 'Tal did not say anything about going outside.'

'Quite right, Lucinda, I didn't.' Tal's deep voice started Gertrude trembling again and she closed her eyes, not wishing to face him. 'Sam, I will have to sneak you into Nell's kitchen. The queen has offered a reward to anyone who brings her a dead dog. Lucinda, darling, keep an eye on *her*. Give me five minutes and then meet me outside. Sam, with me.' Sam trotted off with him.

'Just who the hell does he think he is?' said Gertrude.

'Well, I am glad one of us had sense,' Lucinda sniffed. 'Sam could have been killed. We cats think about things before rushing into anything. That is how we have nine lives.' Jim squawked.

'Eight too many if you ask me. I'll catch you blighters later. I got things to do, people to see, places to go … you know.'

'I don't know. Who?' said Gertrude

'None of your business. Keep out of trouble. And Gertrude mate?'

'Yes, Jim mate?'

'You can trust Tal with your life.' He flew off through the door.

'Bloody bird.' Gertrude lay there staring at the ceiling for a while until Lucinda made a noise. Raising herself carefully onto her elbows, she saw Lucinda looking hungrily towards the exit, her tail flicking. 'Go on, out you go. I'll get changed and meet you outside.' Lucinda sprang off, running down the stable.

Gertrude pulled the bag towards her and pulled out a dress. It was forest green, long and silky. She tore off her clothes, only stopping to get her breath back, as another dizzy spell hit her. Standing up and offering a silent prayer that the dress would fit, she pulled it over her head. It rippled down and settled on her. She had no idea what she looked like and hoped she did not look like a marrowfat pea. In the bag were some soft shoes that matched the dress. She hid her school clothes in the corner of the stable. Taking a steadying breath, she squared her shoulders and stepped through the door.

She walked down the stables, smiling at the horses, who all put their heads over their stalls to watch her pass. A huge black horse bowed his head as she passed and she paused as she recognised him from the beach.

'Hello, sir.' The horse tossed his head.

'At last, you are here, flower bride. Go on now. He will be waiting for you. We will talk soon enough.' With a bow, she left him.

Outside the warm sun greeted her. The air smelled of spring and the scent of delicious food wafted over to her. Her stomach growled. Instinctively she put her head to one side to listen to the birds. There were none. No birds sang or talked and she could not hear any trees whispering. She stepped onto cobbles and found herself in a castle courtyard. Tall turrets climbed towards the sky and flags fluttered in the breeze. Hearing music on the air, she turned and, lifting up her dress, followed the sound. Mrs Eccles had been right; the air was lighter. She almost floated along. Her body felt lighter and she moved with a grace that astonished her. Fighting would be easier here. Rounding a corner, the castle opened into the main courtyard and Gertrude gasped with delight.

She had walked straight into a fairy tale. The women wore colourful gowns, like her own, and the men wore billowing white shirts. A group of children were dancing in a circle and a sole fiddler played the music that made them wheel around. A jester leant against the wall, whispering in the ear of a giggling, brown-haired girl. His bells tinkled on his hat as he leant forward. Everywhere people were bustling around. The whole place had an air of celebration and Gertrude put her hands to her eyes to look up at the turrets. She could see the flags better now and for a moment expected to see animals on them. Instead, there was a woman's head. The flags were white and the woman's head was black, with hair streaming behind her, so it looked as if her hair blew in the wind. Gertrude shivered and tore her eyes away, but she felt as if the flags watched her.

Searching the crowds, she spotted Tal standing by an enormous white horse whilst talking to a man. Lucinda sat by his feet, watching his every move.

Tal bent down and picked up the horse's hooves one by one. They flashed silver in the sun. Standing up, he nodded. The other man fumbled around in his pocket and dropped something into Tal's hand. He turned and left. Tal reached up and held the white horse's face in his hands. Smiling, he leant forward and whispered something into its ear. The horse put his nose down and nuzzled Tal on his neck. Tal and the horse turned and walked back towards the stable. Catching sight of her, he stopped and his eyes swept up and down her body. Gertrude pulled herself up to her full height and lifted her chin. She gave him what she hoped was a defiant stare.

'Hello, flower bride,' said the horse.

'Green always suited you,' Tal said and carried on walking. As he passed her, she heard him murmur something under his breath that sounded like *always did.* He turned his attention to the horse. 'Come on, Apollo, this way.' His white shirt ruffled in the breeze and he walked with a feline grace she thought only Lucinda possessed. He threw his arm up around the horse's neck as if they were two great friends out on a stroll. The horse was even bigger up close. His long white mane almost reached the ground and again, Gertrude caught a flash of silver hooves through the white feathers that covered them. The horse stumbled and Tal held him tight, stroking his neck.

'Beautiful, isn't he?' said Lucinda coming to stand by Gertrude.

'The horse is lovely.'

'That is not who I meant.'

'I know who you meant.'

'Tal is the blacksmith here and if you had seen the way he handled that horse … amazing. Apollo was so nervous. Tal just laid his hands on him, and he went still and calm. He is nature's child that one.'

'Good for him.' Another dizzy spell attacked her. She leaned against the wall and closed her eyes. Feeling the need to be close to the ground she slid down the wall. She heard footsteps and someone stopped by her.

'Still dizzy? I did not think it would take you this long to adjust.' Tal's voice barely concealed his contempt. Taking a deep breath and gritting her teeth, she let her eyes travel up the riding boots, black trousers, and white shirt until she focused on the blacksmith's glowering face.

'They are getting fewer and I am recovering quicker. I am sure I will adjust to the energy soon enough.' But looking up at him from the ground brought on another dizzy spell. Not caring what he thought, she closed her eyes and lay down on the ground. Covering her face with her hands, she said, 'I will be fine in a minute.' He crouched down beside her, his breath hot in her ear.

'Come on. Food will help. Let us get you to Nell. She will be complaining I have kept you too long anyway.'

'Is Nell nice or is she like you?'

'Only one way to find out. Come on.' He put his hand under her arm and pulled her up. The back of his hand pressed against her breast and his touch burned her. As if suddenly realising where his hand was, he snatched it away and placed it on her shoulder, but she still trembled at his touch.

'I am so shaky,' she said, not wanting him to read anything into her trembling state.

'I know. Nell will sort you out, she has a cure for everything.' She wished he would take his hands off her. He was not helping and she resented her body for reacting like this. She shrugged off his hands and lifted her chin.

'I can walk now thank you.' Shrugging his shoulders, he let go of her and turned away. She felt bereft at the loss of his touch. Telling herself to get a grip, she hoped that this Nell would do more than cure dizziness. Tal led them through an archway and into another courtyard. The silence stretched taut between them and Gertrude forced herself to make conversation to distract her from watching him walk.

'I hope Jim is all right and is Sam okay?'

'Sam is having the time of his life, and Jim is always all right.' Lucinda ran up to Tal's legs.

'I am not worried for Jim,' Gertrude said through gritted teeth. Jim was *her* friend. How dare Tal talk about him as if he knew him. Tal looked down at Lucinda.

'Jim still causing trouble?' Lucinda snorted. Tal bent down and scooped Lucinda up into his arms. Gertrude looked away and snapped,

'Jim *is* trouble but he is *my* oldest friend.' Tal stopped walking and Gertrude banged into him. 'Sorry,' she muttered.

'Breathe,' he said. Raising her eyebrows at the blacksmith sounding like a tree, she took a deep breath and her stomach growled.

'Oh my god, what is that delicious smell?'

'That is Nell's home baked bread.' Gertrude almost gulped down the smell. Her stomach rumbled again and she hoped introductions would not take too long. She was ravenous.

'Come. Come and be welcome into Nell's kitchen,' and pushing two large doors open, Tal led them into the kitchen.

CHAPTER 33

Gertrude's jaw dropped as she took in the length of the kitchen.

It was vast. Sounds and smells came at her from every direction. A long wooden table dominated the room. People were rolling pastry and throwing flour around, so that little clouds hovered above them. Further down, she saw people chopping. The room was bright, helped by the floor to ceiling windows that run along the length of it. People ran around carrying dishes piled with food. Colourful fruit, vegetables and even a basket of chocolate passed her. Shouts and laughter filled the air and Gertrude could hear someone singing.

Looking down the table, she saw cats wandering around and sitting with the chefs. They tasted and sniffed the food that was being prepared. As she passed by, she saw a white cat dip her paw into a pot and taste what was in there.

'More rosemary, just a touch.' The jolly looking chef nodded and reached up above him. Hanging down from the ceiling, were rows of dried herbs and flowers. Towards the end of the room, copper pans hung down. They glowed as they reflected the sunlight streaming through the windows. As she followed Tal, the light changed. There was an enormous fireplace at the end of the kitchen. Several black pots were hanging off a large branch stretched across the fireplace. Steam came billowing out of them and Gertrude breathed in the rich smell. She closed her eyes.

'That is the most glorious smell I have ever smelled. It's rich and juicy, it's warm and spicy … I am so hungry.'

'Then you must eat, my darling, darling girl.' Gertrude opened her eyes and took a step back in horror. A huge woman stood in front of her. She had yellow teeth that were so long they looked like tusks. They protruded over her misshapen lips. Thick black hair bristled above her mouth and sprouted from several of her chins. Warts covered her face and each one had a thick red hair growing out of it. She was almost bald and the wisps of yellow hair remaining were plastered down on the pink, glistening skull. Her dress strained over the rolls of flesh and she almost blocked out the fire.

Tal came up behind the woman and threw his arms around her. He gave her a massive kiss on her cheek and then glowered at Gertrude as if daring her to say anything.

'May I introduce my Aunt Nell. Nell, this is—'

'I know who this is my love. Let me just have a moment.' The woman's massive hand fluttered up to her chest. Gertrude schooled her features and smiled.

'Aunt Nell, how lovely to meet you. I believe you have a cure for dizziness?' As if on cue, another dizzy spell hit her and she swayed. Moving quickly for a woman of her size, Nell pushed a stool under Gertrude and then sat down on a stool beside her. She took Gertrude's hand in her own and squeezed it. Gertrude met her gaze and felt a smile spread across her face. The woman's eyes were the colour of cornflowers. They danced and reminded Gertrude of Mrs Eccles' eyes. She felt inexplicably safe. A warmth came from the woman, which had nothing to do with the roaring fire behind them, and she smelled delicious.

'As I live and breathe, that I would see this day … my lovely girl, you are so welcome.' She gave Gertrude's hands another squeeze. Gertrude squeezed back and felt tears prick her eyes. She looked down and Nell patted her hands as if she understood. Letting go of her, Nell turned around on the stool.

'And whom do we have here? Sam? Is this golden vision the

great Sam? Companion of my sister? Trusted friend and loyal advisor?' Gertrude looked down when she heard Sam give a low grunt. Nell sat on the floor, rubbing Sam's exposed white tummy. She was making cooing noises and he cooed back. Laughing Gertrude said,

'I thought you two would have met by now?'

'Sam has been too busy eating all the food. He took longer to get down the kitchen than you did.'

'You have a friend for life now.' Nell laughed.

'Good. One can never have too many friends ... of the right sort, and you, my golden boy, are definitely the right sort.' She carried on with her tickling. Lucinda shook her head in disgust and Nell looked up at her.

'Don't get jealous, little one, your turn is next.' Gertrude shook her head.

'Lucinda does not like to be—' but Nell heaved herself up and began to tickle Lucinda under the chin. Her purring reverberated around the room.

'Nell is chin tickling,' said a smooth voice. Spoons and whisks fell and a mass of cats ran up the table towards Nell and Lucinda.

'Oh, you silly lot. Come on then.' Nell opened her giant arms as cats piled around her.

'Now you will all get a turn ... don't push ... Thoth, away with you, let Bast have a turn.' Gertrude smiled and put her head down on the table, letting the purring noises wash over her. The cats sounded like a huge drill. She closed her eyes and breathed in the wonderful smells.

'Eat,' said a deep voice. Raising her head, Tal stood over her, holding a plate. On it was a hunk of bread smothered in yellow butter. She took a small bite. Hunger overwhelmed her and not caring how un-ladylike she looked, she ripped into the bread, swallowing as quickly as she could. The bread was warm and crusty on the outside, fluffy on the inside and the butter was creamy with salt crystals that burst on her tongue. Tal lowered himself onto the stool next to her and watched her devour the last bit. He raised his eyebrows.

'More?' Gertrude nodded and leaning across the table, Tal spoke to the jester Gertrude had seen outside.

'Dafydd, pass me the whole loaf and the butter.' The jester nodded, his bells tinkling. Tal tore off a hunk of bread. Gertrude's heart fluttered, as she watched his hands tear into the bread. 'Here.' She took the bread offered to her without meeting his eyes.

'Simple pleasures,' said Nell and unable to speak Gertrude nodded. Then remembering something she swallowed the bread down quickly.

'Oh! You're *the* Nell that cooked for me. And for Cat and Mrs Eccles.' Nell disentangled herself from the cats and pushed back a strand of yellow hair from her eyes.

'Yes, flower, I am the cook.'

'Mrs Eccles always pretended she had cooked.' Gertrude stuffed more bread into her mouth.

'And I always corrected her,' Sam said. 'I love her but credit where credit is due, madam.' He licked his lips. Nell reached out and stroked him.

'Where are my manners? You and Lucinda must be starving. Dafydd pass the bread and cheese.'

'Gertrude has already polished off the first loaf,' the jester grinned. 'Enjoy?' Her mouth still full, Gertrude smiled. Swallowing the last delicious bit she said,

'That was delicious. I am so sorry if I have been greedy.'

'Never, ever apologise for finishing my food,' Nell said. 'It is the greatest compliment you could give me. And anyway, there is more from where that came from. Any minute now ...' She put her hand to her ear. A bell pinged. 'There. Dafydd, if you would be so kind, and take that blasted hat off. I can't tell if the ovens are going off or if it's you prancing about.' Dafydd grinned and with a bow, swept off his coloured hat, revealing a mane of brown hair. He strolled over to the oven and watching the masculine way he walked, Gertrude could not imagine him prancing anywhere. She turned her head and caught Tal glaring at her.

'Thank you for the food,' she said. When he did not say anything, she looked at Nell. Nell looked between her and Tal. She gave Gertrude a weak smile.

'Grounding, that is all you need. You are still in between worlds. Part of you is still in the In Between.' Frowning Gertrude tried to remember where she had been but could only hear the whispering echo of a voice.

'I am losing you ... again.'

She shook her head trying to clear the sudden sorrow that washed over her.

Dafydd walked over with a new loaf of bread. Tearing it in two, he leant over and retrieved the knife and butter, giving Gertrude a wink. A low noise sounded and Gertrude looked round in amazement. The noise came from Tal. Tal sprung up from the stool, knocking it over. He stormed out of the kitchen, slamming the door behind him. The sound echoed through the kitchen and everyone stopped and looked up.

'Whoops,' Dafydd said and grinned, but Nell shook her head and his grin vanished.

'Dafydd, my boy, do not play with fire. Now, Sam and Lucinda, eat.' They fell upon the bread and when Nell gave them a big chunk of yellow cheese, the snuffling sounds could be heard down the table.

'I love people who love food,' Nell said clapping her hands together. A flash lit up the kitchen and Gertrude fell off her stool.

'Who could fail to love your food ... or indeed you.' A boy stood where the flash had been. He had curly, strawberry blond hair and pointed ears. Gertrude tried to get up off the floor but he turned around and fixed her with eyes of glittering peacock green and she knew what he was.

When the Elven look at you it is as if the stars themselves have noticed you.

His eyes glowed brighter and Gertrude thought there must be a light shining on him from somewhere, as his skin glimmered gold. He smiled, revealing beautiful gleaming teeth and Gertrude thought this is what a young angel must look like. Nell cleared her throat.

'Gertrude, may I introduce, Finn. Finn – this is Gertrude, whom I told you about.'

'I know who she be, Nell.' His voice shimmered. It reminded Gertrude of something. As the boy stared, Gertrude found her face growing warm. His eyes were not those of a child's. They glittered and twinkled and Gertrude realised whom he sounded like.

'You sound like a star I once sung with.' His green eyes flashed.

'You sang with the stars?'

'Just one.'

'The first one?'

'The first one of that evening.' He bowed down to her.

'The first one has a beautiful voice, so I thank you for that. But the last one … the last one sings most beautifully of all.' Gertrude did not know what to say so she favoured him with a smile. Nell gave a slight cough.

'Finn is a pixie … at the moment, although the goddess knows, it won't be long now. Finn, help Gertrude up please.' Gertrude found she could move again and accepted the offered hand. He pulled her to her feet with such force, she would have fallen forwards if the pixie had not held her. His eyes were level with her breasts and he smiled up at her and then returned his eyes to their gazing.

'Finn! Enough.' Finn let go of Gertrude and a slow smile flowered over his face as he looked at Nell.

'Jealous, my heart?' Nell huffed, puffed, and then broke out into a raucous laugh.

'Yes, terribly. Now away with you. Go and help someone do something.'

'This flower has not rooted. May I suggest a visit to our garden? You need carrots for the stew, no? Nothing grounds like food from the ground. Let her get her hands dirty. Let her feel the land underneath her fingertips.'

'Good idea.' Sam made to move but Finn held up his hand.

'Sam the myth and Lucinda the legend, it is an honour.' He bowed deeply and both Sam and Lucinda made a strange noise.

'That is what delight sounds like,' murmured Nell to Gertrude. 'I've sounded like that a couple of times myself when he's looked at me.' Finn favoured Nell with a deep smile and sure enough, she made the strange noise. He turned back to Sam and Lucinda.

'Both of you stay here. There will be enough time to put yourself in harm's way, but for now, enjoy the sanctuary that is Nell's and mine kitchen. Glory in it and eat to your heart's content.' He turned to Gertrude and held out his hand. 'My lady of spring, this way if you please,' and picking up a wicker basket he led her towards the door. Sam and Lucinda hardly noticed she was going. They were too busy watching the food being prepared. Nell stroked both of them.

'Go, Gertrude. I will look after these two. Or perhaps they will look after me. Go and enjoy our garden. And be most welcome in it.' With a smile, Gertrude let herself be led outside by the pixie.

CHAPTER 34

As they stepped outside, Finn took her hand. Gertrude breathed in the air. It was not as warm as when she had first arrived and for a moment, a chill wind blew reminding her of winter. Then the wind died and the warm spring air came bouncing back. Finn led them through the courtyards and she tried to take it all in, glancing at everyone who came her way.

'Whom are you looking for, flower bride?' said Finn

'No one, I am just taking it all in.'

'Liar.'

'No really. I am looking at all the different dresses.'

'Liar. He is in the stable anyway, shoeing the white horse god.' When Gertrude did not reply, he shrugged his shoulders and tugged at her hand. 'Nearly there.'

They entered a quiet courtyard. A stone birdbath stood in the middle. Two stone doves covered in moss flew above the bone-dry bowl. Finn let go of her hand and went over to a long wall. He moved his hands over it and stopped. Turning his head to make sure they were alone, he motioned for Gertrude to come closer. She stood beside him, flush to the wall.

'Breathe,' he whispered. He took a deep breath and breathed onto the pale wall. It was as if someone had lit a match to paper. Colour spread along the wall and following his lead, Gertrude breathed onto the stone. The pale wall turned dark red and an arched wooden door appeared. Clapping his hands,

Finn skipped over to it and turned the round metal handle. The door opened silently and he turned, beckoning her. When she reached him, Finn pushed her through the entrance and closed the door behind him. He breathed on the door and put his ear to it.

'All hidden again. Just me and thee here. Welcome to Nell and Finn's garden.' For the second time that day, Gertrude's jaw dropped.

Trees in full leaf surrounded the garden, giving it a feeling of sanctuary and secrecy. Flowers of pink and purple swayed in the breeze and dandelions seeds travelled on the air. It was as if the garden had captured the sunlight. The air was warm and fragrant. The trees sighed as they moved back and forth and butterflies chased each other through their branches. Bees hummed and one huge bumble bee lazily made his way to a pink flower. Landing on it, his body weight made the flower bend halfway down to the ground and for a moment, she was transported back into Mrs Eccles' conservatory. Finn skipped ahead and twirled around, throwing his arms out.

'Oh, Finn, it is so beautiful.' He winked.

'And so secret. Nell is a genius and so am I. Her and I made this garden, right under the queen's nose. She has no idea it exists. It was our little act of rebellion. The gods know there is only so much we can do whilst she and I are here. It is hard enough being undercover but this ... this is our quiet revenge. Nell's garden – hers and mine.' Gertrude cocked her head to one side, listening.

'Finn, where are all the birds?'

'On a mission. Come, walk with me. Smell these herbs.' The herb bushes gave off such a strong scent, Gertrude thought they might be showing off. To let them know she appreciated them, she stopped at a plant and buried her face in it.

'Rosemary! You smell wondrous.'

'Rosemary is lovely, is she not? And she does not just smell good either. She tastes wonderful with new potatoes just out of the ground.' Finn opened his arms and indicated the rows of vegetables laid out before them. The plants were in such neat rows, it was if they had all sorted amongst themselves, where they were going to grow.

'That's exactly how we did it. Nell and I just made the space and told them to sort it out amongst themselves.' Gertrude smiled politely but realising Finn had read her thoughts, she told herself not to think of Tal. So, of course, that is exactly what she did. Finn laughed and pulled her along.

Rows of dark green cabbages and pale green lettuces greeted them. Rows of runner beans climbed up their wooden sticks. Finn skipped ahead of her down the path that ran between the vegetable beds. He stopped at a piece of earth where feathery fronds waved in the breeze.

'Hello, carrots.' He gave a flourishing bow. 'Do you know how to pick them?'

'Not a clue.'

'Watch.' The pixie put the basket down and stepped onto the earth. He crouched down by one of the green fronds. He stroked the feathery leaves and bent down, whispering,

'Wake up, it's time.' Gathering the leaves, he pulled. The carrot burst out of the ground in a shower of earth. They were the brightest carrots Gertrude had ever seen. 'Almost as bright as your hair, flower bride.' Finn kissed the carrot and placed it in the basket. He patted it, saying, 'Thank you. Right your go now.' Gertrude stepped onto the soil and knelt. She stroked the trembling leaves.

'Are they scared?'

'No, darling. Excited. They have been grown with so much love they cannot wait to love us back.' Gertrude put her mouth to the fronds and whispered,

'Wake up.' She pulled the leaves. The carrot jumped out of its bed, showering her with earth. She took it over to the basket. 'Thank you,' she said and placed it with its brother. 'Can I do the next one?' Finn stretched out on the ground and turned his pointed face up to the sun.

'Please do. I am going to talk to the sun for a while.' He

smiled, closed his eyes, and put his hands behind his head. Gertrude picked up the basket and jumped back onto the earth.

Each time she bent over and whispered, '*Wake up,*' the carrots would jump higher. She reached the last bunch and watched, amazed, as they leapt into the basket on their own. She laughed and turned to Finn, who was no longer dozing but watching her intensely. He lay on his side, his head supported by his hand.

'The stories are all true. You are beautiful,' he said. Gertrude snorted. 'You are almost as beautiful as Nell.'

'Well in that case … er … thank you, although I think you need your eyes tested.' The pixie leapt up into a crouch, his peacock green eyes flashing.

'Would you like to test my eyesight, flower bride, who has been kissed by the sun? I am an Elven. Are you really so ignorant of our ways? Have you been gone so long, Queen of Sorrows, to forget that my kind can see an acorn falling off an oak from the other side of the forest? Or that I can spot a crow cleaning his feathers in the next village? Or watch a storm gather out over the sea, three days before it hits the shore?'

'Is pixie another name for Elven?'

'A pixie is a young Elven. My change will come upon me soon enough – sooner than I would like … although if you mention that to anyone, I shall deny it and name thee a liar.'

'I won't breathe a word.' His stare deepened. There was a wildness in his look, one that exhilarated and scared her.

'I want to be Elven,' she blurted out.

'Knowing you, my lady of spring, you probably have Elven blood flowing through you already.' Gertrude looked down at her hands and then turned them over to look at the blue veins in her wrist.

'Do you think so?'

'I know so. Now come. The sun tells me that Nell is winding herself up into a frenzy. She needs me back. But first, we replant. What we take, we always give back.' He reached into his pocket and pulled out a handful of seeds. Walking over to where they had pulled the first carrot, he crouched down and placed some seeds in the hole.

'Sleep. Sleep, grow and dream. And become that dream.' He filled the hole and patted down the earth. His eyes twinkled once more. 'Your turn.' Gertrude copied his actions and between them, they replanted every carrot they had pulled. They stood up and wiped their hands on their clothes. Gertrude felt content and more than that, she felt connected.

'Come, take my hand, Queen of the May, and let us go back to the kitchen.' Grabbing Finn's outstretched hand Gertrude smiled.

'Love to.'

✽ ✽ ✽

The kitchen was in an uproar when they got back. They found Nell shouting orders, tasting this, and smelling that. The kitchen staff ran around, banging pans and spoons. They were taking plates down, kneading bread and whisking in bowls. Gertrude tried to find Sam and Lucinda amongst the chaos. Finn tugged at her hand and led her over to Nell, who was dipping her finger into a batter and shaking her head.

'Thoth, what do you think?' A haughty grey cat padded down the table and dipped a paw into the mixture. He licked it and put his head to one side.

'More salt … about five crystals would do it.'

'Not six?'

'No, madam, six will take it just over the edge.'

'Five it is then. Finn, thank the gods you're back. We are not going to make it. We have the whole castle to feed and the villagers will be coming in tonight, as the queen is not in residence, so that is at least another hundred mouths to feed and who knows, perhaps the people from across the lake may come and the gods only know how I will feed them. I am running behind, no one is listening to me and I am never going to get it done.' The grey cat shook his head and looked at Finn.

'Every day the same.'

'Every day, Thoth, the same panic,' Finn replied. 'And yet every day, my darling Nell, you create miracles. It is time.' Finn let go of Gertrude's hand and caught Nell's hand, bringing it to his mouth for a kiss.

'Time,' repeated Thoth narrowing his blue eyes. 'Time for your speech.'

'Get this kitchen into order, Nell.' Finn released her hand.

'You're right.' She cleared her throat. 'Attention everyone.' Cats, maids, cooks, and chefs stopped what they were doing. Nell heaved herself up onto a chair. Gertrude ran forward and helped her. 'Thank you my dear. Right ... phew ... let me get my breath. All right ... oh ...dear me.' No one moved. Her staff were too busy gazing at her. 'Right, everyone. Last meal is approaching. We have a castle and a village to feed. So, everyone, do what you need to do.'

'Do it well,' said Thoth.

'Do it with flavour,' said Finn.

'And above all—' and Nell put her arms out.

'Do it with love,' everyone in the kitchen sang together. Nell grinned, her blue eyes dancing.

'Anyone would think you've heard that speech before.' Everyone laughed, including the cats, which was a sight to see.

The kitchen erupted into action. After the initial clanging of saucepans and clashing of utensils died down, someone began to sing and soon everyone was singing. In contrast to the chaos before, the whole kitchen now moved in harmony. It was like watching a choreographed dance. A person would put their hand out and another person would give them the thing they obviously required. A chef would finish one step of the recipe and then pass the bowl to the next chef to take over. Cats wound in and out giving instructions and purring and Gertrude found her foot tapping to the song.

'A cooking song,' Nell said. 'Now, my dear, help me back down off this chair.' As she clambered down, she put her big hands on Gertrude's shoulders. Gertrude's knees buckled under the weight.

'Can you cook, flower?'

'No, but I am willing to learn.'

'Right, let's put you on carrot duty.' She showed Gertrude how to peel and chop the carrots and left her to it. Gertrude was so absorbed in her work that she did not realise Lucinda had jumped up beside her until the cat spoke.

'Are you feeling better now, Ginger?'

'Yes, I do actually. Finn was right. I just needed to feel the earth beneath my hands.' When Lucinda did not reply, Gertrude followed her gaze and saw Sam deep in conversation with Thoth. 'Jealous?' Lucinda sniffed.

'Do not be absurd.' As if feeling her gaze, Thoth turned round and gave Lucinda the full benefit of his blue eyes.

'Madam, please come over here and help me explain to this … canine, the difference between sweet and sour.' Lucinda pranced forward and settled down next to the grey cat who, after a moment, shifted himself closer to her. Gertrude smiled, glad that at least one of them had found a friend. Mind you, Sam looked happy enough, even if she felt that the cats were just tolerating him. She went back to her task. Sam bounced over.

'Nell, why are there no dogs in this kitchen?' asked Sam. Nell stopped whisking and took something off the table. She threw it at him and Sam gobbled it up. Smacking his lips, he said,

'That was delicious. What was it?'

'That's why, my golden boy.' Sam smiled.

'Are there any dogs in this land?' Everyone fell silent and Nell put her whisk down.

'If there are, they are in hiding. A few moons ago, the queen took a sudden dislike to dogs. She gave an order that they were to be killed on sight. The queen has no time for those who love, and dogs love most of all.'

'Cats, of course, do as well,' said a beautiful white Persian, 'But we hide it better.' Gertrude nodded.

'About the queen, Nell, I—'

'Hush, my darling flower. Here is neither the time nor the place to discuss these matters.' Nell gestured to her staff. 'I trust all those present with my life, but to discuss *her* in her castle? Who knows who else may be listening? Just you carry on chopping those carrots.'

Gertrude grabbed the knife and sliced it down so hard the knife stuck in the chopping board. No one ever gave her a straight answer. However, being with a knife when angry is never a good idea and as she pulled the knife free, she somehow managed to slice her thumb. Finn flashed in front of her and grabbing her bleeding thumb, thrust it into his mouth. His eyes shone. Without taking his eyes from her face, he grabbed the knife and sliced open his own thumb. He brought it up to her mouth and Gertrude parted her lips and let him enter her mouth.

The noises of the kitchen faded away.

Time stopped.

There was no one else in the room. His blood tasted sweet, not coppery like hers. The room spun and Gertrude could hear whisperings and talking from far away. She even caught a song on the wind. Coloured lights danced in front of her. He took his thumb from her mouth and released her. The noise of the kitchen came rushing back and Gertrude fell onto a stool. She covered her ears. Finn moved forward and moving her hands, put his mouth to her ear.

'Now, my May Queen, you have Elven blood,' and with a flash, he disappeared.

CHAPTER 35

Gertrude tried to catch her breath.

Tremors came upon her in waves. Everything was too bright. Too loud. It reminded her of how she had felt after the bath in Cú Chulainn's blood. Glowing lights twinkled around everyone in the kitchen. The cats glowed purple, but the people radiated different colours. Most had red and orange lights around them. Gertrude did not have far to look for Nell. Lights of emerald green, shot through with gold, radiated from her. Nell's voice cut through her reverie, booming, even though she was halfway across the kitchen.

'Where on earth have you been? I have had to make Gertrude do your share of the work and she's a guest.' A figure pranced down the kitchen. The lights around it glowed a dark murky pink, mixed with brown. Gertrude shuddered. She shook her head and the coloured lights faded and disappeared. She recognised the figure as the pretty brunette, who had been giggling with Dafydd, the jester. Gertrude got to her feet.

'I really don't mind helping,' said Gertrude, giving the girl a weak smile.

'I know you don't, flower,' replied Nell, 'but – are you all right, Gertrude? I knew I should not have made you work so hard. You have only just arrived. Elaine, my girl, you begged for a position in my kitchen and now you feel you can just breeze in whenever you like. Where have you been?' The girl gave Gertrude a sly smile that showed off her dimples.

'With Tal,' she simpered and reaching up she slowly pulled a strand of hay from her hair.

It was as if someone had punched Gertrude in the heart. *He's mine,* her thoughts screamed. She sat down, hoping the other girl had not noticed her reaction. Elaine had a kitten face and shining brown hair. The girl's eyes were soft blue and she had a full mouth that looked sulky rather than pouty.

If he likes that sort of thing, good luck to him. He doesn't belong to me. I don't even know him. Ridiculous. If they like to do whatever they do in the stable, well just get on with it. They deserve each other. She listened to her thoughts chattering on, but her heart screamed something different.

'I'm sure Tal did not thank you for the distraction,' Nell said. 'He has enough to do. Now come and meet Gertrude properly. Elaine this is Gertrude—'

'I know who she is. Question is, does *she* know who she is?'

'Elaine,' said Nell with a warning note in her voice, 'Don't start stirring, unless it's soup.' Gertrude stood up, lifted her chin, and looked down at the girl. She extended her hand.

'Hello, Elaine, nice to meet you.' Elaine did not take the proffered hand and gave her a sweeping look up and down. Then seeing Nell's scowling face, she leant forward and shook Gertrude's hand in a weak handshake. Nell grunted in approval.

'Now I am sure you two will grow to be true friends.' As Nell turned away, Elaine and Gertrude both looked at each other in horror. *Well, that is one thing we agree on,* thought Gertrude and she pulled her hand away.

'What do you want me to do then, Nell?' Elaine asked.

'Nothing. You're too late. Go and help Dafydd with the bread. Dinner is almost done.'

'Just as well as there is a queue outside,' Elaine said as she sashayed down the kitchen.

'A queue? Already? But it's not even time. We have half an hour to go yet.' Nell looked at Gertrude. 'News travels fast. Let me look at you. Dare I? Yes, I dare. Thoth?'

'Yes, madam,' said the grey cat from halfway down the table.

'Take Gertrude to the baths.' She turned to Gertrude and smiled showing her yellow teeth. 'We want you looking your best. I have a feeling tonight people will have travelled a long way to see you and I know I would want to look my best. Thoth will take you to the baths. Don't just stand there, chop chop!'

'Can I go?' Sam said. 'I feel like a spare part here. Apparently, I have ruined Bast's soufflé and she keeps giving me the evil eye.' Gertrude followed Sam's gaze and saw a ginger cat glaring at him.

'Go then, but Thoth?'

'Yes, madam?'

'No lingering. Make sure she is in and out and afterwards take her into the little chamber next door. I will make sure there is a fresh gown. Now go, the lot of you.'

'But surely there is not time, Nell?' Gertrude said. Nell gave her a wink.

'I'll make time.'

* * *

When the doors to the kitchen finally flung open, Gertrude did not think the kitchen would hold all the folk that streamed in. However, Nell seemed to have a knack for making things fit. Not only had she fitted in Gertrude's bath, but she had personally attended to her. She then found time to feed the remaining soldiers of the queen. There were some, apparently, who were guarding the castle in their monarch's absence. Gertrude had not seen a soul when she had followed Thoth through the winding corridors to the baths.

'They are here all right,' said the grey cat. 'Let us just say they are very tired at the moment.'

The bath had been astonishing. It was the size of a small swimming pool and Gertrude had dived in – after Sam – into steaming, fragrant waters. Swimming on her back, looking up at the paintings of dolphins and fish, she felt all the tension of the last few days drain from her. She was home.

Later as Nell brushed out her hair, she shared her joy.

'Of course, you're home, flower. You've been gone so long it must feel good to be exactly where you're meant to be. Now stay still while I get out all these storm knots, although there are only a few. Vivienne's shampoo has done wonders.'

'I miss her so much. Where is she?'

'Hush, not here.' Nell lowered her voice. 'Morgan is still looking, but let us not discuss this now. Do you feel better being here, being home?'

'Yes, but I never knew this place existed until a month ago.'

'You may not have known, but your soul did.' Nell helped her step into a gown of green and gold. Catching Gertrude's sudden frown she said,

'No, flower, I would not dress you in *her* clothes, fine though they are. This is yours, made for you.'

'Where is the queen?'

'Away and that's all that matters.'

'When will she be back?'

'Too soon,' and she cut the conversation short as she hurried Gertrude back to the kitchen. Nell and Dafydd left to feed the castle's unseen guards.

'Sleeping like the dead,' Nell had said when she came back.

'Yeah, funny that,' said Dafydd catching Gertrude's eye and winking. Gertrude smiled and then smiled, even more, when she caught the petulant look on Elaine's face.

Now, with still with five minutes to spare, Gertrude stood by the bubbling pots hanging over the fire, with a ladle in one hand and a cloth in the other. As the guest of honour, it was her place to feed the hordes of people who had gathered for last meal, for Nell had said,

'There is no greater honour than to feed folks. To fill up their bellies with warm, good food made with love. If you can do that, you are blessed.' Nell stood at the head of the table.

'Right, everything off the table? Finn?' A flash and Finn

appeared at the other end.

'Here I am, my love.'

'On the count of three. One, two, three.' They both raised their arms and looked up. A green tablecloth came floating down from the ceiling and draped itself over the huge table.

'Best silver?'

'Gold, darling, surely in the circumstances.'

'Gold it is.' Finn and Nell both held their hands in front of them and mimed eating with cutlery. Gertrude looked up, but nothing hovered above the table. She heard a clink and looking down, she watched as gold cutlery appeared, laying itself beautifully.

'Crystal?

'Yes, red and green.' Finn and Nell gave each other a nod and mimed drinking. By each place setting, a beautiful crystal goblet appeared. Catching the sun, streaming through the windows, they threw red and green lights up and down the kitchen.

'Bowls, Nell?'

'Yes, green glazed, rimmed with gold.' They mimed holding a bowl. Green bowls began to appear.

'Stop! We did not warm them,' and with a sweep of Nell's hand, they disappeared. Again, the two mimed holding a bowl, but they breathed gently on the imaginary crockery. The bowls popped back onto the table. Gertrude reached over and touched one. It was warm. Once the last bowl was in place, Nell and Finn bowed to one another. As Nell straightened, she looked at her staff, who gazed at her in worship.

'My loves. It is time. Open the doors and let us do what we do best.' The huge doors opened and people flooded in. Everyone found a bowl and formed two queues, one leading to Nell, the other to Gertrude. Looking at the queue and looking down at the black pots simmering, Gertrude did not know how they were going to feed everyone, but she had seen enough that day to have faith that Nell would somehow make it happen.

As the first person reached her, she took the lid off, wincing as it was hot, and ladled the thick golden stew into the waiting bowl.

'One ladleful only, Gertrude,' Nell said. It filled right to the top and the young man blushed and stammered his thanks. She recognised him as the fiddler she had seen earlier. An older man with a white beard stepped up.

'Come on, girl, give us two ladles.' Gertrude laughed.

'I can't fit anymore in.'

'That's what the pirate's wife said to the gypsy,' and he roared with laughter. Nell let out a raucous laugh and a cat fell off its chair.

'Oh, away with you, Gwyn and stop tormenting the poor girl.' Gertrude filled bowl after bowl and she loved the way the people thanked her as if she were doing the most amazing thing in the world.

'Thank you, Nell, I am famished.' The deep voice floated over to her and with a start, she glanced up and saw him in Nell's queue. She stared at the back of his dark head.

Of course, he did not come to my queue. Probably looking for Elaine. She dumped some stew into the next bowl, splashing the woman standing in front of her.

'Ouch,' said the woman.

'I am so sorry.' Gertrude offered her cloth to the woman to wipe herself. She watched as Tal took his place near the head of the table. Elaine went and sat next to him. She leaned over and whispered something that made him smile. *His whole face transforms when he smiles. Like the sun coming out from behind a cloud. I wonder if I could make him smile?*

'My lady?' said a soft voice. Gertrude looked around. There was no one there.

'My lady?' said the voice again. Gertrude looked down and saw the ginger cat that had been glaring at Sam earlier. She had a bowl in front of her.

'Sorry.' Gertrude picked up the bowl. She filled it to the top and held it out to the cat, who took it in her mouth. The cat walked away, and jumped onto the table, next to a young man, without spilling a drop. Finally, the queue ended. Nell poured a bowl and gave it to Gertrude.

'Now you pour mine.' Gertrude did so. Nell bowed to her and Gertrude gave a little curtsey, which pleased the crowd as they all clapped. Nell took her place at the head of the table and placed Gertrude on her right, opposite Tal on her left. Lucinda sat on the table next to Tal, and Sam jumped up on the stool next to Gertrude.

'Hands up for red?' Nell said and then patting Gertrude's hands added, 'I mean wine, dearie, not you.' She chuckled at her own joke. Hands went up and Nell made a sweeping gesture with her hand, as did Finn sitting down the other end. The glasses in front of them filled with a deep, plum-coloured liquid.

'Hands up for white?' Again, those who put their hands up had their goblets filled with a citrine yellow liquid.

'Gertrude?'

'Er ... red please.' Finn gestured and her glass filled. The bouquet mingled with the scent of the stew and Gertrude's stomach growled. On the table were loaves and pots of yellow butter. Nell put her hands together and bowed her head. Everyone followed.

'We thank thee, gracious Goddess, for thy bounty. May the love that made this food sustain us through the dark times and keep us strong in our endeavours. Blessed be.'

'Blessed be,' murmured the people and the cats.

'A toast,' said Nell raising her glass. 'To those who have been found, our guests, Sam, Lucinda, and Gertrude—'

'And me!' croaked a voice. A black object hurtled down from the ceiling. Men cursed, women screamed and some cats hissed. Only Gertrude, Sam, Lucinda, and Tal did not flinch. Finn burst out laughing.

'Jim,' Nell said jumping up and grabbing a bowl that had just appeared. She filled it with stew. 'You black demon.' She fussed and crooned over him, stroking him under the chin.

'Nell, you ugly monster, I have missed you.' Nell threw her

head back and laughed.

'Still a charmer.'

'Yes indeed. That he is,' said Lucinda

'Silver-tongued I would say,' Sam said. Gertrude reached over and stroked the crow.

'Jim, you absolute sod, where have you been?' Nell sat back down and raised her glass again.

'I'm sure Jim will tell us in good time. I have not finished my toast yet and people are getting hungry. To friends old—' and here she nodded to Jim, 'And new—' she nodded to Sam and Lucinda. Gertrude wondered where she fitted in. 'And to absent enemies. May they remain absent a day more.'

'Friends and absent enemies,' everyone repeated and sipped their wine. The fragrant wine rushed down Gertrude's throat and into her stomach, where it blossomed into a warmth that crept up to her face. She felt a tingling begin in her fingertips. Everyone fell silent and began to eat. The stew was steaming hot. It was thick and rich with a slight spice that caught pleasantly in her throat.

'Like a hug on the inside,' sighed a woman further down. Raising her eyes, Gertrude watched as Tal leant over and grabbed a loaf of bread. He tore it into four chunks and spread the butter. He placed one hunk next to him and gave one to Lucinda. He reached over and placed one by Nell and then, without meeting her eyes, he leant over and offered one to Gertrude.

'Thank you,' murmured Gertrude and shot a glance at Elaine. The brunette glared back.

'Stop staring at him,' Sam said, already licking his lips as he had devoured the stew in moments.

'Just eat your food, Sam.'

'I have.'

'I wish you would take your time. It's not right the way you wolf it down.'

'Gertrude, I am descended from wolves, how else am I to eat it? Like a cat, all finicky? Or perhaps you would prefer it if I used a knife and fork? But seeing as I do not have opposable thumbs—'

'Okay, okay, point taken.'

'And do not snap at me just because I caught you staring at Tal.'

'Sorry.' She took a sip of her wine and carried on eating.

Halfway through her bowl of stew, she emptied the last drops of wine down her throat. She did not feel snappy anymore. On the contrary she, almost, loved everyone.

Not Elaine, of course. But even Tal.

Especially Tal.

Her stomach fluttering like a newborn baby bird, she put her spoon down with a clatter that made people look up. She fixed Tal with a stare. He was listening to Elaine witter on, whilst he stroked Lucinda. Feeling her look, he glanced over at her and went still. His grey eyes widened and then blazed. Gertrude stood up and pushed back her stool. She made it halfway across the table before Sam caught her dress and Nell grabbed her arms.

'What's the matter, flower?'

I want to hear him say my name. I want to run my hands through his hair and pull his head back. I want to kiss his throat, his ears, his face, and his mouth. I want to smack Elaine in the face and shove her spoon where it will hurt. All these thoughts raced through her mind in a moment, but all anybody heard was a groan of such longing, the woman next to Sam looked over at her husband and winked.

'Sam, has Gertrude drunk wine before?' asked Nell, as she wrestled with her on the table.

'Yes, Mrs Eccles gave her meadowsweet wine once,' but to answer he had to let go of Gertrude's dress. She crawled further towards Tal. Tal jumped up and stared down at her. His eyes darkened and he seemed to be having trouble breathing.

'No you don't.' Nell heaved Gertrude back onto her lap. She grabbed Gertrude's glass and sniffed it.

'Oh, by Dionysus – Finn!' she yelled.

'Yes, my darling?'

'How could you? Fireflower wine? On her first day? When the moon is three days off from being full? What possessed you?'

'Finn. You had no right,' said Tal turning to the grinning pixie at the end of the table.

'Just helping things along,' said Finn and he gave a little wave. Tal scowled and then with one final, burning glance at Gertrude, he stormed out of the kitchen.

CHAPTER 36

Gertrude wrestled with Nell, trying to chase after Tal, but the cook held her fast.

'Dafydd, get me some water, quick. Now you look at me Gertrude, that's right, now breathe—'

'If one more person or tree tells me to breathe, I am going to scream … oh look, the pretty colours …' said Gertrude looking up.

'Water. Now.' Nell raised a glass to Gertrude's lips.

'Down in one, my flower. That's it. Big gulps. Fireflower wine should only be drunk on certain occasions and only under supervision. It can make you do weird and wonderful things—'

'As Nell will gladly tell you,' said Jim.

'Thank you, Jim. Finn is a terror. I shall ban him from the kitchen. Yes, I will, I shall ban him.'

'Oh, please don't.' Gertrude wiped her mouth and sat on her stool. 'I feel better now, and he is such a pet.'

'Pet? Good gods, girl, he's a pixie less than two moons off his changing. You think he's trouble now? Wait until he becomes full Elven. I will lose most of my kitchen maids, and quite a few of the porters,' she said nodding towards a young man who was dabbing his mouth with a white napkin. 'He will become a different creature, and Finn will be one of the most powerful this land has ever seen. I have never beheld a pixie with as much magic as he has. I once saw him stare at a flower and a ship miles away got caught in a storm and sunk down onto the ocean's bed. That *'pet'* you speak of, is the son of the Elven queen and king and one day Finn will be king of the Elven himself.' Nell looked down at her hands.

'You are going to miss him.' Nell looked up, her eyes glittering with tears.

'More than you will ever know.' She took out a huge hankie and blew her nose so loudly a cat fell off the table. 'Still, he's a terror and that was a naughty thing he did there.'

'I don't know, I felt rather wonderful. Mad, but wonderful.' For an answer, Nell harrumphed. She took Gertrude's chin in her hand and peered closely at her.

'All right, the fire has gone.'

Gertrude was no longer hungry and took the time to observe the people around her. Elaine had disappeared, no doubt scurrying after Tal. It soon became apparent that warm and cosy as the kitchen was, the people and the cats were not acting normally. They laughed too loud and too long and when they thought no one was looking, their faces became sad or angry. Once or twice, a noise made most of them jump.

'These people are scared of something,' said Sam.

'Or someone, obviously. No one will talk to me about the queen.' answered Gertrude. Lucinda padded across the table.

'What on earth is going on here, Lucinda?' Sam asked. 'Has Tal told you anything?'

'No, not a word. He wants to tell me though. He keeps looking as if he is about to say something, and then he shakes his head.'

'I found the same,' agreed Sam. 'When you were getting carrots, people would stroke me and go to speak and then they would shut up. And I wish there were more dogs. I am surrounded by cats. I will be coughing up hairballs soon and washing myself every ten minutes.'

'You say that as if it is a bad thing,' murmured Lucinda and to make a point she licked her paw and put it over her ear.

'Jim knows,' Gertrude said. They all looked over to the crow. He nestled up to Nell finishing a joke.

'… and the drunk at the end of the bar says, "Yeah, I'd like to try it but I don't think I can hold my mouth open for that long!"'

Nell fell off her stool. Gertrude jumped up and tried to pick her up but Nell laughed so much, that Gertrude could not manage. She ended up laughing as well because Nell's laugh was so infectious. She managed to heave her up a little and then Jim, who was still chuckling at his own joke, rolled over. Unfortunately, it was onto Thoth, who had come over to help. Thoth swatted him with a sheathed paw. That made Nell laugh even more and she flopped back down on the floor. A couple of the men stood up and with great tenderness heaved her up. They settled her on the stool. Wiping tears away, Nell said,

'Everyone finished?' and everyone murmured yes, except the old bearded man, Gwyn, who said,

'Almost.'

'Anyone still hungry?' but not one person said yes and looking pleased with herself, Nell and Finn made a sweeping gesture and the dirty bowls and spoons disappeared.

'Anyone want desert?' There was a slight pause and the whole table nodded. Nell laughed and looked over at her staff, who were seated amongst the townsfolk.

'The strawberry cakes, if you please.' Soon everyone had a slice of fluffy, vanilla sponge, topped with the freshest, juiciest strawberries Gertrude had ever tasted. Thick clotted cream accompanied it and the whole table oohed and ahhed.

'*Now* is everyone finished?' and with the nods, Nell and Finn cleared the table of the cloth, bowls, and cutlery.

'Hey, I hadn't finished,' yelled Gwyn.

'There is always one, and it is always you, Gwyn. Anyway, you could do with losing weight.'

'You're a fine one to talk, Nell.'

'Cheeky. And now … dancing.'

People clapped and stood up. Looking down at the clean table, Gertrude took in the sheer size of it. It was one complete piece of wood.

'What tree did that come from?' she asked Sam.

'Dafydd told me it came from a king oak. It was a present to Nell from the Elven king.'

'Elven king? Good lord! Elven king, pixies, evil queens … what have we stepped into?'

'Animals will be speaking next,' Sam said with a wink. Gertrude tickled his ears. Nell and Finn stood opposite each other at the head of the table.

'On my count, Finn. One, two, three.' They parted their hands in a sweeping gesture and the table disappeared. 'And now, let's dance.'

Instruments came out of cupboards and drawers. There were flutes, lutes, a bodhran and two fiddles. Gwyn took his place with a small golden harp and counted everyone in. The young fiddler sprang over to them, his foot already tapping in time. The kitchen filled with dancers. Men grabbed girls and some girls grabbed men. The dancers wheeled each other round and weaved in and out of each other, often getting themselves in a tangle and falling over. No one seemed to mind.

Gertrude sat in a corner watching the people dance. Her feet kept tapping and she smiled watching everyone having fun. She looked up through the large windows and saw the red streaked sky. It was a beautiful sunset. At some point, Nell disappeared and when she asked Thoth where she was, he replied,

'Nell goes at sunset every night and where she goes is no one's business except hers.' Sam called him a pompous puss. A pretty blonde maid hauled the retriever onto the dance floor and he jumped around barking.

After the third dance, Gertrude realised, with her heart sinking, that no one was going to ask her to dance. She caught the eyes of some of the men but they flushed and looked away. Some of the women smiled and some stared with outright hostility. Gertrude sighed. Why should here be any different? The music finished and the dancers flopped down to rest, puffing, and blowing.

A single note from a harp sounded. It hung in the air, trembling and just as it faded, the trill of a flute chased it. The harp sounded again, low, and golden and again, the silvery sound of a flute responded. This time the harp replied quickly as if being persuaded by the flute to hang on and join it. Gertrude heard some people gasp and she looked up.

Tal sat by the musicians with a small golden harp on his knee. Finn stood opposite him with a shimmering silver flute to his lips. The two musicians stared with such intensity at each other, that Gertrude glanced away, ashamed at barging in upon their intimacy. But she could not look away for long. The flute slowly drew the harp out, until the harp entwined itself with the flute and began to do the chasing. It was a tune of longing. It was a tune of desire and of desperate passion. The bodhran joined in and Gertrude's foot began to tap. Some people stood up and swayed, as though hypnotised by the music. The fiddler and Gwyn added their instrument's voices and the tune picked up speed. The dance moved into Gertrude's blood until she found herself on her feet. She looked about her with desperation and Dafydd caught her eye.

Smiling, he ran across the room and, grabbing her by the waist, pulled her into the dance. She heard Tal's harp waver a little as she joined in and then it came back stronger and faster. Dafydd spun her until her hair streamed out behind her. She laughed and felt, rather than saw, Tal look at her. As Dafydd spun her, the music caught up with them, or perhaps they caught up with the music. Just as she thought it could not get any faster or wilder, it did.

Dancers dived under each other's arms and jigged. Men swung their partners higher into the air. Gertrude closed her eyes and felt the music flow through her. She never wanted it to end. With that thought, she realised she could not stop even if she wanted to. Feeling a tremor of fear, she tried to catch the musician's eyes, but she wheeled around so fast, that everything blurred. *I am going to fly. I am going to leave the ground and soar into the air.* Just as she gathered herself for lift off, the music stopped and she fell crashing down on the floor, along with everyone else.

Silence. Then a huge round of applause sounded, but Gertrude did not have the strength to get up or even clap. Sam bounded over to her and licked her face. Lucinda jumped on her head. Laughing Gertrude said,

'That was wild.' Sam rolled over, exposing his tummy.

'That was crazy.'

'That was mad,' Lucinda said. 'I asked Sam to dance.' Gertrude gave a mock gasp.

'Oh my god, Lucinda, what dark magic was it?'

'Bloody awful, Elven, pixie, troubadour, god forsaken, wild magic,' Jim said, landing next to them. 'I flew around in circles so much I smashed into a window and slid down it. A sodding cat laughed so much he fell into a pot of custard. That Finn is a son of a biscuit and as for your Tal—'

'He's not my Tal—'

'I don't blame you after this. Bloody blacksmith.' Jim wobbled away, cursing to himself. Dafydd stood up and leant over, offering his hand. Still panting, Gertrude grabbed it and he pulled her up. Dafydd sketched a bow and Gertrude dropped into a deep curtsey with her hand to her chest.

'My lord.'

'My lady,' and smiling at her, he took his leave.

Feeling Tal's stare, she looked over and caught his eye. She dropped into a curtsey and smiled. After a moment, he bowed his head to her. Tal looked over at Finn and with a nod, they began to play again.

They played a lullaby. Finn's voice soared and Gertrude wondered at the beauty of it. It sounded like the star she had sung with, but there was a wild yearning as if for unnamed things, threaded through it. Tal joined in and, like their instruments, the deep voice, and the ethereal voice, entwined. Some people said goodbye and stepped out into the night. Others moved to the end of the kitchen and from a cupboard, pulled out pillows and blankets until the whole kitchen floor resembled a giant bed. People lay down and the cats lay between them.

Gertrude, Sam, and Lucinda wandered down and found a free corner. Sam snuggled in and after a moment, Lucinda jumped in between them. The song finished on a note that made Gertrude's skin tingle. Goosebumps broke out all over her skin. She closed her eyes, but it was no use. All she saw was Tal's face and the way his eyes had blazed when she had crawled over the table, to get to him.

It was going to be a long night.

CHAPTER 37

'**Z**eus, get out of the blasted way.'

The snarling voice shocked Gertrude awake and she bolted upright. Tal was trying to get into the stall they had been sleeping in. The enormous black horse that Gertrude had bowed to yesterday, stood across the entrance, like a gate with muscles. 'Where the hell have you been?'

Taking her time, Gertrude stood up and brushed the hay from her gown. Straightening, she met Tal's grey stare over the horse's back, but only just. The horse filled the entrance.

'We could not sleep in the kitchen, so we came in here.' In actual fact Gertrude had fidgeted so much last night – making Lucinda hiss – that she had been asked to leave – not very politely – by some grumpy villager. Not knowing where else to go, Sam had trotted off towards the stable where at least they would be warm and in a place they had already been.

'You stupid girl. Zeus could have killed you.'

'Zeus was not here when I chose this stall.' Tal raised his eyebrows.

'Zeus?' The stallion looked at Gertrude in a manner that could only be called sheepish. Laughing, she stepped forward and ran her hands down his long nose. The horse snuffled and buried his nose in her hands.

'Zeus?' Tal asked again.

'I wondered who had come in, so I went to have a look and when I saw who it was … well that crow was not much of a sentinel. He fell asleep and fell off his perch.'

'Oh my god, Jim.' Gertrude dropped to her knees and rummaged in the hay. 'You haven't stood on him have you, Zeus?' The hay beside Lucinda moved.

'Here I am. Panic over.' Jim burst free and shook his wings. Lucinda jumped back.

'Please tell me you have not slept next to me all night?'

'You made a nice pillow. I like you better when you're asleep. But you still smell.' Lucinda shuddered and Tal pushed around Zeus. He crouched down, opening his arms and Lucinda sprung into them. He stood up and let her nuzzle his neck.

'Do not disappear like that again, my dark darling. I was out of my mind with worry.' Gertrude was sick of herself for feeling jealous. She went back to stroking the black horse, but not before she had glimpsed his golden hooves.

'Zeus is very dangerous,' said Tal. 'He is not like the horses you have in your land.'

'Dangerous to my enemies,' the horse said. Gertrude dropped a kiss onto his nose.

'I think you are beautiful and thank you for looking after me. I had another friend like you, called Duke and he guarded me whilst I slept as well. You would have liked him. He is the fastest horse in my land. Once, he let me ride him. We were rescuing—'

'Go and get changed,' Tal snapped. 'You can't help Nell in that getup.'

'—Sam and Lucinda's kittens. Well, Lucinda's kittens. I don't mean that Sam and Lucinda had kittens together, that would just be silly. Maybe you will let me ride you one day?' Zeus jerked his head out of her hands and stepped backwards, narrowly missing Sam. Tal put Lucinda down and reaching forward, caught the horse's head.

'Zeus, it's all right, my love. No one has to ride you.' Turning to Gertrude he said,

'Get out. Now. Go and help Nell. Now, I said.' Gertrude tried to push around them but ended up pressing herself into Tal's back. With an impatient shake of his head, he hauled Zeus out of the way and she made her escape.

'Come and ride me this afternoon, flower bride.' Gertrude took in Zeus' huge frame. The thought of riding anything so powerful filled her with dread, but she realised she had just been given a gift, and Tal's face was worth it, so she gave a curtsy.

'Zeus, my friend, it would be a pleasure,' and trying to hide the tremble in her legs she made her way to Nell's kitchen.

CHAPTER 38

'**H**old those emotions!' Nell yelled at Gertrude. Gertrude stood by the kitchen fire, clenching her fists.

'Good morning, Nell,' she said through gritted teeth. 'I was ordered to come and help.' Nell clapped her hands in glee and came over carrying a bowl. She took out a ball of dough and placed it on the table in front of Gertrude.

'Knead.' Gertrude punched the dough. The table shook.

'Sorry, Nell.'

'Oh no, I pray for angry people in the morning. Bread is going to be good today, folks.' Some of her staff laughed. 'Sam, come with me. I will fetch your breakfast.' The kitchen was already in full swing, even though it was early. After pounding away for ten minutes, Gertrude felt the anger leave her. Dafydd brought her a steaming cup of something brown, which gave her a rush of energy, and Nell gave her a little sweet cake that tingled on her tongue. She wondered if she could still see the glowing lights around everyone and found when she relaxed her eyes she could. *I must thank Finn when I next see him. Mind you, I don't know how it can help with anything.*

The great arched kitchen windows were open and a myriad of little birds sat on the windowsills. Most of them radiated a brilliant blue light. They sang and chirped, whilst the kitchen staff came over with bits of cheese and bread. Gertrude realised the birds were giving snippets of news.

'A titbit for a titbit,' said a sparrow. Dafydd listened intently to a thrush. He suddenly jumped up and clapped his hands.

'Nell! Rhiannon has had a son. She has called him Pryderi.' Nell burst into tears, making two cats fall off the table.

'Well, of course she has.' She blew her nose so loudly another cat fell into a bowl of custard. 'Quick, a toast everyone.' Nell clapped her hands and little glasses of amber liquid appeared in front of everyone. Even the cats. 'To Rhiannon and Pryderi. May he blaze a light all his days.' Everyone with opposable thumbs raised their glasses and downed the drink in one. The cats lapped their glasses dry and then knocked them off the table. The rest of the staff threw their glasses onto the floor. Gertrude did the same. The broken glass vanished.

'I am going to stay here all day,' she sang. 'I love this kitchen.'

'Thank you, my lovely,' said Nell, 'but you are not staying here all day. Tal is going to take you out of the castle later.'

'Why?'

'To get some kitchen clothes and to show you around. You need to see what is out there. I think it is too soon, but Vivienne said you must be shown everything, and judging by the cold weather, the queen is on her way. The sooner we have you dressed in dowdy kitchen clothes and looking less like a queen, the sooner I will be able to breathe.'

'Can't you take me shopping?'

'Bless your heart, I never leave this kitchen.'

'You left last night.'

'Except at sunset. Now keep kneading. I have twenty more batches to do and—oh lordy.' The kitchen doors banged open and in strode Tal and Lucinda. Putting Lucinda down gently, Tal stood with his fists clenched, glowering at everyone. A muscle in his cheek flickered. Nell glanced at Gertrude and then back at him.

'Tal! Hold those emotions.' She waddled down the kitchen, coming back with two bowls. As she passed Gertrude, she winked.

'That's at least ten batches worth there.' Gertrude refused to look at him, but his kneading made the table shudder. Elaine appeared and glided over to him with his breakfast. Looking out of the corner of her eye, Gertrude watched as Elaine attempted to feed him. He jerked his head away, reminding her of Zeus' reaction. Elaine flounced off. Grinning, Gertrude carried on kneading and did three more batches. Wiping her hands on her green gown, she looked down at the mess. She definitely needed some other clothes. If only she was not going with Tal.

'Sam, Lucinda, I'm going out to find Jim. I want to know what is going on.'

'I would like to know what is going on too,' a smooth voice said. Nell shoved Sam under the table and the kitchen came to a standstill.

A tall thin man stood by the door that led into the castle. A hook nose dominated the man's cruel face. His little dark eyes flitted around the room, taking everyone and everything in. He wore black tails and a red waistcoat, which made him look like a butler. He looked ridiculous and yet he dominated the room, commanding attention. Two men came in, carrying trays with cloths draped over them. They set their load down on the table and, with a bow, walked out. The thin man slowly looked around the room. A sparrow squeaked. The man sneered.

'I will have order.' He clicked his fingers. All the birds flew away and the cats scattered. Nell opened her arms.

'Come back, friends, please,' she whispered and the birds fluttered back onto the windowsills. The cats jumped up on the table and glared at the tall man, their tails flicking. Nell walked up to the man and put her head back to look at him. 'This is my domain, Edric. Now say what you want and kindly leave.'

'Your domain, wench? Everything in this castle and beyond belongs to her majesty … even you. This is her domain, not yours.' Tal moved in front of Nell. Edric flinched. 'Bit unhygienic cooking with the blacksmith, isn't it? I hope you made him wash.'

'I will wash myself thoroughly when you leave,' Tal replied.

'Hurry up, Edric, I have a castle to feed,' Nell said. The butler's eyes flickered back to Nell and he smiled.

'You have her majesty and her troops to feed. She returns tonight and she wishes you to cook these.' He whipped off the cloth covering one of the trays and Gertrude leaned forward to see what was in there. She instantly regretted it.

In the tray, lying as if asleep, were three spring lambs.

'Born only yesterday,' Edric said. 'Killed this morning. Oh, you should have heard their stupid mothers bleating ... heart breaking.' Nell sagged and Tal held her up. 'Her majesty wants them slow-cooked in herbs, so you better get a move on. And do not overcook them, you know her majesty has a tender mouth.'

'Get out,' Tal said. Edric stood, looking down his nose. A movement caught Gertrude's eye.

'Oh my god, one of them is still alive.' She jumped onto the table to get at it. Edric pulled her off and brought his fist down onto the lamb's head, shattering the skull and covering Gertrude in blood. He did not stop but grinned as he punched the lamb again. Gertrude flew at him, pulling his arm back. He turned on her, slapping her across the face with such force she fell to the floor. Sam sprang from his hiding place reaching for Edric's throat, but Tal got there first. Sam had to make do with an arm as Tal bent Edric backwards onto the table and squeezed his throat with both hands. The butler's legs thrashed and the rattling noises from his throat cut through the silence.

'Tal,' Nell said softly. 'Tal, my love, stop. If he dies, it will be the worse for us. Tal? Sam? Please stop.' However, Tal and Sam carried on as if she had not spoken.

'Tal, Sam, please stop.' Gertrude gasped. Tal instantly let go of the man. He made a gesture and Sam let go too. Edric slid to the floor, gasping for breath, and clutching his throat with one hand and his ripped sleeve with the other. Tal crouched down next to him.

'You do not touch her; you do not look at her and you do

not think of her. I will know it if you do. Thank you, Sam, for your help.' He stepped over the butler's prone body and walked out of the kitchen, squeezing Nell's shoulder as he passed. Gertrude was now at eye level with Edric and she recoiled at the hatred she saw in his eyes.

Edric slowly got to his feet. Every member of staff had a kitchen knife in their hands. He straightened his waistcoat and pulled himself up to his full height. He pointed at Sam and then brought his arm up making a slicing motion across his throat. With his back ramrod straight, he walked out through the door he had come. Nell dropped to her knees and pulled Gertrude into her arms.

'Oh, by the Mother, my flower, are you ok?' Gertrude nodded unable to speak. 'Dafydd, a cloth please, and fetch the arnica.' Dafydd ran and came back with a damp cloth and a little blue bottle. Nell poured a few drops onto the cloth and pressed it to Gertrude's burning cheek.

'That has made my mind up … it's definitely time to go. No more spying, no more sneaking around. Edric won't let that go unpunished for long and he has seen Sam. Your coming here has changed everything. There now, all better. There won't be any bruising. Let's wipe that blood off you.' She dabbed at Gertrude's face and then pulled her into a bone crushing hug. 'Now off you go to market. Today was meant to be an education for you, to show you what you are up against. My sorrow that you had to learn so soon and in such a painful way.'

'But Tal—'

'—Will be waiting for you outside. Don't press him or ask questions. Don't even thank him … not yet. Just watch and listen to what he shows you. I will see you back here.' Dafydd pulled Nell up and then helped up Gertrude. Nell wrapped a brown cloak around her. Sam moved to go, but Nell stopped him. 'Sorry, my golden boy. They are going out of the castle and the law demands that any dog is to be killed on sight. Edric has now seen you, so I want you by me at all times. I have grown very fond of you.' She scratched his ears.

'I will be all right, Sam, honestly.' Gertrude said, taking in the brown pleading eyes. 'I don't want you putting yourself at risk.'

'I did that the moment I met you,' Sam replied.

And to that, Gertrude could not answer.

CHAPTER 39

Gertrude found Tal outside the kitchen.
He stood with his hands on his hips and his head tilted back, looking at the sky. Wrapping Nell's cloak tighter around her, Gertrude took the opportunity to study him. She took in the proud face, the sculptured lips, and long eyelashes. His black hair hung down behind him in thick waves and she had to stop herself from reaching forward and running her hands through the silken mass.

Tal is like a storm. Beautiful and exciting to look at, but you would not want to be caught up in it. Sensing her at last, he let out a deep sigh and brought his head round, imprisoning her with his stare. She waited for him to speak.

'Right, rules. You keep your hair up and your head down. If anyone speaks to you, let me handle it. I will tell them you are a mute. You stay close to me at all times. You do not leave my side. Ever. And you do everything I say.' Gertrude raised her eyebrows.

'Everything. Do you understand?' Gertrude nodded. With another sigh, he strode towards her and pulled up her hood, pushing her mass of hair into it.

'You stick out like a sore thumb.' Gertrude bit back a retort, mindful of what Nell had said. This man had nearly killed another man for hurting her and she did not mind admitting she was in awe of him. She gave him a smile, hoping she looked friendly.

'Stop smiling. Where we are going, no one smiles.' He turned and headed off towards the drawbridge.

Running, to keep up with Tal's long strides, and wrinkling her nose at the stagnant water in the moat, Gertrude finally saw what was beyond the castle.

It was a wasteland. Over the drawbridge, there had once been a wood surrounding the castle. Blackened trees, like grotesque, burnt corpses twisted into strange shapes, reached up to the sky, as if pleading for mercy. They smelt of burnt flesh and looking amongst them, Gertrude could see human and animal forms. She passed a huge mound of charred corpses, piled on top of each other. Flies buzzed around them and the smell of rotting flesh stuck in her nostrils and the back of her throat. Looking closer, she could make out what they were.

She vomited.

Dogs. Hundreds of them. Their skeletal jaws were open as if screaming. For a moment, she thought she heard them and shook her head to drive the pleading voices out. Tal handed her a handkerchief and she wiped her mouth. Looking up at him, she saw him gazing at the dogs, a muscle flickering in his cheek. How worse for him? He had lived here. She wanted to say something but what could she say? She murmured a thank you and straightened up.

'Stay close,' Tal said and they moved off again.

As Gertrude entered the market, she felt her mood lift a little. There were brightly coloured flags and bunting on the stalls. However, looking closer, she saw that the stallholders were sullen and rough looking. Some looked downright fierce and she moved closer to Tal. They grinned and grimaced as she passed them. A man stepped out, halting them on their path, his face splitting into a toothless grin. A dirty bandage covered his head. His wound oozed yellow and Gertrude could smell the pus and his body odour. She put her hand up to her mouth to stop herself from retching again.

'Something for the pretty lady, sir. Some earrings perhaps or maybe this bracelet.' He held up a delicate rose gold bracelet, studded with red stones. Gertrude moved to touch it, but Tal reached forward and snatched it out of the man's grasp. He turned it over in his hand.

'Where did you get this?'

'I made it.'

'I will ask you again. Where did you get this?'

'I made it—' Tal's hand pressed a point on the man's neck and the stallholder fell to his knees with a cry.

'I bought it. It's mine. I was given it. That butler at the castle – Eric something – he give it me. I bought it off him.'

'It was not his to give. This belongs to my aunt.' A crowd had gathered around them and the man scrambled to his knees pointing at Tal.

'Robbery! I am being robbed. Help.'

'You'll get over it,' and grabbing Gertrude by the hand, Tal walked on, ignoring the man's outraged cries and the mutterings of the crowd.

'Which aunt?' asked Gertrude, running to keep up.

'Vivienne. The Elven made this for her on one of her birthdays. Edric has her stuff. Remind me to go back to that stall and check for more. She loved this bracelet.' He stopped and turning to her, rolled back her sleeve, and put the bracelet on her. The minute it touched her skin, the stones glowed.

'You can keep it for her and give it to her when she comes back.' He held her wrist looking down at the bracelet.

'Do you think she will come back?'

'Yes … she has to. She has too much to do and I refuse to think she is …' He still held her wrist in a firm grip. Gertrude became aware of the heat coming from his hand. They stood still for a while and he seemed lost in thought, unaware that his thumb caressed the delicate skin underneath her wrist. Hearing the catch of her breath, he blinked at her and dropped her hand. He strode off, causing her to run after him.

She kept a respectful distance, as being near him was causing her head to ache. It was like the intense pressure before a thunderstorm and she did not want to be the one that caused the storm to break. Tal came to a stop and Gertrude just managed to avoid banging into him.

'Raine,' he said quietly, and stepping aside, he revealed a woman standing by a market stall.

She was tall and slender and looked at Gertrude without smiling. Gertrude raised her chin and looked the woman square in the eyes. After a long moment, the woman gave her a nod and beckoned to her. Up close, the woman's eyes were citrine coloured. Her mass of white hair was twisted up in intricate coils. It framed a delicate, fine boned face.

'We have not much time and you are slimmer than I was told. Here are your clothes. A kitchen outfit for Nell's, complete with a cap to hide all that hair and a little something from me. A gown that I have been keeping for you. I hope you will forgive an old lady's indulgence.' The woman smiled, but there was sadness in the smile and Gertrude did not feel cheered.

'Thank you,' she said, taking the offered bag and bobbing a curtsey. Tal grabbed her by the elbow and shook his head.

'We are always being watched, and stallholders do not get curtseyed to.' The woman looked at Tal.

'Do not scold the child. She knows who I am, even if she does not realise it.'

'With all due respect Aunt—' The woman gave an impatient gesture with her hand.

'Until we meet again, child.' She turned and went behind her stall, the interview plainly finished. Gertrude gathered the bag to her chest and waited. Tal stared at the woman as if willing her to look up, but she ignored him. With a sigh, he turned and went still. A strange look came over his face. Gertrude followed his gaze.

Three knights on horseback were making their way through the market. The first two knights wore armour that shone, even in the weak sunlight. The first knight's armour glimmered gold, the second knight's shone a lustrous black. However, Tal's yearning look was for the third knight. His red armour did not shine. It was dull and dented. Gertrude found her eyes drawn to the red knight and, as if sensing their gaze, the red knight stopped and turned his head towards them. His visor hid his face, but Gertrude felt the touch of that look and her breath stuck in her throat. She trembled and willed herself to stay upright. The knight moved on, releasing her.

'Who are they?'

'Agravaine, Balin and Rufus, the queen's most loyal and feared knights.' He gave her a sharp look. 'I am sure you would love a knight in shining armour.' Her eyes followed the red knight.

'On the contrary, give me the knight with the armour that is dull and dented. At least I know he can fight.' Tal raised an eyebrow.

'You will see them at the feast tonight. Cat will have told you that as a warrior, you must know two things; know thyself and know thine enemy. Those three are the enemy.' Yet as he spoke, his eyes followed the red knight's progress as if he could not bear to look away.

'A robbery! I have been robbed. Good knights, please I beg you,' a voice rang out.

Tal pushed Gertrude behind him. The stallholder, who had lost the bracelet, held onto the stirrup of the black knight. The black knight brought his gloved fist down on the man's face. The man stumbled and fell to the ground holding his nose. Gertrude looked round to find Raine, but she and her stall had vanished. Hearing the man's yells, she turned her attention back to him. He scrambled up and bowed several times to the black knight.

'Good sir, sorry, sir. Please I have been robbed.' The gold knight lifted his visor.

'Balin, do not be in such a foul mood.' The gold knight's voice drawled, as if already bored of the whole thing. 'The poor peasant is obviously in some distress. Speak then, but for god's sake don't touch him. Sir Balin hates to be touched … unless you're under ten that is,' and he laughed.

'I have been here selling my wares like any good honest man

—' the man jumped back as the black knight aimed a kick at him.

'He is lying, Agravaine. There are no honest men in this market.' The gold knight chuckled, his shoulders moving up and down.

'Carry on, dear chap, but for your own sake, get to the point.'

'Him! Him over there with that redhead. He's the one who robbed me.' All heads turned towards Tal. Tal paid them no heed. He still gazed at the red knight who, in turn, gazed back at him from beneath the visor.

'Well, if it isn't the blacksmith,' the gold knight said. 'Come forward, man. That's right, so we can see you.' Tal walked towards them. He moved with such grace, that he looked out of place amongst the rough crowd that had gathered. The gold knight leaned forward on his horse. 'Now then, this man accuses you of robbing him. Is this right?'

'How can I steal what is rightfully mine?'

'You will address Sir Agravaine with respect,' the black knight said and he pulled his fist back. As the fist came down Tal, almost as an afterthought, stepped aside, causing the black knight to fall off his horse. The crowd burst into laughter. The knight leapt to his feet, drew his sword, and beheaded the man nearest to him. Balin kicked the head into the crowd.

No one moved. Turning to Tal, the knight stepped forward and took a swipe, meaning to give Tal the same punishment. Tal bent back and the sword whistled through the air where his head had been. Cursing, the knight swiped again. Tal sidestepped, ducked, and twisted away from each of the knight's desperate attempts to attack him. The black knight panted as he swung and stabbed, but he was always met with thin air. The red knight kept still, but the gold knight shifted uneasily in his saddle.

'Balin, for god's sake make an end of it. I'm hungry and that hag in the kitchen may be uglier than a stuck pig, but her food surpasses anything that we have had lately.'

Tal stopped and looked up at the gold knight.

'That is my aunt you are referring to and you will address the Lady Nell with respect.' With a roar, Balin grabbed his chance and flew at Tal.

Tal spun round and with his hands caught the sword's blade. He twisted the sword out of Balin's hands. Balin fell to the ground and Tal stepped over him, placing the knight's own sword at his throat. He turned back to Agravaine.

'As I said, that is my aunt you are talking about and she deserves respect. And the bracelet I have been accused of stealing belongs to another aunt. I am her rightful next of kin and the bracelet, in her absence, rightfully belongs to me. So again, I ask you, how can I steal what is rightfully mine?' The gold knight moved his horse back.

'This bores me. Keep the cursed bracelet. Balin, get up,' but Tal did not move the blade from the black knight's neck. The gold knight leant down.

'Blacksmith, you are lucky I am in a good mood, and who wouldn't be after the sport I have had this afternoon, but do not push that luck. Put the sword aside.' Tal tightened his grip on the sword. The red knight lifted his visor. From where she stood, Gertrude could not see his face, but she heard him.

'Let him go, blacksmith. You fought well.' At the sound of the rich, deep, voice, Tal's head snapped up. The red knight inclined his head. Tal moved back, lowering the blade. The black knight scrambled up off the ground and reached his hand out for his sword. With a deep bow, Tal handed it back to him.

'This is not over,' growled Balin and mounted his horse. With a kick to its flanks, he took off at speed.

'Come, Rufus, we better get going or that oaf will eat everything.' With a flick of his reins, the gold knight moved off at a trot.

The red knight did not move. Tal and him stared at each other and then, at an unspoken command, the red knight's horse walked off.

'God, you can bloody fight.' The stallholder wiped his bloodied nose on his sleeve. He shook his head in admiration.

Tal looked at him.

'I am sorry that black-hearted bastard hit you. It is not your fault you are here. I hope this covers any costs,' and he dropped some coins into the man's hand.

'Thank you, sir. God, when I was brought over here, I was promised riches and enough girls to satisfy me.'

'Where were you before?' The stallholder grinned.

'At another majesty's dwelling.' Tal frowned.

'Jail,' Gertrude said, walking over to him.

'And what were you jailed for?' Tal asked. The man looked over at Gertrude and licked his lips.

'I like little girls.' Gertrude turned away. It took Tal under a minute to render the man into unconsciousness.

CHAPTER 40

Walking back towards the castle, Gertrude could not stand the silence between them anymore.

She cleared her throat.

'All your aunts are lovely. Raine, Nell and Vivienne. Is Cat an aunt?' Tal barked out a laugh.

'Aunty Cat? I would love to see her reaction if I called her that. Yes, in a way she is … or more like an older sister – a bullying older sister. I still bear the scars.'

'Did she teach you how to fight?'

'Cat teaches everyone how to fight. I can still hear her voice ringing in my ears, "Never leave your guard down. Keep your centre of gravity close to the ground—"'

'"Bend your knees over your toes."'

'You too?'

'Yes, drill after drill. I miss her terribly. Where is she? I thought I would have seen her by now?'

'Tomorrow. It is all arranged, but let us not talk here. Just be patient.'

'I am trying to be, but I feel that everyone knows what is going on except me and I am getting tired of it. Like those knights. You tell me to learn everything about them and that they are the enemy, but how am I supposed to make a difference to anything if Cat and Vivienne can't? I mean that gold one seems cruel and the black one? He's an animal and—'

'What did you say?' Tal halted and turned to face her. They

had reached the burnt forest but it was the look on Tal's face that made her mouth go dry.

'It's a figure of speech,' she stammered. 'I did not mean anything by it, and I am shocked myself that I even said it. I am sorry if I have offended you ...' Tal's grey eyes grew dark.

'And therein lies the problem. It is that attitude that has caused all this. And if even *you* can forget, then what hope does humanity have?' He gestured to the blackened forest. 'People from that other gods-forsaken Britain think they are better than the trees and the animals. Do you know, we never even had a name for animal, until the queen's kind came? They are our brothers and sisters, our four-legged siblings.'

'We're not all bad, in that other Britain. There are some of us who are good.'

'You mean the artists and the poets? The witches and the seers? Oh yes, and we know what that world does to anyone who sees beyond the veil. You persecute them and hunt them down. You kill them ... or they kill themselves, because the few people who have faced the truth of your banal existence, must be terminated for the greater good.

'Those who believe in magic, and the Elven and the unicorns are torn apart, either with longing or being shunned by your society.

'You kill anything you cannot understand. You kill plants and your furred and feathered brothers and sisters without a thought. You feed yourselves on junk; junk for the body and junk for the mind. If you cannot see it, you dismiss it. If you cannot understand it, you destroy it. You shut yourselves in boxes and then find ways to numb yourselves in order to cope.' He turned away from her and looked out across the burnt forest, a muscle flickering in his cheek.

'This was once one world,' he said softly. 'Elven and unicorns used to walk on your world too. But you betrayed yourselves. You turned your back on nature. With your pristine gods, you sought to conquer nature. Now, one of your kind is trying to do that to my world.

271

'This was the last sanctuary, a place of love and life. Now it is being destroyed by a human who is not content on adding to the destruction in her own world, but has to unleash her own vision of hell onto mine.' His voice cracked. Gertrude moved closer to touch him, but then lowered her hand.

'Tal, I am not one of them.' He turned and stared at her.

'But you are not one of us either. Not anymore.'

She turned and ran.

She ran straight over the drawbridge, through the gate, passed the guards and even when Sam came bounding out of Nell's kitchen, she did not stop until she reached the stables.

'Zeus? Is that offer of a ride still there?' The black horse stepped forward.

'I have been waiting for you all afternoon, flower.'

'Gertrude, do not do this,' Sam said. Lucinda ran into the stable and jumped up on a table.

'What is she doing?'

'She is going out on Zeus. You heard Tal. He said he was dangerous.'

'Only to my enemies,' Zeus said, tossing his huge head.

'Point taken, sir, but Gertrude, you do not know how to ride.'

'I rode Duke.'

'And nearly died, you told me.'

'This Duke, what did he teach you?' asked Zeus.

'Grip with my thighs, hold onto his mane, listen to my body.'

'Then you know how to ride. Get on. What are you looking for?'

'A bridle.'

'I would rather you didn't.'

'Gertrude, I shall tell Tal,' Lucinda said.

'Tell him. He hates me.' Lucinda shook her head.

'It is not hate. I have seen the way he looks at you. It is the same look, no doubt, that I have when I have spotted a wounded bird.' Gertrude picked up a stool and standing on it, pulled herself up onto Zeus' back.

'I am coming with you,' Sam said.

'No, Sam, stay here, you will get yourself killed. I just need to get away from here.'

'I am still coming with you.'

'Sam—' but she did not get to finish her sentence. Zeus surged forward and her speech whipped away from her mouth as the black horse took off.

I am going to die. Zeus galloped out of the stable. The guards saw them coming and shouted. They ran to the gates to close them, but Zeus sped through them, missing the metal by inches. They clattered over the drawbridge and then turned left towards the market. Gertrude saw the astonished look on Tal's face as she passed him and felt a burst of delight. They left him standing, open-mouthed, in a cloud of dust. People scattered in all directions as they sped through the stalls. Zeus followed the path around. Fear and instinct made Gertrude hold on with her thighs, as he made the sharp turns.

'Match your heartbeat to mine,' the horse said. Feeling her heart back in her chest, she focused on its beat. She laid her hands on Zeus' neck and closed her eyes. She reached down and felt his strong hammering heart, through his skin. Her heart stumbled and fluttered like a butterfly's wing. It paused and then broke into the horse's beat.

Only then did she open her eyes and smile at the sheer exhilaration of riding a wild horse, whose heart answered her own. They rode on and on and Gertrude never wanted the wild ride to end, but eventually, Zeus came to a stop on a hill. Gertrude looked down onto a wasteland of sand and blackened tree stumps. In the distance, water glimmered.

'I'm Elven,' Zeus said.

'Elven?'

'Yes, that explains my golden hooves that you have been wondering about. I am also a spy.'

'A spy?'

'Who better to spy on these dumb creatures than another *dumb creature*'? These cretins do not take any notice of us with wings or four legs. We let them ride us and work us and all the while, we report back. The base of the resistance is in the castle. Is that not genius? Morgan said the best place to hide is in plain sight, so that is what we do. Of course, I am now an outcast amongst my people.'

'Why?'

'The Elven have retreated. Queen Mab called us back. She has seen this before and no pleading on Morgan or Vivienne's part would persuade her otherwise.'

'Why did you come then?'

'Finn. Tal. Nell. In that order.' A question hovered on Gertrude's lips when Zeus' head came up.

'Company.'

'Oh god, who?' Zeus put his head to one side.

'Apollo and Tal.' Gertrude looked down the hill.

'You cannot escape flower. We are on an island. But we can have a race.' He began to circle. Gertrude could see a cloud of dust moving towards them.

'They are very fast.' Zeus snorted.

'That upstart with his white gleaming coat and silver hooves? Yes, he is fast. However, we are faster. You and I are one. Say it.'

'You and I are one.' Zeus stopped circling and faced the oncoming pair.

'Say it again. Close your eyes. Chant it. You and I are one.'

'You and I are one. You and I are one.'

'Feel me beneath you. Feel my heart beat in you. I am you. You are me.' A slow smile spread across Gertrude's face.

'I have you.'

'You are ready. Open your eyes, for they are almost upon us.' Gertrude focused on Apollo and Tal galloping towards them. She gripped her knees.

'Not yet,' but she felt Zeus tremble. Her body joined in, until they were both quivering beings of energy, waiting to be released.

'Hold ... hold ...' Apollo and Tal came over the crest of the hill. Tal opened his mouth to shout.

'Now!' Zeus wheeled away, moving from standstill to full gallop in the time it took Gertrude to draw her next breath.

Zeus had been holding back she realised.

This was not riding. This was flying. Her hood fell back, her hair came undone, streaming out behind her, and yet she was not afraid. Her heart rate rose a little, but that was because Zeus' had. As they came down the hill, the ground levelled out and Zeus exploded forward.

'*How are we doing?*' he said, but no words came from his mouth. She shifted her mind to allow him room there and she heard him sigh at his own power. She looked behind her.

'*They are still following and seem to be gaining,*' she answered with her mind. At least Zeus had had a rest. How was Apollo still keeping up?

'*Excuse me. Forget about them. Give yourself over to me. They do not exist. Only you and I exist.*' Gertrude turned and looked down at the flying black mane and put all thoughts of Tal out of her head.

Where did she begin and Zeus end? Was he galloping or was it her? When he made a sharp move, to avoid some twisted vegetation, she knew he was going to move a split second before he did. They raced on through the wasteland.

Gertrude jumped as something moved at the corner of her eye. Somehow, incredibly, Apollo and Tal had moved alongside. Fascinated, she watched as Tal swung his leg over and pulled his knees up close to his chest. Holding onto Apollo's mane, he waited until he was level with Zeus.

Then he jumped.

He landed behind her. Her heart stumbled and fluttered and she knew she had lost the connection with Zeus. Tal reached around her and placed his hand on the horse's neck.

'*Slow, my love.*' Gertrude shook her head, as she heard Tal in her mind. Zeus slowed and came to a standstill, his breath coming out in gasps. Apollo drew near in the same state.

'I would have beaten you, Apollo, if he had not jumped on me and broken the connection.'

'You know I am the fastest horse Zeus ... well except one other.' The white stallion said this without any arrogance. 'But even so, that was the most brilliant race I have ever had in my life. Legend you are and legend you remain.' The white horse put his leg out and bowed deep. Zeus tossed his head and then went still.

'Nay lad, legend you are and legend you will become.' Watching this exchange Gertrude realised she had leant back onto Tal. She could feel his heartbeat in her back. She leapt down from Zeus and ran across the plain.

'Will you stop running away from me?' Tal jumped down and caught her by the waist.

'Get off me, you son of a motherless goat.' Tal let go of her, only to catch her by the shoulders and turn her round to face him.

'One of Jim's I suppose?'

'Yes. I could do with Jim now. Jim! Jim? Come and curse this ... this ...'

'Fudge knocker? Blasted farnation? What about son of a sheep lover? Although having said that, there has never been anything wrong with loving sheep.'

'Spoken like a Welshman.'

'I am not Welsh. I do not think I have ever been Welsh.'

'Mores the pity. What do you want, Tal?' Tal let go of her shoulders and looked down at her.

'To say I am sorry. I meant every word—'

'That's not much of an apology.'

'—except the last bit. You are one of us. You would not have been able to ride Zeus if you were not. And you belong here.'

'You hate me.' His eyes flickered and grew hard.

'Yes. With all my being.' She felt an overwhelming sense of sorrow as she stared into the grey eyes, but she could no more read the depths of them as she could read the clouds.

A movement drew her attention away.

'Sam!' She crouched down and the golden retriever leapt into her arms. After licking and kissing each other, until they both had wet faces, Gertrude sat up cradling him in her lap.

'You did not run all the way, did you? Were you seen?'

'No, I had a lift. We were galloping so fast no one would have seen me in Tal's arms.' He looked up at Tal. 'He dropped me at the bottom of the hill, as he knew he would have to race to catch you. He did not want me falling off. I am safe out here as no one comes this far out.' Gertrude glanced up at Tal, but he was not looking at her. He was looking at the ground where they had been standing. His stare made Gertrude push Sam from her lap and look round. Where Tal had caught her, there was a circle of little white flowers.

'How pretty.' She got up and went over to them. Crouching down she brushed their petals releasing a sweet fragrance. Putting her ear to them, she listened.

'Nothing. They must be newborns. It is strange. I did not notice them.'

'That is because they were not here a moment ago,' Tal said in a strange voice.

'Are they rare?' Tal seemed to be having trouble speaking. Zeus walked over and nuzzled her shoulder.

'Little flower, nothing has grown here in sixteen years.'

'Well, in that case, flowers, you are very welcome.' She leant over to brush them again. This time she heard them sigh and she laughed.

'Stand up.' Tal stood over her. 'Please.' He stretched out his hand. Hesitating a moment, she took it and allowed herself to be pulled up. For a moment their chests touched and she moved back to avoid any awkwardness.

'Walk over there, to the remains of that tree.' She walked over to where Tal pointed. She turned to face him.

'Now what?' but no one was looking at her. All eyes were on the ground. She looked down and saw the miracle happen.

Right along the path, where she had walked, white flowers popped out, like stars in the early evening sky. Where there had been sand, now lay a trail of white flowers, releasing their sweet scent and beginning to sigh and laugh. Tal's eyes shone.

'We have to get back. We speak of this to no one, understand?' Zeus shook his head.

'Flowers …. flowers growing on the plain of destruction. I thought I would never see the day.'

'Let us go. Now.' Tal threw his arm over Apollo and said over his shoulder, 'We will walk part of the way, to give these two gods a rest. I will take Sam when it becomes busy.' Zeus did not follow. He walked up to Gertrude and bowed deep before her.

'Legend you were and legend you will be again.' He pushed her arm until she raised it to him. They turned and walked away, leaving the white flowers sighing softly in the breeze.

CHAPTER 41

The kitchen was in an uproar again, when they got back. Nell was yelling orders and whipping up mixtures in several bowls at once. Gertrude sat by the fire, grateful for its warmth, as the day had grown colder. On the way back, the stallholders in the marketplace had been packing up. The people kept glancing at the dark clouds that gathered over the castle. Gertrude sat with a half-peeled carrot in her hand and watched, as the chefs, the maids and the cats all moved with speed and grace. She itched her side, as the heavy coarse dress rubbed at her skin. The outfit Raine had given her, was two sizes too big. She had found a piece of string in the stable to act as a belt. Tal had taken one glance at it and declared it showed off her waist too much. He ordered her to take it off and then stormed out, saying he had the soldiers' horses to attend to. She felt dowdy and heavy and it did not help that Elaine was flouncing around, pulling down her blouse to show off her smooth white shoulders. Elaine had been prancing and preening all afternoon and when Gertrude had asked Dafydd why the girl was so happy, he had grinned.

'The soldiers are back.'

'But they are the enemy.'

'Still men and Elaine loves to be admired.' Gertrude sought out Dafydd now and found him staring out of the window. She went to call him, but his name caught in her throat. He had become unnaturally still as he looked up into the sky. Slipping off her stool, she fought her way through the darting bodies to arrive at his side. Following his gaze, she saw the dark clouds hovering over the castle. Nell came to join them and then Dafydd made a small noise as the first snowflake floated down from the dark sky and landed on the ground. It did not melt but lay there until it was joined by another, and then another.

'And so, she returns,' whispered Nell. Dafydd reached across Gertrude and brought her and Nell into a hug, holding them in his trembling arms.

* * *

Nell had braided Gertrude's hair so tight, her head hurt. She had tried to tuck the hair under her cap, but it kept trying to escape. Nell had protested about Gertrude seeing the queen, but Tal silenced her, saying knowledge was power. Nell could not argue with that.

And so, Gertrude found herself standing in the great hall, pressed up against a stone wall, awaiting the arrival of the queen. Dafydd stood to her left and Tal stood in front of her. Shielded as she was, she could see the blue crystal throne that dominated the great hall. Elven made, Dafydd had told her. It looked dull and lifeless.

Outside the clouds were so dark, it looked like twilight, even though it was the middle of the afternoon. Crystals lamps, set into the walls, gave out a faint, half-hearted glow. They offered no comfort with their wan light. Banners hung along the length of the hall, high above, with the same design as the flags Gertrude had seen outside. The dark shape of the woman, whose hair streamed out behind her, seemed wild and untamed and, despite being fearful, Gertrude's curiosity outweighed her fear. She wanted to see this queen with her own eyes.

A hush descended on the hall as the temperature plummeted. Something soft fell onto Gertrude's nose and she wiped it off. Then something fell on her cheek. She looked up at the high vaulted ceiling and watched, as snowflakes fell. No fanfare sounded, no one made an announcement, but as one, the queen's subjects bowed as a tall, graceful figure swept down the centre of the hall.

The queen wore a hooded cloak of dark blue, trimmed with white fur. Gertrude relaxed her eyes and tried to see which colour light surrounded her but there was only a swirling darkness. She quickly looked at the congregation and found, to her shock, she could no longer see the colourful lights around people. It was as if the queen's darkness had not only swallowed all the light but the ability to *see* the light.

As the queen passed, the crystal lamps flared into light. Dafydd's hand came up and forced Gertrude's head down into a bow. There was complete silence, for the queen's footfalls did not make any noise. Then as one, the whole room came out of their bow.

The queen's hands came up and pushed back the fur-trimmed hood. She shook out her hair and it fell to her knees. The frost white hair shone with highlights of silver. It glimmered, like the crystals that burned in the walls. Her pale face was exquisite, almost childlike in its fragile beauty. Her lips were full and red and the blue eyes glittered like midnight frost as she took in the whole room with a wintry glance.

And then the queen smiled.

Gertrude's mouth went dry. Her heart hammered so loudly, she felt sure someone would hear it. A cold sweat broke over her skin and she shook. She sunk down onto the floor. Tal instinctively stepped back, closer to her, as did Dafydd, to shield her from prying eyes. Hidden from view, she pressed her burning forehead to the cold stone floor, trying to breathe deeply. Waves of nausea and panic crashed over her.

For she knew who the woman was. The woman, whose beauty shone like a star in winter. From the moment the glacial eyes had flashed and the red lips had curved upwards, it had confirmed, what she realised she had always known.

The Queen of Albion was her grandmother.

CHAPTER 42

The queen sank down onto the throne.

It flamed brilliant blue at her touch. She gave a slight inclination of her head and footsteps echoed through the hall. Striding down the aisle, walked the black knight. He bowed and stood, legs astride, arms crossed, on the step below the dais. Dafydd pulled Gertrude to her feet and she had time to take in the black knight's hawk-like nose, black beard, and small black eyes. He laid his hand on the sword that, only that morning, Tal had pointed at his throat. Gertrude took strength from the image. At least he was not invincible.

'Sit,' chimed the queen. Chairs scraped as people settled themselves. Tal looked at Dafydd and with a nod, they swapped places. Gertrude swayed as she sat down and Tal put an arm across her, to hold her in place.

'Breathe,' he whispered, never taking his eyes away from the seated figure at the top of the hall. Gertrude took in gulps of air, but the trembling would not stop. Dafydd turned round in his seat and pressed a small brown bottle into her shaking hands.

'Drink this.' She took the cork out and tipped the contents into her mouth. At once, the trembling ceased and a sense of calm came over her. She reached over and squeezed Dafydd's shoulder. Dafydd grinned.

'Thank Nell, later.' Tal grabbed her hand off Dafydd and placed it back on her lap, all the while not looking at her. Gertrude did not blame him. She could not tear her eyes away from her grandmother either.

'Proceed,' the queen said.

'Bring in the first tribute,' Balin said. A scrawny man came shuffling down the aisle, followed by a little girl who skipped. She had dirty blonde hair that fell to her waist in ringlets. Despite being thin and filthy, she was a pretty child. She stood, singing to herself, oblivious of the looks she attracted. The man dropped to his knees and pulled the little girl down with him. Their noses scraped the floor and they stayed there until the queen gave an impatient gesture with her hand.

'Get up,' Balin said.

'Your Most Highly Esteemed Majesty. Your beauty, as they say, is—'

'Who says?' asked the queen. The man wrung his hands.

'Poets, songwriters and the like. Your Majesty—'

'Quote me something.' The man looked down at his hands but the girl jumped forward.

'They say your beauty is like a star at midnight. They say your lips are as red as the twilight rose. They say your eyes sparkle like snowflakes on diamonds.' The girl gave a clumsy curtsey. The queen gave her a half smile and leant forward.

'And tell me, child, do they say I am the fairest in the land?'

'Oh yes ... yes ... except for—'

'Yes, Your Majesty, of course they do,' interrupted the man, but the queen's eyes did not leave the little girl's face.

'Except for ...?'

'Except for she who will bring back spring and summer. The flower bride, the land's beloved.' The girl hummed and twirled. The queen raised a hand and the girl froze, mid-turn, with her thin arms stretched out and her head tilted back. Swinging her gaze back to the scrawny man, the queen raised one white eyebrow.

'Forgive me, Your Majesty. She's my sister's child and she's a bit strange, but I thought she could work in your kitchens, which I have heard are the best in the land. Or perhaps she could run errands for you.'

'I have Balin for that,' said the queen and Balin flushed.

'She doesn't know what she's saying. She's always talking to herself and seeing things, but her mother is dead and—' Balin leapt off the step.

'You dare to bring a retarded child to the queen, expecting her to feed and clothe it?' Drawing his fist back, Balin hit the man in the face. Standing over him, the black knight shouted,

'What on earth do you think the queen would do with a child? She hates children.'

'Balin, on the other hand, loves them. Would you like a gift, Balin?' The queen's voice was soft and sweet, but Gertrude felt only horror at its sound.

Balin stepped over to the motionless girl and walked around her. He poked her once and came to a stop, in front of her upturned face. Leaning forward he licked her from chin to forehead and wiped his mouth.

'A bit dirty, but nothing a good bath won't sort out.'

'And no doubt I can leave that to you. So shall it be. The girl is yours. But Balin … I have no wish to see her again.'

'Your Majesty,' he said with a bow, 'no one will see her again.'

'Now, look here,' the man said, scrambling to his feet. 'She is strange, I grant you, but she's my only kin and—' Balin raised his fist again.

'Which you wanted us to take off your lazy hands. We have done so. Leave us.' The man backed down the aisle, bowing and muttering thank you, whilst wiping his bloody face. The queen waved her hand and the girl came to life again, twirling. She stopped when she saw the man leaving.

'Uncle?' she said in a small voice. Balin came to stand by her and put a black, gloved hand on her shoulder. The girl buckled under the weight.

'I am your uncle now.' The girl wheeled round to face the queen and the queen gave her another cold smile.

'There are flowers growing on the plain of destruction,' the girl said. The queen's smile froze.

'What did you say, girl?' Balin asked. The girl paid him no

heed, her gaze only for the queen.

'There are flowers growing on the plain of destruction. Your end is beginning.'

Gertrude dug her nails into her palm to stop herself from screaming. The queen's left eye began to twitch, a sign Gertrude knew only too well.

The queen took a breath and exhaled in the girl's direction. The girl faltered back, but she drew herself up, lifting her chin. The queen breathed in and light from the girl's body poured up into the air above her. The light took the form of the girl. The ghostly shade reached out a hand to Balin, who reached up to touch her. The queen made a slicing movement with her hand and the ghost girl came apart with a scream. The girl's body collapsed in a heap on the floor. The queen stood and her eyes sought out the man who had brought the child. He had stopped down the aisle, his face a mask of horror. She flicked her wrist. The man's body flew up, towards the ceiling and impaled itself onto one of the banners. The pole stuck out of his chest. His blood dripped down onto the floor and onto some of the heads of the congregation. No-one moved. The drips echoed in the silent hall.

Balin stepped forward and scooped the girl into his arms. At the queen's frown, he said,

'She's still warm. Warm enough for me. With your leave, Your Majesty?'

'Do what you must, Balin.' She looked out to the congregation.

'When I say tributes, I mean money, jewels, livestock. Never children and never *girl* children.' A faraway look came into her eyes. 'Anyone who knows me will know that I have had enough of little girls to last me a lifetime.'

CHAPTER 43

'Why did no one tell me?' Gertrude whispered.

They were in Nell's kitchen huddled at the top of the table. Sam sat as close as he could to Gertrude, whilst Lucinda watched Tal who was leaning against the mantelpiece, staring into the fire. He had not said a word since they had returned to the kitchen. Nell was eating her way through a loaf of bread, her eyes never leaving Gertrude's face. Every now and then, she would absentmindedly hold a piece out to Sam, who gobbled it down.

Gertrude had asked this question several times but no one had answered her yet. She raised her eyes to Nell, who gulped down her bread and went to pat her hand. Thinking better of it, Nell stopped and went back to tearing up the loaf.

'She deserves an answer,' Tal said. Jim flew onto the table.

'And she will get all the answers she needs, but not here and not now.' He looked at the kitchen staff, but they were all busy preparing for the feast to take any notice of them. Gertrude stroked Jim's chest.

'Did you know Jim?' Jim cocked his head.

'Yeah, of course I did.

'Did Mrs Eccles – I mean, Vivienne – know?'

'Yep, and Cat did.'

'Why did you not warn me?' Jim hopped from one foot to another.

'I have been over this before, I *couldn't.* My geis demands I can't tell you. I can't speak for Viv or Cat, but they will have had their reasons.'

'I am so tired. I am so tired of secrets, and half-truths and riddles. I am so tired of finding myself in a story that everyone knows the details of, except me. If you don't tell me everything there is to know, then I swear, I will pack my things tonight and head home to *my* Britain. At least I can deal with my grandmother there. At least I know what I am up against.'

Nell gulped down a chunk of bread.

'Now, flower, don't be rash. You will know. I myself will tell you everything I know. But please, believe me, I did not know the queen was your grandmother and I cannot say I understand what is going on myself.'

'There is no need, Nell, for you to trouble yourself,' Jim said. 'It's all arranged. I have summoned them all and those who can come will come. Then we can talk. But not here. Not a word here.' Tal raised his head and turned.

'You speak the truth, Jim?'

'Yeah, of course I do, you cheeky blighter. A guide will arrive tomorrow. All you lot have to do is stay safe and get through the feast tonight.'

'I do not think she should serve tonight,' Tal said, addressing Nell. Gertrude stood up.

'I will serve. Hiding me from harm has not done me any good so far, so we may as well stop all of that. And I will not allow anyone to make decisions for me anymore. Will … *she* be there?'

'No, flower,' Nell replied. 'The queen will take her meal in her chambers and Edric will serve her. She does not let the serving girls or me near her. She cannot abide prettiness in others.'

'That's why I have never served her,' Elaine said, flouncing up to the table and throwing Tal a smile. Gertrude felt a pang of jealousy. Not for the smile, but for Elaine's uncomplicated life. *Her whole world turns on the smile from a man. My path is always dangerous and dark. Oh, Elaine, how I envy you.* Gertrude began to stuff her hair back into her cap, but her hands trembled so much she could not do it.

'Here let me.' Tal stood behind her, whipping off her cap and re braiding her hair.

'You can do mine after, Tal,' Elaine said.

'If you wish me too.' He wound a band around the end and coiled up the heavy plait, before putting the cap on her head.

'You will do, but keep that hair of yours hidden and do not do that thing with your eyes.'

'What thing?'

'That sidelong look you do, underneath your lashes.'

'I do not do that.'

'Oh, darling, you so do,' Dafydd said, sitting down at the table and giving her a grin. 'Tal, you can dress her down and bind her hair as much as you like, but she still shines like the first daffodil of spring.' Gertrude looked down and up again, rewarding Dafydd with a smile. He threw his head back and laughed.

'You just did it! The look!' Gertrude shook her head and laughed along with him. Nell, sensing the ease of tension, decided she had eaten enough. Smiling she looked up and caught Tal's face looking at Gertrude and Dafydd laughing together.

She reached for another loaf.

CHAPTER 44

The noise hit Gertrude first.

Men's voices, cursing and laughing, echoed around the dining hall. The smell hit her next. Sweat, mixed with beer, mixed with the odour of a hundred bodies that had not bathed for days. She stood at the end of a long table, looking down at men spitting and slurping. She noticed that although they laughed, their eyes looked dead.

'Are you posing for a statue or are you actually going to pour me a drink?' She felt a hand go round to her backside and slipping out of her reverie, Gertrude looked down at the man who had spoken. He had spit on his chin and, to hide her revulsion, she bobbed a curtsey, as she had watched Elaine do. She poured beer into the proffered tankard. The man looked into his tankard and grimaced.

'More.'

'But it's nearly full.' The man grabbed her arm and pulled her down onto the table. She was level with his face and, unfortunately, his breath.

'Do you know how many people I killed today? Killing is thirsty work. I'm going to teach you some manners.' He stood up, knocking his chair back on the floor. His hands went to his trouser belt and Gertrude scrambled up off the table. She backed straight into another man, who held her tight by the shoulders.

'Gwen, are you flirting? Stephen, for god's sake, put it away.

It is what my dumb cousin is after and you have already used it too much today.' The table burst into laughter.

'Too right I have, blacksmith. I have been busy with my sword,' and he mimed a sword thrust, 'And I have been busy with my *sword*.' He gave a pelvic thrust and Gertrude felt Tal's hands tighten on her shoulders.

'Then you must be thirsty. Give this good soldier some more beer, Gwen, which is what he really wants. You are not for the likes of him, my girl. He is far too good for you.' Tal released her and, with a slap on her behind, shooed her away.

'Silly cow!' he yelled after her and all the men joined in with his laughter.

Gertrude did not have much time to think after that. The men never seemed to have enough to drink and she ran back and forth to the kitchen. Every time she entered, Nell would look up and say,

'Still intact?'

'Just.' Finn was helping Nell open bottles of beer and pouring them into huge earthenware jugs. Sam and Lucinda looked on.

'What in the name of Bacchus is this stuff?' Finn said, sniffing a bottle. Gertrude laughed.

'Lager, beer. It is very popular where I come from.' Nell snorted, and a cat fell off a stool.

'They're welcome to it. I would rather they drink this cursed poison than take all my reserves of dandelion mead.'

'Gertrude, do you want to try some dandelion mead? It will help you get through the night ... and beyond?' asked Finn, his astonishing green eyes twinkling.

'No, she does not, you wicked pixie.'

'Oh, to Hades with this bottle opening. Stand back, flowers of mine.'

'Finn don't—'yelled Nell, but the pixie ignored her. With a gesture, every top on the beer bottles popped off. Foam bubbled up and cascaded down onto the tabletop. Sam jumped up on the table to lick the spilt beer. Nell pursed her lips.

'Finn, the queen will sense magic.'

'And to Hades with her too. We leave tomorrow anyway and I for one cannot wait.' Nell lowered her face and carried on pouring the bottles into the jugs. Finn glanced over at her. 'I cannot wait to leave this castle,' Finn said softly, his eyes gazing at the top of Nell's head, 'but you know how my heart stands as regards to leaving you.' Gertrude tried to pretend she was not there and wiped up some of the spilt beer that Sam had missed. Nell blew her nose on her hanky and Gertrude knocked over a bottle at the sound. Sam grinned and sprung over to help clean up. Nell plastered a smile on her face, but it looked fake.

'Shush you, I am not going to cry. Here, Gertrude, take these in and send Elaine in, will you? I have only seen her once.'

Entering the dining hall, Gertrude looked for Elaine, but the girl was nowhere to be seen. She soon had too much to occupy her thoughts, than the whereabouts of the flirtatious kitchen girl. The men's hands went everywhere and Gertrude stopped blushing or even noticing. What she did notice, however, was that wherever she was, Tal was never far away. He would slip into conversations and arm wrestle with the men. He even led a group in song, but whatever she was doing, she would look up and he would be there. She leaned over and poured some beer into an outstretched tankard.

'You're new, aren't you?' She jumped and spilt the beer on the table. 'I like my beer in my tankard please.'

'I am so sorry, let me wipe it for you.' She took her cloth and mopped up the liquid. She glanced at the man and was surprised to see a kind face smiling back at her. He looked younger than the other men. He had sandy hair and warm brown eyes that danced in amusement.

'Do not worry yourself, sweetheart. I have had worst spilt on me.' Gertrude gave him a smile and his eyes widened.

'Oh, sweetling, you should smile more often. It is like the sun breaking through the clouds.' Before she could reply, he stood up, along with every other soldier in the room. All the men looked towards the dining hall entrance. Gertrude followed their gaze and saw the three knights she had seen earlier in the day, standing there.

Agravaine, dressed in a gold doublet and cloak, came prancing in. His long yellow hair hung down to his shoulders and he waved as he moved up the hall. His high cheek boned face gave him an aristocratic look. Gertrude felt he was good looking enough if you liked that sort of thing. He arrived at the top table and stretched his arms out, encompassing the hall in his smile.

'Didn't we do well?' The men, as if released from a spell, banged their fists and tankards on the table, chanting his name. He sat down and closed his eyes, allowing the adulation to wash over him. Tal grabbed her by the waist and pulled her back to the entrance of the kitchen.

'We can watch unobserved from here. Now, look to the men at the top of the table on the right-hand side.' Gertrude sought the group out and saw a cluster of young men, all dressed in red shirts wearing black gloves. They were not yelling or smiling and with a start, Gertrude saw Elaine and Dafydd with them. Before she could point this out to Tal, Agravaine spoke again.

'Balin, you black bastard, come and eat, for you will be famished after your escapades today.' The men roared with laughter and chanted the black knight's name at the top of their voices. Balin swaggered and grinned his way through the dining hall. He caught the hands of the men in handshakes and palm slapping. He gave a little bow to Agravaine and sat down on the gold knight's left, shaking his fist in the air as he did so. Gertrude looked back at the men in red. They were perfectly still, looking down at the table.

'Apart from the men in red, the soldiers love him.' When Tal did not answer, she looked over to where he was staring.

And so, Gertrude laid her eyes for the first time on the face of Rufus the Red.

He filled the entrance and towered over every other man in the room. Despite his size, he stepped in with a grace that amazed her. His red shirt stretched tight across his arms. The front laces of his shirt were undone and showed his gleaming onyx skin. Dark as he was, he seemed to draw all the light in the room. His tight curls were jet black and she watched, entranced, as he surveyed the room. His eyes lit on her face and she stopped breathing. They were startling. Golden, they blazed in a face full of angles. The light bounced off his cheekbones as he held her in his powerful gaze and she felt nailed to the floor, unable to move. It was like being noticed by a panther. His eyes slid over her and moved on. Gertrude took a shuddering breath.

'Rufus the Red,' breathed Nell.

'I think he's misnamed,' Gertrude whispered, thinking of his beautiful, glistening ebony skin. Tal made a noise.

'You have not seen him fight. It is as if the god of war himself has stepped forward.'

Rufus moved slowly down the hall, like a lion moving amongst cattle. No one banged their tankards or chanted his name, but he held the room still. Not one pair of eyes looked anywhere else but at his graceful form. He came to the group of men in red and with a warm smile, greeted each one in turn. He even grasped Dafydd's hand.

'The Reds,' Tal said, 'The most elite group of warrior knights this land has ever borne witness to. They make Balin and Agravaine's troops look like toddlers playing with wooden swords.' She looked up at Tal.

'You want to be one of them.'

'Yes.'

'But they are the enemy.'

'They are … different. They have honour and morals. They protect and we have caught them doing things that mark them as different.'

'Like what?'

'When they practice archery, they use targets. Agravaine and Balin use—'

'Please do not talk about it,' Nell said. 'I once saw Rufus pick up a mouse and move him to a place of safety when they were training. I am sure he spoke to it.'

'I think that may be wishful thinking, Nell, but we are hoping we may be able to turn him to our cause.'

'Our only cause at the moment is to feed these blighters, otherwise, we will have a riot on our hands. Chop, chop.' Gertrude turned reluctantly away.

Throughout the next hour, between running back and forth to the kitchen and being groped and pawed at, Gertrude found her gaze being drawn to the golden-eyed man on Agravaine's right. She wished that it was only Rufus who dominated her thoughts, but for every glance she gave him, she gave two to Tal. Tal followed her around the room, laughing and talking to the soldiers.

'How can Tal bear it, talking and joking with these men?' she asked Nell, whilst loading up a tray with bread.

'I sometimes don't think he can, flower. Now two loaves to each table. Go.' Gertrude ran back out. She had tried to avoid serving the three men at the top table, but she found herself passing them whilst distributing the bread.

'There's that bastard blacksmith,' Balin said to Agravaine, totally ignoring Gertrude. 'I'll whip him like a whore the next time he looks at me.' Agravaine laughed.

'Careful, Balin. He will turn your horse from you. Like him or not, and I myself do not, I have never seen a man handle horses like he does. And we all know what happened to Melwas.' Balin tore into the bread.

'Melwas was a posturing fool, but I refuse to believe that the blacksmith had anything to do with his death.' Rufus slowly turned his head to look at Balin.

'How else do you explain the fall from his horse?' Gertrude willed him to carry on speaking so she could listen to the deep, rich voice. Balin snorted and shoved the bread in his mouth.

'The horse hit a stone,' he said, showering the table with crumbs.

'That horse,' Rufus continued, 'threw Melwas down on the

ground and then broke his neck by standing on him.' Rufus took a sip of his wine. Agravaine laughed.

'At least we put the black beast down.' Rufus put down his goblet.

'That horse is still in the stables and if anyone does try to destroy such a horse, I myself will break their neck. The blacksmith is a better fighter than you will ever be, Balin, and you will just have to learn to live with the shame.' Balin stood up and across Agravaine's head, aimed a punch at Rufus' face. Without looking round, Rufus shot out his hand, catching the fist before it hit his face. He twisted it so that Balin let out a cry of pain. One of the Red's, a man with a mane of yellow hair, jumped to his feet. Agravaine sighed.

'Children, do stop fighting. Balin sit down. Have you not fought enough for one day? Rufus, have done and let the cretin go. Tell your man to sit. Fighting over the blacksmith like a couple of sluts on heat, I ask you.' Rufus obeyed and Balin sat, nursing his hand. The red warrior, who had jumped up, glared at Balin. Rufus gave a slight shake of his head and the warrior sat down. Agravaine turned to Rufus.

'You have hurt his pride. Now he will be insufferable unless I praise him.' He picked up a fork and hit the side of his goblet. The hall fell silent, as Agravaine rose.

'How splendid you were today. Another two rebel villages annihilated. They won't be complaining about our laws again.'

'They won't be complaining about anything again,' yelled a man and the hall erupted into laughter.

'Agreed, agreed. But, my good men, my toast must go to the man on my left. Balin the Black.' He turned to the seated knight. 'No one takes out old women like you.' The soldiers roared their approval, laughing and banging their fists. Agravaine raised his voice over the noise. 'The old witch would have herbed us to death with her lotions and potions, had you not been so quick, dear friend.' Gertrude looked at Rufus. He concentrated hard on his goblet, turning it in his hands by its stem. The Reds also looked down at the table. All except the yellow-haired warrior who stared with outright hostility at Balin. A slight dark-haired boy sitting next to him nudged him and the yellow-haired man dropped his eyes. The laughter died down.

'But I must admit, Balin,' Agravaine continued, 'I never knew your carnal lusts ran to old women. Way over your normal target age.' Balin nodded and grinned.

'The old bitch blinded one of my men with her witches' potions. Seemed the honourable thing to do. Although there were times, when she was struggling beneath me, I could have sworn it was a young slut who was screaming.'

'All in your head, you old dog. A toast.' Everyone stood up.

'To Balin the Black, bastard and grandmother lover.' Gertrude heard something drop in the kitchen. Tal leapt over a table and ran towards the noise. Gertrude put her tray down and followed him. Over the chanting of Balin's name, only two men observed her departure.

Both were part of the dangerous, dark path she had chosen to walk upon.

CHAPTER 45

Gertrude fled through the kitchen in pursuit of Tal. She found the kitchen deserted. She ran through the open door and stood shivering in the cold courtyard. She could not see him in the dying light of the day. To her right, she heard a noise and ran towards it. Rounding the corner, she found him. He stood behind a woman, her long, honey blonde hair gathered up in his hands. She was bending over, vomiting, and in between the violent retches, she sobbed.

'Hush, please hush,' Tal said, as he rubbed her back. Gertrude felt she was intruding, but did not want to be noticed, so she stood, rooted to the spot. The heaving stopped and the woman straightened, clinging onto Tal's shirt.

'Brighid. Oh gods, Brighid. She used to soothe your headaches and nightmares do you remember Tal?' She buried her face in Tal's chest. Gertrude caught a glimpse of the woman's face and even in the fading light, she could see that the woman was astonishingly beautiful. She stepped back and Tal's head jerked up.

'Gertrude, what are you doing here? Go away. This does not concern you.'

The woman's head came up and she looked straight into Gertrude's eyes. She reached out a hand towards Gertrude.

'Of course it concerns her.' The voice sounded familiar and Gertrude frowned. She took a step forward to touch the outstretched hand. Tal turned the woman away, blocking her from Gertrude.

'Go back to the dining hall. Now. It will look suspicious if too many of us are missing. Go. Now.' Gertrude turned and ran back the way she came.

First Elaine, now this blonde woman, how many more women do you have? Gertrude cursed herself for a fool. He probably had not been protecting her tonight. He had probably been following her around the hall to make sure she did not do anything stupid. She had thought there had been a change in his eyes tonight, as he watched her move around the tables, but she had been way off the mark.

'You ugly, minging fool,' she said to herself. She fell back as she banged into someone. An arm reached out to steady her.

'I've been waiting for you,' a pleasant voice said. Peering closer, she saw the young sandy-haired man whom she had been serving earlier. He stood by the doors to the kitchen. A slow smile spread across his face and she could just make out his brown eyes, still dancing in amusement at her.

'Why do you look so shocked, sweetheart? I saw you leave in a rush and since you smiled at me the way you did, I knew that where you go, I must follow.' Gertrude tried to slow her breathing. He tipped his head to the side. 'It has grown noisy and hot in there. I thought I would take a walk and would be honoured if you would join me.' His eyes had not left her face and Gertrude found herself smiling back.

'I would love to.' Reaching up to her cap, she removed it and unbraided her hair. The man's smile faded and a look of wonderment came into his face, as she let the mass of red curls fall to her waist. She raised her eyes slowly and gave the man the full benefit of her green eyes. His eyes swept up and down her body.

'I knew you were a beauty; anyone could have seen that. The way you move and the way you speak, but I had no idea just how beautiful you were. If there is indeed a goddess of love, like these fools believe, then surely she looks like you.' Gertrude suddenly felt uncomfortable and realised she had been stupid. This man was the enemy. He may even have assisted in the violation of the old woman. She took a step back, but he grabbed her wrist and pulled her near.

'Shall we walk, goddess?' Not knowing what else to do, Gertrude took his proffered arm. 'My name is George.'

'Mine is Ger—Gwen—Gwendolyn.'

'Well, Ger-Gwen-Gwendolyn, you have a lovely name to go with your face. Welsh, I believe?'

'Yes, I am Welsh. I mean my family are from there. Where are you from?'

'London … you know, in that other world. Are you from there too or are you an Albion?'

'I am from everywhere really. What brought you here George?' George looked over at her and frowned.

'You really are new here, aren't you?' They walked across a courtyard. Gertrude glanced up at the sky. The clouds had gone and she could see the first star of the evening twinkling. She remembered singing to the star in another world. Had that really been only a few days ago? She felt sad and homesick and then shook herself. This was meant to be her home.

'Penny for them?'

'What?'

'Your thoughts. You were miles away and here I was, thinking I had entranced you with my charm.'

'I am sorry. You were saying?'

'The queen of course.'

'Pardon?'

'In answer to your question. The queen brought me here. She brought all of us here.'

'Have you met her?'

'Yes.'

'What is she like?'

'Up to a few minutes ago, I would have said she was the most beautiful woman I had ever seen. And I have seen a lot.' He drew in a ragged breath and stopped. He took Gertrude by the shoulders and looked down at her. His hands shook and she felt her ego revel in the effect she was having on him. But it dawned on her that she was in the middle of an unfamiliar courtyard, with one of the soldiers who had laid this land to ruin. And then, he was not the only one who was trembling. He raised his hand and drew his finger across her cheek, his breathing becoming shallow.

'The queen is like the moon, but you are like the sun.'

'Thank you, but I must be getting back. They will be missing me.'

'But Gwendolyn, the night is young, as are we.' She stepped back and smiled.

'I need this job.'

'Ah well, who am I to come between a girl and her money? Of course, you must go back, but may I ask just one thing from you?' Gertrude's mouth went dry as she nodded. 'A kiss? One kiss, that is all and then I shall return you to your kitchen, dear, beautiful Ger-Gwen-Gwendolyn.' Swallowing Gertrude leaned forward and pressed her lips to his. She was surprised, but thankful when his lips remained closed. She pulled back and smiled at him.

'Slut,' he said. He pulled her into a fierce embrace. His mouth crashed down onto hers, forcing it open. He plunged his tongue into her mouth, making her gag. One of his hands tangled itself in her hair and the other moved at his waist. He yanked her head back and Gertrude felt the cold blade of a knife at her throat. She forced her eyes open to look at him. His face twisted and his eyes bulged.

'Do you know what the queen promised me when she brought me here?' Gertrude shook her head, wincing as his grip on her hair tightened and the blade cut into her skin. 'All the women I wanted. I am going to love you, Gwendolyn, and when I am done loving you, I will take part of you with me. Right now, I'm torn between your ear or your perfect little nose.' He ran the knife down her body. Gertrude went still. No one was going to hear her scream. It was just her and him. She let her weight sag, trying to get closer to the ground, as Cat had taught her.

'*Use their strength against them.*'

She closed her eyes, trying desperately to remember what else Cat had said, but fear froze her mind. He moved her back against a wall and travelled the knife up her body. He placed the tip of it by the hollow of her throat.

'My angel, my baby girl, I am going to love you to death.'

Gertrude pushed him and as he went backwards, she swung her leg back and kicked him between the legs. He fell forward and she reached out, grabbing him by his shirt. She pulled him in and let go at the last second. His body crashed into the wall. She turned and ran, but his foot came out and caught her ankle. She fell, face down, on the ground. Blood seeped into her mouth and he straddled her back. She knew she had lost. The kick alone should have disabled him. He lifted up her skirt and she writhed beneath him, trying to knock him off her.

'Oh yes, baby girl, that's right. Fight me.' He yanked her head up and round and kissed her mouth.

Then he was no longer on top of her. She got to her knees and saw Sam pulling the man away from her by his shirt. Sam released him and went for his throat, but a figure flew over her and Tal fell on the man and pulled him upright. He pulled his fist back and smashed it into the soldier's face. The soldier's nose shattered with a crunch and warm blood spurted onto her face. The soldier fell back onto the ground and Tal straddled his chest, his hands around the soldier's throat. The soldier made a strange noise and with a shiver, Gertrude realised he was laughing.

'What's so funny, bastard?' Tal asked, loosening his grip.

'That you hate me for doing the thing you want to do. We are not so different, you and I, blacksmith.' The soldier's hand moved and Gertrude saw the knife come up to stab Tal in the ribs. With a snarl, Sam flung himself at the moving arm and bit down. The soldier yelled and dropped the knife. Tal looked at Sam and the soldier, seizing his chance, brought his fist crashing down onto Tal's head. Tal slumped forward and the man twisted out from underneath him. He jumped up and moved towards Gertrude, leering at her. Sam flung himself between them. The soldier kicked the dog across the courtyard and Sam landed, crumpled in a heap. He did not get up.

Gertrude ran and dropped into a roll, picking up the fallen knife. She sprang forward and plunged it straight into the soldier's heart. At exactly the same moment, Tal jumped up and took the man's head in his hands. He twisted it and snapped his neck.

For a moment time stopped. They gazed at each other, the limp body of the soldier between them. Something leapt in Tal's eyes but the look vanished in a flash and his eyes grew hard. Tal released the body and it fell in a heap on the ground.

'You stupid little girl. What in Hades were you thinking? You could have got yourself killed or worse. What on earth possessed you to go walking with a soldier?' Tal's eyes blazed, his face white. He pulled his hand back and flinching, Gertrude ducked. He slammed his fist into the wall behind her. He put his forehead against the wall.

'I do not think I can go through this again.' Gertrude tried to walk over to Sam but her knees gave way.

'Sam. Sam, please get up.' She crawled over to the prone dog. Sam moved and crawled on his belly to meet her. 'Oh, Sam.' She buried her face in his fur, breathing in the warm golden smell. *If I close my eyes and put my head on the cold ground, maybe it will snow, and they will find me here in the morning. Still and white. Me and my Sam. Would it be such a bad thing? To die in this land could not be as bad as living in it.*

'Sam, my Sam,' she whispered. She closed her eyes. Strong arms lifted and carried her. Tal sat down with her on his lap and leant against the wall. She wound her hands around him and buried her face in his neck, breathing him in. Sam snuffled into Tal's side.

'Cry,' Tal said.

'I honestly do not think I can.'

'Scamp ... let the tears flow. They are just watering your

path,' Sam said. Listening to the warm voice, she let the tears come. Tal rocked her, murmuring words of comfort and then softly began to sing to her. The song seemed achingly familiar. He held her tight, as her body racked with sobbing. When the last tear rolled down her cheek, she gratefully gave herself up to oblivion, falling asleep wrapped around him.

And still he sang.

CHAPTER 46

'Is she ok?' asked Finn.

'Shock I think.' Gertrude could feel Tal's voice vibrating in his chest.

'First time she has seen you kill?'

'First time *she* has killed.'

'Already? Cat will be proud.'

'Cat will string her up by her hair for putting herself in danger in the first place.'

'And you, my friend? You look as pale as the moon.' Tal tightened his hold on her.

'Ah, Tal, the sacrifices we make for them.' It was at that point Gertrude thought she had better open her eyes. It was impolite to eavesdrop. She shifted in Tal's arms, feeling awkward and he let her go. She crawled out of his lap and sat down next to him, leaning against the wall. Sam walked over to her. She smoothed his silky ears and gave Finn a weak smile. Behind his crouching form, she could see the dead soldier, illuminated by the moon that was now riding high in the sky. The soldier's body faced away, but his head was twisted back and his eyes stared at her from between his shoulder blades. She felt sick and closed her eyes.

'No,' said Finn, grabbing her hand. 'Look into his eyes. Keep this moment; burn it into your brain for evermore. This was your first kill, flower bride. Mark it well.'

'Will it get easier?' she asked.

'Yes,' said Tal

'No,' said Sam.

'Perhaps,' said Finn. Lucinda slunk out of the shadows.

'We need to get rid of that thing.' She padded over to Gertrude and laid a paw on her knee. 'Always dispose of your dead.'

'Where?'

'The moat,' croaked a voice and everyone, except Finn and Gertrude, jumped. Jim landed on Finn's outstretched hand.

'For all the bastards in hell!' barked Sam. Jim laughed.

'Oi, your language, furball, is disgusting.'

'Jim is right,' said Finn, smiling as Jim climbed up his arm and balanced on his head. 'Whatever it is that lives in the moat, will feast tonight. Slime deserves to live with slime. I will distract the guards. Sam, if you please, a little help is required.'

Gertrude and Tal dragged the body through the courtyard. They waited whilst the panicked soldiers ran to defend themselves against what sounded like a pack of wolves. In amongst the howling noises, Gertrude and Tal upended the body over the barrier and watched as the dark, stinking liquid sucked the soldier down. The surface bubbled and Gertrude thought she saw something white raise its head. Tal grabbed her hand and they ran back to the courtyard to wait. Finn and Sam skidded around the corner, grinning and panting.

'The fools,' Finn said, a note of sorrow creeping into his voice. 'There has not been a wolf heard in these parts for sixteen years and yet still they run. Sam, you are Merlin clever. You would make a good Alpha.' Finn bowed low and Sam bowed back. Gertrude looked up at the moon. Everything up there looked peaceful, but she was down here amongst the pain, the noise, and the fear. A fragment of a voice echoed in her mind, but it escaped her before she could grab it. She looked down at her arms and saw dark bruises flowering on her pale skin.

'Is Balin still at the feast?' she said. Tal grunted.

'Of course. He will be the last to leave. His capacity for

drinking is legendary.'

'That little girl …' She looked up at him. When he looked back at her his eyes were haunted.

'I know. I have been thinking the same thing.'

'I am coming,' said Finn.

'And me,' said Sam and Lucinda together.

'If you're up to mischief, count me in too,' said Jim. Tal pushed his hand through his hair.

'We cannot all go.'

'You need me for the lookout,' said Lucinda.

'You need me to watch Lucinda's back,' said Sam. He and Lucinda bowed to each other.

'I'm the secret weapon. No one ever expects me,' said Jim and Sam growled. Gertrude laid her hand on Tal's arm and then removed it quickly as his head whipped around.

'It is because of me she is dead.' Tal looked down to where she had touched him. He nodded and looked over at Finn with a raised eyebrow.

'She is one of mine, Tal.' Tal's eyebrows shot up. 'The little darling had Elven blood. How else did she know about the flowers on the plain? How else did she see what she saw?' Tal sighed.

'Right, we go in, we go out. Simple and fast. You do what Finn and I say, understand?' They all nodded. Gertrude tied her hair up.

'Stop worrying, Tal. I killed a man tonight. Surely it cannot get any worse?'

CHAPTER 47

It was worse.

Sam and Lucinda stood guard by the door whilst the others huddled around the four-poster bed that dominated the room. Jim perched on the end of the bed, and all of them looked down at the young girl, lying on top of the covers. The little girl looked clean. She smelled sweet. She wore a white robe that was too big for her, making her look even smaller. Her arms lay by her side. Her legs were spread.

Balin's room was a surprise. Rich tapestries and rugs adorned the room and hundreds of candles flickered. The bed's thick burgundy curtains hung in folds to the ground.

'Takes his loving very seriously, does Balin.' Tal said. Gertrude reached out to touch her.

'She is still warm.'

'The queen's gift to her favoured knight,' said Tal.

'Promise me I get to kill him.' Finn said. Tal shook his head.

'Cannot do that, my friend. I owe him for Brighid.'

'Tal, I owe him for Brighid, this little one and the sacred groves. I hate him so much his name stinks in my nostrils.'

'I'll be the one to kill him,' Gertrude said. Tal went to answer, but Sam gave a soft bark.

'Can we keep this debate for another time? I can hear movement.' Tal leaned forward but Finn got there first, showing strength beyond his size. He scooped the little girl up in his arms and looked down at the pale face.

'She looks like a closed flower.'

'What will you do with her?' asked Gertrude

'What we do with our dead is for us Elven to know alone.' Echoes of another voice came back to her and Gertrude looked over at Jim.

'I told you,' he said, 'Always the innocents first.' Tal grabbed Gertrude's hand.

'Come on, let us move. I would rather get out without resorting to Finn having to cast an invisibility spell. The queen will sense any magic used.'

'I already used magic tonight, Tal.'

'Then we are in more danger than I thought. Move. Now.'

'Can't we destroy the bastard's room?' asked Jim 'Can't I at least leave an offering on the bed?'

'There will be a day for Balin's destruction. Today is not it, my feathered friend. Move.'

Whether it was luck or just the knowledge Tal had of the castle's corridors, they found themselves safe and unobserved in the courtyard under a dark sky. The snow clouds had returned and they shivered in the wind. Finn thanked them. With a nod to Jim, he turned and walked away. The crow flew low by his shoulder. Gertrude watched the girl's hair swinging from side to side and felt overwhelmed with sorrow and exhaustion. Without a word, Tal scooped her up and carried her to the stable.

Hours later, she lay awake. Sam and Lucinda snored and Zeus and Apollo snuffled in their sleep. She stared up at the ceiling and could not understand why sleep eluded her and what she was feeling. She chased the emotion down and found it.

It was fear.

But of what? She went over the day's events.

The queen is my grandmother. Terrifying. I kissed a man and then killed him. Awful. Then there is Balin, who thinks nothing of assaulting women, whatever their age. Dreadful. But when she found the reason for her fear, she became even more frightened. She could not breathe.

As they had looked at each other over the dead soldier, Gertrude had read an emotion in Tal's eyes. He had, for a moment, dropped his mask and what she had read in his eyes was not contempt, nor hatred, nor even the cold indifference he normally showed her.

It was need.

A need so deep and primal, it shook her to her very core. If the soldier had killed her, Tal would have lain down and willed himself to die alongside her. She knew this, just as she knew it would snow tomorrow and Sam would wake up hungry. To be needed that much by someone, was as terrifying as not being needed at all. Panic settled on her chest, like a bird of prey, making her feel trapped.

When sleep finally came, it was troubled. She dreamt of three men. One with eyes of gold and one with eyes that changed colour. But the one she reached for, the one she chased down through the corridors of time and space, was the one whose eyes were like storm clouds on a summer's day.

CHAPTER 48

'Where's Tal?' Gertrude asked the next morning. The kitchen was quiet. Only a couple of the staff remained, along with Thoth, Finn and Dafydd. Nell stopped filling a huge bag with food and gave Gertrude a sharp look.

'Out practising his moves. Lucinda went with him. By the Morrigan, you look awful. You look as pale and drawn as he does. What happened last night?'

Gertrude sank down on a stool, near the fire. As she knew it would, snow had fallen overnight and showed no sign of stopping. Her green dress was not as warm as her kitchen clothes. The wind whistled through the chimney. Sam lifted his head from a bowl of porridge, oats dripping off his nose.

'I did not realise Tal took dancing so seriously,' he said. Nell burst into laughter.

'Not dancing, you daft flower, his fighting moves. Rufus is back and every morning he trains his men. Tal will be up on the walkway, watching and practising with them. If you are going up there take this with you.' She thrust a basket into Gertrude's hands. 'Bread, milk and cheese. If that comes back untouched, I will box both your ears. And don't either of you come back until you have colour in your cheeks.'

'Yes, Mum.' Nell's face split into a massive grin.

Sam came with her, keeping to the dark corners of the courtyard. Using his sense of smell ('I can smell that damned cat anywhere!') they climbed the wooden steps onto the walkway that ran around a large courtyard. Gertrude placed the basket down on the ground and glanced below. Rufus shouted instructions, as the Reds went through their drills. Their red shirts stood out as the snow fell around them. After that cursory glance, she forgot about them. Her whole attention focused on the man before her.

The elegance of his movements captivated her. She had seen him beat a man and she had seen him kill a man, but she had never seen him like this. His sword blurred with the quickness of his thrusts and parries. His feet moved with intricate steps as if dancing to a song only he could hear. She started to discern a pattern to his movements and recognized Cat's handiwork. Lucinda sat, tail curled neatly about her, watching his every move.

'Damn', Tal said, stopping, 'I always mess that last bit up.'

'You are moving back on your heel. Try the ball of your foot.' Rufus' voice floated up to them and Tal looked over at Gertrude. They went still.

'See, Oscar, like this.' Rufus demonstrated a move to the slight, dark-haired young man Gertrude had seen last night. Tal and Gertrude let out their breath.

'He is right though,' Tal murmured, 'I need to use the ball of my foot.'

'I brought you breakfast.' Gertrude crouched down, hiding her face behind her hair. 'Nell says if we do not eat it, she will box our ears.'

'I believe she would too.' He crouched down opposite her. She pulled apart the bread and pressed a hunk of cheese into it. She held it out to him. He reached out and took it, his eyes not leaving her face. His fingers brushed her own and, furious at the heat she felt in her cheeks, she hid her face again. She focused on making her own makeshift sandwich.

'Are you all right?' he asked softly. 'After last night I mean.'

'I do not think I will ever be all right about it, but I will survive it. I am alive, which is more than I can say for that little girl … and your friend Brighid.' They ate in silence for a while, sharing their breakfast with Sam and Lucinda, who were oddly quiet.

'You look tired. Bad dreams?' asked Tal. She looked up, taking in his dark shadows under his eyes.

'Not bad … troubled.' He gave her a long look.

'And me.' She looked away first.

'Are you ever worried you will be spotted up here?'

'No. I checked. The shadows are so dark up here no one can see me.'

'Break over. Back to practice.' Rufus' deep voice reached them. Gertrude smiled.

'Are you sure he cannot see us?' Tal smiled back and jumped up. He fell into the same drill pattern as the men below him. After a while, Gertrude rose and joined him. She could not keep up with him, but she fell into the routine Cat had taught her.

'Watch yourself,' he said, turning to her, 'You are leaving yourself wide open there.'

'Don't you find it boring?'

'No. Never. You do these moves over and over until they become a part of you. Your body does them automatically so you do not have to think about them. In a fight, you can let the energy flow right through you, whilst your body takes over, leaving you to look around and seize any opportunities you would have missed.'

'I miss my training, although there were times I hated it. I miss Cat.'

'Hopefully, we will see her soon and no doubt she will shout at both of us for not practising enough.' Together they fell back into their routines watched by Sam, Lucinda, and a pair of golden eyes.

CHAPTER 49

They returned to a deserted kitchen.

Only Nell and Finn remained. Thoth and Dafydd had left to check that the gates were unlocked. Nell blew her nose on her hanky and Gertrude tripped over a stool at the noise.

'Where is everyone, Nell? What about the people who danced with us? The castle is deserted as well.'

'All gone,' Nell sniffed. 'I would be hard-pressed to find them myself. We Albions know how to hide and the minute *she* returns, they vanish. All my staff and my cats. And now I have to leave, because of Edric. I'm going to miss this kitchen.' Tal squeezed Nell's shoulder.

'There will be others, Nell.'

'But this was my kitchen, Tal. Mine, where I taught you and fed you. My pots, my pans. I cannot believe I am leaving my copper pans. Can't I take them with me?'

'Nell, you have almost packed the kitchen sink and—'

'Oh, my sink! Do you think I could take that too? My lovely deep kitchen sink.' Tal walked away over to the fireplace and stood looking down into the ashes. Gertrude took Nell's hands in her own.

'Nell, wherever you are, whether it is in a little room or out in the forest around a fire, that will be Nell's kitchen. You are what makes it the heart of the home, not the actual room.' Nell patted her hand.

'Bless you, flower, but my pans, Gertrude ...' and she started sniffing and putting pasties in a bag that was already stretching at the seams.

'Enough, darling,' said Tal placing his hands on her shoulders. 'You have given us enough food to feed an army.'

'Oh, Morrigan protect you all, what if you meet the army? There must be an easier way to get to the gathering. Can't you come with me?' Finn, who had been looking out of the kitchen window, turned, his peacock green eyes glistening with unshed tears.

'Each of us must take our own path now, feather in my wing. We knew this day would come.' Nell returned his gaze and fat tears rolled down her cheeks. Lucinda jumped up onto the table, her eyes wide.

'The guide has arrived.' She looked at Sam. 'You are not going to believe who has turned up.' Nell grabbed Sam and hid him underneath her skirts, whilst telling Dafydd and Finn to stay to look after her pans.

Gertrude fell to her knees when she saw who had arrived.

A unicorn stood, pawing the snow-covered ground. A shimmering white light emanated from its white horn. Little blue flowers adorned its white mane. Against the dark snow-filled sky, it shone like white fire. As if catching their scent, the unicorn turned and looked at them. Its eyes shone with a dark flame and all the joy and the light of the world was in that look. A joy Gertrude had never known. It looked straight at Gertrude and she felt every defence, every wall and barrier come tumbling down. Under its gaze, there was nowhere to hide, so she laid it all out for the unicorn to see. Her fears, her passions, her past and her present. Her dreams and desires. Everything she wanted and everything she needed. She hid nothing and let the unicorn have it all. The unicorn closed its eyes as it probed her soul. When it opened them again, a sob caught in Gertrude's throat at the look of sadness that had replaced the joy, and Gertrude knew, deep in her soul, that she had denied herself joy in many lifetimes. Queen of Sorrows, the water spirit had called her.

The unicorn walked over to where she knelt and came right up to her until its nose was a breath away from hers. Two large tears dropped from its eyes and fell onto Gertrude's folded hands. She brought her hands to her mouth and tasted them. The tears tasted sweet. The unicorn pressed its nose to Gertrude's and then, knees buckling, it sank to the ground and laid its head carefully in her lap. Trembling, Gertrude touched the unicorn's horn and watched in wonder, as it glowed silver, then gold and then pink. It was not white, as she had first thought, but iridescent. The unicorn released a deep sigh and nestled further into her lap. The two of them let their tears flow freely, like warm summer rain.

How long they lay wrapped around each other, Gertrude did not know, but a movement to her right broke her entranced stare. Looking up, through blurry eyes, she watched Tal step forward and she saw the naked need in his eyes once more. She held out her hand and drew him close. Taking a deep breath, Tal, who had loved horses all his life, crouched down on his haunches and reached out a hand to run it through the white mane. The unicorn opened its eyes and fixed Tal with the same piercing gaze. Tal stopped breathing and went still, the colour draining from his face. After a few moments, apparently satisfied, the unicorn gave another sigh and closed its eyes again. Tal moved onto his knees and he and Gertrude entwined their hands in the soft white mane, letting the peace flow through them. Lucinda edged nearer the unicorn and said,

'Excuse me, dearest, do you not think you should get up? Are we not a little conspicuous?'

'Look around you, Lucinda,' said Nell. 'No one has noticed anything. The few people left here belong to the queen and they can't see anything sacred. All they see is a kitchen girl on her knees and the blacksmith kneeling beside her. They can't see him, petal.'

And it was true. Not one of the queen's servants or guards looked their way. The kitchen door opened behind them.

'Holy father of trees,' said Dafydd and he dropped to his knees behind Tal. The unicorn opened its eyes.

'Rhiannon sends her love, brother. She asks that you would see the bairn soon. He grows stronger every day.'

Gertrude had heard many beautiful voices. Mrs Eccles' musical Irish lilt, Nell's deep voice, as warm as her kitchen. Tal's voice, with its stormy wildness and Rufus' rich dark voice, but no voice could compare with the voice of the unicorn. If Tal's voice was of the storm and Nell's voice of the kitchen fire, this was the voice of the earth itself. All the joy and the bounty of the land echoed within that voice. If there was a god, she hoped he or she sounded like this unicorn, otherwise she would laugh in disappointment.

'Thank you, Your Sacredness.' Dafydd drew a shaky breath. 'Thank you. I will see her soon.'

'Course you will, lad,' said Nell fiddling with her apron.

'Cariad,' said the unicorn moving its head off Gertrude's lap and looking at Nell. 'It has been a long time.'

'Too long.'

'You know I do not eat, Lady Nell, but if it would please you, I would have some water.'

'Dafydd, hide Sam.' She whipped her skirts off the golden retriever. Nell waddled away, returning with a bowl. She placed it on the ground and stepped away. The unicorn turned its head and placed the tip of its horn into the water. The water glowed, like liquid moonlight, and the unicorn lapped it up.

'More?'

'No, cariad, that was enough.' It laid its head once more in Gertrude's lap and closed its eyes. Nell knelt and placed her hand on its neck, stroking it. Lucinda curled herself into its stomach and began to purr. Only Sam did not come near. He sat facing away, his face pressed into Dafydd's leg. A shiver passed through his body.

'Sam, come close,' said the unicorn. Sam turned and Gertrude shrunk back from the expression on his face.

'I have done such things, such terrible things,' he said in a

317

shaking voice. The unicorn raised its head and looked straight at Sam. On and on dog and unicorn stared at each other.

'Sam, come close. You have travelled so far.' Not understanding any of this Gertrude reached out her hand, desperate to soothe Sam. He slunk over to her and lay down, covering his face with his paws. Gertrude and Lucinda exchanged a glance, none the wiser.

'Bloody hell, One Horn. It's good to see you!' Jim dived down from the sky and landed on the unicorn's horn. The unicorn laughed, soft and low.

'Well met, Jim, noble crow, keeper of secrets. Your heart weighs heavy with them, dear friend.'

'Ain't that the truth? Where we going then?'

'As far as the crow flies.'

'Still got your sense of humour I see.'

'Sometimes, Jim, laughter is all we do have.' Sam raised his head.

'Laughter is the language of the survivor.'

'Oh, in that case, two deaf men walk into a bar—'

'No!' everyone shouted, but the unicorn shook with laughter. Everyone, except Sam, joined in. Nell wiped her eyes on her apron. The unicorn got to its feet and Gertrude felt bereft as the warmth left her lap.

'Well, friends, that has halved our journey already. Let us be gone. Tal, fetch your friends.' With a deep bow, Tal strode off towards the stable.

The unicorn's head whipped round at a noise and gave a delighted whinny. It pranced and danced about the courtyard. Gertrude looked behind her and saw Finn emerging from the kitchen.

The pixie jumped in front of the unicorn and joined in the dance, mirroring the unicorn's steps. They took turns in changing the dance and each one followed the other. The snow continued to fall around them, but Gertrude was unaware of the cold as she gave herself up to the beauty of their dance. At last, they both stilled and Finn took the unicorn's head in his hands. He looked deeply into its eyes. He nodded and let go, his shoulders slumping. Slowly he turned and made his way towards Nell, dragging his feet.

'It is time, flower of mine, sun in my sky.' Nell let out a pained cry.

'No, Finn. You were to journey part of the way with me. You said.'

'It is not to be, Nell. My mother is calling and my time is upon me and I cannot – I *may* not – be with you during my changing. You know that.' Nell nodded. Finn turned to Sam.

'Sam, come here.' Sam went up to the pixie and Finn crouched down. He kissed him on his wet black nose and made a movement with his hand.

'There. You are gone, for the next few days, hidden from eyes that have no right to see you. No one will see you unless love burns bright in their heart.' He stood up and looked at Nell who was twisting her apron in her hands.

'Yes, Finn … yes of course … you must go,' she said. 'We knew it was soon. May the gods speed you on your way and I wish you every luck in the future.' She held out her hand. Finn ignored it, his eyes never leaving her face.

'Will you come back, Finn?' said Gertrude.

'You think you could keep me away from Nell's honey cakes?'

'Sounds rude,' said Jim. Finn laughed too long and too loud. He held out his shaking hands, his eyes glittering as Jim flew onto them. He looked back at Nell and Jim flew off, landing on Gertrude's shoulder. Nell bunched her apron in her hands and as Finn went forward to speak to her, she put a finger on his lips.

'Don't. Don't say it. I can't bear it.' Finn removed her finger.

'But you must. You must bear it for both of us. Only for a while.'

'Go. Change. Become who you must be. No promises, no oaths to bind. You will feel different once you are changed.'

'Ah, woman, for all your wisdom, you do not understand the Elven at all do you?' He pressed his lips to her hands, breathing in her scent.

Then he vanished.

Nell's eyes closed as she tried to control the grief sweeping over her. Gertrude turned away, not understanding and not wanting to.

'How far are we travelling?' she asked the unicorn.

'You have already travelled far.' She waited for it to continue.

'How much further must I go?' It gave her another searching look.

'For you, so much further.' Jim leant down and whispered in her ear.

'It will take a day and a half at most. He's a lovely fella, but he speaks in riddles all the bleedin' time.' Gertrude struggled to her feet, the cold making her stiff. Nell went inside and came back with a big dark green cloak. She wrapped it around her.

'There, with your green gown, you look like a queen.'

'Won't I stand out?'

'No, you will merge with the trees wearing this.'

'But there aren't any trees.'

'Not here, but where you're going there are plenty.' Tal came up, leading Zeus and Apollo. 'Tal, good, you put your cloak on. Keep it on. This snow is here to stay.' At seeing the unicorn both horses extended their forelegs and took a deep bow. It bowed back and the three horses stared at each other. A strange sound came from the unicorn. Zeus and Apollo joined in.

'They're laughing,' Jim said. 'Horse humour. Very dry, very swift and totally unfunny to the rest of us.' Zeus shook his head, sending his mane flying and Apollo pawed the ground.

'We are ready, My Sacredness.' Zeus said.

'Are you sure?' the unicorn asked softly. Zeus stilled.

'I will not know I am ready until I try.'

'And I can only try my best,' said Apollo.

'And that is all any of us can do.' The unicorn looked up at one of the turrets and Gertrude saw him shudder. 'We must go. Now.' He turned, facing the entrance of the courtyard. Nell scooped Gertrude up into a bone-crushing embrace.

'Goodbye, Nell, thank you for everything,' Gertrude managed to gasp out.

'Now stop with the goodbyes, I will be seeing you soon. Dafydd and I are following on. We just have to shut up my kitchen and protect my pans, so no one steals them, and then we will be following on. I'll be there before you.'

'Why can't I come with you?'

'Each of us must take our own path now,' and tears welled in her eyes. 'Now have you got enough food?'

'Yes, Nell, more than enough,' said Tal pulling Gertrude out of Nell's arms. He helped Gertrude up onto Zeus. 'There is too much in this bag as it is.' Nell stroked the horses' noses.

'I put carrots and crystallized sugar in there for you both.'

'Are you sure you packed enough?' asked Zeus.

'Yes!' said Tal and Gertrude together. Sam and Lucinda licked their goodbyes to Nell and Dafydd. Nell pulled Tal in for an embrace.

'Be safe. Keep them all safe for me,' she said in his ear. 'And yourself, my boy.'

'Good journeying, Aunt.' He leapt onto Apollo. Thoth ran out flicking his tail and Lucinda ran over to him and purred something into his ear. She ran back to Sam and gave him a haughty look. Sam chuckled.

'You and Thoth?'

'None of your business, dog.' Jim made a retching noise.

'Ugh, cat's kissing. Gawd no. Let's go then.' He took flight. No one moved. He turned and flew back. He landed on Zeus's back, in front of Gertrude.

'I have no idea where we are going, do I? It changes every time. Lead on, Guvnor.' The unicorn chuckled.

'I will have need of your keen eyesight later on, Jim.' The unicorn danced forward. Gertrude looked back and waved at Nell and Dafydd. They were holding onto each other whilst Thoth sat on the ground between them. Gertrude glanced up at the turret that the unicorn had looked at earlier.

And a cold entered her bones that had nothing to do with

the falling snow.

CHAPTER 50

Up high in the turret, a figure stands by the leaden window.

Wrapped in the furs of an alpha wolf and his mate, she has to keep leaning back from the glass, as her breath leaves ice crystals on the window pane.

Looking at the unicorn, blazing like a fallen star, she feels a pang of yearning that makes her clutch her chest. She chases the feeling away.

Not for her. Never for her.

Concentrating on the red-haired figure, dressed in green, she takes that yearning desire and changes it into hate. She focuses every part of her being onto that small figure on the black horse and her desire and hate becomes a living thing that grows.

She feels it breathing beside her. Turning, she observes the dark shadow. She looks back out of the window, at the little group leaving.

'Follow,' she whispers.

The creature beside her bows and disappears.

CHAPTER 51

An hour and several dirty songs later, courtesy of Jim, they stopped for food.

Gertrude spread out a rug on the snowy ground. The burnt twisted trees offered no shelter, but the rug felt warm beneath her. She shared out the mountain of food, almost covering the rug completely. Nell had packed pasties, cheese, bread, grapes and even a glorious sponge cake. For the horses, there were carrots and a tub of red sugar cubes. Gertrude thought it tasted like strawberries. Tal raised a glass of lilac wine.

'Much as I moaned, I am starving, so here is to you, Nell.'

'To Nell,' everyone said. No one said anything for a while as they ate their way through the feast. The unicorn stood, looking off into the distance. Tal wiped his mouth on the back of his hand and followed the unicorn's gaze.

'It is a wasteland, isn't it?' The unicorn let out a sigh.

'And spreading every day.'

'This island was not always an island,' Tal said looking at Gertrude. 'The queen raised the waters and cut it off. No one can get near her stronghold without her knowing. When Vivienne taught here, she could raise the waters to please herself, but she never had them like this.'

'Mrs Eccles lived here?'

'They all did. Cat, Morgan, Vivienne, Brighid ... this was a centre of learning and magic.' A wistful look came over his face. 'I grew up here.'

'So, we have to cross water?' Lucinda asked.

'Yes, my love.' Lucinda shook her head.

'I am not swimming.' Tal looked at the unicorn.

'We are not going to swim … unless you found another way?' The unicorn turned, his great dark eyes taking them all in.

'We must cross with the ferryman.'

'Oh gawd,' Jim said. Lucinda nestled close to Tal.

'Listen, I do not care if that ferryman is the seventh demon from hell, I am not going in the water.'

'He is the sixth, actually,' said the unicorn. He looked off into the distance again. Sam stood up and walked over to him. They exchanged a long look.

'Would you like some food, Your Divineness?'

'No thank you, Sam, but it is kind of you to ask.'

'What is your name?' asked Gertrude. Surely, he had a name and Gertrude needed to say it. She wanted to feel the purity of it in her mouth and form it with her breath.

'I could say it, but you would not hear it.'

'Try us,' said Lucinda smugly. The unicorn turned to face them and spoke one word.

Gertrude immediately felt a warmth spread from within her as the word moved over her like a deep contented sigh. Everything felt wonderful. Everything was happening just the way it should be. She caught Tal smiling at her, the corners of his grey eyes crinkling. The moment passed and they all shook their heads.

'I caught the first bit,' said Zeus.

'I caught the last bit,' said Apollo and both horses looked extremely pleased with themselves.

'I caught the fifth letter,' Lucinda said. Jim snorted and puffed his feathers up.

'I heard it all.' The unicorn laughed.

'Really, little friend?'

'Nah, but I hates smug horses. Didn't hear a bloody thing,

but I felt full of worms when you said it.'

'So, what shall I call you?' said Gertrude.

'What your heart tells you.' Gertrude thought for a moment.

'Star.'

'Friend,' said Lucinda.

'Compassion,' said Sam.

'Lord,' said Apollo.

'Vengeance,' said Tal. No one said anything for a while after that.

❋ ❋ ❋

'Jim, if you sing one more dirty song,' Sam growled, 'I swear I will bite your wings off. There are ladies present.' Jim made a great show of looking around.

'Where?'

'Tal, please, for the love of whatever god you worship, you sing instead.' Tal thought for a moment.

'All the nice girls love a candle —'

'Oh, good god, there is no hope,' Sam cried. Tal laughed. Gertrude looked over, astonished to hear him laugh. It was rich and deep and she found herself laughing in delight.

'Maybe when we are on our own, Jim.' Jim guffawed and Lucinda and even Sam joined in the laughter.

'Bless you all,' said the unicorn, 'That is taken some more time off our journey.' They rode on in companionable silence. Gertrude could not stop herself from smiling and she turned to Tal. He gifted her with one of his rare and dazzling smiles.

'I feel ...'

'Lighter? Freer?' Tal said, nodding. 'It is getting out of her shadow.'

'I have lived in that shadow all my life.' Tal said nothing for such a long time she thought he had not heard her.

'I found you so late,' he finally said.

'You were looking for me?' Capturing her eyes with his, she

felt terrified again at the intensity she saw there.

'Always.'

'I see the lake!' called Jim. 'Well, when I say see it, I mean it is here. Bloody thing always covered in mist because that despot doesn't want anyone getting on her island. Oh yes, cover it in mist, make it hard to get to, because that will stop people finding you. Well, it didn't stop me. I come and go as I please, you crazy, mad as a snake's arse, twonking old bollocking, hag.'

'Yes, thank you Jim and now everyone knows we are here as well.' Sam said.

'There's no one here, you stupid furball. There's just us and— oi, One Horn? Is he here yet?' The unicorn lifted his head.

'He is coming.' Gertrude slid off Zeus and wandered to the edge of the lake. Only the water lapping at the shore made a sound. She sensed Tal beside her and dared not look up at his face. *Always,* he had said.

The prow of a boat broke through the mist. On its prow, a strange creature painted dark blue parted the fog. The figure in the boat wore a black hooded cloak and the hands that gripped the pole were those of a skeleton.

'Charon? From Ancient Greece?' Sam asked.

'Maybe,' said Gertrude, 'But Charon fetches the dead.'

'Maybe we are dead,' said Lucinda, pacing by Tal's feet. Jim snorted.

'Well, I ain't bloody dead. I can still eat worms.'

'Spoken like a true philosopher,' muttered Sam. Gertrude stroked his silky ears.

'Scared, Scamp?'

'Yes. You?'

'He would be a fool if he was not,' Tal said. Tal gathered Lucinda up in his arms and watched the boat come in. It did not make a sound, even when it stopped, just offshore. The cloaked figure stood still; his face obscured. The unicorn made a move forward but Tal put out his hand.

'Let me,' and with Lucinda snuggled in his arms, he waded out to the boat. The ferryman put out a bony hand and one by one, his skeletal fingers unfurled. Tal looked back at the unicorn.

'You have to give him a gift, Tal.' Lucinda scrambled up Tal's arms and wrapped herself around his neck like a fur collar.

'Oh my god, do not even think about it.'

'You daft darling.' Tal fished around in his pockets until he found two coins.

'Who would want a cat as a gift?' said Jim.

'I have no idea,' Sam replied. Tal flipped a coin over for Gertrude to catch, but Jim caught it in his beak. He gave it to her and Gertrude closed her hands around the gold. Tal placed the coin in the ferryman's hand and the fingers curled over it. The ferryman placed it in an unseen pocket. He beckoned to Tal, but as Tal went to jump on, the ferryman put a hand out and pointed to Lucinda.

'I do not have any more coin, sir.' Tal looked over to the unicorn.

'He will want something else from your brothers and sister. He does not expect them to carry coin.'

'Give him a hairball, Lucinda,' shouted Jim. Gertrude walked over to Nell's picnic bag on Zeus.

'You are not helping, Jim. Here, Lucinda, give him a grape.' She threw a plump black grape over. Tal caught it and put it in Lucinda's mouth. She placed it in the bony hand. Again, the grape disappeared into a secret pocket and the ferryman beckoned the two friends on. Lucinda jumped off Tal and hid underneath a seat.

'You next, brother,' said the unicorn and Apollo splashed forward.

'I give you the wind from my mane,' and he shook his head so his mane flew around the still figure. The ferryman moved back and beckoned the horse on board. The boat did not even tilt as Apollo jumped aboard.

'Poncy twatfish,' Jim croaked.

'I am not as arrogant,' Zeus said, 'So I am going to give the ferryman what I would like as a gift. Gertrude, if you please, some sugar.' Gertrude reached down into the bag until she found the red sugar cubes and placed one in Zeus' mouth. The horse gulped.

'Sorry. Can I have some more?' She got out another bit, but Zeus ate that too.

'Zeus, try to control yourself.' This time Zeus managed to hold onto it and waded over, dropping it into the ferryman's hand. He jumped on beside Apollo and bent down to talk to Lucinda.

'Jim?' said the unicorn.

'What are you going to give him?' Gertrude said.

'A joke, what else?' Jim flew over to the dark figure. He alighted on the prow and the ferryman leaned closer.

'Two deaf men walk into a bar—' Gertrude put her hands over her face, looking through her fingers.

'The nerve of that bird,' said Sam. Jim continued whispering in the ear of the ferryman, laughing so much at his own punch line, that he fell off the prow with a splash.

The ferryman did not laugh. Sam shook his head.

'Perhaps he is deaf and that joke has backfired. Serve him right.'

'No, he likes it. He's let him on.'

'Bloody bird. Right just you and me now, Scamp. Ladies first.'

'No, Sam, your turn,' said the unicorn

'What is your gift, Sam?'

'I am going to tell him something I once read, long ago.' Sam trotted through the water. He went up on his hind legs, his front paws resting on the side of the boat. The ferryman leaned down and Sam whispered in his ear. The cloaked figure straightened and did not move.

'Oh god, Sam, what did you say?' Gertrude murmured. After a long moment, the figure nodded and Sam clambered aboard. It was only Gertrude and the unicorn left on the shore now.

'Now you, flower bride.' Gertrude stepped forward into the icy water. Looking up she realised how tall the ferryman was.

'Here, sir, a coin for you,' but the ferryman kept his hand

closed. 'Sir, a gold coin for you, my lord.' But the hand remained closed.

'What would you like me to give you?' she whispered. The fingers unfurled and nestling in the bones, she saw a tiny seed. Looking up into the dark space of the hood, she said,

'Do you wish me to take it?' Silence. She took the seed out of his hand and without thinking, she breathed on it. She placed it back into his hand.

At once, the seed sprouted. A green shoot curled out and up, followed by three more. The seed expanded and the green shoots burst into leaves. A long stalk grew out of the seed. The stalk grew thorns and as it grew longer, a bud appeared at the top. The petals unfurled and a dark red rose lay in the ferryman's hand.

The ferryman still did not move. In desperation, Gertrude grasped the rose and yelped as the thorns pricked her. A drop of her blood fell onto his white bones and lay there, glistening.

Like the seed, his hands sprouted fibres and muscles until flesh covered his hand. The flesh moved up the ferryman's arms and he gasped and dropped the rose. She caught it and he swayed back and forth, as flesh began to clothe him. The other hand gripping the pole changed and she saw he had beautiful hands with long fingers. The pole dropped over the side of the boat with a splash. The cloaked figure gave a scream that turned into a roar of such passion and anger, that Gertrude fell back into the water. She watched, unable to move, as the arms came up and ripped the hood back, finally revealing the face of the ferryman.

CHAPTER 52

A young bearded man stood, with chestnut hair falling to his shoulders and bright hazel eyes. Leaning down he stretched out an arm to Gertrude and said in a golden-throated Welsh voice,

'Though you are small, you are gifted.
From the sea and the mountain, from rivers' depths
God sent bounty to the blessed.'

He broke into a smile. 'Get out of the river's depths, Jenny, and come into my arms.' He pulled her up into the boat and planted a firm kiss on her mouth. Tal stepped forward.

'As I live and breathe … Taliesin.' The man let go of Gertrude and enveloped Tal in a bear hug. He threw his head back and laughed.

'I might have guessed you would not be far away. Well met son, oh well met. Oh, to touch again, to smell again, to feel sweet flesh again.' He grabbed Gertrude and buried his nose in her neck, growling, 'By all the gods, the scent of a woman.' Tal pulled him away and Taliesin grinned.

'Stop worrying. I know better than to mess with your destiny.' Winking, he released Gertrude. Taliesin looked over the prow at the unicorn standing by the shore.

'My dear, wonderful friend.' He gave a deep bow. The unicorn walked across the water without splashing.

'And what gift shall I give you, ferryman?'

'None, dearest heart, I have all that I need. Get on and I shall take you across. Where are you all going anyway?'

'Across,' said the unicorn springing up onto the boat. He moved over to the prow and looked towards the shore. Taliesin walked over to him and caressed the carved beast at the front.

'Come, Prydwen, take these seven to safety.' He looked at the unicorn, 'I need hardly ask for your safety, but of course, I wish you safe passage as well.' The boat moved backwards and turned. Gertrude settled down on a seat facing the prow. Lucinda crept out from under her seat and jumped onto her lap. Taliesin waved his arms around.

'Let's get rid of this confounded mist, shall we?' The unicorn lowered his head over the side and blew onto the water. It was like watching paint spill. The water near the boat turned blue and spread across the lake. The mist glowed gold and evaporated.

'Great stuff.' Taliesin rubbed his hands. 'I don't suppose you have any food?'

'Just a bit,' laughed Tal. He removed the picnic bag off Zeus and threw it over. 'Help yourself.' Taliesin dived in and sat down opposite Gertrude, stuffing a pasty in his mouth.

'Ah, Jenny,' he said, showering her with crumbs, 'You can't beat a pasty. One of Nell's I take it?'

'My name is not Jenny, sir.'

'What is it this time then?'

'Gertrude.' Taliesin spluttered and leant over to wipe the crumbs from her front. Gertrude blushed as he brushed her breasts.

'Really? And what's with all this sir stuff? Call me Tal.'

'I can't, that's his name.' Taliesin turned round and gave Tal a searching look.

'Tal? Short for Taliesin?' Tal's eyes narrowed and he shook his head.

'Talfryn.'

'Really?' He looked back and forth between Gertrude and Tal

and shrugged.

'Who am I to interfere? But I can't make much of a song with those names. What rhymes with Gertrude for muse's sake?' Tal sat down next to Gertrude and Lucinda crawled from her lap into his.

'What happened to you, Taliesin?' Tal asked. 'Vivienne was so worried. When she sent you into the castle and you never returned, we feared the worst.' Taliesin shivered.

'It was the worst.'

'Why on earth did Vivienne send you to the queen?' asked Gertrude.

'I am a bard, darling heart, remember? What better spy is there? We creep in and out unnoticed … well not unnoticed,' and he winked. Jim guffawed. Taliesin looked over at Jim and then slapped his thigh. He threw his head back, roaring with laughter.

'Country and western! Brilliant Jim, just brilliant.' He wiped tears from his eyes. 'It's good to laugh again. It's good to feel again. Any more pasties?'

'Only enough for a battalion,' replied Tal.

'Which of course you are,' he said, spluttering them all with crumbs. 'A small one, I grant you, but one nonetheless. Now Jen – I mean Gertrude – remember us bards can come and go as we please and many a lady and gentleman takes us into their confidence. For the right price, we can obtain certain information and pass it on. Now, sometimes the other side asks us to do the same and then we have a right to-ing and fro-ing.'

'Is that not disloyal?' said Sam, leaning up against Gertrude's knees. Taliesin fixed Sam with a stare.

'Sir, the only loyalty I have, is to the word.'

'But are you not breaking your word?' Lucinda said.

'Gods, Talfryn, where did you find these two? You must understand there is only one group of people I am loyal too and a couple of them are on this boat. May I continue? Being *the* bard, the bard to end all bards, I naturally drew attention from the queen. The fact that I wrote a song praising her wintry beauty helped. She called on me to perform and the whole castle was in a state of excitement.' He threw out his arms. 'This lake is testament to that fact, as they all wet themselves in anticipation of my stanzas.' Gertrude laughed and felt Sam shake with laughter beside her. 'So, in I come, harp in hand, best seat by the fire, and I begin.' He stuffed the remains of the pasty in his mouth, gulping it down. 'I started with a rousing ballad and brought them to a fever pitch. I moved the energy up and up until people's hearts were beating and sweat broke out on their lips.' Taliesin leaned forward and everyone on the boat moved closer to him as he dropped his voice to a whisper.

'Then, I brought them back down with a mournful song, so that the tears ran so much that this lake swelled. I completely entranced her.' He leant back on the bench and crossed his arms. After a while, Gertrude asked,

'And then what happened?' Taliesin cleared his throat.

'I went to sleep and woke up in this boat as a skeleton. Don't suppose there is any wine in that bag?' Tal placed his hand on Taliesin's knee.

'What happened?' Taliesin ran a hand over his face and looked down at the floor. Suddenly he jumped up, raising his arms to the sky, making Lucinda run for cover.

'Damn' your questions, Talfryn. I never could lie to you.' He wheeled round pointing at Tal, his hazel eyes blazing. 'Mind you, you could never lie to me either could you?' He sat back down. 'The queen asked for a private performance, and I gave her one.' Jim laughed and then stopped at the agonised glance Taliesin gave him.

'Yes, my Jim. In all ways.' He stared at the floor. 'She asked me to sing of Tristan and Isolde.' Tal's head snapped up and Taliesin nodded.

'Aye, that song.' He turned to Gertrude. 'You remember, I was Tristan and Isolde's confidant. I would visit King Mark in Cornwall and sing a love song that I had written with Tristan. He always had an ear for a song, you remember, Tal?' Tal nodded. 'I would sing this song for Mark. Everyone would clap and cheer and he would never notice his wife in the corner, trembling, with tears streaming down her face. Then Isolde would come to me and tell me her reply. I would fashion it into a song, go back, and sing it for Tristan. The men would cheer and clap and no one would notice Tristan, pale and shaking in the corner. Through my songs, they would arrange places to meet and make love. Not the first time I have been used for that purpose and no doubt it will not be the last.' He turned and gave Tal a piercing look. Tal looked away over the water.

'You sang for the queen?' said Zeus.

'Yes, I sang for her. I sang my ballad of Tristan and Isolde. I let my guard down because I loved them both and therefore, I sang from my soul rather than my head, as I had done in the great hall. And she knew. She knew who I was and why I was there. She looked at me with her glacial eyes and she lay down on her bed. I placed my harp down and I went willingly. I was on fire, as Tristan and Isolde had been. I burned for her and I lay on that bed, covered with the furs of my wolf friends. I touched her to quench my thirst for her.' He buried his face in his hands and his shoulders shook as he started to sob. Gertrude slid off the bench and knelt in front of him.

'She is a difficult person to say no to.' He raised his head and Gertrude read the gratitude in his eyes.

'The moment I touched her … the moment she took me … within, I felt a numbing coldness spread through me. I looked down. My skin had turned to ice and then broke off, leaving only bone. I think I started screaming then.' He wiped his nose on his sleeve and Lucinda jumped up onto his lap. Sam placed a paw on his knee. Taliesin hugged Lucinda and then wiped his nose on her fur. She sighed but did not move.

'I became what you saw, a living death. She stood over me and she said in that voice of hers, soft with an undertone of horror—'

'I know it well,' said Gertrude.

'—she said, "There will be no talk of love in this room. There will be no talk of love in this castle or in this land. I have killed love … for love has killed me.'" Gertrude leant back.

'She said that? Are you sure?'

'Lady, I have forgotten my clothes. I have forgotten where I have placed my drink. I have forgotten which lady I am meant to be bedding. I once even forgot my harp, but I have never, ever forgotten words. Every word said in my presence is here, preserved for eternity.' He tapped his head.

'Forgive me.'

'Forgiven. She told me, as I liked travelling back and forth, I was to become her ferryman, to take people back and forth to her kingdom. I was to remain her ferryman until the day I died, which she said would never come. And that is what I have been doing, ferrying the rapists, the murderers, and the child killers to her castle, silently screaming and praying for death … until I saw you, radiant flower and realised what the seed was for.'

'Where did you get the seed?'

'An old woman gave it to me and said I would know who to give it to when the time was right.' He slapped his hand to his forehead, knocking Lucinda off his lap.

'Fool! It was Morgan, wasn't it?'

'It sounds like it,' said Tal, picking up Lucinda, 'But it could have been any of the sisters.'

'Where *are* you all going?'

'To meet up with them, I hope.'

'Oh, this is too much, too much to hope for. Will … *she* be there?'

'I hope so,' Tal said. Taliesin stood up and made his way to the prow of the boat. He stood with the unicorn, talking quietly. Gertrude looked up and found Tal staring at her, his grey eyes reflecting the lake. She tried and failed, as always, to read their depths. She turned her head and jumped up.

'Sam, do you see what I see?' Sam jumped up on the bench.

'Good god.' The island was receding into the distance, but seen from here, it seemed familiar. On top of the hill, stood a tower.

'Where has the castle gone?'

'It is still there, but it is veiled,' Tal said.

'Help me, Sam, why do I know this view?'

'Glastonbury Tor.'

'But that is in our world.'

'But this is your world,' shouted Taliesin, from the prow.

'This is the first version, the deeper version,' explained Tal. 'There will be things you recognise here. Of course, there was not always a tower there and that island had a different name once.' The sadness in his voice made Gertrude look over at him.

'What name?' His hands gripped Lucinda and without taking his eyes off the island he said,

'The Isle of Apples, the Fortunate Isle.' He turned to face her. 'Avalon.'

CHAPTER 53

'**R**ight, let's get off this boat, find an inn and give them a sing-song they will never forget.

'How about it, Talfryn? For old times' sake?' Taliesin slapped Tal's back and jumped off the boat as it drew slowly to the shore. Splashing through the water, he reached the shore and, kneeling he kissed the ground.

'Land. To be on land again. I am never leaving land again. Solid earth, terra mater, Gaia, my mother, my sacredness, dirt, soil ...'

'Passionate fellow ain't he?' Jim said. 'Personally, the land stinks. Give me the air. Oh, to be flying free like the wind, in the breeze, in the vapours, riding the thermals ...' Lucinda shook her head.

'Don't you go all bardish on us, crow. One bard is enough.'

'Just because you have no poetry in your heart, you cruel dark feline from hell, you utter abomination, you demon incarnate, you—'

'Somebody make him stop. And get me off this boat. Now, if you please, *Talfryn*.'

The boat drew to a stop and everyone disembarked and made their way to shore. The unicorn remained standing in the water. Taliesin stood up and stared, wild-eyed, at the boat. It turned and moved of its own accord back across the lake.

'Prydwen, voyager of my soul, whence will we meet again?' Taliesin took a shuddering breath and turned to the unicorn.

'You asked me what gift you should give me?' He stretched out his arms. 'Purification.' He dropped to his knees again. 'I can still feel her, you see,' he said in a ragged whisper. 'I can still feel her cold grip around me.' The unicorn gave Taliesin a long look. Taliesin shook his head.

'No, my friend, do not look on me with compassion. I went willingly, do you understand? In one moment, I forgot everything and everyone I have ever loved, even *her*, my most beloved. There was just the queen and I could not see past her.'

'Taliesin,' Gertrude said, 'She dominates your thoughts. I can vouch for that.'

'Then how come Talfryn was able to resist her? I wasn't the only one Vivienne used.' Tal grew still. Taliesin looked over at Gertrude and back at Tal. He gave a crooked smile.

'Ah, my friend, if only I had your singleness of purpose. You are blessed.'

'Cursed,' snapped Tal and looked away.

'Come into the water, Taliesin, Bard of Bards and Wordsmith of the Universe,' the unicorn said. Taliesin stood and waded into the water. 'Kneel, child.' The bard knelt with a splash, his black cloak spreading like oil around him. 'There is nothing to forgive, Bard of Bards. Nothing at all.' Taliesin bowed his head. 'Gather some water in your hands.' Taliesin scooped up the water and held it out to the unicorn who lowered his horn into the outstretched hands. The water gave off a golden glow. 'Drink.'

Taliesin gulped the golden water down. As he did so, he began to glow. He tore off the cloak and threw it up into the air. The unicorn caught it on his horn. A flash illuminated the lake and black-winged creatures flew out across the water, back towards the tower on the hill. The unicorn put his head down and immersed his horn in the lake. He tossed his head and a showering arc of water came down on Taliesin's head and bare shoulders. The water caught the light and it looked as if Taliesin was bathing in a rainbow. The unicorn tossed the water over him three times. On the last time, a flash of brilliant light obscured him and when Gertrude could see again there stood the Bard of Bards, fully clothed, in soft brown trousers, with a white billowing shirt and knee-length brown boots. A brown cloak settled about him and in his hand, a small golden harp appeared. Taliesin ran his hands over the strings, caressing the music out of it. The notes hung over the lake and with it, Gertrude felt a memory stir. A long-forgotten echo of a song.

'I am back,' he said.

'You are back,' replied the unicorn.

'She took. I never gave. I am back.'

'Now the music can begin again,' Jim sniffed, wiping his eyes on his wing. Taliesin bowed to the unicorn, who bowed back. He splashed through the water, onto the shore.

'Right, who's for a rousing verse of *"All the nice girls love a candle?"'* Jim and Tal laughed and joined in the song as he and the horses walked down the shore. Sam sat shaking his head and Gertrude knelt beside him, the memory of the song now vanished into silence.

'What did you say to Taliesin when you entered the boat?' Sam looked over at the unicorn. Again, they exchanged a long look.

'I told him, "We set out to be wrecked."' Gertrude watched Tal walking away, his feline grace making her breath catch.

'Oh, Sam … don't we just?'

CHAPTER 54

They made camp just after they entered a forest.

Icicles hung from the branches and lumps of snow fell on them as they passed underneath the first few trees. Gertrude placed her hands on them, but the trees did not speak. Before the forest fully took over, they found themselves in a clearing. The unicorn sat down and refused to move and therefore, Zeus and Apollo did likewise. Gertrude and Tal dismounted.

'The forest needs to feel that we are friends, not foe,' the unicorn said. 'The land is dying but it will die no more today.' With a sigh, the unicorn fell asleep.

'It is a testament to the queen's power that even this forest cannot escape her coldness,' Taliesin said. He plonked himself down on the ground, pulling Gertrude down with him and flung his arms around her. 'Keep me warm, Jenny.' He tickled her face with his beard. Gertrude giggled and then stopped as she caught the stormy look on Tal's face. Taliesin pushed her away from him.

'Goodness, Jen – Gertrude, leave me alone, girl.' But Tal did not join in with the laughter. He went over to Zeus and removed the picnic bag.

'Sam, Lucinda, Jim, with me. Let us go and search for food.'

'Do we not have enough?' Sam said.

'Taliesin has demolished most of it. Taliesin, gather some firewood, but only wood that—'

'Is lying on the forest floor, yes, *Talfryn*, I have been here before you know.'

'Then you will know how to conduct yourself.' He walked into the forest with the others scampering to catch up with him. Gertrude watched the graceful retreating figure.

'Has he always been like that?'

'You should know that better than anyone. One minute there are blue skies and the next the storm clouds gather. However, he is a prince amongst men, and I am wrong to play with his emotions. It's just I feel so ... so...'

'Alive?'

'Lustful,' and he winked at her. 'This must be how the trees feel after a long winter when you are back from the dead and your lifeblood, your sap, is pulsing and rising. Food tastes better; drink is like nectar, and to feel warm skin and a soft body in your arms ...' Gertrude smiled, but her eyes looked over to where Tal had gone. She hoped he would be quick.

'Tell me your story,' Taliesin said in a different voice. Gertrude looked over at him and found him staring at her.

'What do you want to know?'

'Everything.' He crossed his legs and placed his hands in his lap.

And so, she told him, slowly at first, but then every detail came tumbling out. Her grandmother and Jim. Meeting Mrs Eccles and Sam. The baths and Ariel and Cat. The fight at school. Mrs Eccles' disappearance and her journey into Albion. Taliesin never interrupted, even when she revealed who her grandmother was, but she could see him absorbing every word, rearranging it, and finding the thread that ran through it all. She could sense him weaving her tale into a tapestry that he could revisit and look at whenever he wanted.

The only thing she kept to herself was the golden-haired man with the eyes that changed colour, for he was hers and hers alone. Years of not mentioning him had locked him deep into a place even she would have trouble unlocking. Afterwards, she sat back against a log, exhausted, but feeling lighter.

'You are missing so much out.' Taliesin said.

'It is mine, and mine alone.'

'I respect that, and that is not what I am referring to. Whatever *that* is I will not pry. What I am referring to is all the other stories you have locked within you. You are not even aware they are there and I cannot access them, so there has to be a reason. Buried stories unearthed at the wrong time can lead to madness.' They sat together for a while in silence, listening to the gentle snuffling of the horses. 'Come on, let's gather wood before Talfryn comes back. Look for branches and sticks that have fallen on the ground. Do not break any off the trees.'

'Is this forest safe?'

'Is any forest? If we show it respect, it will do us the same courtesy. Anyway, we're both Welsh, my girl, so the forest is bound to love us.'

When they had gathered an armful each, Taliesin made a fire and wrapping her cloak around her, Gertrude gazed into the flames. The wood crackled and threw out sparks. Looking up through the trees at the approaching twilight, Gertrude was glad of it. Taliesin edged nearer to the fire.

'It's magic, isn't it? Our most ancient gift, our stolen salvation. You may be lost, with no hope of ever being found, and you may have travelled far, but if you have a fire, you have a home.'

'Be the fire in the hearth,' murmured Gertrude.

'When you met Cat, did she mention me?' Taliesin's eyes were pleading in the firelight.

'No, I am afraid she didn't, but she was so busy teaching me, we never had much time to talk.'

'How did she look?'

'Fierce.' He burst out laughing.

'But did you know her mouth is as soft as the wings of a dove?'

'She used that mouth for telling me off, more than anything

else.'

'Believe me, she does the same with me.' As they laughed, Tal and the others returned with a haul of berries.

'Did you find them all on the forest floor?' asked Gertrude.

'No,' said Sam. 'Tal explained the scent to us and I sniffed it out—'

'With help from me,' added Lucinda.

'I spotted it from the air you mean,' said Jim.

'Yes, yes, anyway Tal sat and talked to the bush for a while and then all the berries just rained down onto the ground.' Taliesin jumped up, and clapping Tal on the back, he drew him aside to speak to him.

'What are they talking about?' Sam asked. Gertrude shrugged, but when Taliesin glanced over towards Gertrude, she had some idea. She watched as Tal put his hands on his hips and looked down at the ground. He shook his head and then thrust his hand into his hair, pushing it back. Taliesin stood with his arms outstretched and Tal, after a moment, allowed himself to be enfolded in them.

'Bloody sappy twats,' Jim scoffed. Lucinda snorted.

'This, coming from the bird who hung around with Fred, Sid and the rest. You crownies were always hugging.'

'Shut up, cat. Just because you ain't got any friends.'

'I have no need of friends, nor do I want them.'

'Thanks for that,' said Sam.

'You know what I mean.'

'No, I do not. After all we have been through—'

'I love the way we disguise love with anger,' said the unicorn raising his head. He fixed Gertrude with a penetrating look. She looked over to the two men again and her heart contracted at the sight of Tal lit up by the fire. She turned away and looked back at the unicorn.

I can't help myself, can I? But the unicorn did not reply.

Later that night, as they settled down to sleep, the unicorn's words kept coming back to her. Was that why Tal was so angry with her all the time? He had said that he had always been searching for her. *Always.* She lifted her head and saw the shape of him, wrapped in his cloak, on the other side of the fire. To reach him she would have to reach through the flames. *I am not ready to be burned again* and she wondered where that thought had sprung from. But, as sleep crept upon her, she knew it was too late.

He had set her soul alight from the moment she had seen him by the church, standing with Zeus, on the first day of spring – a lifetime ago.

CHAPTER 55

Feathers floated down from the sky, landing on Gertrude's face, and waking her up.

Of course, they are not feathers. They are snowflakes, making my nose tickle. Except they are not melting. Someone yanked her up from the ground before she could open her eyes.

'Jenny! Look around you. Look. Wake up. Look at the wonder of it!' She opened her eyes a crack and would have fallen back down in shock if Taliesin had not been gripping her firmly.

Blossom covered every tree in the forest. From the palest pink to the deepest fuchsia, the trees blazed with colour. Overnight the snow had melted. She had fallen asleep on a winter's night and woken up on a spring morning. Petals danced in the soft breeze and Gertrude laughed when she saw Lucinda trying to catch them. Sam sat still, his face upturned to the falling blossom, letting the petals land on his nose. The horses and unicorn were gazing at each other, whickering softly.

'It's beautiful,' said Gertrude.

'Beautiful,' said Tal. His grey eyes shone and he smiled at her.

'How did this happen?' she asked.

'You. You happened,' he replied. 'You once asked me how you could make a difference. This is how. This is what you do. You bring back spring. You bring back life.' Taliesin turned round and flinging his arms around Tal and Gertrude, pulled them both into his chest.

'Ah, my loves, it is good to be alive, no?'

'Talking of good things, is there any breakfast?' asked Sam. Taliesin laughed.

'Of course, there is. Is there?'

'I will sort something out.' Gertrude removed herself from his embrace and hurried off to find the picnic bag.

When they were all stuffed, they covered the fire – after Taliesin said thank you to it –and carried on with their journey through the forest. The trees grew close together making it difficult to find their way through. The unicorn suggested that they sang, so Taliesin and Tal led them in various songs and soon the journey became easier. Gertrude even felt the forest was helping them. She was sure she saw a tree root pull back before Zeus stepped over it. Paths suddenly appeared and if they felt lost, a bird would land ahead of them singing, 'Over here,' before flying off. Jim called them nosey, bloody, bleeding, blighters but even he seemed relieved.

'You hardly need me,' the unicorn said, but Taliesin disagreed and they all said how grateful they were for his guidance.

'Apollo and I have loved talking to you, Sacred One.' Zeus said.

'Yeah, what have you silly tarts been talking about?' Jim asked. He was riding like a king, perched on Apollo's head. 'It's rude to speak a different language when we can't understand.'

'You would not understand anyway, crow,' Apollo answered. 'There are no words to describe the kind of subjects we have been discussing.' For an answer, Jim pecked Apollo on his head and Apollo tossed him off into a bush. Gertrude jumped off Zeus and retrieved the swearing crow.

'Stop winding people up,' she laughed and then fell quiet as she thought she heard something laugh back. She put her hand on a neighbouring tree and listened. It sighed but did not speak.

'I thought with the blossom they may have woken up.'

'Perhaps they take a while to come round like bloody

Lucinda does. You can't talk to her until she's had a third bowl of milk.'

'I heard that, crow,' said Lucinda 'I am not a morning person.'

'I don't think you are an anytime person. I think you are a miserable sod of smelly underpants whatever the time.' Lucinda did an about-turn and chased Jim out of Gertrude's hands. He managed to fly onto a tree just in time and then swore as she began to climb it.

'Children, children, do stop,' Sam sighed. He yelped and ran as Lucinda and Jim chased after him. Gertrude was laughing so much, it took her a while to realise that everyone had gone silent. They had moved into a large glade and even Jim, Sam and Lucinda stopped chasing each other and became still.

'We are here,' the unicorn said. He sank onto the grass and promptly fell asleep.

Taliesin moved forward and twirled in the centre of the glade. He threw back his head and closed his eyes, letting the warm sun caress his face. Blossom fell about him and he smiled. Gertrude looked over and found, as she knew she would, Tal staring at her. She smiled but he did not return her smile. To cover her embarrassment, she wandered over to the oak tree that dominated the clearing.

No blossom adorned it. Its gnarled trunk was the size of a house. Green moss covered it and its bare branches stretched far up into the sky. Gertrude felt dizzy looking up at it. To steady herself, she placed her hand on its trunk.

'Breathe,' said a deep-rooted voice and the earth trembled. Gertrude clapped her hands in delight.

'Yes, sir, yes I will breathe. Hello.' She flung her arms along the vast trunk and kissed the knotty bark. Pressing her body to the tree, she took in a deep breath. The tree answered by taking in a shuddering inhale. Three times she breathed on the tree and three times it breathed on her. On the final time, it said,

'Enter.' Gertrude stepped back. The tree shook as if to adjust itself. Hearing a noise from above, Gertrude looked up and watched as the miracle unfolded.

The branches began to creak and twist. Slowly they parted and Gertrude saw what looked like a turret appear above her. One of the tree's branches expanded sideways and high above her, a round room appeared, complete with arched stained-glass windows. On the other side, another turret appeared and then rooms, turrets, and walls burst out all over the tree. A spiral staircase wrapped its way down and around the tree and came to rest before Gertrude's feet. Standing further back, Gertrude could now see a small castle nestled in the branches of the huge oak. She could not tell where the oak ended and the castle began. Hearing a noise, she looked up the steps and saw an apple bounce down to land at her feet. Leaning forward she picked it up and smelt it.

'Food!' Sam bounded up to her and Gertrude went to give it to him.

'No,' shouted Tal and Taliesin at the same time.

'You have to give it back,' Taliesin said. 'Go on, up you go.' Her eyes sought out Tal.

'Come with me?' She saw something flash in his eyes and he moved forward, but Taliesin put out his arm, stopping him.

'She must do this alone. Go, flower bride, go and meet your sisters.' She trod on the first step. Sam and Lucinda joined her on either side.

'You did not think to leave us, did you?' Sam said.

'Ha! Just think what mess she would get into,' Lucinda said. Sam pressed his trembling body close to Gertrude's and she put down her hand to smooth his head. She turned back to look at the two men and the horses that were watching her. The unicorn had woken up and gazed at her, love shining from his eyes.

'Where's Jim?'

'Here, on the ground. I won't fly in front, because this is your moment, Queen Girly, but I will hop behind you, as long as that dirty demon feline leaves me alone.'

'She'll leave you alone, won't you, Lucinda?'

'As long as he does not hop on my tail.'

'Right. Shall we go up then?' and clutching the apple tight in her hand, she began to climb.

Round and round the tree they went as she watched the ground fall away. She had underestimated the size of the tree, as they seemed to be climbing up for a very long time. They stopped and looked across the treetops. Her three companions did not rush her, although she could sense Lucinda's coiled energy. They let her set the pace. Sam lifted his nose to the air.

'Can you smell something? No ... it cannot be ...'

'What?' Gertrude said.

'I thought I smelt pasties.' Lucinda let out a snort.

'Good goddess, dog, do you ever think of anything but your stomach?'

'Madam, I know your sense of smell is inferior to mine, but try yourself.' Lucinda muttered under her breath and then stopped.

'You are right, I can smell pasties.' Gertrude laughed and started climbing again.

'Maybe it is a magical place where you can smell what you most desire. Maybe there will be a room full of pasties when you get there.'

'Or birds,' said Lucinda

'Oi, shut it, hairball,' Jim squawked, 'it's pasties all right.'

'A room full of birds would have been preferable and—oh my goddess—' Lucinda jumped forward, hackles up as the staircase ended. She hissed at the figure there.

'Cat to cat if you harm any one of us, I will hunt you down and destroy you.' The lion that waited for them at the top of the steps jumped back in surprise. A small grey head peered from between the lion's paws.

'Cat to cat, you really need to start trusting us.'

'Thoth?' The grey cat moved forward and licked Lucinda's nose. Jim made a retching sound. The lion roared into laughter.

'*Cat* to cat, I do not intend to harm any one of you. Well met, little Lucinda and Gertrude ... blessed be, you are here at last.'

'Ariel.' Running forward, Gertrude flung her arms around the lion, pushing him to the ground. He licked her face and she showered kisses all over his mane.

'I wanted to be your guide, little cub, but the unicorn and I fought over it and he won this time. Sam, good day, sir, how are you? And Jim, stop loitering and let me see you. You all look well and I am so glad you made it. Cat and I were so worried.'

'Cat is here?'

'Yes of course she is. Come in, come in and be welcome. You too, fierce Lucinda. We have been wanting to meet you for a long time. Welcome, friends. Welcome to Camelot.'

CHAPTER 56

Singing floated in the air as Gertrude followed Ariel and Thoth.

She stepped into the round room with the stained-glass windows. It was larger than it looked from the ground, but cosy, with a friendly fire crackling in the grate. Tapestries hung on the walls, and rugs lay across a stone floor. In the middle of the room was an enormous round table groaning with food and standing by it was the singer.

The woman smiled. Her glossy, honey blonde veil of hair hung down to her knees. The cornflower blue dress matched her sparkling eyes and she swayed as if showing off her curvaceous body. She looked as if you bit into her, milk and honey would flow. She was delicious. She held out her hands and Gertrude placed the apple into them.

'Oh, flower, you made it,' said the woman in a voice Gertrude had grown to love in the last few days.

'Nell?'

'The same.' The woman enfolded Gertrude in a perfumed embrace. Sam and Lucinda rushed forward and the beautiful woman knelt and gathered them into her arms.

'Nell?'

'Yes, little ones, me. Do you like?' She stood up and twirled around, letting her hair fly out about her. 'I know, flower, you're shocked but it *is* me. It's a long story to do with spells and enchantments and only being able to be beautiful in the day or in the night, depending on who I am with.' A note of sorrow crept into her voice. 'But this is me. Here I can be lovely all the time and—oh, Gertrude don't look like that. Don't tell me, you prefer Cook Nell? Why does everyone prefer Cook Nell?'

'Because Cook Nell cooks better than Golden Nell,' said a voice and a tall woman strode out of the shadows.

'Cat!' Gertrude flung herself at the warrior, only to be flung onto her back with a knife at her throat.

'What have I told you? Never, ever, let your guard down. You've met the queen; you know what she is capable of and yet you run towards me leaving yourself wide open for attack. And why is your hair down? I thought Tal would have more sense.'

'Tal's here?' said a voice from the other side of the room. Gertrude turned her head and saw Elaine hopping from one foot to another.

'I left him downstairs,' Gertrude said through gritted teeth. Elaine ran off, followed by Jim. Cat pulled Gertrude to her feet and looked her up and down.

'Cat, I know I have not been training since I got here and Nell's food—' but she did not get to finish as Cat pulled her into a fierce embrace.

'I have been so scared,' she whispered into Gertrude's ear. 'The queen sealed the veil and I could not get back. I should have been there. I should have saved Vivienne.' Sam bounded over to them.

'Cat, I should have been the one to save her and I failed.'

'Sam, if you could not save her, then maybe no one could have.' Cat crouched down and hugged the retriever to her chest.

'Do we know where she is?' asked Gertrude. 'I thought she might be here?'

'No one knows where she is. Morgan is looking for her everywhere.' Cat released Sam from the embrace. 'I have something for you though.' She reached behind her and produced Gertrude's sword.

'Joyous Guard! Oh, thank you. I thought I had lost it.'

'Wear it at all times from now on. Now, we need to work on some more moves, because I should never have been able to throw you on the floor like that. Now if you bend your knees—' Nell stepped forward.

'Cat, let the girl eat first. And there are the others she has to meet. Gertrude you already met Raine in the market. Here she goes by her true name, Igraine.' The tall woman stepped forward, but she was no longer the old woman from the market. The fine-boned face was recognisable, but her mass of coiled hair was auburn rather than white. She had smooth porcelain skin and a golden net held the heavy auburn hair in place. Her regal beauty and the citrine stare intimidated Gertrude. She made herself meet Igraine's eyes full on, raising her chin. A small smile played around Igraine's mouth and she stretched out her hand. Gertrude walked over and taking the hand, sank into a deep curtsy. She stayed there with her head bowed until Igraine said,

'We are all queens here. Arise, child,' but Gertrude saw she looked pleased. The gurgling of a baby made Gertrude turn around and she came face to face with a slender woman with long, straight brown hair and huge dark blue eyes.

'He wants to meet you,' the woman said in a soft voice.

'This must be Pryderi, Dafydd's nephew. And you must be Rhiannon.'

'Yes, how lovely for you to remember.'

'Where is Dafydd? I thought he was travelling with you, Nell?'

'He had to take a detour,' said Nell. Gertrude turned her attention back to the baby, who was reaching a hand out towards her. He had bright yellow hair and the same big blue eyes as his mother.

'Would you like to hold him?'

'May I?' and she held out her arms. The baby was a warm weight in her arms and she looked down. He gurgled and fixed his eyes on her. Slowly a smile spread across his face and his chubby hand reached out to touch her. Gertrude felt a powerful yearning and swallowed to rid herself of the lump forming in her throat.

'He likes you,' cooed Rhiannon.

'Of course, he bloody does, who doesn't?' Cat snapped. Gertrude laughed.

'You want a list? My grandmother, Tal—'

'I thought maybe on the journey you two resolved your differences.' Nell said. Cat kicked a stool.

'Give over, Nell. It's not a bloody fairy tale.' Nell's face fell. Gertrude placed a hand on Nell's arm.

'It is what it is, Nell. He hates me. He told me.'

'When?'

'On the plain of destruction.' Nell fixed her with a look.

'There is a fine line between love and hate, and I fear that Tal walks upon it every single day.' Cat paced up and down the room.

'Nell, enough. Now feed Sam because he looks like he is going to explode. And, Gertrude, aren't you going to introduce me to your friend?' Gertrude handed the baby back to his mother.

'Cat, meet the other cat in my life. This is Lucinda.'

'And a true warrior if ever I have seen one,' said Ariel. Lucinda inclined her head and stalked over to Cat, who had crouched down.

'Don't touch her, Cat,' Sam said. 'She hates it.'

'Same here. Very few people touch me.' Ariel placed a huge paw on Cat's shoulder and pushed her over. Cat sprang up and wrestled Ariel, who banged into the table. Nell steadied it with her hands and shot Cat a sharp look.

'Cat for the love of Cú Chulainn, stop. Why must you always cause chaos wherever you go?' Hearing Nell repeat what Mrs Eccles had once said, made Gertrude miss the old lady even more. She felt safe in this room, as safe as she had in Mrs Eccles' house, but the old lady's absence felt like a gaping wound.

Camelot.

When Ariel had said the name, Gertrude had felt something pull at her memory, like a child pulling on an adult's sleeve. She took in the tapestries and saw that each one portrayed the women.

Rhiannon's showed her standing with a white horse. Igraine's showed the regal lady holding out a crown. Cat's tapestry showed her in a fighting pose, with Ariel dancing alongside her. Gertrude did not get any further. Nell made a sound and flung herself across the room. Tal gathered her up and wheeled her around. Seeing them together, Gertrude realised the identity of the beautiful, sobbing, blonde woman she had seen with Tal the night of the feast. Gertrude wondered if he had greeted Elaine like that, but seeing the look of hunger on Elaine's face as she entered the room, made Gertrude think not.

'Look at you, Miss Golden,' Tal said, placing Nell down on the ground.

'Gertrude prefers Cook Nell.'

'We all prefer Cook Nell. Your pasties taste better.'

'Did you have enough food? Are you hungry because we are still waiting, but I am sure you could have a little bit now?'

'No, I will wait thank you. Hello, Thoth. Well met, sir. And this must be Pryderi. Congratulations, Rhiannon.' He walked over and kissed Rhiannon on the forehead. He held the baby's hand and leant down.

'Hello, little one. Ridden your first horse yet?'

'Give over, he is only a few days old,' Rhiannon said, smiling.

'Well, you are in good hands when you do ride, as your mother knows all about horses.' He turned his attention to Igraine and bowed.

'Aunt.'

'Nephew.' He walked over to her and kissed her on both cheeks. 'Do not be so formal, boy, you make me feel old.'

'Well, aren't you?'

'Aren't we all?' He nodded and turned and looked at Cat. She had stopped pacing and glared at him. Her sudden stillness made Gertrude nervous. Tal opened his hand and walked over to her.

'Hello …. Aunty.' A flicker of movement and Gertrude yelled out his name, but it was too late. The knife sliced through his shirt, leaving a red trail.

CHAPTER 57

Ariel growled and Lucinda hissed.

Cat brandished her knife with a wild look on her face. Tal grinned and hurled himself at her. She tried to sidestep, but he anticipated her move and shoved her up against the table. Nell yelled out,

'Not near my sandwiches!'

'Stuff your sandwiches, Nell,' Cat said, through gritted teeth.

'I did. It took hours. Get out, up to the hall, if you want to fight.' Tal and Cat stared at each other. Then, with a nod, they ran through the room and bolted upstairs, pursued by Ariel and Lucinda. Elaine hesitated and then followed, with Thoth racing behind. The remaining women all looked at each other in silence.

'Three coins on Cat.' Rhiannon said. Nell put out her hand.

'Five coins on Tal.' The two women shook hands and Nell ran upstairs. Igraine put her arms out and Rhiannon placed her son in them. Muttering thanks, she followed Nell. Igraine cooed to the baby and caught Gertrude's eye.

'Go. It will be worth seeing.' Gertrude and Sam ran toward the sounds of fighting.

They found themselves in a bright and spacious hall, with sawdust on the floor. Three crystal chandeliers festooned with candles gave off a warm yellow light. Weapons lined the walls, but there were no weapons in the fighters' hands. Gertrude had watched Cat fight with Ariel and she had seen Tal fight the soldier who had assaulted her, but nothing prepared her for the savage beauty that unfolded before her. They circled each other and every now and then, one of them would hit out, only to be blocked by the other. Their eyes fixed on each other and they moved closer together.

At an unspoken signal, the rhythm of the fight changed. Their bodies became a blur as their arms and legs entangled around each other. It was hard to tell where one person ended and the other one began. They separated and then clashed again, as Cat pushed Tal back down the room, kicking up clouds of sawdust as she went.

'To soak up any blood,' whispered Rhiannon. Tal had his back to the wall. He skirted underneath Cat's arms and attacked her from behind, smashing her into the wall. With a yell, she whipped around and knocked his feet from underneath him, but as he hit the ground, he anticipated her jump and rolled out of the way. She landed on the floor with a whack. Letting out a hoot of laughter, she sprang back up and launched herself into a series of forward flips, which had her wrapping her thighs around his neck. She yanked his hair and laughing, he grabbed her waist and flung her from him. She sailed through the air and rolled into a somersault.

Hooves echoed in the hall as the horses, the unicorn, and Taliesin entered. Jim flew over to Rhiannon who made a fuss of him.

'Hello, Rhi. What odds are we on?'

'I've bet Nell three coins that Cat wins. She has five on Tal.' Jim nodded.

'Five coins on the Cat, please. I'd love to see Tal get his arse kicked for once.'

'Yes, that would be nice, but when you are the greatest knight the world has ever seen it is not likely is it?' Gertrude was about to ask Rhiannon what she meant when she saw Cat run around the room.

Halfway up the wall.

Tal frowned. He took a running jump and leapt, grabbing

the middle chandelier. He swung back and forth, gathering momentum, and let go. He tumbled through the air, just as Cat leapt from the wall. They met in mid-air and fell into a mass of limbs only to separate.

'Had enough, boy?'

'Just warming up, Aunty.'

'By all the gods and goddesses isn't she wonderful?' said a booming, deep voice next to Gertrude.

It was Cat's undoing.

Her head snapped round to see Taliesin smiling at her. Tal took his chance and pounced, knocking her to the floor. In one fluid movement, he unsheathed her knife and sliced her upper arm.

'I win.' Cat let out a roar of anger. He released her and she jumped up.

'Damn it to Hades and a curse on you and all your kind.'

'Why did you attack me in the first place?'

'You let your guard down. How many times do I have to tell you and Gertrude, never, ever, let your guard down?'

'And how did I win?'

'Because I let myself become distracted.' Tal rolled his eyes.

'And how many times do I have to tell you—'

'Come here, you glorious child,' and she leapt at him. He caught her by the waist and wheeled her around. She jumped out of his arms.

'That leap from the chandelier. Genius.' Tal grinned and looked so proud he looked like a little boy. Gertrude felt her lips tug upwards.

'What about you running around the side of the wall,' Tal said grabbing Cat's upper arm. 'I mean how? You will have to show me.'

'That first move, brilliant. How did you know I was going to move that way?'

'I read your ears.'

'What?'

'Your eyes tried to fool me, but I watched your ears and

therefore your head moved a different way.'

'Damn.' Tal threw back his head and laughed.

'You taught me that.' Cat shook her head.

'Did I? Damn, I'm good.'

'The best.'

'And that move you did, the one where you stuck your leg out—'

'My love, am I going to have to fight you to get your attention? Is that what it will take?' Taliesin's rich voice echoed through the hall. Tal smiled over at him but Cat stared ahead as if she had not heard him.

'My angel, please. I have travelled so far and—'

It happened in a flash. One minute Taliesin stood there and the next he sprawled halfway across the hall, from the punch, blood pouring from his mouth.

'That had to hurt,' Sam said. Jim nodded.

'Should never cross Cat.'

'Or indeed, any cat,' said Lucinda. Tal moved forward to grab Cat's hand but she pushed him off.

'Don't you dare say anything to me. I thought he was dead.'

'I was dead. I was a living death,' said a choked voice across the room. Taliesin caught his blood in his hands. Nell moved towards him, but Cat stopped her with a look.

'You left me,' she said in a strangled voice.

'You know why, my love.' A taut silence stretched between them until Cat's raw voice broke it.

'You slept with her.' Taliesin wiped his bloodied mouth on his sleeve.

'I won't deny it. I don't deny it.'

'You forgot me.'

'I forgot my name, I forgot everything. She overwhelmed me and overpowered me. I did not go willingly. She took. I did not give.'

'Lies.'

'Truth,' the unicorn said. Cat's head whipped around, tears flying from her eyes.

'He did not go willingly. I looked. She numbed his mind and she numbed his heart. She took what was never hers. Your face was the last image he clung too, before he went under.' The unicorn's eyes of dark fire held Cat's until she bowed her head.

'She is destroying us. Ripping us apart, one by one.' Taliesin shook his head.

'She's trying to. But we have something on our side.' Cat lifted her head and glared at him.

'What?' He wiped his mouth again and held his hands out to her across the room.

'Love.' Cat spat onto the sawdust.

'Love? And that will turn winter into spring, will it? That will bring back the dogs, the wolves, and the sacred groves? That will crush her army of murderers and rapists? Will Vivienne come skipping through the door through love?' Taliesin lowered his arms.

'It's a start. She hates love. She is trying to destroy it. She fears it more than magic. She made me into a living death because of it, because I sang of love. But she lost. She will lose, because on my knees, bleeding from your hand, looking up at you, I know she lost. Woman of mine, I have a fire burning inside of me again, where once there was ice. I loved you before I went away, but that is nothing to what I feel now. When I saw you sail through the air like an angel on fire and—' Cat made a cutting gesture with her hand.

'You and your words.'

'You and your swords. Are we so different? Don't words and sword contain the same letters?' Cat made a noise and ran across the room. He gathered her to him and pulled her down on top of him. He said her name over and over, between ferocious kisses and winces of pain, his mouth still bloody. Nell looked over at Rhiannon and raised her eyebrows.

'You owe me five coins I believe, Rhi.'

'You bet against me?' Cat's voice yelled across the room.

'You've been like a lion with a sore paw since you got here and you were rude about my sandwiches.' Cat kissed Taliesin again and sprang across the room to stand before Nell.

'I haven't eaten for days. What with worrying about Vivienne and if Gertrude was all right. I am a sod when I am hungry.' Nell took Cat's face between her hands.

'My darling girl, why did you not say? Get downstairs right now and eat. Everyone who is going to come is here. Come on, all of you eat. I wish you had said, Cat, I would have given you something.' Taliesin came over and took Cat's hand. Cat smiled at him and turned to Nell.

'You said we were not to touch anything until everyone was here.' Nell stood on tiptoes and kissed Cat's nose.

'Since when have you ever listened to anything I say?'

CHAPTER 58

They ate solidly, renewing friendships and forging new ones.

Jim had already been told off for trying to teach the baby rude words. He, Sam, and Rhiannon were now huddled together by the fire, deep in conversation, the baby gurgling in Rhiannon's arms. Ariel and Lucinda showed off their leaps, to a delighted Cat and Taliesin. The reunited lovers sat on one chair, wrapped around each other. Thoth kept shouting out instructions, so Lucinda told him if he thought he could do better, then to do so. Thoth climbed onto the back of the chair and leapt onto the lamp, making it swing. Everyone felt disorientated as the light swung back and forth and Nell yelled at him to get down.

Igraine and Nell chatted over the table with Zeus and Apollo. It was a while until Gertrude noticed that the unicorn had gone. Only Tal seemed as isolated as she did. He stood looking out of the window. Elaine, who had long given up trying to talk to him, sat sulking in a corner, stuffing her face with chocolate cake.

'A toast,' said Nell hitting a knife against her glass. 'To friends. To new ones, to old ones, to found ones,' and here she nodded at Taliesin, 'To passed on ones ... ' Nell trailed off and looked down at the floor. Then she took a breath and squared her shoulders. 'To missing ones and to ones who bloody didn't bother to turn up.' She raised her glass and everyone followed suit.

'To friends.'

'To friends.'

The door swung back with such force it bounced back, obscuring the figure that stood there. It opened again, revealing a woman. Her crow black hair rippled to her small waist and contrasted sharply with her moon pale skin. The full lips that curved upwards, were as red as the gown she wore. White light blazed around her and Gertrude's head exploded with pain. The woman's eyes roamed across the room, alighting, and pausing on Gertrude. Gertrude felt the power in that sapphire blue glance. It was like being noticed by the sea. Her headache vanished as suddenly as it had arrived and her stomach flipped. The woman was too much, too powerful, and too forceful. The room was not big enough to hold her. It would be like trying to put the ocean into a jar. A smile flickered on the woman's lips and then dismissing Gertrude, she looked across the room to the fireplace.

'Morgan the bloody Fey,' said Jim.

'Jim the bloody crow,' the woman purred. Gertrude watched as her oldest friend flew across the room to land on the woman's outstretched arm. The woman laughed and Jim made soft noises as she stroked his chest and whispered kisses onto him.

'Get this bloody geis off me.' The woman made a movement with her hand and smiled.

'It is done, beloved.' Jim coughed, cawed, and croaked.

'Thank Gawd for that! I can spill secrets again.' Taking in all the staring figures in the room, the woman said,

'Have I missed the party?

They were like figures in a tableau. No one moved, no one spoke. Gertrude tried to still the thudding of her heart. Her eyes had not left the black-haired woman and she wondered if she would ever tear them away from the beautiful pale face. 'Is no one going to welcome me home?' Nell, who had been clutching her gown, moved forward.

'Forgive our manners. You have travelled far. Do you want a pasty?' She was met by silence and an intense stare. Then Morgan threw back her head and laughed.

'Nell, thank the goddess some things never change. I would love a pasty. I dream of your pasties.' She placed Jim down on the arm of a chair and gathered Nell in an embrace. Nell let out a sob and Morgan patted her on the back.

'I am here now, hush, I am here. You have been so strong, so brave.' She let Nell go and dried her tears with the sleeve of her red gown. 'Our spy in the kitchen. Not one of us has had to be near the queen for so long. Your bravery will be the stuff of songs.'

'And I shall sing them.' Taliesin's powerful voice flowed across the room. Cat unfurled herself from Taliesin's lap and they stood up together, holding hands. Morgan clapped her hands.

'Taliesin, oh, great day. You escaped? You found the way?'

'Thanks to your seed, yes. I should have recognised you.'

'No, you shouldn't have. The sisterhood has always loved our old women disguises. No one takes notice of old ladies. You were not meant to recognise me. Well met, Bard of Bards, well met.' Coming forward Morgan flung her arms around him. He lifted her off the ground. Placing her down, Morgan turned to Cat and held out her arms.

'Sister, you must be relieved to have him back.' A quiver of movement from Cat and then another from Morgan. Cat's knife hung, suspended in the air between them.

'Almost,' whispered Morgan.

'Almost. But not quite. Never quite. Welcome home, sister.' Morgan handed the knife back to Cat. The women hugged in a violent embrace. Freeing each other, Morgan turned and wrapped her arms around Ariel. He dissolved into a golden heap on the floor, taking her down with him. His purrs made the room shake and he licked Morgan all over her face.

'Fierce as ever I see,' she laughed. At the sound of that musical laugh, Gertrude's head began to throb.

'To my enemies, yes.'

'Now where is my nephew?'

Rhiannon stepped forward.

'This is Pryderi.' Morgan disentangled herself from the lion and stood up.

'Hello, little one. Well spun, Rhiannon. He is beautiful, just beautiful. He has your eyes.' She lifted the baby from Rhiannon's arms and held him up, speaking in a language Gertrude did not recognise. The baby gurgled back and Morgan spoke some more. The baby giggled and waved his arms. Morgan laughed and handed the baby back to his mother, kissing Rhiannon on the cheek.

'Now for goddesses' sake, Rhi, don't misplace this one.' Elaine let out a gasp and everyone froze. Then Rhiannon let out a raucous laugh that was in contrast to her delicate beauty. The baby joined in and nervous laughter filled the room. 'He is good, Rhiannon, good and strong and clever. He will be—'

'No. Do not tell me. I know you see far, sister, but let me just enjoy him as a babe. Let me live each moment with him, without knowing about the next one.' Morgan nodded.

'You have always been wise, Rhi, but heed this advice, don't let Jim near him. Pryderi already knows two swear words, and they are the worse two.' Jim puffed himself up. Morgan turned to Igraine, who had been standing silent since her entrance. A long look passed between them.

'Mother,' said Morgan and sank into a graceful curtsey.

'My dear, it is good to see you.' Morgan raised an elegant eyebrow and went over to kiss her mother on both cheeks.

'Have you seen him? Your brother, do you know how he does?'

'His plans are not my plans, mother.'

'But you two are joined at the hip.'

'Not this time it seems.' She turned her attention to Elaine. Elaine wiped her chocolate-covered hands on her yellow gown and stood up.

'Sister,' she simpered. Morgan stared at her.

'So, you have been initiated into the sisterhood?' Nell cleared her throat.

'Not yet. But she is here to take the place of Brighid.'

'No one can take the place of Brighid,' Morgan said, still staring at Elaine.

'Of course not, but—' Morgan held up a hand and Nell fell silent. She held out her hand and Elaine hesitated and kissed the ruby ring on Morgan's hand.

'I will not let you down.' Morgan's face went blank and a faraway look came into her eyes. She pulled her hand away from Elaine and gave her a cool smile.

Gertrude shook so much it was noticeable. She put her hand on the back of a chair and wished the ground would swallow her up. She knew Morgan would come to her soon and she did not want to show how affected she was by her presence.

Morgan crouched on the floor.

'Sam and Lucinda.' Sam bounded into her arms, whilst Lucinda trotted over.

'Brave, wise, Sam. Vivienne searched high and low for one such as yourself. You have travelled so far and so long, more than any of us perhaps. It is good to feel the love of a dog again.' Sam rolled over, exposing his stomach, which Morgan rubbed.

'And Lucinda, you brilliant cat, making out you were evil incarnate when all along you were a hero in disguise. It is a trick I myself have used, in many lifetimes. Welcome, dark one.' Lucinda bowed her head. Morgan rose from the floor.

Any moment now. Morgan turned, but not to Gertrude. She spoke to Apollo and Zeus in a language that was beautiful, but alien.

'High Elven,' whispered Jim, but Gertrude could not reply as she felt a wave of dizziness crash over her. The two horses turned and ran from the room. Tal came forward.

'You brought Hermes.' Morgan spun and gazed at him.

'Rather Hermes brought me.' Walking over to him, she took his head in her hands and kissed him full on the lips. She did not hurry and Tal did not struggle. Igraine pursed her lips and

Elaine looked murderous, but Taliesin broke into laughter.

'Hello, Aunt,' said Tal.

'Hello, darling,' Morgan purred and she let him go. Her head fell forward. A veil of black hair fell, obscuring her face. Her shoulders sagged and she let out a long sigh. The trembling had grown so strong now, that Gertrude felt she was going to pass out. Her blood raced through her veins and her head spun.

'How is it that every time you return, you are more staggeringly beautiful than the last?' It took Gertrude a moment to realise that Morgan was talking to her. Morgan held Gertrude with her sapphire eyes. 'Light to my dark, spring to my winter, sun to my moon, land to my sea, my love, what took you so long?' Gertrude's knees gave way. She willed herself to stay upright. 'What name have you been going by this time?' Gertrude drew a deep breath and hoped her voice would come out strong.

'Ger – Gertrude.' Morgan barked out a laugh.

'By the goddess, that bitch hates you.' At Gertrude's frown, Morgan moved closer. Her scent of the sea and jasmine overwhelmed Gertrude. 'You do not know, do you? They have not told you?' Nell stepped forward.

'We thought we would wait for you, we thought you might ...' Nell's voice trailed off. Morgan ignored her. The sapphire blue eyes crashed into Gertrude's and Gertrude felt she was being pulled under the sea by a strong current. 'Would you know your true name, flower bride? Would you know, Queen of the May, Queen of Sorrows, who you are and all the burden that goes with it?' Gertrude's mouth was dry. She nodded. She heard a buzzing in her ear.

In the end, Tal said it. After all, it had lain on his lips the moment he had seen her on the first day of spring.

'Guinevere.'

As she stared at him across the room Gertrude knew, finally, who he was. How could she not? They shared the same soul. As she stared at him, his mask dissolved and his need for her and his vulnerability shone from his grey eyes. All the years and the heartbreak were there to see. One single tear rolled down his cheek and she was aware that a single tear rolled down her own.

His name sprung from her heart and worked its way to her lips and at last, she could call him by that most beloved name.

'Lancelot.'

He sank down on one knee, his eyes never leaving her face. The hurt and the passion, over so many lifetimes, came crashing through the wall that her mind had made to protect itself. Her head exploded in pain. Everyone in the room bowed low.

There was no protection here. She was no longer safe. The dam burst and the memories that came pouring through carried her and swept her out to sea. There was nothing to cling onto. She was lost, adrift and beginning to drown.

'Lancelot,' she said again. And gratefully she allowed herself to go under the waves, passing into dark oblivion.

EPILOGUE

A graceful figure steps out from behind a tree.

'My Lord,' says the tree, but the figure does not answer. His eyes focus on the turrets and the rooms, high up in the great oak. He flashes his eyes from blue to brown, to hazel, until they turn the same shade of forest green as the one he has come to find.

Except she has been found by another.

The other.

He sniffs the air, catching her scent on the breeze. Closing his eyes, he reaches out and senses her pounding heart.

Her heart is leaving him.

The spark of her consciousness is extinguished, so he creeps into her dreams, as he has been doing so since she was four.

He finds her, as always, waiting for him. The grey-eyed man is there too, as he always is, but today he is strong. Instead of hiding in the shadows, he is bright and shielding her.

They have found each other.

A blast of heat leaves a scorch mark on the earth and the grass catches fire. An owl flies from the tree. The tree shakes.

'Forgive me, my child,' the golden-haired man says. He opens his eyes to gaze once more up at the room where she lies. The tears come, flowing down his face. He is so lost in the waves of grief he does not see the shadow creature who steps out behind him. The creature, who has sorrows of its own, becomes still and watches. The golden-haired man's tears extinguish the fire he has made from his hands. Both of them turn their faces to the room where she lies, afloat on the waves of unconsciousness.

One wishes to burn her; the other burns for her.

The golden-haired man vanishes, leaving the shadow creature alone.

The blossom begins to fall, and a lone magpie takes flight amongst the trees.

ACKNOWLEDGEMENT

A huge thank you to my Beta readers, Natalie-Ann Jones, Alex and Aimie-Leigh Mogg and Alice Robb. Thank you for your invaluable feedback.

They say your first novel is a love letter to the author you love the most, but I have two. So, with deep gratitude for the magic you brought into my life, C. S. Lewis and Guy Gavriel Kay, this is for you.

To my three step-children, Gemma, Nick, and Kyle, who welcomed me into their hearts and soon got used to me dashing from the room to carry on writing. Thank you.

To my two fur babies, Alfie and Oscar. Your company whilst I wrote was so loving, even if I did have to stop to walk you both.

Massive hugs to my daughter, Megs, who fell in love with Jim almost as much as I did. You are a pixie if ever I saw one.

Lastly, thanks to my husband, Barrie. Your patience in losing your wife for hours whilst I wrote this was unending, as is the love I have for you.

ABOUT THE AUTHOR

A. E. James

Like many writers, A. E. James has held down a myriad of different jobs to keep a roof over her head. She has worked for museums, banks, dentists, the pharmaceutical industry, and accountants, as well as being a professional tarot reader, and an astrologer. But she has always been a writer.

Born in Scotland, she grew up in England (and then Scotland again), before finally moving to Wales. Moving around Britain gave her a love of the myths and legends of this land, so it was no surprise when her first novels turned out to be about the Arthurian legend.

She currently lives in Wales with her husband, her daughter, two dogs, and a crate of wine.

She would love to hear from you and you can reach her on:

Her instagram account, @aejamesauthor

Her facebook page, A. E. James, Author

Her website, aejamesauthor.com

or contact her directly on her email at info@aejamesauthor.com

THE LIVING LEGENDS SERIES

What if you were a living legend and you had no idea?

Queen Of Sorrows

It's tough being a living legend.

It's even tougher when you have forgotten which legend you are.

Orphan, Gertrude Springate, is plump, ginger, and as bright as lightning.

She is also mad.

Because no one else can hear the trees whispering to her or her best friend, Jim, King of the Crows, swearing like a sailor. Bullied at school by a vicious group of girls and at home by her abusive grandmother, Gertrude's life changes when an old lady and her book-loving golden retriever move next door. For the old lady can also hear the trees whispering and the crows swearing.

Gertrude discovers that she and Mrs Eccles are from another Britain called Albion. A Britain where all the legends such as King Arthur, Morgan Le Fay, and Robin Hood are still alive. Mrs Eccles reveals that she too is a legend – Vivienne, The Lady of the Lake, but refuses to tell Gertrude who she is. Nevertheless, she needs Gertrude's help, for Albion is in the wintry grip of an enchantress.

Soon, Gertrude is sinking into magical baths that bestow powers and being trained in hand-to-paw combat by a massive lion. But her connection to Albion and its Ice Queen will shock Gertrude to her very core.

And just who is the dark-haired horseman she keeps seeing? Or the golden-haired man who visits her in her dreams?

Blending Celtic and Arthurian mythology with historical fantasy, Queen Of Sorrows is an imaginative retelling of the Arthurian myth and book one in the Living Legends series.

It is also a story that should never have happened.

God Of Sorrows

It's tough being a living legend.

It's even tougher when you realise which legend you are.

When Gertrude's true identity as Guinevere, Queen of Sorrows, is revealed, she is urged by the Ladies of the Lake to take up her crown and take her rightful place as Albion's and Arthur's queen.

But Gertrude does not want to be Guinevere again. Guinevere brought nothing but sorrow to Arthur and his knights of the round table, and the obsessive love she shared with Lancelot has led to Lancelot still dancing on the edge of madness.

But take up the crown she must as the Ice Queen is threatening Albion's very existence.

Trusting only her three friends; Sam, the book-loving golden retriever, Jim, the King of the Crows, and Lucinda, the powerful cat, Guinevere reluctantly takes up her crown again to find that Albion is not the only thing that needs saving.

For the whole universe is under threat from a long-forgotten god.

A god that is not supposed to exist. A god who hides at the end of the universe. A god who has haunted Guinevere in her dreams for years. And just where are King Arthur and Merlin?

Blending Celtic and Arthurian mythology with historical fantasy, God of Sorrows is the heart-breaking conclusion to the Living Legends Series.

It is also a story that should never have been told.

Printed in Great Britain
by Amazon

27397873R00219